# CLAIMING CARTER

A WAVERLY WILDCATS NOVEL

JENNIFER BONDS

This book is a work of fiction. Names, characters, places, and incidents either are the product of the author's imagination or are used fictitiously. Any resemblance to persons, living or dead, business establishments, events, or locales is entirely coincidental. The author acknowledges the trademarked status and trademark owners of various products referenced in this work of fiction. The publication and use of these trademarks is not authorized, associated with, or sponsored by the trademark owners.

Claiming Carter: A Waverly Wildcats Novel



**Cover Design by Cover Ever After**
**ISBN (Amazon): 978-1-953794-00-0**
**ISBN (B&N): 978-1-953794-25-3**
**ISBN (Ingram): 978-1-953794-29-1**
**First Edition 2020**

**www.jenniferbonds.com**

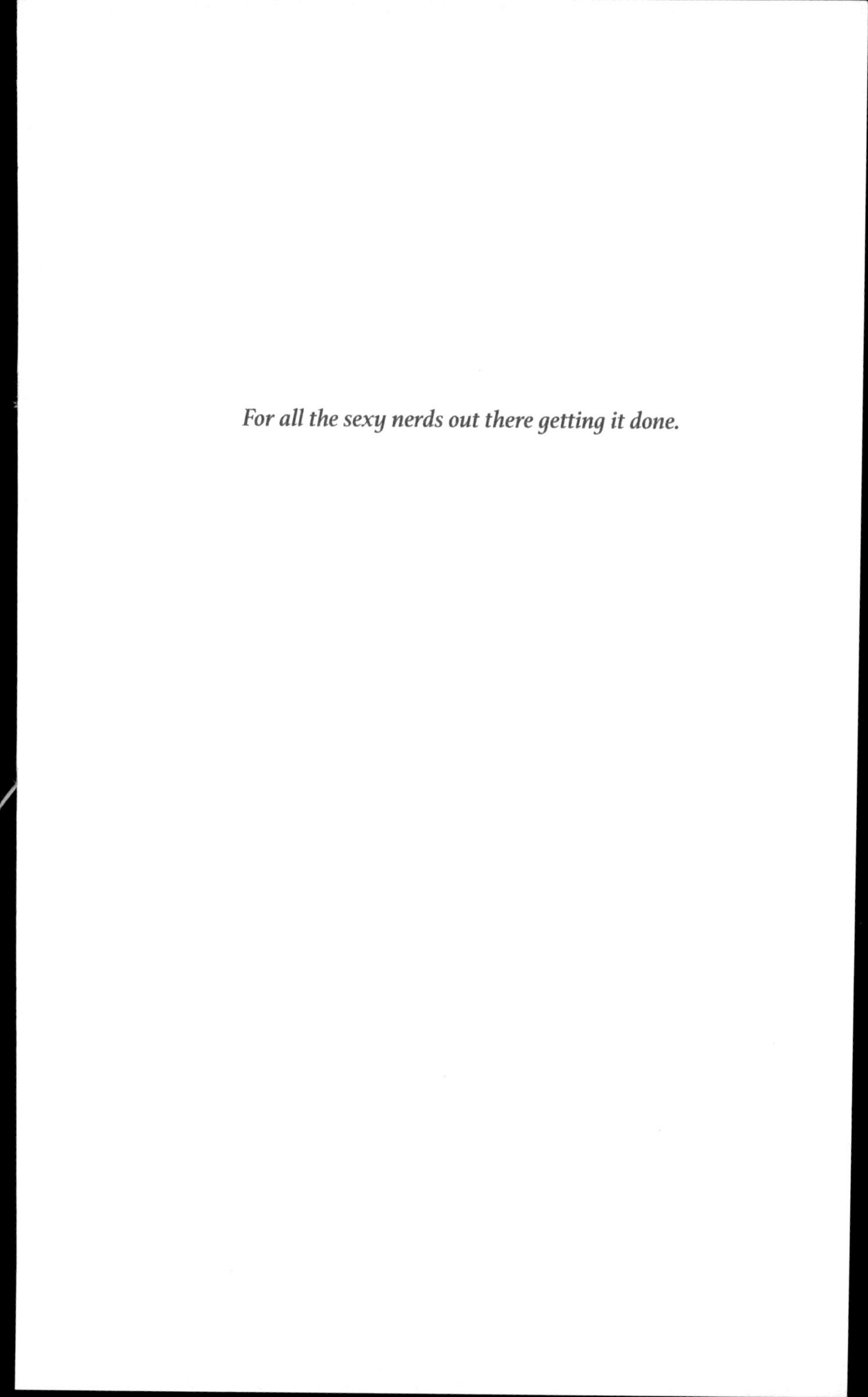

*For all the sexy nerds out there getting it done.*

# 1

# AUSTIN

DESPERATE TIMES. Desperate measures. I never really understood that phrase—*until now.*

"Why the fuck did you drag me up here, Reid?" Coop crosses his arms over his chest. He scans the soccer field before turning to meet my stare, a smirk twisting his lips. "Dude, I'm not making out with you under the bleachers. You've gotta at least buy me dinner first. Maybe get me some flowers."

"You wish, asshole. You're not my type."

I let my gaze drift back to the field. Not exactly what I had in mind, but training camp ran late and we missed the men's soccer practice. The women's team is warming up, and, yeah, I'm that desperate to find a new placekicker for Wildcat football.

"Bullshit." Coop scoffs before turning to wink at me. He's the only guy I know that can pull off a wink without looking like a complete douche—and he knows it. "I'm everyone's type."

"You actually believe that shit, don't you?" I snort and shove him toward the bleachers. Coop's the best wide receiver Waverly has seen in a decade. He's also the king of casual sex. The result? An ego to rival the Grand Canyon. "Let's go, Casanova."

We climb the metal steps two at a time and plant ourselves at the center of the stadium, midway up. It's trimmed in blue and white—Waverly University colors—and there's a Wildcat head emblazoned over the player's tunnel. Big Ten flags hang limply at both ends of the pitch, a quiet testament to the heat wave that's smothering the campus. The afternoon sun is brutal and the seats are hot as balls, but we've got a perfect view of the field and the players on it.

Coop leans back and rests his elbows on the bench behind us like he's out to get a fucking tan.

*Must be nice.*

I don't have the luxury of kicking back.

Not when my last shot at a national championship—and my future—is on the line.

I lean forward, resting my elbows on my knees to get a better look at the women on the field.

Or, more specifically, their legs.

*This has to work.*

Otherwise, we can kiss our season goodbye and any hope of a bowl game with it.

*No.* I have to deliver a winning season. I've worked too hard, sacrificed too much to watch it all go down the drain because of a drunken dare.

"Spellman really screwed us," Coop says, reading my mind.

"Tell me about it." I nod even as guilt gnaws at me. I'm not exactly thrilled Spellman's shit choices could tank our season, but I'm not without a heart. After all, the guy's wearing a fixator, and from what I hear, the brace is hella painful. "What's done is done. It's up to us to unfuck the situation."

And by us, I mean me.

After all, I'm the team captain.

It's my job to lead Waverly to victory, to ensure we play like a team and have each other's backs. It's up to me to make sure drunken shenanigans don't cost the seniors a national title or their NFL draft positions come spring. Coach Collins made that perfectly clear when he ripped me a new asshole about Spellman's busted leg.

Like I was the jackass who dared him to jump off the roof.

Man, was Coach heated. In the four years I've played ball at Waverly, I've never seen him so angry. Not even when a couple of linemen pissed hot during drug testing sophomore year and the news outlets were gobbling it up like a crack epidemic.

So yeah, it's day four of camp and I'm third-and-long.

*Down but not out.*

"Are you going to explain what we're doing here?" Coop jerks his chin toward the field. "Or am I supposed to guess?"

"We need a kicker. Soccer players have the best legs on campus." I rub the back of my neck, reluctant to throw the new guys under the bus. "You saw the freshmen. They're too green. Not enough power and zero poise."

"Poise?"

Poor choice of words. I can tell Coop wants to make a joke about bladder control, but I cut him off.

"You know, mental toughness. They'll crack under the bright lights." It's not their fault. They should've had a year to develop. "There's a reason we have redshirts."

Coop shrugs, unconvinced. "Since when does Special Teams make or break us?" He snickers and holds his fist up like a microphone, doing a poor imitation of our game day announcer, his voice high and nasally. "With Austin Reid leading Waverly's offense, the Wildcats have a real shot at a national championship this year!"

I roll my eyes. Waverly hasn't won a national title in fifteen years, but this is our year. Even the talking heads are saying it.

"I'm not taking any chances. You know as well as I do that football is a game of inches. We're going all the way, and we need a decent kicker to make it happen. One with range."

Coop leans forward, his eyes bouncing from me to the field and back again. "You really think this will work, don't you?"

"It'll work." I've never failed at anything in my life, and I'm not about to start now. There are too many people counting on me. Not that I mind the pressure. Starting quarterback for a Big Ten university is nothing compared to growing up in the shadow of a future Hall of Famer. "We need power and precision." I point to midfield where the women are running passing drills. "They've got it."

"Doesn't hurt that they look a helluva lot better in shorts than Spellman ever did." Coop snickers and shakes his head. "I'm gonna need a front-row seat when you pitch this whack idea to Coach."

A tall brunette jogs onto the field, ponytail bouncing, and drops her bag on the sideline.

She immediately starts to stretch, keeping her head down as she bends at the waist and plants her palms on the grass.

Coop gives a low whistle.

Can't say I blame him. Her perfectly toned legs are a goddamn mile long. My dick twitches, reminding me it hasn't seen any action in weeks. Something I can remedy later.

First, I've got to find a kicker.

"You're late, Carter!" the coach yells down the sideline.

I check the time. This chick's almost fifteen minutes late. Coach would have my ass for that kind of tardiness.

"Sorry." The brunette straightens her spine and grabs her left foot, pulling it back so it's nearly touching her perfectly round ass. "I came straight from work."

"You know the deal." The coach blows her whistle and gestures to one of the other players before turning back to the late arrival, a hint of warning in her tone. "Don't let it happen again."

The brunette doesn't respond, but my curiosity is piqued.

What kind of deal do they have that allows a Division I athlete to work during the season? That would never fly in the football program.

Coach Collins has a zero distractions policy.

It's a wonder he hasn't made Coop quit Sig Chi.

We watch the practice in relative silence, studying the players to see who has the strongest leg and best accuracy. The goalie's got a canon, but even I'm not delusional enough to believe we have a shot at recruiting her. She's probably on scholarship.

"Pull up the roster." Like the football program, the soccer team will have headshots, bios, and stats for each player posted online. Makes it easier for jersey chasers, reporters, and scouts to do their thing. It'll make it easier for us to poach too.

Coop pulls out his phone and begins typing furiously on the screen as the women scrimmage. "Well, if we don't find a kicker, at least I'll have some new material for the spank bank."

"You're a real charmer, you know that?"

"Nah, I'm just a leg man." He looks up and points to the field without an ounce of shame. "I'd be a fool not to appreciate those beauties."

It's hard to fault his logic. For all his bluster, Coop's a straight shooter when it comes to hookups. Like me, he prefers women who have a healthy appetite for sex and who aren't looking for commitment.

No time when you're chasing a national title.

When I return my attention to the field, the less than punctual brunette is squaring up behind the ball. She takes three steps forward and plants her left foot. Then she draws her right leg back and kicks the ball, her foot connecting with a soft *thwump.*

I watch, not daring to breathe, as the ball sails forty yards down the field. It lands directly in front of her teammate, who springs into action, dribbling toward the net.

I elbow Coop, keeping my gaze locked on the field. "Did you see that?"

"No, because I'm fucking blind."

"Who is she?" I ask, ignoring the sarcasm.

Coop glances down at his phone, scrolling through the roster. When he finds her headshot, he holds up the phone. "Kennedy Carter."

Carter, huh? Up close, I realize she's got a lot more going on than just the legs. She's got this whole girl-next-door thing, with warm brown eyes, a wide smile that shows *all* the teeth, and a few blonde highlights that complement her olive complexion.

Not my usual type, but I'm kind of digging the natural look.

"That's our girl." I stand and stretch my legs, determination coursing through my veins. "She just doesn't know it yet."

# 2

# KENNEDY

SWEAT TRICKLES down my forehead and I wipe it away with the back of my hand. Central Pennsylvania humidity is a bitch, and it's so hot I swear my boob sweat has boob sweat. Despite the heat wave, Coach isn't cutting us any slack.

Or maybe it's just me. You know, since I was late.

*Again.*

"You want a ride back?" my roommate, Becca, asks, looking fresh as a daisy.

*Shit.* Apparently Coach *was* riding me extra hard.

I silently vow to be on time tomorrow. My body can't handle another workout like today.

"Thanks, but I'll catch the Loop." I check my watch, confirming the next bus is due in twenty minutes. "I've got a tutoring session on campus tonight."

My last of the summer session, thank God.

"Have fun with that." Becca scrunches her nose, a not-so-subtle reminder that I need to haul ass if I'm going to squeeze in a quick shower. Because, you know, underclassmen generally prefer it when their tutors don't smell like eau de student athlete. "I'll see you back at the apartment."

"Later." I wave as she slings her bag over her shoulder and turns to the lot.

Then I zip my bag and head for the locker room.

"Hey, Carter! Wait up!"

Instinctively, I slow my steps, glancing back over my shoulder at the two lumbering giants cutting across the field. No one I know. At least, not personally. But even I recognize the face of Waverly's darling quarterback, Austin Reid, as he jogs across the field, covering the distance in smooth, graceful steps.

"I'm kind of in a hurry." And I have zero interest in chatting it up with douchey football players.

The giants slow to a stop a few feet away, assuming a casual stance, their feet spread wide, arms dangling loosely at their sides.

If I didn't know better, I'd think they've had coaching on how to look unthreatening.

Or as unthreatening as possible, given they look like a Captain America-Thor matched set.

*Mmm. Chris Hemsworth.*

"This won't take long." Reid flashes a disarming smile. One that has surely relieved a few (hundred) Waverly women of their underwear.

Austin Reid is even better looking in person than in *The Collegian*. The grainy black-and-white photos in the student paper don't do him justice. The guy's a beast, towering over my five-foot-ten frame by a good six inches. With muscles for days and electric-blue eyes that dance with barely contained energy, it's no wonder women flock to him like freshmen to a rush party. I take satisfaction in the fact that his normally spiky hair is drooping in the humidity, falling over his forehead in a dark wave.

After all, I'm a big ball of sweat, so it only seems fair.

"I'm Austin and this is Cooper."

"You can call me Coop," the Hemsworth doppelgänger says, extending his hand for me to shake. Judging by his size, another football player. He's got broad shoulders, shaggy blond hair, and eyes like sea glass. And like Reid, he's stupid hot.

*If* you're into meatheads.

Which I'm not.

I grip my bag tighter, ignoring the proffered hand.

"We play football," Coop says, his lopsided grin reminding me of Becca's mischievous Labradoodle.

"And?"

If he's looking for someone to stroke his ego, he came to the wrong place.

"We saw you play today." Austin—*Reid*—smiles, and his eyes crinkle at the corners. "You've got a powerful leg."

"And damn fine accuracy," Coop adds, crossing his arms over his muscular chest.

"I've been playing soccer since I was five," I blurt out, cursing myself for offering the information when I have no idea where this conversation is going. Not that it matters. Whatever they want, I'm not interested. "What's your point?"

"Look, I understand you're in a hurry, so I'll cut to the chase."

I raise a brow. Quick, this one.

"Waverly football needs a quality kicker." Reid takes a step forward, as if all that bottled-up energy is propelling him into motion.

"And?" I shift my bag, impatience getting the better of me. If I don't hit the shower, I'm going to miss the bus. "I'm still not seeing what this has to do with me."

"Really?" Coop smirks, looking me over from head to toe as if he's sizing me up. "You're a mechanical engineering major. Pretty sure you've got the brainpower to put two and two together."

Before I can decide if I should be offended or flattered, Reid pins his buddy with a withering glare. "What my teammate is trying to say is that we want you to try out for the football team."

This time I actually laugh out loud, making no attempt to stifle my hysterical giggles even as tears leak down my cheeks. Because, come on, it's ridiculous.

Me? On the football team?

They can't be serious.

When I finally catch my breath, I realize they aren't laughing.

*Maybe they're high.*

"Have you been smoking?" I ask, because, *no filter*.

They look at each other and then back at me. "Smoking?"

"You know, weed? Pot? Or whatever the cool kids are calling it these days," I finish, noting their surprisingly clear pupils.

"I'm serious." Reid plants his hands on his hips, expression unreadable.

"We don't smoke during the season," Coop chimes in like he's immensely proud of this show of restraint. "Gotta keep our reflexes tight."

*Fucking ballers.*

"In case you haven't noticed"—I look pointedly around the field—"I'm already on a team. Besides, I don't even like football."

Or football players.

"Seriously?" Reid shakes his head in apparent disbelief. "Everyone likes football. It's America's favorite pastime."

"Pretty sure that's baseball."

"Debatable," he says as Coop mutters, "Baseball is for pussies."

Reid and I both ignore him. The rivalry between the two teams is legendary at Waverly.

"What'll it take to convince you?" Reid asks.

"A miracle." I smile sweetly and turn on my heel, but before I can take a step, Reid grabs my arm.

A spark of awareness shoots straight to my belly, reminding me it's been a while—seven months and twenty-three days to be exact—since a guy touched me. His grip is gentle but firm, his calloused fingers wrapped around my forearm. It's not threatening. If anything, it reeks of desperation.

*Just like his absurd suggestion that I try out for the football team.*

"Look, I know it's unorthodox, but I'm serious." Frustration flashes in his eyes, like it's the first time in his life he hasn't gotten his way, and he doesn't know how to deal. "We need a quality kicker to save our season."

"Trust me, I'm not your girl." I twist out of his grip, breaking the unwanted connection.

"How can you be so sure?"

I smirk. "Oh, let me count the reasons." I hold up my fingers and begin ticking them off as I go. "I'm a soccer player. Your last kicker is bedridden." I pause, forcing myself to look him in the eye. "And let's be honest, you've probably had one too many concussions if you think this is a good idea."

Coop snorts, pressing his fist to his mouth to stifle a laugh. It doesn't work.

A smile tugs at the corner of my own lips, and I give myself silent props for hilarity.

Reid ignores his teammate, eyes locked on me. The smile is back in place, even broader than before, this time accompanied by a tiny dimple in his chin. A dimple that, were it not attached to a football player, would totally be my kryptonite.

*Talk about a waste of a perfectly good dimple.*

"I watched you kick. It's not that different," Reid argues. "If you can kick a long ball, you can learn to kick a field goal. And while our previous kicker may be laid up, that's because of an asinine dare, not the game."

I roll my eyes. "Shocker. A bunch of irresponsible football

players getting wasted and doing dumb shit? I can hardly believe it."

"Hey, I never said we were wasted." Reid throws his hands up defensively, like he's worried I might quote him to the paper. "And for the record, I told him not to take the dare."

"He obviously didn't value your opinion much if he ignored it," I point out, earning another laugh from Coop.

"I like her." He elbows an annoyed-looking Reid. "She's going to fit right in."

*Like hell.* "This has been fun and all, but I have to get to work. Good luck with your search."

"Didn't you just come from work?" Coops brow furrows. "We heard—"

He swallows the rest of the sentence, a sheepish grin on his face.

My cheeks heat, and I do my best to stuff the embarrassment down deep. So what if they heard Coach dressing me down for being late?

"Yes, well, my soccer scholarship is only a partial." A sigh escapes before I can stop it. I'm bone-tired and the fall semester hasn't even started yet. I straighten my spine and slam the door on that line of thinking. Carter women don't do self-pity. I've got three years under my belt. I can do one more. I give Reid an icy glare, because, *arrogant quarterback.* "Those of us who live below the football gods actually have to work. And now you've made me late."

This time, he doesn't try to stop me when I turn to go.

"Spellman had to withdraw this semester, which means he won't be playing ball this year. He had a full-ride." Reid's words are quiet, but there's no mistaking the emphasis he places on the word *had.* "It's too late to recruit a placekicker. The football program has scholarship money available."

I freeze midstride. A full-ride?

"Remind me, Coop. What's the going rate on a football scholarship?"

"Thirty-six grand. Give or take."

No, it's ridiculous. No one is going to give a woman a football scholarship at a DI school.

Not one who's never played a day in her life.

And certainly not one who despises the sport.

"If you had a full-ride, you could quit working and focus on the game," Reid says, sounding every bit like a snake in the garden as I turn to face him.

Manipulative ass.

I chew my lower lip, mulling over his words. We may have different priorities, but he's right about one thing. If I had a full-ride, I could quit working—*and put more focus on my academics.*

"You make the team, they'll probably make one of those inspirational TV movies about you," Coop quips, although I suspect he's only half joking about the enormity of what they're suggesting.

The thought is sobering. This is a big freaking deal.

*It's also utterly ridiculous.*

"Last I checked, the team captain doesn't have the authority to make player selections or award scholarships."

Reid shrugs. "True. But if you come out to camp tomorrow, Coach Collins will give you a shot." He tucks his hands in the pockets of his cargo shorts and lowers his voice to a conspiratorial whisper. "Under all that bluster, he's a big old teddy bear."

Somehow, I doubt it. The man is regularly in the news for his sideline antics and is as likely to be seen throwing a clipboard as yelling at the refs.

"What do you say?" Reid asks, a hopeful note in his voice.

What can I say? As ridiculous as it sounds, a full-ride is what I've always wanted, but they're few and far between. I could've gotten one at a lesser school, but soccer isn't my endgame. I need to be somewhere with a strong engineering program and that's Waverly, even if it means Mom and I both have to work our asses off to make ends meet.

But a full-ride? Now?

It would mean less work study. And it would ease Mom's burden. She wouldn't have to take so much overtime and God knows I'd do anything to lighten her load.

The real problem is that even if this batshit-crazy idea works, I'll have to give up soccer.

There's no way I can do both, and I can't screw the team by quitting.

"Not interested." I adjust my bag and steel my resolve. I can't afford to risk my soccer scholarship for a pipe dream.

Besides, me hanging with a bunch of swaggering football players?

Never going to happen.

Reid's face falls for an instant, but the cocky quarterback smirk is back in place before I can blink.

"Why don't you sleep on it, Carter?" He nudges Coop and they turn to go. They make it a whole three steps—yes, I counted—before Reid looks back at me over his shoulder, a challenge burning in his eyes. "Camp starts at eight tomorrow. You can meet us on the practice fields when you change your mind."

The arrogant bastard actually says *when*.

Not if, *when*.

"Spoiler alert, Reid. I won't change my mind." I plant my hands on my hips, determined to get the message through his thick skull. "I'd rather streak across campus naked than play ball with you."

# 3

# AUSTIN

THE DAY'S shaping up to be another scorcher and I'm already sweating through my pads thirty minutes into practice. Coach is putting us through the wringer with speed drills, and I'm not the only one dripping sweat. Coop's looking good, and I give silent thanks that at least my top receiver's got his head in the game, because the O-line looks like shit.

If I didn't know better, I'd think they were out partying last night.

"Come on, Jones! Get your balls wet!" I yell at the sophomore running back who's going to see real action for the first time this year.

He picks up the pace, and I clap my approval.

Coop approaches and I lift my helmet, letting it rest on the crown of my head so I can get a little fresh air. Sweat runs down the back of my neck, but I don't bother wiping it away.

*Plenty more where that came from.*

"What's got your shorts in a twist?" Coop asks, offering me a water bottle.

"Coach's been riding my ass all morning." I squirt a cool

stream of water into my mouth, and return the nearly empty bottle.

"This wouldn't have anything to do with a certain Lady Wildcat shooting you down, would it?"

The question sounds innocent enough, but the shit-eating grin on his face tells me he knows exactly what's driving my foul mood.

"She'll be here," I say, sounding more confident than I feel. "She needs the scholarship."

I don't bother to point out that we need her just as much as she needs us. Because if I have to watch the freshman front-runner—*Jones? James?* I can never remember the kid's name—shank another field goal, I'm going to slam my head into a locker. The kid's got potential, and he'll be good—maybe even great—with time.

Unfortunately, time's a luxury we don't have.

Our home opener is in three weeks. We need a pressure player now. And Carter's a pressure player. I read up on her last night, and I'm more convinced than ever that she's exactly what this team needs.

"You did everything you could." Coop claps me on the shoulder. "We'll find a way."

"We always do." I give him a fist bump and return to the line of scrimmage, slipping my helmet on as Coach yells at us to run a few plays.

*Time to work.*

I take a couple snaps, giving the guys a chance to practice running their routes as I warm up my arm. Most of these guys, even the ones who didn't see much action last year, could run the playbook blindfolded. Seeing the team run plays like a well-oiled machine improves my mood, and I'm pumped when Coach Collins calls for The Gauntlet.

The guys line up in two rows, creating a narrow path parallel to the sideline. Coach instructs a couple of defensive tackles to get in the middle and the O-line gathers at the mouth of the human gauntlet, preparing for their individual runs.

Coop goes first, tucking the ball under his arm and barreling down the shoot.

Wyant, a junior who's built like a Mack truck, moves to block the run, but Coop spins at the last minute and blows by without too much trouble before juking past Bates.

They'll have to be faster than that to have any hope of stripping the ball.

I watch with pride as a few more of my guys destroy the drill.

By the time it's my turn to make the run, the team is worked into a frenzy, shouting and shoving and taking bets on whether I'll make it past the two thick tackles. I flash the cocky grin they expect from their captain and grip the ball, holding it tight to my right side as I plant my left foot and wait for the piercing shriek of the whistle.

Coach Collins lets it rip and I shoot forward, knowing my speed and height will be an advantage. Wyant charges and I drop my shoulder, like I'm prepared to go right through him.

*Wouldn't be the first time.*

He goes low, diving for my feet. I jump over him, clearing the first hurdle easily enough. Bates is more experienced and will be harder to fake out. He's holding his position at the end of the tunnel and the guys are cheering him on, encouraging him to put me on my ass.

*Not gonna happen.*

I take two short steps and turn up the heat, deciding to rush him at full speed. He's a big mofo, but we're evenly matched and I like my odds. The cheering dies down and I glance to my left—rookie mistake—to see Carter through a break in the line of players.

Bates takes advantage of the distraction and plows his

shoulder into my midsection, driving me right through the line and onto my ass.

There's a chorus of "Dayyyummm!" and "Oh shit!" but I barely hear them.

*She came.*

I heave a sigh of relief as Bates leans down and offers me a meaty paw, pulling me to my feet with little effort.

"Sorry, bro."

"Don't sweat it. I lost my focus." Understatement. I didn't even put up a fight and he knows it. "Nice tackle. Next time it won't be so easy," I say, pointing the ball—which is still clutched in my right hand—at him.

"I'm counting on it." Bates gives me a devious grin and there's no doubt he's going to be rehashing his victory for days.

Worth it. Carter's here, and she's going to try out.

"Get your damn head in the game before Bates takes it off!" Coach barks, arms crossed over his chest. "We can't afford another injury because you've got your head up your ass, Reid!"

"Yes, sir."

The Gauntlet continues and I jog to the sideline, where Carter stands awkwardly, shifting her weight from one foot to the other. I can feel the stares of the guys on my back. They're far from subtle as they hoot and holler, speculation running rampant.

To be fair, it's not often we have women show up at practice and when they do?

Well, they usually fall into one of three categories: water girl, jersey chaser, or athletic trainer.

Carter sure as shit doesn't look like a jersey chaser with navy athletic shorts and her dark hair falling over her shoulder in a tightly woven braid. Total wishful thinking on the part of the guys, hoping she's searching for a hookup. And judging by the look on her face, she's not exactly flattered. Her lips are pressed into a flat line and there's a little wrinkle in her brow like she's thinking of bolting.

Okay. Not getting off on the right foot. I turn and glare at my teammates, giving them the universal gesture for *knock it the fuck off.*

I join Carter on the sideline and strip off my helmet, tucking it under my arm. "You changed your mind."

She keeps her gaze leveled at the field, refusing to meet my eye as she toys with the end of her braid. "Believe me, I'm as surprised as you are."

*Oh, it's like that?*

"Practice started at eight. You're late." I smirk, remembering her parting shot last night. "Streaking across campus naked?"

She arches a brow, her dark eyes flashing with annoyance—which is kind of hot—as she turns to face me with a tight-lipped smile. "I'm here now."

"Indeed." I turn back to the field and cup a hand to my mouth. "Hey, Coach! There's someone here I'd like you to meet."

When Coach finally makes his way to the sideline, I've decided the direct approach is best. No sense beating around the bush, not when hard and fast is more my speed.

"Coach, this is Kennedy Carter. She'd like to try out for the team." To Collins's credit, his jaw only falls half-open. "As a placekicker, sir."

Carter's eyes are bugging out, and I can see the moment she realizes Coach had no idea she was coming. Like I was going to put my neck on the line with zero guarantee she'd show?

*Not fucking likely.*

"Is this a joke, Reid?" Coach looks from me to Carter and back again, his face growing red. "I am not—"

"It's no joke, sir." I glance at Carter, giving her a reassuring smile. I'd hate to see her take off now. Once Coach sees what she can do, he'll be singing a different tune. Coach and I? We speak the same language: football. "She's been playing soccer since she was five. She's got a strong leg."

Coach says nothing, just studies her face as if he can read her intentions and level of commitment.

Hell, maybe he can. The guy's been doing this for ages.

Thankfully, Carter keeps her mouth shut. Coach isn't big on sass. He'll pump the brakes on the whole damn thing if she starts spouting off now.

Finally, he steps back and looks her over from head to toe. Carter stands tall, chin lifted, shoulders back, unwavering in the face of his physical assessment.

"You ever kick a football before?" Coach asks, narrowing his eyes.

I can't fault the guy for being skeptical. I'm not the only one under pressure to deliver a national title and this isn't some campy feel-good movie where success is guaranteed.

It'll take blood, sweat, and a bucket of tears to claim the honor.

"No, but I'm a quick study." She meets his gaze with unflinching confidence. "What I lack in experience, I'll more than make up in determination."

"Sir, she can kick a ball." I don't mention that she's probably got a better leg than both freshmen combined. I doubt he'd appreciate my assessment, even if it's spot-on.

"Walk-on tryouts don't start until after camp," he says, rubbing his chin.

"I know it's unusual, but I thought it best given the circumstances."

I don't dare mention Spellman's name. No need to remind him of my role in that mess with a whole day of practice ahead. Not when he's already busting my balls.

Coach grunts. "Let me talk to Coach Jackson. Wait here."

Carter stares at me expectantly.

"Jackson is the Special Teams coordinator. He'll be the one coaching you."

She nods, but says nothing, her gaze drifting back to the field where the team is running agility drills with the defensive coordinator. She looks wary as hell, which makes no sense.

It's not like she's got anything to lose.

# 4

## KENNEDY

I CAN'T BELIEVE I'm actually doing this. It's unhinged. Doesn't help that my stomach's twisted up tighter than a Philly pretzel.

*Stupid nerves.*

Or maybe it's guilt. Kind of hard to tell the difference right now.

Between Reid's intense stare (which is bordering on stalker-iffic) and Coach Collins grunting my way as he talks to a bald dude rocking fluorescent green kicks, I can hardly think straight.

The only thing I know for sure? This is the last place I want to be.

A smirk tugs at the corner of Reid's lips. "Nervous?"

"Hardly." I cross my arms and shift my weight, wishing the coaches would just make up their damn minds because I'm starting to feel like a show pony.

"Liar." He leans close, his hot, spearminty breath whispering across my cheek. "I can see it in your eyes, Carter."

I lift my chin. Austin Reid will not get the best of me.

"If we're going to be teammates," he says, giving my arm a playful shove, "you need to lighten up."

"That's a big *if*," I mutter, gaze locked on the field, determined not to yield another goddamn inch to the obnoxious BMOC.

"Naw." His voice takes on an "aww, shucks" quality. "It's practically a done deal. Look at Jackson. He's all but drooling over your leg."

I snort. Hardly looks like a sure thing from where I'm standing. Maybe the universe is going to spare me the humiliation of this experience and send me packing.

Reid spins and steps in front of me, blocking my view of the field and forcing me to meet his eyes. We're so close I can see the tiny white lines that streak across his blue irises like an electrical storm. "What changed your mind?"

We just met like five seconds ago. If he thinks I'm going to open up and share all my personal shit, he's got another think coming. "Has anyone ever told you that you have serious boundary issues?"

He laughs and adjusts the white headband that's completely failing its mission to absorb the sweat dripping from his hair. It's kind of sexy, but I'd die before admitting it aloud. "It's not a trick question, Carter. You don't have to get all defensive."

I shrug, striving for indifference.

Like hell I'm going to admit the only reason I'm here is because my mom's working seventy hours a week and it's still not enough to make ends meet with my tuition bills. Or that her POS car—which is eight parts rust, two parts steel—is back in the shop.

When I called to check in last night, it sounded like she was about to drop. She'd never admit it, but I could hear it in her voice. She's exhausted.

And probably working herself to death.

*For me.*

So, yeah, I didn't exactly have a choice when it came to showing up this morning. If I have any chance of landing a full scholarship, no matter how long the shot, I have to take it. Even if it means screwing over the soccer team.

Guilt rears its ugly head and I swallow it back down, throat burning. I have to do this for my mom. She's all I've got.

*Just one more year.*

One more year and I'll have my diploma.

As long as I keep my grades up, I'll be able to land a good job. A salaried job. The kind that will allow me to help Mom with the bills and relieve the constant financial pressure.

But if I had a full scholarship, I could help now.

Coach Collins and Coach Jackson are staring at me again, faces unreadable as they approach. And Collins? He looks just as intimidating as those crappy *Collegian* photos, with a square jaw and flat brows and a mouth that seems stuck in a perpetual frown.

Then it hits me. Coach Collins has RBF. Resting bastard face.

A nervous laugh escapes, and I press my lips flat.

*So not the time.*

"Moment of truth," Reid whispers, revealing a crack in his cocky demeanor for the first time.

"So much for being a done deal." I wipe my sweaty palms on my shorts and throw up a quick prayer, hoping they'll at least let me try out.

"Get your ass back on the field, Reid." Coach Collins jerks his head and Reid bolts, tugging his helmet on as he jogs across the field to join the rest of the team. Then Coach Collins turns to me. "Miss Carter, this is Coach Jackson. You'll be working with him today."

My spirit soars. "Thank you. Sir," I add hastily, knowing I'll need every bit of goodwill I can scrape together.

"Get warmed up and meet me in the end zone," Coach

Jackson says, gesturing toward the upright as if he thinks I might need directions to find it.

With a herculean effort, I manage not to roll my eyes.

*Probably best not to piss off the man who holds my financial freedom in his hands.*

I begin my stretching routine, doing my best to block out the sounds of practice and focus on my breathing as the warm glow of the sun heats my skin. Easier said than done. Between the crash of helmets and pads, there's no shortage of trash talk. Or speculation. The guys are still wondering exactly why I'm on their field.

Pretty sure I also catch something about my ass being firm as a melon.

Nice. It's only been five minutes and already they're living down to my expectations.

Not that I expected much.

I've always known football players are creeps.

*Just like dear old Dad.*

I grit my teeth. Doesn't matter.

Today, only Jackson matters. I can deal with the rest later.

When I finish stretching, I catch Reid watching me again. He nods, but I don't return the gesture. He's not the one I have to impress, and I doubt Coach Jackson will be so easily wowed.

I know my leg is strong, but it's not like I've ever kicked a football before. Not that I'm entirely unprepared. I read up on the process last night and did some web research (thanks, YouTube), but that's hardly the same as actually doing it.

I jog toward the end zone where Jackson is working with two other players. They're both tall and lanky, but seriously lacking muscle tone. Ten to one, they've been given strength training programs to bulk up, because even I have more definition than they do.

Jackson looks up as I approach.

I slow to a walk, stopping a few feet short of where he stands with his arms crossed over his chest. Dude looks like he'd rather be anywhere else, and I can't blame him.

Still, I give him a bright smile because I need the guy to like me.

"So what's your experience, Carter?"

"I've been playing soccer since I was five," I say, deciding this isn't the time for modesty, "and I've got the best long ball in Wildcat soccer. Men's and women's."

He nods and narrows his dark eyes. "What's your training regimen?"

I run him through my strength training exercises and throw in a few kicking drills that have helped hone my accuracy. He grunts, and I'm starting to wonder if this is a secret form of communication in the land of Neanderthals.

*Should've asked Reid for the secret decoder ring.*

"Sir, I need this scholarship. A full scholarship," I clarify. "I'm a quick study and can learn the fundamentals if you'll give me a chance." My words are wrought with confidence, and hell, even I'm starting to believe I can do this. After all, how hard can it be?

"Don't tell me." Jackson nods at the field where one of his players is preparing to kick a field goal. "Show me."

I watch as the guy sets himself up, taking three steps back and two to the left. He sucks in a deep breath and studies the upright. When he releases his breath, he takes three quick steps forward, closing the distance to the ball and booting it into the air with a smooth sweep of his leg. What he lacks in muscle, he makes up for in flexibility, his kicking foot flying higher than his shoulder as the ball sails through the upright.

"You're up," Jackson says, voice giving nothing away.

*If he's expecting me to fail, he's in for a surprise.*

I take my place on the field and set the ball in the holder, laces out, just like the tutorial recommended. Apparently kicking the back seam maximizes compression for better height and distance. Who knew?

I walk off the steps, same as I would for a soccer kick. The sounds of practice die down behind me, but I don't dare turn to look. I'd have to be an idiot not to realize all eyes are on me.

Or possibly my ass.

I draw a deep breath, inhaling the scent of fresh-cut grass and willing my racing heart to slow. I have to make this kick. It's only twenty-five yards. Hardly a challenge, even for the skinny dude who's now watching me as intently as Coach Jackson.

Of course, he probably has years of practice under his belt.

But so do I. It's not *that* different.

I release my breath and take my approach steps, keeping my eyes on the ball as I swing my leg back and plow it forward.

My cleat connects with the ball and it rockets off the ground, blasting through the upright.

*Team Carter, FTW!* It's all I can do not to pump my fist in the air.

Coach looks pleased.

The kid next to him? Not so much. Probably wondering if I'm about to steal his job.

"Again!" Coach calls, his smooth baritone giving nothing away.

I put two more through the upright before he has me move the ball back five yards.

Thirty yards. It's nothing. I could do this in my sleep. I take my position with greater speed and less hesitancy this time.

Only this time, the wind grabs the ball and I watch in horror as it sails wide.

*Shit*. Where did that breeze come from? College Park isn't exactly the Windy City.

I sneak a peek at Coach Jackson. He shakes his head, disappointment clouding his eyes. "You have to account for your surroundings, Carter."

I'm well aware of this fact, but the freaking wind came out of nowhere, so I bite my tongue, clenching my jaw so tight he'd need the Jaws of Life to get a response.

"You've got plenty of power," he adds, sounding slightly more encouraging this time. "Give it another try."

So I do. This time, I nail it.

I kick three more for good measure before moving the ball back another ten yards.

Coach grunts in what I can only assume is approval.

Forty yards requires greater concentration and I take my time, ensuring I'm accounting for the August breeze that continues to kick up in sporadic bursts. I'm four for five with one of the balls pinging off the upright.

*Stupid wind.*

Coach Jackson remains unreadable when he signals for me to stop.

I quickly do the math. I made eleven of my thirteen attempts. That's eighty-five percent, if you round up. Which I do. But is it good enough?

"Thanks for coming out today, Carter." He extends a hand and I shake it, hoping he doesn't notice my sweaty palms. "I'll be in touch."

*That's it?*

My stomach bottoms out. It's got to be the shortest tryout in the history of tryouts.

## 5

# AUSTIN

I'M DRAGGING ass by the time practice ends and not even a cold shower can revive me. I'm going to crash as soon as I get back to the apartment, but first I need to see Coach Collins. He hasn't said jack about Carter's tryout, although Coach Jackson seemed pleased enough when she cracked forty yards without breaking a sweat.

Not bad for someone who's never handled a pigskin.

I weave my way through the locker room, taking note of the somber mood. Most of my teammates look as spent as I feel. There are none of the usual antics or shouts.

It's depressing as hell.

Like, one step up from losing-a-game depressing.

I roll my shoulders, trying to ease the tension that's settled in at the base of my neck. Seeing Coach will have to wait. Duty calls.

"Yo, Smith." I throw a balled-up towel at the back of the tight end's head. It bounces off his locs and drops to the floor. He spins to face me, signature grin fixed in place. I match it with my own cocky smile. "Xbox tourney at my place tonight. You owe me a Madden rematch."

Smith tosses his head back and laughs. "For real? You know I'm gonna whoop your ass again, pretty boy."

"Yeah, yeah. Big talk from a guy who won by a fucking point," I counter, knowing the team needs to see the swagger. It's good for morale. And hell, if Smith can smile despite everything he's been through, I guess I can too. Sure, I'm tired, but the team comes first.

*The team always comes first.*

Might as well get it tattooed on my ass, I've heard it so many times from my old man.

"Loser buys pizza," Smith says, doubling down on his mad Xbox skills. "Unless your arm's too tired?"

"Don't you worry about my arm." I smirk and point at him. "You're going down."

"Hell, yeah!" Coop shouts, snapping a wet towel against Smith's ass. "I'll pick up a case of beer on the way home."

A ripple of excitement spreads through the locker room.

Coach has firm rules about partying during camp, but a little Xbox and a couple of beers hardly count as partying. Besides, most of these guys could use a night off. No way this many ballers will fit in the town house Coop and I share with Parker and Vaughn, but most of the upperclassmen live at College Park Apartments since it's close to the fields and they'll all open their doors for a little team bonding.

"Count me in," Parker yells. "You know I'm always down for seeing Reid get his ass beat." He turns and grins at me. "Good for you to get that ego taken down a few pegs."

"S'all good." I shrug and strut toward Coach's office. "Plenty to go around."

I arrive just in time to see Jackson slip through the door. Talk about perfect timing. I take up a post outside Coach Collins's door, figuring I'm within my rights to listen in since I'm the one who found Carter.

Fortunately, Collins takes the open-door policy literally and rarely closes it. Today's no exception, and he instructs Jackson to leave it open.

I inch closer, catching a glimpse of Collins behind the oversize desk before I press my back to the wall. He looks like shit. Apparently the coaching staff is also feeling the effects of the blistering heat.

"Well, how'd it go?" Collins asks, skepticism clear in the tone of his voice.

There's a long pause, as if Jackson's mulling over his answer. My heart thrums in my chest, an unwelcome reminder of the situation I need to fix.

"Carter's got a good leg," he finally says.

"But?"

"No but. First time kicking a field goal and she hit four out of five from forty." Jackson pauses. "Her accuracy's good and the soccer coach says she takes direction well. I can work with that, assuming she can handle the pressure."

I grin, my spirits finally lifting.

"Only one way to answer that question," Collins says. "You want to offer her Spellman's spot on the roster, it's your call."

Jackson doesn't respond immediately, and my palms begin to itch. "There is one other matter we need to discuss. Carter is looking for a scholarship."

Coach grunts and slaps something down on the desk. "Out of the question. She's unproven and we've got men on this team who've been playing three and four years, hoping for a shot at scholarship money."

Fuck. I should've seen this coming. Collins might be a hard ass, but he takes care of his guys.

I let my head drop back and it *thunks* against the wall.

"Quit hovering and get your ass in here, Reid."

*Busted.* But maybe I can make it work to my advantage.

I straighten my spine and stroll into the office like I was just waiting for an invitation. "Coach."

Neither of the men says anything, but Jackson studies me, head tilted and brow furrowed, like I'm a puzzle he can't solve.

*Good luck, bro.* I haven't figured my shit out either.

I don't know Jackson well since he works with Special Teams, but I've heard good things about him from Spellman. And hey, if he wants to give Carter a scholarship, that makes him good stuff in my book.

After a beat, Collins clears his throat. "What the hell are you doing listening at my door, Reid? I know your mama taught you better than that."

His words land like a jab to the solar plexus, and it's all I can do not to flinch. As soon as the reprimand is out of his mouth, it's clear he regrets it.

After all, my mom's dead.

That shit hurts, my chest tightening at the loss like it was yesterday. Or maybe it's the prospect of disappointing her that burns white-hot.

I take a deep breath and embrace the pain.

It's up to me to make this thing with Carter happen.

A lot of people are counting on me. Coach. The team. My dad. The fans.

It's a lot of fucking pressure, and I can already picture the headlines if the team stumbles.

*Nope. Not gonna happen.*

"Austin—"

"Sir," I say, cutting off what will no doubt be an awkward apology.

*Hard pass.*

Got enough of those to last a lifetime when the cancer took my mom.

"I understand there are guys on the team who would appreciate scholarship money, but I think I speak for everyone when I say we want a national title more."

Collins nods. He wants it too. I can see it in his eyes.

"The guys voted me captain because I'm a leader, so I could be the voice of the team. The way I see it, we can't expect to win a national title without a kicker. James"—*fuck, I hope I got the new kid's name right*—"will be good eventually, but we need Carter now."

Jackson shifts in his chair, but says nothing.

"You realize this is highly unorthodox?" Coach asks, rubbing the gray stubble on his jaw.

"Sir, I'm a sucker for a good underdog story. I'd throw my lot in with Carter all day long. She needs the scholarship and we need her leg. We can make this work." I pause, meeting his eye and hoping like hell he can see the determination that's burning in my gut. "I can make this work."

Coach narrows his eyes, but when he throws his hands up, I know I've convinced him. "You're the captain, Reid. It'll be on you to explain it to the rest of the team. And I don't want any damn funny business in the locker room. You feel me?"

I snort. No danger of that happening. Carter's made it clear she doesn't exactly hold football players in high regard.

Coach grunts, and I realize he's waiting for an answer. "No funny business. Got it."

"A woman on the football roster." Coach shakes his head. "I never thought I'd see the day." He turns to Jackson. "It's up to you to work out the logistics. And make sure she understands I won't tolerate distractions of any kind. First sign of trouble, I'll yank that scholarship so fast her head will spin, same as the men."

"I'll get the paperwork started." Jackson climbs to his feet, looking pleased at this turn of events. "Then we can make the call."

Coach shakes his head and scrubs a hand over his face. "This girl really wants to play college ball?"

"Yes, sir." Assuming Carter hasn't changed her mind again.

After all, her record is 0-1.

# 6

# KENNEDY

"Hey, Mom." I do my best to sound cheery despite my roiling stomach. Unfortunately, the greeting comes out more like the croak of a dying frog.

*Good one, Kennedy.*

"Hi, sweetie." Her melodic voice is a balm to my frazzled nerves. "Just calling to check in. I thought you had your first practice with the football team today?"

"I'm on my way there now."

I glance out the bus window as we leave the ivy-covered brick buildings of campus behind and take University Drive out to the football building. I've never been inside the modern stone and glass behemoth, but I've heard it's a state-of-the-art facility on par with pro athletic teams.

*Go Wildcats!*

"Nervous?" she asks. It's been just the two of us for as long as I can remember and it doesn't take her long to suss out my moods.

"Of course I'm nervous." No point lying when she already knows the answer.

I was shocked when Jackson called to say he wanted to work

with me. Apparently he was impressed by my raw talent (because sixteen years of soccer and strength training don't count as experience) and somehow convinced Collins to award me a full scholarship. I still can't believe it, but I agreed to give him my all, dumping soccer and work study.

Fortunately, I've got a little money saved up from my summer internship, which should get me through the semester, if not the year.

"It's not too late to change your mind. I'm sure—"

"I'm not going to back out." I sigh and let my head flop back against the headrest. "We talked about this. It's a full-ride. I can't walk away from that kind of money. Not when you're working your fingers to the bone at the hospital." Nursing might be a noble profession, but it's also grueling, especially when you pick up every double shift you can to cover your kid's tuition. "It's just one season. Twelve weeks."

If you only count the regular season.

"Twelve weeks is more than enough time to get hurt," she snaps, catching me off guard.

We're both silent for a beat.

The only time Mom raises her voice is when she's tired. Her short temper reinforces my decision to take the scholarship.

When she continues, her voice is gentler, but I know what's coming before she even says the words. "You know how I feel about football players, Kennedy."

How could I not? She's been telling me my whole life.

"Don't worry. I have zero interest in dating a player, Mom."

Why would I? My father was a deadbeat quarterback more interested in chasing the NFL dream—and the women, drugs, and parties that came with it—than raising a family. And don't even get me started on the linebacker I dated in high school.

Cheating asshole got a random jersey chaser knocked up senior year, and I had to find out about it on Insta.

#Loser.

So, yeah. No players for me.

*Been there, done that, have the emotional scars to prove it.*

Besides, Coach made it clear if I step out of line, I can kiss my scholarship goodbye.

"Promise me," she says as the bus pulls up to the stop. "Promise me that you will not get involved with any of those boys on the team, Kennedy. I don't want to see you end up like me."

"I promise." I sling my bag over my shoulder and climb to my feet. I hate it when she says that. I know she loves me down to the marrow in her bones—I've always known it—but I can't help the guilt that claws at my throat every time I hear those words. What would her life have been like if she hadn't gotten pregnant with me? "I have to go, but I'll call you tomorrow, okay?"

"I love you."

"Love you too."

I disconnect and stuff the phone in my bag.

My heart is beating double time and Mom's little pep talk didn't exactly help.

I exit the bus and stand on the sidewalk, staring up at the home of Wildcat football. The heat wave from hell continues and the afternoon sun glints off the front of the two-story building, forcing me to squint.

Thanks to a massive fundraising effort, the building was renovated a few years ago to the tune of twelve million dollars. Seems excessive to me, but then again, I'm a nerd at heart, so I can think of about twelve million better ways to spend that kind of cash than dropping it on an eighty-nine-thousand square foot sports facility with a thirteen-thousand square foot weight room.

*Why do they need four practice fields anyway?*

Shit. I'm so nervous I'm doing the numbers thing, letting my brain default to facts and figures because it's what I know best. Some people do yoga to relax. I do numbers.

I gulp down the humid air, solidifying my resolve.

I'll count my way through the whole damn practice if I have to, but I've come this far and I'm not going to back out now.

I march right into the building, doing my best to ignore the flashy decor (this place is rocking some serious Wildcat pride), and give myself props for finding the locker room without too much trouble.

*Go me!*

Coach Jackson is waiting at the door when I arrive.

We exchange curt greetings, and I follow him into the nine-thousand square foot locker room, which is home to one hundred thirteen players.

All of whom seem to freeze when I enter.

That's two hundred and twenty-six eyes fixed on me. Not counting the coaching staff.

The locker room is split into three wide rows, with one row of white lockers running across the back wall, the better for everyone to get a look at me.

Not that I care what they think, but all those eyes?

It's a lot of pressure.

I resist the urge to shift my bag and straighten my spine, forcing myself to meet the stares of my new teammates.

Talk about awkward. Scratch that—*it's awkward as hell.*

Thankfully Coach Collins enters, disrupting the stunned silence. The locker room devolves into chaos, but he quickly squashes it, calling for attention.

"Listen up." His gritty voice carries easily through the large space. "This is Kennedy Carter. She'll be joining Special Teams as a placekicker, working with Coach Jackson. Carter will take Spellman's spot on the roster," he says, turning my way to ensure he's got my attention, "and just like everyone else, she'll be fighting for a starting position."

I meet his stare. *Message received.*

He pauses and the room erupts again, louder than before. I only catch a few snatches of conversation, mostly shock at the prospect of a female joining the team.

No surprise there. It's a first for me too.

Pretty sure I also hear something about making the Wildcats the laughingstock of the conference.

"Is this shit for real?" a guy with a fauxhawk mutters.

My cheeks blaze. I should have realized this would be an issue.

Because fauxhawk? He doesn't look like the kind of dude to embrace feminism.

"Watch yourself, Langley." It's Coach Collins who speaks first. "Carter is a member of this team and will be shown the same respect you'd give any other player. You feel me?"

"Yes, sir," Langley agrees, though the look on his face is anything but compliant.

Reid steps forward, positioning himself to my left. It's a show of solidarity from their captain, and I have to admit I appreciate it.

"All right. Settle down!" Reid waves his hands, gesturing for his teammates—*our teammates*—to bring it down. "Now, I'm proud to be a Wildcat, and it's an honor to lead this team."

He stands tall, shoulders back, and scans the room, making eye contact with each of his guys. I hadn't noticed before, but he's got a strong jaw and it's lined with the slightest bit of stubble, like he didn't have time to shave today.

Normally I'd find it sexy, but he's a football player, so, yeah.

"We've got the best offense in the Big Ten," he bellows, starting back up. He pauses and the guys to my right whoop their agreement with a few shouts of "Hell, yeah!" thrown in. His attention shifts to the players gathered on the left. "And we've got the best defense, am I right?"

The response from the defense is even louder and someone sets off one of those roaring sound effects that sounds just like our Wildcat mascot.

"Special Teams caught a tough break losing Spellman," he continues, and a wave of agreement passes through the room.

I figure I'm the only one questioning the use of the phrase *tough break* because, hello, drunken dare?

Curiosity takes root, and I make a mental note to get the full story from Reid.

"Replacing Spellman won't be easy, but if we want a national championship, we've got to explore all avenues to fill his spot. We've busted our asses to make this team the best in the conference. I sure as hell don't want to lose a game over a missed field goal."

There's a rumble of assent from the team and Coop hollers, "Got that right!"

Then the cocky bastard winks at me.

I pretend not to notice and flip the end of my ponytail over my shoulder.

Reid turns to me then, a half-smile playing across his full lips.

"Carter's got a decade and a half of experience playing on the soccer field and she's got a damn fine leg. We're lucky to have her on the team. I expect every one of you to welcome her with open arms. Let's show her the hospitality and class that makes Wildcat football the best in the country!"

By the time he finishes, he's practically shouting, but his enthusiasm is infectious and the team responds to it, stomping their feet and doing the school cheer.

"This is our year!" he thunders, cheeks flushed, eyes alight, totally in the zone as he pumps his fist in the air. "I want that national title. Who's with me?"

The noise level in the locker room reaches a deafening roar, and I'm impressed by how well Reid commands the room.

But I shouldn't be.

He was born and bred for this.

The son of a legendary quarterback (yes, I Googled him), he grew up in this world. And he probably knows better than anyone that winning means more parties, more women, and more privilege...something I've never experienced.

The cocky QB may be talking me up to the team, but I'm not naive enough to think he's doing it for my benefit. His endgame is clear. He's doing it for a shot at a national title, one he thinks I can help deliver.

*What the hell have I gotten myself into?*

# 7

# AUSTIN

Morning practices are a bitch, but they're better than hitting the weight room at six in the morning, which will start next week with the fall semester. The life of a DI athlete isn't nearly as glamorous as people think.

Our schedules are grueling.

Every minute of the day is packed with training activities, leaving just enough time for basic necessities like eating and showering.

I scrub a hand over my face, trying to throw off the last dregs of sleep, and open my locker without acknowledging Coop.

He's flexing his biceps in the mirror—again.

Lucky for him, I'm too damn tired to bust his balls about it.

I drop my bag in the bottom of the locker and kick off my sneakers, adding them to the carefully contained mess.

Coach instituted a new rule this year: clean locker rooms. It's part of his Sweep the Shed philosophy.

Not that I'm complaining.

The man's got a point. The mess in the locker room has a tendency to spill over into other areas of our lives and onto the field, which is the last thing we need.

"Never have I ever seen a bigger douche," Vaughn says, slapping Coop on the back. Vaughn slams the door to his locker and tucks his helmet under his arm, eyes narrowed. "Don't you ever get tired of admiring yourself?"

"Hell no." A slow grin spreads across Coop's face. "Word of advice: you're going to have a hard time getting laid with that ugly-ass beard of yours."

"What's wrong with my beard?" Vaughn looks genuinely perplexed as his gaze flits from Coop to me and back again.

"Aside from the fact that it needs its own zip code?" I ask, shamelessly piling on.

Vaughn's a good sport and despite his intimidating appearance, he's one of the nicest guys I've ever met. He's the kind of guy who will do anything for a friend and has impeccable manners, even in the locker room where anything goes.

"Seriously, bro. Just because you're from West Virginia doesn't mean you have to look like a mountain man," Coop says, shaking his head like he's an expert on the subject.

Then again, he does have a pretty large female following on campus, so maybe he actually does know what the hell he's talking about.

"You think a girl wants all that," he continues, gesturing to Vaughn's overgrown beard, "scratching her special place while you're going down on her?"

The air quotes he makes when he says *special place* draws a burst of laughter from the guys surrounding us.

Vaughn blushes, his cheeks growing scarlet above the dark scruff. "Fuck off."

"Don't shoot the messenger," Coop calls as Vaughn retreats down the aisle, giving us the one-finger salute over his shoulder.

Okay, so that thing I said about Vaughn's manners? They're usually flawless, but Coop's made it his mission to, as he puts it, "loosen the guy up."

So far, it doesn't seem to be working.

I strip off my T-shirt, pulling it over my head, and slip into my shoulder pads, making quick work of the straps.

*You should've gotten up earlier.*

As team captain, I should be the first one on the field, not the last.

"I hear Special Teams is practicing with us today," Coop says, closing his locker and leaning a shoulder against it.

I glance up at him, not sure where he's going with this. "So?"

"So, that means we'll get to see Carter in action." He grins and wiggles his brows. "I hope she's wearing shorts today."

"Don't be an asshole." I glare up at him as I step out of my shorts and toss them in the locker. "It's one hundred fucking degrees outside. Of course she'll be wearing shorts. And no one's going to say shit, got it?"

"That's what I thought." Coop smirks. "The lady doth protest too much."

I shake my head and grab my jockstrap. The thing ain't pretty, but it gets the job done. "As usual, I have no idea what you're talking about."

"*Riiiiigght.*"

I drop onto the bench in front of my locker and brace myself for more of Coop's brand of wisdom, but it never comes.

"What the fuck?" He stares down at his pants in confusion. Then he does a weird little shimmy and before I know it, he's jamming his hand down the front of his pants, scratching his balls. "What. The. Actual. Fuck!" he howls, going to town on his johnson.

Parker shoots me a *WTF?* look before turning back to Coop with a wicked gleam in his eye. "I told you to double bag that shit. Bet it burns when you piss too."

"I don't have an STD, asshole." Coop yanks his pants down and stares at his junk. "I always wrap it before I tap it."

The volume in the locker room begins to climb as he kicks off his cleats and strips.

When he raises his jockstrap for inspection, I avert my eyes.

I'm used to being surrounded by naked dudes, but I don't need his dick right in my face.

"Which one of you assholes put itching powder in my jockstrap?" he yells, brandishing the flimsy garment. "That shit's not funny!"

Yeah *fuckin'* right.

It's hilarious considering Coop is one of the biggest pranksters on the team.

"Payback's a bitch," Parker says, extending his closed fist so I can bump it. Then his face goes slack and he glances down, a look of panic on his face. "Oh shit."

I inspect the jockstrap in my hand and decide not to risk it. I'd rather free ball it than spend the day with my hand down my pants. I toss the jock on the bench and tug on my practice pants.

The locker room erupts in chaos and Coach storms in, no doubt wondering why the team is standing around with their dicks in their hands when they should be on the field.

"What the hell is going on in here?" he roars, glancing around at his half-dressed team. He narrows his eyes in my direction. I'm not sure if it's because I'm captain or because I'm the only one wearing pants. "Reid, care to tell me why you aren't on the field yet?"

*Not really.*

I sigh and rub the back of my neck. After the Spellman incident, Coach made it clear he expects us to toe the line. If he finds out who did this, there could be a suspension involved.

"Well, sir." I stall, forcing myself to meet his steely gaze. "It seems—"

"Spit it out, son." He waves his hand impatiently and my gaze slides to Coop.

He's too busy scratching to crack the joke Coach just set up and I know we're in deep shit.

"Someone put itching powder in our jockstraps," I admit, relieved I narrowly avoided the same fate as my teammates.

*How's that for loyalty?*

"Fuckin' pranks." Coach shakes his head. "Who did this?" he demands, face flushing a deep shade of crimson as he scans the locker room.

I seriously doubt anyone's going to step forward, but the truth will come out eventually.

It always does over a couple of beers and a solid brag.

"Y'all wanna win a national title and you're wasting my time with this kind of romper-room bullshit? You have ten minutes to take care of business and get your asses on the field. And when I find out who did this..."

The rest of the threat is lost in the pandemonium of the locker room as he stomps back to his office.

"Who do you think did it?" Parker asks, using a towel to dust off his junk.

"No clue." I glance around to see if anyone else dodged the itching powder bullet. "But I hope it's not one of our guys."

Or worse yet, Carter.

Four minutes later, I take the field fully dressed. I'm nothing if not an overachiever.

Most of the guys are still washing up, so it's just me, Carter, and a few of the support staff.

The sun's already high in the sky, and I can feel my temperature rise as I swagger down the sideline to where Carter's stretching, waiting for the team huddle.

"It's about time," she says, not bothering to look up.

She's sitting on the ground with her legs spread, stretching her hamstrings. Her blue shorts are, well, short, not leaving much to the imagination and reminding me of Coop's suggestive comments.

Carter's got great legs. They're long, golden, and perfectly toned.

I'll bet they're smooth as hell too.

Desire stirs in my gut and I drag my eyes from her shapely legs, instead fixing them on her face—or rather, the back of her head, since she's not looking at me. Her dark hair is braided, falling over her shoulder, and she's wearing a headband, not unlike the one circling my own forehead.

"I can't believe you had the nerve to give me crap about punctuality when I'm literally the only one who showed up on time today."

"There was an incident," I say, trying to keep the edge from my voice.

"Oh?" She looks up—and interested—for the first time. "Do tell."

I study her carefully, searching her dark eyes for any sign she might have been the one behind the prank.

After all, as she so quickly pointed out, she was the only one who showed up on time today.

Kind of convenient, isn't it?

Most of the guys have been cool with Carter's presence on the team, but there are a few, like Langley, who still need to be brought into line. Couldn't exactly blame her if she was looking for a little payback, although I'd rather put on a Buckeyes jersey and stroll across campus than admit it out loud.

"Come on, spill," she prods with a grin, her full lips tilting up at the corners.

Damn, she has a nice smile.

*Too bad those lips are dedicated to the forces of evil.*

I could think of better ways to put that mouth to use than all the snark she's been dishing. Much better ways.

Shit. I sound like Coop.

I sigh and rub the back of my neck, feeling like an asshole.

"Someone put itching powder in the guys' jockstraps," I say, going on the offensive. The last thing I should be thinking about is Carter's lips. Coach would have my ass. Besides, I've got a national title to win, which would be a helluva lot easier if my teammates weren't in the locker room scratching their balls. "You wouldn't know anything about that, would you?"

Carter snort-laughs. "Priceless."

She tosses her braid over her shoulder and climbs to her feet. She's not quite tall enough to look me directly in the eye, but she comes closer than most girls, which is kind of hot. Some of the guys on the team are into short girls—spinners, they call them—but I'm a leg guy all day long.

"I wish I could take credit, but sadly, the thought never even crossed my mind." She smirks. "But I'd love to meet the evil genius behind the prank, because she's clearly awesome."

I rake a hand through my hair. "You think it's a chick?"

"Chick? Really, Reid." Carter wrinkles her nose. "Do better."

I lift my brow. So, what, now *chick* is derogatory?

It's like the equivalent of *dude* or something. I stare at her, but she doesn't budge, just meets my defiant gaze with one of her own. Like two twelve-year-olds in a staring contest.

Fine. Whatever. "You really think it's a woman?"

"Totally." She nods her head, the thrill of victory shining in her eyes. "You know what they say, hit 'em where it hurts."

# 8

## KENNEDY

It's day one of senior year and my schedule is bananas. I was late for my first class and after spending hours reviewing syllabi, I'm seriously questioning my sanity.

In a moment of blind ambition, I signed up for eighteen credits of upper-level mechanical engineering classes—a necessary evil if I want to graduate in May—which, coupled with football, is...unhinged.

Seriously. No one in their right mind would willingly sign up for this schedule.

Which totally explains why most of the guys on the team take the minimum credit hours during the season.

Unfortunately, I don't have that luxury.

Not if I want to graduate on time and start paying down my mammoth student loan debt.

So, yeah, fall semester is already kicking my ass and it's only day one.

*First class, then football.*

Special Teams doesn't always join the main practice, but when we do, I swear Reid spends half the time scrutinizing me, no doubt judging my progress and wondering if he made a mistake.

Well, he can suck it.

I've been busting my ass to perfect my technique and with Coach Jackson's help, I'm currently seventy-thirty on the long-range kicks, which is better than the freshmen. Bonus: my accuracy skyrockets to ninety-three percent inside the thirty-five, which is the best on the team.

Still, Reid's lingering gaze is a distraction I can live without.

Thankfully, practice is over, and I've got the visiting team locker room to myself.

It's just as nice as the home team locker room, with the same pristine white lockers, industrial blue carpet and overwhelming scent of disinfectant, but it's kind of lonely—I swear to God there's an echo every time I so much as pee—and for the first time, I miss the women on the soccer team.

Miss having Becca by my side after a tough practice.

Miss the singing and dancing and ridiculous victory celebrations reserved for wins over conference rivals.

I glance around the empty locker room, heart sinking. I didn't realize how much I valued the camaraderie on the soccer team. It's unlikely I'll be participating in any locker room celebrations this year, but you know what they say about hindsight.

*It's a bitch.*

Not that I'm complaining.

Because, hello, full-ride scholarship.

Coach Collins was decent enough to assign me a locker in the home team locker room. But it's mostly a token gesture for inclusivity and game days since getting naked with a bunch of football players is against my personal code of conduct.

Sure, there are women who'd give their left ovary to get in that locker room—including Becca—but I'm not one of them.

I drop onto the heavily padded bench in front of my locker

and let my head rest against the solid white door. My locker in the team room glows with the number ninety-three, my jersey number, but this one is plain. Anonymous even. The complete opposite of me.

I stick out like a sore thumb around the football building.

*Nothing new there.*

I'm used to being the odd woman out in a major dominated by men.

The only thing that matters right now is my scholarship.

And that means taking care of my leg. Which is currently feeling a little tight.

Okay, screaming for relief would be a more accurate description, but I'm not about to tell Coach Jackson. Our first game is this weekend and Collins made it clear I'm fighting for the starting position.

So, yeah, no whining.

No, what I need is a trainer.

Too bad they're all in the men's locker room. If I want a rubdown or ice or any sort of assistance, I'll have to brave all that peen or wait until the guys leave and hope to catch a trainer.

*Which is total bullshit.*

I sit up straight and square my shoulders. Why should I have to wait until the guys leave?

We're teammates. I have just as much need of a trainer as they do.

It's not like I haven't seen a naked man before.

I sling my bag over my shoulder and climb to my feet. I'm a badass, and I'm totally doing this.

A nervous laugh escapes as I weave my way toward the door.

Becca is going to die when I rehash this later. By her own admission, she'd sell her soul to get up close and personal with the kind of muscles these guys are packing.

Plus she has a thing for asses, and there's no shortage of those on the football team.

When I reach the door to the team locker room, I pause, taking a deep breath to calm my racing heart. Maybe this isn't such a good idea after all.

*Don't be such a chicken! Get your ass in there and take care of business.*

Right. My leg. The one that feels tighter than a brand-new rubber band.

I suck in one more fortifying breath and steel my resolve. Then I push the door open and saunter into the locker room like it's no big thing, like I belong.

That feeling of belonging? It's lasts for about point four seconds.

It doesn't take the guys long to notice me standing in the doorway.

A few grab for their towels, but most just stare at me like they've never seen a woman before. Or, more precisely, a woman in their locker room.

*Talk about déjà vu.*

Whatever. They have to get used to me being here at some point, right?

I lift my chin, determined to see this through and find the trainer. Still, it's impossible not to notice all the cocks in the room. Heat flares at the back of my neck, and I do my best to keep my eyes up, but come on, it's a total dickfest.

Big dicks, hairy dicks, bald dicks, thick dicks. Tiny dicks, too.

At least now I know why Langley has such a chip on his shoulder.

I eye his baby peen and arch a brow. His girlfriend must be so disappointed.

The tops of his ears turn red and he scrambles to wrap a towel around his waist.

*How's that for laughingstock, asshole?*

Feeling smug—and, okay, a little bitchy—I turn toward the trainer's office.

"It's about time you joined us." Coop saunters up in a pair of mesh shorts with the Waverly logo on the leg. His shaggy hair is damp from the shower, but at least he's got pants on. He leans in close and whispers, "I figured it would take you until at least October to work up the nerve."

"And I figured it would take you until at least October to remember my name, given the parade of women trailing you around campus." I flash him my brightest smile. "I guess we were both wrong."

To my surprise, he throws his head back and laughs. It's a deep, rich sound, like it's coming straight from the pit of his belly.

"You slay me, Carter. If I were the settling-down type, I'd totally let you be my wifey."

"Don't flatter yourself." I roll my eyes and grudgingly return his fist bump. Nothing sticks to this guy, but I have to admit he's growing on me. Kind of like that little spot of mold in the shower I just can't get rid of. "I'm here to see the trainer, not provide the entertainment."

"Don't let me hold you up." He throws his palms up in surrender, an expression of innocence transforming his face from wicked rogue to choirboy. "Get your shit taken care of. We need you in top form on Saturday."

*Holy crap.* Did Cooper DeLaurentis just compliment me?

I watch in dismay as he retreats to his locker.

And here I thought the guy didn't take anything seriously.

I weave my way through the locker room, keeping my eyes fixed straight ahead. Little good it does, because when I turn the corner, I crash boobs first into the solid, slippery chest of Austin Reid. I stumble back and my stupid feet get tangled in the strap of a half-zipped duffel bag, sending me careening toward the floor.

Reid leaps forward, quick as lightning, and grabs my shoulders, slowing my descent and preventing me from falling flat on my ass.

*Just like a real-life Captain America.*

I look up, mortification burning my cheeks, and do a full-body scan. My mouth is drier than the Sahara, and I doubt I could form a proper sentence if I wanted to.

*Damn.* The guy really does have muscles for days, and I can see them all because he's practically naked.

Not that I'm looking—*much.*

"You okay?" He gives my shoulder a squeeze, the sinewy muscles of his biceps flexing in the process.

Water drips from his hair and I watch, entranced, as a droplet slides over his well-defined pecs and down the front of his washboard abs, the V-cut pointing directly to the danger zone. The tiny droplet disappears into the white terry-cloth towel wrapped around his waist, snapping my brain back to reality.

"Huh?" I ask, pulse thundering through my veins.

"Are you okay?" he repeats, speaking more slowly this time.

"I'm fine." Though I should probably get up off the floor. People are starting to stare.

Reid's grip on my shoulders is gentle, and my flesh burns through my Waverly tee as if his calloused fingers were infused with fire.

*Danger! Danger!*

What am I thinking? Reid's a football player. And a QB to boot.

Okay, no need to panic. So he's hot. There's no rule that says I can't appreciate a guy who's got ripped muscles and a great—okay, godly—physique.

He may look like Adonis, but no harm done.

*Shit.* That's probably what my mom told herself back in the day.

Is this how things started between her and my father? An innocent touch here. A fiery kiss there.

Not that I'm thinking of kissing Reid. Just speaking hypothetically, of course.

"Are you sure you're okay?" Reid narrows his eyes suspiciously. "You didn't hit your head, did you?"

He reaches for my chin like he's going to inspect me for a concussion. I bat his hand away, finally finding my voice.

"I'm fine. Other than my pride." I glance at his towel, which has slipped dangerously low on his hips, damn near giving me a full frontal in his crouched position. "Why don't you take care of that," I suggest, waving a hand toward his crotch, "before you flash the whole locker room."

Reid smirks, the corners of his lips lifting just enough to reveal his dimple. "Trust me, it's nothing they haven't seen before."

"Yes, well, I have no interest in seeing it." I climb to my feet and smooth the front of my T-shirt. Reid stands and gives me a once-over, so I return the favor.

*Big mistake.*

Huge, actually, because I can't help but notice the bulge behind his towel. No baby peen for Reid. The guy's packing, which probably explains the way he swaggers around campus like he's God's gift.

I jerk my gaze back to his face, ignoring the way my belly flips at the thought of his...package. If he notices my stare, he says nothing. I offer a silent prayer, thanking sweet baby Jesus himself Reid can't hear my thoughts.

"No need to be embarrassed." He casually drapes a hand over the spot where his towel is tied. Then he steps closer, getting all up in my personal space before continuing in a husky voice, "You know, you can join us in the team locker room any time you want."

I snort, something I would never do in front of a guy I was actually attracted to—hormones notwithstanding. "Thanks, but no thanks."

"Your loss." He shrugs a shoulder, and my gaze darts to his smooth pecs, which are devoid of hair. Does he shave his chest? Probably. "It would really help you get better integrated with the rest of the team."

My temper flares.

*Typical.* Just when I was starting to think he wasn't a complete ass—he did break my fall, after all—he goes and proves me wrong.

"I don't think having them ogle my breasts is the golden ticket to team bonding."

The moment the words are out of my mouth, I know it's hypocritical, because hello, I just checked him out. But honestly? I doubt these guys care. According to the gossip mill, they're dropping their pants for women all over campus.

Me? Not so much. I can count my hookups on one hand.

"Jesus, Carter. Give me some credit. I meant for pregame meetings and halftime and shit." His eyes darken with...disappointment? What the hell? How was I supposed to know it was a serious offer? He sidesteps me and struts halfway down the aisle before turning and calling over his shoulder. "See you at study hall. I'll save you a seat."

# 9

# AUSTIN

I ROLL into study hall with my backpack slung over my shoulder and a smoothie in my hand.

I'm running late because I had to swing by the nutrition bar and grab snacks for my roommates. I've learned the hard way if they aren't eating, they're talking, and I can't get shit done. I feel like a goddamn babysitter, bribing them to sit still and behave for two hours, but whatever.

I've got a shit ton of reading to do for my career management class, which I wouldn't be taking if it weren't required. I don't want to fall behind, even if the class is a joke. Like some prof is going to be able to help me figure out how to manage my career in the NFL.

*Un-fucking-likely.*

That's what sports management firms are for.

Hell, I've already got a dozen trying to woo me into signing once my NCAA eligibility expires, despite the fact it's a foregone conclusion I'll sign with my dad's agent.

The library's second-floor reading room is mostly empty, a first day perk that won't last, but it makes spotting the guys easy enough.

Not that they'd be hard to spot even if the room were packed.

They're big, loud, and completely at odds with the old-school space that probably hasn't been updated in decades.

Mahogany bookshelves line the walls, broken up only by the half-dozen floor-to-ceiling windows that allow the last light of day to filter through. Row after row of heavy oak tables fill the room, each surrounded by neatly arranged chairs with wide backs and seats that are as uncomfortable as hell.

Still, it's nice to get out of the academic center—where the underclassmen are required to sign in for study hall—once in a while.

Parker notices me at the door and waves.

"Saved you a seat!" he calls, deep voice carrying across the open space.

The thing about the reading room? It's supposed to be a silent space.

So even though the room is mostly occupied with football players, there are a few studious types shooting the O-line pissed-off glares as they toss a foam football back and forth over the green table lamps.

*Assholes.*

I'd tell them as much, but there's no point.

For every pissed-off stare, there's one filled with adoration or lust, which means they'll keep the antics up all night and I won't get shit done.

I shake my head and weave through the long tables, making my way to the back corner where my roommates are camped out, books spread across the table to create the illusion of studying.

Parker slides his shit over and makes room for me. I take the seat at the end and unzip my bag, dumping my haul onto the table. Protein bars, single-serve nuts, cereal, and a bunch of other crap spills out on the table, sending the guys into a frenzy as they grab for snacks.

"Vaughn's mama ain't got nothing on you." Parker grabs a protein bar and shoots Vaughn a toothy grin.

Vaughn, whose mom still sends care packages despite the fact that her son is now a senior, flips him the bird and tears open a tube of trail mix, pouring the entire contents into his mouth.

"Yeah, well, I actually need to get some work done. I figured this was the best way to keep you assholes quiet." I pull a couple of notebooks and texts from my bag and drop them on the table before opening the side pocket to search for a highlighter and pen. "You can show your gratitude by keeping the volume to a minimum."

"Dude, it's day one." Coop rolls his eyes like I'm the diva here. "Chill out."

Ignoring him, I crack open my career management text and begin reading, highlighting passages that seem likely to pop up on an exam, because unlike Coop, academics don't come easy to me. I have to bust my ass to make grades.

Waverly's got a long tradition of academic achievement among student athletes and as team captain, I'm expected to set a good example, which means I have to make the Dean's List.

I'm halfway through my reading assignment when Coop nudges me in the shoulder.

"What?" I ask without looking up.

"Carter's here," he stage-whispers, leaning close. "Figured you'd want to do your captain thing and roll out the welcome wagon. Unless, of course, you'd like me to do the honors?"

He's jerking me around. I know it, and still I rise to the challenge, shoving my chair away from the table. "On it."

Because no, I don't fucking want Coop anywhere near her.

It's a feeling I refuse to consider beyond my role as captain.

Carter's hovering near the door, chewing her bottom lip as if she can't decide whether she should sit down or make a run for it. Her dark hair tumbles over her slender shoulders in loose waves, and she looks more relaxed than usual, despite the indecision written all over her face.

I catch her eye and nod as I make my way across the room, smiling at a couple of jersey chasers—Leslie and Gemma—who wave as I pass their table. They're regulars at the football house, but who am I to judge?

They're cool as hell and I'm a fan of no-strings sex myself.

I may not be the most evolved guy on the planet, but I can sure as hell appreciate a woman who's not afraid to take what she wants, society's double standards be damned. If anyone's being used, it's the players. Women lose their shit for the muscles we work so damn hard to carve and there are plenty of females on campus who just want to bag 'n' brag.

"Fans of yours?" Carter asks, rolling her eyes.

"More like acquaintances." I stuff my hands into my pockets and immediately regret the words.

I know what it sounds like, despite the fact that I've never hooked up with either of them.

Carter presses her lips into a flat line, and I can practically hear her calling me a pig in her head. "So."

"So, we saved you a seat, as promised."

I gesture to the table where my roommates are doing a piss-poor job of pretending they aren't watching us.

They aren't the only ones.

Several heads jerk away when I turn, and I know half the damn team is staring. The thing is, they're curious about Carter. She hasn't exactly made an effort to fit in, and after today's little stunt in the locker room, most of the guys view her as a wild card.

Not exactly ideal heading into our first game.

Carter's gaze sweeps the room and settles on an empty table that's about as far away from my own as she can get. "I've got a lot of reading to do. I think I'll just go sit over there where it's quiet."

I can't exactly fault her logic, but fortunately, her stomach growls at that exact moment. Most women I know would be mortified, but Carter appears unfazed. Still, it's an opening and I'm not about to let an opportunity pass.

"Come on." I nod toward the back corner. "We've got snacks, but Vaughn's likely to devour them if we don't get over there."

She bites her lower lip, seeming to debate the offer, before finally shaking her head and relenting, her dark eyes wary. "Thanks, I missed dinner."

We fall in step and her elbow brushes mine, a jolt of awareness sliding up my arm before settling low in my gut.

The guys scoot down and make room for Carter, giving her the seat directly across from me.

We settle back in as she unpacks her bag, hefting a textbook that must be three inches thick onto the table.

"Holy shit! You carry that thing around with you? It must weigh like twelve pounds," Coop says, a look of disbelief on his face. Then he reaches out and squeezes her biceps. "These scrawny things must be stronger than they look." He flashes her a mischievous grin that's helped him score in more ways than one. "You know, I could show you a few good exercises to—"

"My arms are fine." Carter swats his hand away. She's not wrong. Her toned arms are golden brown from the summer sun, and there's nothing scrawny about them. "And if you touch me again," she says, giving him a saccharine smile, "I might accidentally drop that book on your foot."

I'm pretty sure she's serious, but Coop just laughs and shakes his head.

"Now that I'd like to see." Vaughn grins at Carter and

extends his giant paw. She shakes it, looking only slightly intimidated by our token mountain man. "I'm Vaughn, by the way. Nice to meet you."

"Same," she says, though her stilted reply lacks the sincerity of Vaughn's words.

"And that troublemaker over there," I say, nodding at the last of my roommates, "is DJ Parker."

"S'up?" Parker lifts his chin in greeting.

"Hey." Carter grabs a bag of trail mix from the pile of snacks and tears it open. She pops a handful in her mouth and chews ravenously.

Two ounces of nuts does not a dinner make, so I toss another bag her way.

It lands on her textbook, and Vaughn leans in for a closer look.

"Mechanical engineering, huh?" He studies her with a new appreciation. "Tough major."

"Damn, girl. You must be a brain," Parker chimes in. "Me? I'll take the soft subjects every day of the week."

Yeah, right. Parker may be studying communications, but he's no slouch. The guy's super smart and could easily handle a more rigorous major, but it would be a waste of time since he's hoping to work in sports broadcasting where he can put his charm to good use.

Carter shrugs, pretending it's no big deal despite the telltale blush creeping up her neck. "It's not so bad. I've always enjoyed STEM classes."

"STEM?" Vaughn asks, leaning forward with genuine interest.

"Science, Technology, Engineering, and Math." Carter opens her book. It's clear she's done with the interview portion of the evening, but the guys aren't letting up. I consider intervening but decide to keep my mouth shut. Getting to know one another on a personal level is an important part of team bonding and Carter could sure as shit use some friends on the team.

Besides, the guys are on their best behavior.

Parker grabs one of her notebooks—clearly not worried about the threat of a twelve-pound textbook—and holds it up for inspection. "So what's the deal with your name anyway? Kennedy Carter? Your parents hoping to raise the first female president or what?"

Carter shifts in her seat, not meeting his gaze.

Parker's teasing is harmless, totally in good fun. Anyone who knows him would see that, but the thing is, Carter doesn't know Parker. She doesn't know any of us beyond her preconceived notions, which I'm pretty sure she'd sum up as *douchebag football players.*

That attitude irritates the shit out of me, but Carter's part of the team. I owe her the same support I'd give any of the guys.

"Knock it off, Parker." I grab the notebook and hand it back to her. "Some of us actually need to study and you're disturbing the peace."

I glance over his shoulder and lift my chin, indicating a particularly pissed-off looking guy who's glaring at us over the top of a physics book.

"You know what?" Carter scoops up her books and clutches them to her chest. "I'm going to grab another table. It was really nice meeting you," she says, looking from Vaughn to Parker, "but I really work better on my own. I guess I'll...see you at practice."

Well, fuck me.

# 10

## KENNEDY

I SETTLE my things at a new table on the far end of the reading room and haul ass for the stacks. I don't actually need anything other than a break from the intense stares and endless questions of my teammates. Having all those guys looking at me, constantly probing?

It's uncomfortable as hell. Even if a few of them do seem kind of nice.

And, okay, funny.

Whatever. It's probably just a front.

After all, I know exactly what kind of guys they are, and I'm not going to make the same mistake as my mother.

*Hard. Pass.*

I've suffered enough heartbreak and disappointment at the hands of ballplayers to last a lifetime, thank you very much. Like the time my father promised to take me to the zoo for my seventh birthday and never showed. Or the time he bailed on the fifth-grade father-daughter dance because he got tickets to a playoff game. Oh, and then there was the time he showed up drunk to my high school graduation with a woman half his age in tow.

At least by then, I was old enough to understand I wasn't the problem.

So, yeah, the last thing I need in my life is more ballplayers.

Shaking off all thoughts of my deadbeat father, I wander past the stacks and head for the water fountain, glancing up at the clock as I pass by. I'll get a drink and then head back to my table. Only fifty-four minutes to go.

*Easy peasy.*

Except this is only day one.

Which means I have to face another fifty-nine study halls with these guys.

I suppress a groan. No way am I going to get through twelve weeks of study halls without more awkward encounters like the one tonight.

Shit. Maybe I can get a private room at the academic center. That's a thing, right?

I stop at the fountain and twist my hair before tossing it over my shoulder and bending to get a drink.

*Ugh.* Why are the water fountains so low to the ground? I know I'm tall, but come on, I feel like my ass is on display for the whole library to see.

*That's what you get for leaving your water bottle at home.*

Pushing the thought aside, I press the metal button and lower my lips to the stream of icy cold water, doing my best not to dribble on the front of my shirt.

As I'm drinking—okay, fine, guzzling—a pair of preppy deck shoes stroll into my peripheral vision, lingering just to the left of the fountain.

*Um, hello, personal space?*

I release the button for the water flow and straighten my spine, pulling myself up to my full height, where I find myself face-to-face with Reid.

Should've known. He's not one to give up easily.

"Do you stalk all your teammates, or is this a special privilege reserved just for me?" I plant my hand on my hip and cock it to the side for maximum impact.

Total waste of effort, because as it turns out, his gaze is locked on my mouth.

*Oh hell.* Do I have water dribbling down my chin?

I lick my lips, praying I don't have water on the front of my tank top. Kind of hard to be badass when you've got water spots on your shirt.

Reid swallows, his Adam's apple rising and falling, before his hooded eyes meet mine. "We need to talk."

"No, we don't."

I turn and head for the stacks, hoping to ditch Reid. The only thing I need right now is space, and it's clear he isn't going to give it to me. He's right on my heels, easily matching my long stride. I hook a left, turning into the stacks like I totally know where I'm going (spoiler alert: I don't.)

I steal a quick glance at the shelves and realize I don't even know what section we're in. The library has three floors, plus a basement, and houses five-point-four million books, so yeah, I feel sorry for the poor sucker who has to do the reshelving, but mostly I feel sorry for my directionally challenged self at the moment.

"You can't outrun me," Reid says, his words tinged with laughter.

Crap. He's right. It's a dead end.

I slow my pace and stop in front of a random shelf, studying it with purpose, like I've arrived at my intended destination.

Reid stops a breath away—literally—using his giant body to crowd me in the narrow space. With towering bookshelves pressing in on either side, he's effectively blocked my escape with his broad shoulders.

Judging by the shit-eating grin on his face, he knows it.

From my periphery, I can see him glancing around, taking in our surroundings like he's never seen the inside of a library before.

*Or he's casing the place to see if there will be any witnesses to whatever he's planning.*

My pulse quickens.

"Are you really looking for a book or are you just trying to avoid me?" he asks, the words a husky whisper as they skate across my cheek.

"Book, obviously," I lie, keeping my attention fixed on the shelf before me.

I've always been a shitty liar. It's ridiculous to cling to this pointless charade, but my stupid pride refuses to admit defeat.

After all, if Harry Potter can take down Lord Voldemort, surely I can best Austin Reid.

"Really? What book?" He inches closer, the fresh, spicy scent of his cologne tickling my nose. "I'll help you look."

"No thanks." When I turn to meet his gaze, our mouths are dangerously close. *Nope, nope, nope.* I snap my attention back to the bookshelf. "I've got this."

"I'll bet." His voice is a low rumble as he reaches around me, fingers skimming across my biceps, and pulls a book from the shelf. A shiver races up my spine, and I can't bring myself to look at him as he scans the cover. "What's a mechanical engineering major need with a bunch of psychobabble bullshit?" He holds up a psych book with a picture of an abstract brain on the cover.

The smirk on his face says I'm totally busted.

Pulse racing, I wipe my palms on my thighs, certain it's annoyance making my heart beat double time and not Reid's dimple.

"Well, what do you know?" I snatch the book out of his hand and clutch it to my chest like a golden ticket. "Just the one I was looking for."

"Uh-huh," he deadpans, shifting his weight and crossing his arms over his chest. "Look, I'm serious. We need to talk about your role on the team."

Clearly he's not going to let this go, so I decide to roll with it. Whatever *it* is. "What about my role on the team?"

"As team captain, it's my job to make sure the team gels and plays like a cohesive unit." He pauses, blue eyes scanning my face for understanding. "That works best when everyone pulls together. It's good for morale and winning games."

I tilt my head, completely lost. "I have no idea what you're trying to say, but I'm not some delicate flower you have to worry about crushing. Just give it to me straight, okay?"

It'll be less painful for both of us.

"You're a wild card." He heaves a monumental sigh and plants his hands on his hips. "It's messing with team morale. The guys don't know you and therefore don't trust you."

I open my mouth to protest, but he holds up a hand and plows forward.

"Look, I get it. Kickers do their own thing at practice, but it wouldn't kill you to act like part of the team once in a while. There are some pretty good guys back there." He hooks a thumb over his shoulder, pointing toward the reading room.

"Really?" I challenge, indignation fanning a fiery ball of outrage in my belly. "Because I hear the talk. I know what football players are like."

He quirks a brow. "Do you?"

"Oh, come on." I blow a loose strand of hair out of my face. "Langley thinks I'm going to make Waverly the laughingstock of the conference."

"Fuck Langley." He doesn't miss a beat and the passion behind his words catches me off guard. His swift agreement takes some of the wind out of my sail, because most of the guys have been more welcoming than Langley. "He's an asshole."

"I know."

"So prove him wrong." He rakes a frustrated hand through his hair, destroying the artfully messy spike. "Most of the guys on the team want to have your back, but you're not making it easy. These guys have been playing ball their whole lives and for some, it's the last time they'll ever play. The last time they'll have a shot at a national title. So maybe you could act like you give a damn."

That fiery ball of outrage in my belly expands. It's practically a full-scale inferno now.

"I wouldn't be here if I didn't give a damn." I poke him in the chest and do my best to ignore the fact that the wall of muscle doesn't so much as budge. "In case you've forgotten, I bailed on a sport I love for one I hate."

"What do you have against football?" he asks, curiosity lighting his eyes.

Or maybe it's disbelief, because how could anyone not love football, right?

"That's irrelevant." I lift my chin and cross my arms over my chest.

We are so not going there.

He narrows his eyes, suspicious. "You're so sure you know what we're like. Have you ever even spent any time with a ballplayer?"

I flinch. The accusation stings, reminding me of my father, whose absence taught me everything I need to know about football players.

"What do you want from me?" I throw my hands up. "I'm learning a new technique, and I'm here busting my ass every day."

"Are you? Because it seems like you've got one foot out the door." He pauses and rubs the back of his neck, suddenly Mr. Fidget. *Serves the self-important ass right.* His voice is soft when he continues. "I stuck my neck out for you. The least you could do is try to fit in with the team."

His words catch me off guard, hitting me like a sucker punch to the gut.

He didn't stick his neck out for me. He did it for himself. For his shot at a national title and parties and women and draft picks and whatever the hell else it is football players actually give two fucks about.

Not for me.

Laughter bubbles up from the pit of my stomach, and for once I don't even care if I'm breaking library rules by being loud. "Let's be honest, you were dead in the water without me. We both know it. So instead of bitching about my team spirit—or lack thereof—perhaps you could say thank you."

I arch a brow for good measure, because, honestly, who the hell does he think he is?

"Okay, that might've come out wrong—"

"You think?" I snort and flip my hair over my shoulder, channeling my inner Veronica Lodge.

"Don't get me wrong, we're thankful to have you on the team —*I'm* thankful to have you on the team—but that's awful big talk for someone who hasn't proven herself yet."

"Seriously?" I knit my brows together and purse my lips. What the hell does he think I've been doing at practice for the last two weeks? "Because Coach Jackson is thrilled with my progress. In fact, he told me today I'm starting on Saturday."

If he's surprised by the news, he doesn't show it. "See me after your first game," he says, eyes blazing, chest heaving. "All those soccer games you played? They're nothing compared to the bright lights and screaming crowds of D1 football. You ever have one hundred thousand fans screaming your name, counting on you to bring home the win? It's pressure like you couldn't imagine, so trust me when I say you'll want the team at your back."

Without another word, he turns on his heel and walks away.

I watch him retreat, his words echoing in my head.

*Pressure, indeed.*

## 11

## AUSTIN

I KNOCK on Coach's door, unease twisting my gut. It's not exactly unusual for him to call me in after practice, and there's no way he could know about the blowup between Carter and me, but...

He waves me into the office. "Come on in, son."

His face gives nothing away except the fact that he's spent too much time in the sun.

I slide into the chair opposite his desk, casually draping my hands over the front of the armrests, and hope like hell this isn't going to be a repeat of the Spellman conversation.

"How're things going with Carter?"

"Fine." Aside from the fact that I can't stop thinking about the way she bites her plump lower lip. Or how bad I wanted to kiss her senseless when she was spewing righteous indignation between the stacks.

*Talk about hot and bothered.*

Just the memory makes me shift in my seat.

Coach tosses his pen on the desk and leans back in his chair to study me. "She fitting in okay with the rest of the team?"

"As well as can be expected," I hedge, avoiding an outright lie.

In truth, the woman is infuriating as hell, a fact that's making me feel like a complete failure as captain, something I refuse to accept.

Coach narrows his eyes to slits, his bushy brows flattening. "Something you want to tell me?"

"No, sir." I'm determined to figure Carter out on my own.

It's rare someone can slip past my defenses and make me lose my shit, but she seems to have a rare gift for pushing my buttons. And vice versa, if I'm being honest. Sure, I'm annoyed, but mostly at myself for screwing things up in the first place.

In retrospect, I probably could've handled the whole teamwork conversation better.

But, honestly? There are a ton of guys on the team who'd give their left nut for a full-ride.

Doesn't she get how big a deal this is?

Even so, I feel like a dick about how we left things at the library. It isn't like me to walk away—from a fight or a teammate—and the last thing I'd want to do is psych her out before her first game.

*Shit. What if she gets performance anxiety because of me?*

Some fucking leader I am.

"Good," Coach says, dragging me back to the present. "I actually called you in to talk shop."

My ears perk up, but I keep my mouth shut.

"Got a call from a scout in Chicago yesterday." He leans forward and rests his elbows on the desk, lacing his fingers together. My heart begins to pound. He's got my full attention now. "You ever think about playing ball in the Windy City?"

Fuck yeah, I have. Like every day for the last two years. They've got a killer coaching staff and although the team is in a rebuilding phase, there's a lot of potential there.

I shrug, not trusting myself to speak.

"They've got a good program in Chicago, despite their

record. Coach Norris is a good man and a good coach. He could really help elevate your game as you transition into the NFL."

I nod, tamping down my excitement. Coach doesn't need to know I'm pissing myself at the prospect of attention from Chicago. "I appreciate the interest, sir, but I don't think it's in the cards. My family wants me to play ball in Pittsburgh."

I've always known that wherever I go, all roads lead to the Steel City. It was all my parents ever talked about when I was a kid, seeing me wear the black and gold one day. Just like my old man.

Hell, I'm wearing a black and gold striped hat and matching blanket in my first baby picture.

No way I'm going to let them down when their—*the* dream is finally within reach.

"Pittsburgh." Coach grunts. "I know it's your old man's team, but you could be part of something special in Chicago. Blaze your own trail, so to speak. Team's got the makings of being great one day. They just need a solid QB to jump-start the program."

He's not wrong. Chicago's always had a first-rate defense.

If they could play both sides of the ball at the same caliber, they'd dominate the NFC North.

But I'm hardly in a position to blaze my own trail, even if the prospect gets my blood thrumming.

Outwardly, the draft will decide my fate. But there will be a shit ton of wheeling and dealing behind the scenes. My father's got friends in high places and I have no doubt he can make Pittsburgh a reality.

It wouldn't be the first time a QB threatened not to sign if he didn't like the draft team.

"Look, I know you've got history in Pittsburgh, but it couldn't hurt to talk to the Chicago scout." He levels me with his eyes, no doubt taking my measure. "You're one of the top players in the country, Reid." What he doesn't say is that I'll also be a top draft pick, but we both know it's true. "And a good leader." Except, apparently, when it comes to Carter. "There are going to be a lot of teams sniffing around this season, son. I wouldn't be doing my job if I didn't encourage you to explore all your options and find the team that's right for you. Not your family, *you*."

I grunt noncommittally, ignoring the disappointment gnawing at my gut.

No sense wasting the scout's time or mine. And definitely no sense getting my hopes up for things that aren't meant to be. I'll be a franchise quarterback, but it won't be in Chicago.

My future was laid out years ago. Now all I have to do is walk the path.

"Anything else, sir?" I rise to my feet, the weight of expectation heavier than usual.

"No, you're free to go."

Coach glances over my shoulder and I turn to find Carter hovering at the door. I freeze, tension coiling in my chest at the sight of her toying with a wet rope of hair.

*How much of our conversation did she hear?*

She clears her throat, but doesn't meet my eyes. Enough then. "Um, you wanted to see me, Coach?"

I shouldn't be surprised by her presence. Coach probably just wants to talk to her about Saturday's game. But football's the last thing on my mind as I take in the guarded look in her eyes.

*The look I put there.*

My breath comes hard and fast. I want to apologize, tell her I'm sorry for being a colossal jackass, but this is hardly the time with Coach breathing down my neck. Besides, there's so much shit between us right now, it takes a superhuman effort just to get my mask of control back in place.

The woman has a talent for slipping past my defenses, I'll give her that much.

Problem is, it can only lead to trouble—*for both of us.*

# 12

## KENNEDY

I STIFLE a yawn and check my reflection in the mirror, making sure my hair is somewhat presentable. It's not something I typically worry about for practice—it'll be a hot mess by the time we're done—but with the home opener tomorrow and all the speculation surrounding little ol' me, Coach thought it would be a good idea to let the media watch practice today.

Oh, and apparently I have to do an interview as well.

Just the thought makes me twitchy.

I'm not great with public speaking (okay, real talk—I suck at it), but Coach assured me it would just be one or two local reporters plus someone from *The Collegian*.

"It's just a regular practice," I remind myself, although the face in the mirror looks far from convinced. Or maybe it's just lack of sleep making my eyes appear flat.

With sixteen-hour days and hardly a moment to breathe, the football schedule makes soccer feel like a walk in the park.

It also means I rarely see Becca, despite the fact that we live together.

Clearly I should have asked more questions before saying yes, because I had no idea the team was expected to be in the weight room from six to eight every morning. Or that there would be morning meetings and afternoon game tape reviews, in addition to daily practices. Or that my day would start at six in the morning and go until nine at night.

*If* I'm lucky enough to get all my schoolwork done in study hall.

And that if? It's a biggie.

*Stupid bananapants schedule.*

My phone rings as I move to shut my locker, and I glance at the clock. I've got a few minutes before practice starts, so I grab my phone and swipe to accept the call.

"Hey, Mom."

"Hi, sweetie." Her words are cheerful, buoyant even. *Someone's in a good mood.* The thought brings a smile to my face. "How's your day going?"

"Good." Because all things being relative, it is a good day. Despite the fact that I'm about to go perform like a show pony for a bunch of reporters. "I've got practice in a few minutes, but I'm glad you called. You sound happy and...well rested."

For the first time in ages, her words aren't weighed down by fatigue.

"That's because the car's running again, and I let my director know I'll be cutting my hours back when the next schedule comes out."

*The light at the end of the tunnel.*

Relief floods my veins, loosening the ever-present knot of worry in my chest. "Good. You always preach the value of self-care. It's about time you indulge in a little."

"I'll certainly have plenty of free time." She sounds excited by the prospect, reaffirming my decision to play football. I may be tired, but Mom's been working her ass off, shouldering the financial burden of our little family for twenty-one years—alone. I can do it for one season. "Who knows? Maybe I'll even take one of those Zumba classes that are all the rage at the community center."

"Whoa, listen to you, wild woman." A smile curves my lips. "Don't get too carried away."

We share a laugh, but her voice is wrought with concern when she speaks again. "Speaking of getting carried away, how're things going with the team? You're not getting *involved* with those boys, are you?"

"Mom!" Heat floods my cheeks, and I turn away from the mirror, not needing to see the evidence of my total humiliation. Thank God my mom isn't into FaceTime, because I'm pretty sure *involved* is code for *sex* and while the only orgasms I'm having are courtesy of two AA batteries, one look at my face would tell her everything she needs to know about my lusty Reid-centric thoughts. "Are we going to have this conversation every time you call?"

I mean, honestly, we've been having the same "football players suck" conversation since I got my first period. And fine, maybe I ignored it to my detriment in high school, but I've learned my lesson. It's time to move on.

She pauses, and I can easily imagine her pursing her lips on the other end of the line, running her reply through the filter I'm sorely lacking.

"I won't apologize for worrying about you," she says, her words filled with that fierce tiger-mom pride that floods my heart with warmth. "You're my baby, and it's my job to protect you. Trust me. They're all the same. I don't want to see you learn that lesson the hard way."

*Like she did.*

I swallow, reminding myself why I agreed to do this in the first place.

"Don't worry. I'm not going to do anything that would jeopardize my scholarship, which is why I've got to go. Practice is starting."

She sighs. "All right. I don't want to make you late. I'm sorry I can't make it to the game tomorrow, but I'll be listening on the radio at work. You're going to do great."

"Thanks, Mom." She may not like that I'm playing football (probably hates it with the fire of a thousand suns), but I have zero doubt her confidence in me is sincere. She's always been my biggest fan. "I love you."

We say our goodbyes, and I make my way to the outdoor practice field where Coach Jackson is already waiting with the reporters. Five of them, to be exact.

Which is two more than I expected.

My belly flips, and for an instant, I think the apple slices I ate on my way over might make a reappearance. Not exactly the kind of headline I want to make today.

"Miss Carter," Coach Jackson says by way of greeting before swiftly introducing the reporters.

Their names and affiliations are lost on me—my brain is stuck on a let's-get-this-over-with-before-I-hurl loop—but I do learn two of them are photographers or videographers or whatever they're called.

So only three interviewers, as promised.

With the introductions complete, Coach Jackson suggests we start with the Q&A.

*Thank you, sweet baby Jesus.*

I'm not sure I could kick knowing they're waiting to play twenty questions.

Just, *no*.

I suck in a deep breath, inhaling the scent of freshly cut grass that lingers in the air. The sounds of practice wash over me. Sounds that have become as familiar to me as my own breathing over the last few weeks. The telltale crash of pads and helmets.

The calling of plays. The grunts and cheers that follow a well-executed tackle. The sun is warm on my face and there's no wind today.

Perfect conditions for a kicker.

*Perfect conditions for me.*

I open my eyes and smile at the interviewers, hoping they won't see straight through me. There are no bleachers on the practice fields, so we dive into the interview where we stand, thirty yards from the end zone where Coach has set up the football and holder. There's a mesh bag of extra balls off to the side, so I know he's expecting me to make several kicks.

*Just like any other practice.*

"Miss Carter, how does it feel to be the first woman to earn a football scholarship to a Division I school?" the first reporter asks.

Her dark hair is pulled back in a severe ponytail and the look on her face is all business. I try to focus on the question, but she's intimidating as hell. Maybe I should've paid more attention to the introductions, because who is this woman?

"Honestly?" I resist the urge to bite my lip. "I try not to think about it most days. Out here, I'm just like any other player on the team. I have a job to do and nothing else matters. It's just me, the ball, and the upright."

Besides, it's not like I'm the first woman to score a college football scholarship, just the first at a DI school.

Coach Jackson raises a brow, and I remember what Austin said about having the team at my back. I still don't want to get close to them, but maybe there's another way.

"Like I said," I continue, pasting a bright smile on my face, "I try not to think about it and focus on the team, but I know I'm fortunate to have this opportunity. There are a lot of guys on the team with more experience than me, who are also deserving of scholarships, but everyone's been really supportive. The team, the trainers, the coaching staff, they've all been very welcoming." Except that asshat Langley. "And I'm honored to be playing for a program with such a distinguished history and wealth of talent."

A smile pulls at the corner of Jackson's mouth, and I know I've said the right thing.

*One down...*

"Coach Collins has announced you'll be starting tomorrow against Idaho," the second reporter, a squat guy with broad shoulders, says. "You'll be the first woman in history to clock actual game time in DI football. How are you handling the pressure?"

Okay, then. No easy warm-up questions here.

"I don't let myself get caught up in hype. I've been an athlete all my life, so preparing for tomorrow's game against Idaho is no different from any other week of training. I've been really focused on technique, distance, and accuracy."

"You stated you've been an athlete all your life," he says, cutting off the *Collegian* reporter before the guy can get a word out, "but you've never played football, isn't that right? You were a soccer player before you tried out for Wildcat football?"

"That's right." I shift my weight and keep an eye fixed on Jackson in case he's got more nonverbal cues for me. "I played soccer for sixteen years, most recently for the Lady Wildcats, before joining the football team as a placekicker." I shrug. "The skill isn't all that different from kicking a long ball in soccer. The same principles apply and my training regimen really isn't all that different either, although there's a lot less cardio involved."

Jackson grins, and I find myself smiling back, a genuine reaction this time.

Because, come on, look at me being all funny and charming.

"You stated that the team and coaching staff have been really supportive," the *Collegian* reporter says, shoving his iPhone closer to ensure he gets a clear recording of my response, "but there are a lot of folks out there who question whether you've got what it takes to compete in the Big Ten, arguably one of the toughest conferences in college football. What do you say to the detractors?"

Fuck you? *No.* Jackson would probably keel over.

"Like I said, I don't get caught up in the hype." Truth. I don't even know what they're saying about me online because I don't have time to worry about it with my bananapants schedule. "My focus is on the game and showing up for the team, but I guess I'd tell them not to count me out. The best kickers in the country have a field goal percentage north of eighty-eight percent and so do I." I hold up a hand before he can argue. "I may not be game tested, but I like my odds." I nod to the adjacent field where the rest of the team is still running plays. "These guys get me in range on game day, I'll prove it."

The *Collegian* reporter nods, doing his best to look unimpressed—and failing. "Percentages can be misleading," he says. "Most kickers can put up those kinds of stats inside the thirty. What's your range like?"

I open my mouth to tell him I'm money from the forty-five, but Jackson answers for me.

"Why doesn't she just show you?" He gestures to the spot in the center of the field where he's set up the football and holder.

*Why not indeed.*

An hour later, I've done my best to impress the reporters, but even I know hitting all my kicks in optimal conditions doesn't exactly carry the wow factor.

We wrap up the interview as practice winds down—thankfully it's a short one today—and I find myself walking in step with Reid as we leave the field.

We haven't spoken since the other night at the library. I don't have the first clue what to say to him, even if I wanted to break the ice. Not that I've forgiven him, exactly.

But after overhearing his conversation with Coach Collins, I can't help but feel a little bad for the guy.

He's clearly under a lot of pressure.

"How'd the interview go?" Reid asks, a warm smile curving his lips. "Did you wow them with your usual grace and charm?"

A week ago, the comment would've had my back up, but I'm starting to get the team's brand of humor. "Guess we'll see when the articles come out, but they didn't seem overly impressed."

"Then they're idiots." He says it completely matter-of-fact. No room for debate. "You're playing ball for a top-tier school with only a few weeks of training. If they can't see how incredible that is, they're idiots."

I freeze in my tracks. It's the nicest thing Reid's ever said to me.

*Is this his version of an apology?*

He pauses and turns to look at me, a question I'm not prepared to answer in his eyes. He takes a step toward me and I chew my bottom lip, trying to decide if it's enough, this proverbial olive branch he's extended.

The rational part of my brain—the part that's cataloged the date and time of every shitty thing my father's done—is screaming at me to keep on walking, chin held high.

*You haven't exactly been a peach yourself.*

I've done everything I can to drive a big-ass wedge between myself and this team. And while Reid might very well be a player, he's treated me with respect since day one.

Maybe it's time to meet him in the middle.

*Just this once.*

I take one step forward, stopping when we're face-to-face.

"The reporters might be idiots, but I think it's safe to say a lot of people are skeptical about my abilities." I shrug it off like it's no big deal, although in truth, the knowledge that people are talking shit about me on the internet is a little unnerving.

"Don't sweat it." He flashes me a dimpled smile that stirs the butterflies in my belly. "If I do my job well tomorrow, you won't have anything to worry about."

# 13

# AUSTIN

Two hours until kickoff and the whole damn town is buzzing with excitement. Coop and I hoofed it to the football building, experience telling us it's the lesser of two evils. With tens of thousands of fans descending on College Park, traffic's a nightmare and there are tailgates on every corner.

It's the first game of the season, and the fans aren't the only ones out in full force.

The media will be waiting in the wings—along with the scouts—to break down every play we make in excruciating detail.

It's nothing new, but it's hard to ignore the constant speculation.

*Can Austin Reid lead Waverly to a national title?*

*Does Reid have what it takes to follow in his father's footsteps?*

*Is Reid in the hunt for the Heisman?*

It's all just noise.

Better to block it out, which is why Coop and I are both wearing headphones. The bulky kind that discourage strangers from stopping you on the street to ask if Waverly's going to win the game. Like, no, bro, I'm kinda hoping we get our asses handed to us today.

Of course we want to win the fucking game.

Short of going undefeated, there aren't any guarantees when it comes to getting selected for the championship game. College ball isn't like the NFL. Championship contenders can't just win their way into the title game.

The top four teams are determined by a selection committee and then compete in a semifinal bowl to determine who will have the privilege of playing for the national title. The road to victory is long, hard, and paved with bruises.

Especially when you compete in a conference that's consistently underrated, despite delivering some of the biggest slugfests week in and week out.

When we arrive at the locker room, my old man is waiting at the door.

*Just one of the many privileges afforded to an NFL legend.*

I gesture for Coop to go on ahead and pretend not to see the flare of jealousy in his eyes. I should be grateful my dad came to watch me play—Coop's dad never shows—but I'm not really in the mood for career advice at the moment. I just want to focus on today's game.

It's Carter's first game, and I all but promised to keep the pressure off her.

"Austin." My father looks me up and down, as usual, concerned first and foremost with appearances.

Although it's a home game, I'm wearing dress pants and a collared shirt, well aware that I'm always in the public eye. I must pass inspection, because his gaze returns to my face without comment, and I make a mental note to thank Vaughn for ironing my shirt.

"Dad." Don't get me wrong, my father's a good guy and I love him, but once in a while I'd like to come before the game. Hell, just once. "Didn't expect to see you until after the game."

"It's the first game of the season," he says, slinging an arm around my shoulder and clapping me on the chest. He's got a half inch on me, but otherwise, looking at my father is like looking into the mirror twenty-five years in the future. Same dark hair, same blue eyes, same dimpled chin. And, okay, yeah, same cocky grin. "I wanted to make sure you've got your head in the game. The stadium's full of scouts today and every game can impact your draft selection."

"I know." I haven't told him about my talk with Coach. There's no point. "I'm feeling good. Should be an easy game."

He squeezes my shoulder and points a finger at my chest, eyes locked on mine. "Don't take anything for granted. Play smart, manage the pocket, no turnovers. Got it?"

"Yes, sir." He's been giving me the same pregame speech for as long as I can remember.

I was probably the only kid in the fifth grade getting professional level coaching on pocket management, but I can't say it hasn't paid off. I'm one of the best QBs in college football and that's not bragging; it's a fact.

"You take care of the ball, son. I'll take care of the rest. We'll get you into Pittsburgh, just like we always talked about."

More like he always talked about.

I nod, keeping my lips pressed flat. If I open my mouth, I might blurt out my interest in Chicago. I haven't been able to stop thinking about what Coach said, but I can't tell my dad. He'd be crushed.

The thing is, Coach Norris is building a powerhouse program in Chicago. The only piece missing is the quarterback. Once they find the right guy, he'll be able to put his stamp on the program, like I've done at Waverly. Taking a team that's on the bubble right to the cusp of greatness, and this year, God willing, a national title.

The same opportunity exists in Chicago—*for the right player.*

I could be that player. Hell, in Chicago, I could play year one. I wouldn't be warming the bench waiting for a franchise player to retire.

"You know, Reiker's only got a year left in him. Two, tops," Dad says, as if reading my mind. "He's a good QB, but he's well on his way to retirement."

"I know."

I step back, putting some space between us. It's not exactly a secret. Reiker's upcoming contract negotiations have been headline news, but I've got a game to play. I can't allow myself to get wrapped up in depressing what-if scenarios.

The team needs me to be on my A game.

*Carter needs me to be on my A game.*

I hitch my bag over my shoulder and nod toward the locker room. "I need to get in there and suit up. Coach'll have my ass if I'm late."

"Go on ahead and remember what I said." He turns to go, but stops, glancing back over his shoulder. I'm not sure if it's a trick of the light, but I swear his eyes are a little glassy. "Your mom would be really proud of you, Austin."

*Thanks, Dad.*

That's what I want to say, but the words stick in my throat.

We've never been the kind of family to talk about our feelings—not even when Mom passed six years ago—so I just watch silently as he retreats down the hall.

Then I take a deep breath and stuff all my personal shit—draft pressure, Heisman speculation, Pittsburgh, Carter—down deep. The team needs a leader, and they've chosen me. I won't let them down by allowing distractions in the locker room or on the field.

That was my commitment when I accepted the role.

I'll be damned if I don't see it through.

Two hours later, when I lead the team onto the field, pulse pounding and adrenaline pumping, the stadium erupts, the noise reaching an earsplitting crescendo of epic proportions. Some sports site measured the sound in our stadium once, and no surprise, it's one of the loudest in the country. It's so loud I can barely hear myself think, but it's the best feeling in the world.

The kind of high you can only get from sex and football.

We power through warm-ups, the noise of the stadium a steady roar that dies down only when the national anthem is played.

I watch from the sideline, hand over my racing heart, and before I know it, I'm jogging onto the field for the coin toss. I've done this hundreds of times, but it never gets old.

I shake hands with the Idaho captain, who promptly chooses heads and wins the coin toss, opting to defer until the second half.

No skin off my teeth.

I prefer to open the second half with possession, but this'll give Carter a chance to settle down and acclimate to the stadium. Although she joined the team for a pregame huddle in the locker room, she was unusually quiet.

In fact, come to think of it, she didn't make a single smart-ass comment.

Probably nerves. Can't blame her. We've all been there before.

I watch the kickoff from the sideline with the rest of the team, helmet in hand.

It's a solid return and we're starting with good field position. The crowd is going nuts and the Wildcat roar damn near rattles the stadium as I slip my helmet on. I give the O-line fist bumps, shouting encouragement as we take the field.

The first drive will set the tone for the game—and the season—and I intend to make one hell of a showing.

Once my guys are settled on the line of scrimmage, I call the play.

The snap is good, the protection even better, and I fire a bullet downfield to Coop, hitting him right in the hands for a forty-yard gain.

*Hell, yeah. Now that's how you win football games.*

# 14

## KENNEDY

FUCKITY-FUCK-FUCK. I cannot believe I'm about to admit this, even to myself, but Reid was right.

I've been playing in front of a crowd for years, but this? The noise and chaos, the charged atmosphere, the near rabid fans?

It's like nothing I've ever experienced.

*So much for being a pressure player.*

Needing a distraction, I crouch down and check my cleats, making sure they're tied tight.

The last thing I need to do is trip over an untied lace in front of one hundred and three thousand screaming fans. One hundred and three thousand and five hundred forty-eight, to be precise. That's the total attendance today, according to the announcer.

Not a record for Waverly, but pretty darn close.

So, yeah, face-planting on the field? Not an option.

I'd be flayed on social media. And possibly ESPN.

Nervous energy churns in my belly, snaking out into my limbs. My freaking hands shake as I re-knot my laces, and I silently curse Reid for reminding me about the size of the crowd.

Granted, I would have figured it out the minute I stepped

foot in the stadium, but now I can't stop thinking about it, and I need an outlet for all these feels.

Reid's as good a target as any. Even if his assessment of the noise and fanfare was no joke. Because let me tell you, it's one thing to witness Wildcat pride from the TV or the stands, but it's another to experience it from the sidelines.

It's oppressive, like I-can't-catch-my-breath oppressive. It's a feeling that has nothing to do with the dense humidity and everything to do with the weight of expectation pouring down from the stands.

I finish tying my shoes and scan the crowd, taking in the exuberant blue and white painted faces. The glint of the sun as it reflects off the band's shiny brass instruments. The Wildcat mascot crowd-surfing through the student section like he doesn't have a care in the world, although he's got to be sweating bullets in that furry getup.

Even so, I'd trade him places in a heartbeat right now, because the anonymity of that mask?

It's looking pretty good.

My attention settles on the scoreboard and my heart leaps into my throat.

Waverly's down by three.

The offense has been strong, but the defense has been a little shaky. It's just a matter of time until I have to make a field goal attempt.

Even Reid can't score on every possession.

Although right now I'm sure as hell pulling for him.

I stand and my gaze darts to the QB who told me not to worry, who promised to play hard today. Not that I'm naive enough to think Reid made the promise for me, not entirely anyway.

He's a freaking powerhouse and a Heisman contender.

*Of course* he plays to win.

Despite my lifetime ban on football players, it's hard not to admire his commanding presence as he drives down the field. The guy's unflappable, appearing cool and confident despite the pressure to tie this game up.

Probably why his teammates voted him captain.

Plus, he's a versatile player, looking equally comfortable running and passing. It's no wonder he's so highly regarded within—

*Oomph!*

One minute I'm watching Reid, the next I'm doing a pirouette reminiscent of my DDR days as an athletic trainer blows past, our shoulders colliding as he dodges a player with a more intimidating stature than my own.

"Sorry," he calls over his shoulder, not stopping to see if I'm okay.

*Note to self: be aware of your surroundings at all times.*

Because the sidelines? Total anarchy compared to soccer.

Every square inch is packed with players and trainers and coaches. And yes, the proverbial bench, where I should be sitting except I'm too nervous to sit still.

Even during halftime, I couldn't shake the nervous energy racing through my veins. I stood through Coach Collins's entire motivational speech, most of it lost on me, kind of like when the teacher talks in those Charlie Brown vids.

*Wah-wah-wah.*

So, yeah, turns out it's a blessing my mom couldn't get time off work for the game.

The experience is proving stressful enough without worrying about letting her down too.

*Shit.* Smith is tackled short of the first down.

I glance at the scoreboard, confirming what I already know. The offense is third and long, which means—

"Get that helmet on," Coach Jackson barks, coming up

beside me. He's got a Waverly hat pulled down low on his forehead, and the man does not look happy. "If they don't convert, we're going to need that leg for about thirty yards."

I stare at him, but I can't do much more than blink. Like some fucked-up Morse code.

*Blink twice for yes, once for no.*

I think I blink twice, but I can't be sure. The roaring in my head is too loud. Or maybe that's just the stadium noise.

Coach shakes his head in disbelief. *Right there with you, dude.*

"It's only thirty yards." He levels his eyes on me, like he can will me to greatness. "You've got this, Carter."

Right. Thirty yards. I could hit it in my sleep. There's not even a breeze going.

Perfect conditions, assuming my heart doesn't beat right out of my chest.

And right now? Definite possibility.

My palms begin to sweat as I slip my helmet over my head, fingers fumbling with the chinstrap like the rookie I am. When I finally get the stupid thing secured and look up, a chorus of "Boo!" fills the stadium.

Reid's been sacked for a loss of five yards and there's a look of disgust plain as day on his face, like he can't believe he allowed himself to go down.

"So, thirty-five then?" I say, hoping I sound more confident than I feel.

Thirty-five is well within my range. I've made ninety-three percent of my kicks from thirty-five or better.

*Piece of cake.*

Jackson moves to slap my ass, but seems to think better of it, instead clapping me on the shoulder. "Just like practice, Carter."

Words to live by.

I jog onto the field, passing Reid on his way to the sidelines.

He looks far too calm and collected for a QB who just got stuffed.

*How the hell does he do that?*

"You've got this," he says, offering a passing greeting. "Tie it up and we'll bring it home on the next possession."

Coop rushes up behind him and gives me a wink. "Yeah, just pretend you're smashing Langley's face."

I grin, unable to help myself despite the circumstances. "That I can do."

And with that, they're gone. Relegated to the sidelines to watch and wait, as I've been doing for most of the fifty-two minutes and thirty-eight seconds of game play.

*Breathe!*

There are still seven minutes and twenty-two seconds left on the clock.

More than enough time for the offense to make another run down the field, just like Reid said.

*This is not do-or-die.*

Except it kind of feels like it might be.

I line up with the upright and walk off the steps. The punter, James, marks the spot I've indicated, the one where the ball will be placed after the snap. I keep my eyes fixed on the upright, doing my best to block out the roar of the crowd.

It's deafening, the volume no doubt driven by the close score and excitement of a new kicker.

After all, not only am I a walk-on, I'm a woman.

Which, it turns out, is a big freaking deal.

After the interview yesterday, I cracked and totally Googled myself.

In hindsight, it was a stupid thing to do. The stupidest, actually, because right now all I can think about is the speculation. The speculation Coach was shielding me from by closing practice up until yesterday.

Too bad the interviews are only likely to fan the flames.

Everyone's dying to see what I'm made of, if I've got what it takes to wear a Wildcat jersey. Half are hoping for a savior. The other half are betting I'll be a total failure, letting the team down in the clutch.

But they don't know me.

I won't fail. *I can't.*

My mom's counting on me and so is this team.

It doesn't matter that I'm not a fan of football players, because this isn't about the guys or my asshole father. It's about the game and the commitment I made to give it my all. It's what I've spent the last three weeks training for, this moment.

I relax my shoulders and exhale, shoving all the noise and pressure and speculation from my brain.

It's an easy kick. One I've made hundreds of times in practice.

The stadium has gone silent like no one dares to breathe.

The ball is snapped and I hear it slap against James's hand before he plants it on the ground, laces out. And then I'm moving, the sound of helmets crashing at the line of scrimmage a distant lullaby as I swing my leg forward, eyes on the prize.

*I've got this.*

## 15

## AUSTIN

*Holy fuck.* Watching Carter set up the field goal is the longest thirty seconds of my life.

I stand with the O-line, hands gripping the collar of my jersey and the pads beneath, because what else can we do but watch and wait? It's not exactly a game-winning kick—we've still got time—but it's tense as hell.

The stadium has reached fever pitch, but the sideline is silent. All eyes are on Carter.

*Moment of truth.*

Did I make the right call convincing her to try out? Was Coach right to start her today?

Everyone's on the edge of their seats, wondering if she's going to crack under pressure. The media's been salivating over the news of Carter's scholarship, churning speculation daily, but with closed practices, no one had any actual facts.

Just a whole lot of conjecture.

Most of it total bullshit.

"Have faith, man." Coop wipes the back of his arm across his forehead. It's hot as balls and we're all feeling it. What should have been an easy game has become a race to score, because no way are we going to lose our home opener. "Carter can make thirty-five with her eyes closed."

"I know." I do, but there's that tiny little ball of doubt zinging around in my head.

*What if...* It's the same damn pattern of second-guessing myself I've always dealt with when it comes to football.

Not that I can let it show. That shit has to stay buried deep.

I'm expected to lead by example and leaders don't sit around stewing over what-if scenarios.

Carter marks her spot and walks off her steps.

The stadium falls silent as the play clock counts down, and I swear to God an eternity passes before the ball is finally snapped. James positions the ball, but Carter stands frozen, taking her sweet-ass time.

If she doesn't get the damn ball up, it's going to be blocked.

Or worse yet, she could get tackled by the defense.

Sure, her body's made of muscle, but that doesn't mean I want to see her crushed by some two-hundred-pound goon who doesn't mind a personal foul. It sure as shit wouldn't be the first time and with all the hype surrounding Carter, I wouldn't be surprised if there are guys in the conference gunning for her.

*Shit.* I should've warned her. Given her a heads-up or something.

Because unlike her, I actually do know what football players are like, and while most are pretty decent guys, there are always a few assholes.

Like Langley.

My gut clenches when the defense leaps forward, closing in fast.

What the fuck is she waiting for? A personal invitation?

I step forward, stopping just short of the field thanks to Coop's grip on my shoulder.

*Thank Christ.* Carter's finally moving.

She springs into action, one short step followed by two longer ones. Her foot connects with the ball, sending it arcing through the air, sailing over the heads of the defensive players with just enough clearance to avoid a blocked kick.

The ball flies through the upright, dead center, and just like that, the game is tied up.

*That's my girl!*

I pump my fist in the air as the stadium erupts, but no one's cheering as loud as the guys on the sideline when the announcer calls Carter's name over the loudspeaker. You'd think we'd won the game by the way the team's reacting. Or that she'd set a new school record.

But I know exactly how they feel.

Like it's all finally coming together. Like this is our season. Like we're unstoppable.

Relief washes over me like a Gatorade shower.

I came through for the team, patching the hole Spellman left and making us stronger for it. I may have gotten lucky finding Carter, but she's with us now and the team is delivering on all fronts.

This is our time, our year.

Carter jogs off the field, and I find myself hanging back as the team surrounds her.

There are high fives and cheers and probably an excessive amount of celebration, but what I notice most? It's the way her cheeks flush and her eyes shine with pride as the guys pile on the congratulations.

She turns to face me. I should give her a fist bump or a clap on the shoulder or...something.

But it's like we're frozen in time.

Just a split second where it's me and her and no one else.

No teammates, no coaches, no crowds.

In that moment of hesitation, something between us shifts.

I feel it in my gut, see it in the way she studies my face, in the tiny wrinkle that forms between her brows.

*Fuck.*

I'm the team captain. I'm supposed to see her as one of the guys, treat her like one of the guys. I haven't forgotten Coach's warning or her feelings on football players or even my responsibility to lead this team to a national title.

But when she looks at me—really looks at me—that beautiful smile lighting her face like a ray of goddamn sunshine, I know I'll do whatever it takes to see that smile again and to hell with the consequences.

## 16

# KENNEDY

I'm STILL FLYING high from today's win—and my totally awesome field goal—when I finally exit the locker room. It's getting late, and I'm starving. The game ran almost three and a half hours, and I got tagged for an ESPN interview before leaving the field.

Which is ridiculous considering my role in the final score was minor.

Reid and Coop, The Dynamic Duo, as the press calls them (super creative, right?), were the real stars of the game, leading the offense and putting up another six points on our last possession.

*As promised.*

But I'm starting to understand that everything I do—or don't do—this season, will be amplified by the mere fact that I have ovaries.

As if they're my defining characteristic.

Like, it's *so* hard to believe a woman can kick a ball because she has **gasp** ovaries.

Thank the stars above I'm not a real ballplayer.

That crap would get old real fast, and I have more important things to worry about, like my GPA and the upcoming ACME

Student Design Competition, now that I've popped my football cherry, so to speak.

*And it was good. So. Good.*

Even better than sex.

Although, to be fair, Two-Minute Mitch wasn't much to write home about, so my assessment could be skewed. (Seriously, my vibrator gives better orgasms than he ever did.) But when that ball sailed through the upright?

The applause was insane.

I swear the ground trembled beneath my feet. And the knowledge that all those people were cheering for me? Talk about a head trip.

Not that I'm turning into Coop or anything (God forbid), but you know what they say: *you never forget your first time.*

When I round the corner outside the men's locker room, freshly showered with my damp hair hanging in limp strands over my shoulders, I'm swallowed up by a sea of bodies. Reid and a few of the guys from the O-line are standing around, messing with their phones and rehashing the game-winning touchdown.

The one where Reid punched through the defense to bring it home.

It was incredible to watch, his muscular body moving with such speed and agility as he plowed through the defenders. I'm sure there were hot-blooded women all over the stadium wishing for a fan, myself included.

"Just the lady we were waiting for." Reid pushes off the wall, rising to his full height.

He's wearing a pair of tight jeans and a collared shirt, the sleeves rolled up over his muscular forearms to reveal a smattering of dark hair. He looks good—all the guys do—making me immediately self-conscious of my worn Converse and cut-off shorts.

Reid's eyes skate over me, and I resist the urge to tug on the hem of my shirt.

*I do not care what Reid thinks of my wardrobe choices.*

A fact that bears repeating after we practically had a moment on the sidelines.

A moment I refuse to consider beyond the weird post–field goal high. Because Reid and I? We cannot have a moment for about a billion different reasons, not the least of which is my promise to my mom.

"We're heading to the Diner to grab dinner and then we're going to hit up a party at Sig," he says. "You should come with."

I hesitate, chewing my bottom lip. I'm starving and the Diner has the best milkshakes in town, but partying? With the football team? So not my scene. And they'll definitely make a scene. Freshly showered—possibly in cologne if my burning nostrils are any indication—and dressed to kill, they look like they're ready to go hard.

*They look like bad decisions and postcoital bliss.*

Definitely a combination I can do without. Especially with the lines starting to blur, with Reid jamming himself into my life —my thoughts—at every turn.

"My treat." Reid fixes me with the dimpled smile that's my kryptonite. "Thanks for a job well done today."

I can feel the expectant gazes of my teammates, although my eyes are locked on Reid. They expect me to say yes, to fall in line as if I'm one of them. But the thing is, I'm not.

Football is a means to an end for me, not a lifestyle.

Sure, I enjoyed the thrill of the crowd today, but I'm not like them.

I thrive on control, order, and commitment.

Not booze, partying, and casual sex.

If I say yes to dinner, I'll let myself be talked into the party. I can already feel interest stirring in my belly, weakening my resolve. It wouldn't take much, because, honestly? It would be nice to just...let go for a few hours. It's been ages since I've gone out, always too busy or too tired from trying to juggle work, studying, and soccer.

For once, the prospect of warm beer and house music doesn't sound so bad.

Which is exactly why I have to stay strong.

This is how it starts. One minute you're hanging with the guys, playing beer pong and ogling the QB's ass, the next you're piecing your heart back together over a pint of Ben & Jerry's.

That's how it was for my mom, anyway.

"I appreciate the offer." I flash my teammates what I hope is a friendly smile. "But I'm going to pass. Have fun tonight."

"Come on." Reid gives me a nudge, sending a jolt of electricity racing up my arm. "We're a team. At least have dinner with us." His eyes are doing that thing again, boring into me like we're *this close* to having a moment.

*Abort! Abort!*

"I have to study," I lie, wrapping my arms around my waist where they're in no danger of touching Reid again.

It's a lame excuse. Even I know that, because, hello, it's Saturday night. Plenty of time to study tomorrow, but I've thrown it out there and now I have to stick with it.

*Stupid. Stupid. Stupid.*

Should've said I had plans with Becca, which would have been far more believable, but Reid's touch seems to have temporarily short-circuited my brain.

"*Riiight*," he drawls, his voice as smooth as Dove chocolate. Heat rolls off his body, and it's all I can do not to fan myself. "You have a three-point-nine GPA, one of the highest on the team. I'm pretty sure you could take the night off if you wanted to. Hell, you've earned it."

Indignation flares, burning hot in my belly. "How do you know my GPA? Have you been creeping on me?"

He shrugs, that sexy smile shifting to an infuriating smirk my li—*fingers*—are just itching to wipe off his face.

"No need to creep. I saw the grade book on Coach's desk." He laughs, a low rumble that sounds like sex personified, falling from his lips. "It was open."

I narrow my eyes and plant my hands on my hips, scanning the group of players, all of whom are suddenly balls-deep in their phones.

*No help there.*

Not that I expected any. He's their ringleader, after all.

"That's an invasion of privacy," I snark, feeling like an asshole.

After all, what do I care if Reid saw my GPA? It's hardly a national secret.

It's just that the idea of him checking up on me, getting to know me more intimately, makes me uncomfortable. Like my skin is too hot, too tight.

"Relax. It's no big deal." Reid hooks his thumbs in the pockets of his jeans, drawing my traitorous eyes south to the bulge behind his zipper. The smirk is back in place, and I know I've been caught looking.

Heat floods my cheeks, but Coop hops on the peer-pressure express before I can die of embarrassment.

"Hell, if I had a three-point-nine, I'd be shouting that shit from the rooftops." He slips his phone into his back pocket. "But, alas, I'm fated to be the stereotypical jock with a pretty face and a big appetite, so can we move this little battle of wills—fascinating as it is—to the Diner?"

The question is directed at me, but it becomes an open invitation and an escape.

A bunch of girls I hadn't noticed step out of the shadows and descend on the guys like bees on a honeycomb. An exchange of greetings ripples through the crowd, and I realize they aren't strangers, which I guess makes sense because these girls are clearly dressed for the after-party Reid mentioned.

A blonde in booty shorts that could give Queen Bey a run for her money slips an arm around Coop's waist and smashes her boobs against his rib cage. She looks familiar, but I can't place her.

"I'm so hot, but maybe a milkshake would cool me down," she says, batting her lashes. "Mind if we join you?"

Another girl, this one a brunette, slides under his other arm.

That's when it hits me. These are the girls from study hall. The ones Reid was talking to.

*Acquaintances my ass.*

"Great game today!" the girl chirps, gushing with more pep than a cheerleader snorting Pixy Stix. "You were amazing!"

A grin slides across Coop's face as he looks from the blonde to the brunette, and I can practically see the wheels turning in his head.

*Oh, for fuck's sake.*

Just what Coop needs, a threesome to further validate his overblown ego. I'd swear it was a scene from some cheesy, Friday night lights dramedy if I weren't witnessing it firsthand.

Coop catches me staring and miracle of miracles, his grin actually gets wider.

For his part, Reid just stands there, still as a statue, neither encouraging nor discouraging the women.

Has he hooked up with them? For some reason, the thought of Reid getting handsy with these girls stings more than it should, and I realize with a sinking stomach that I don't want to know the answer.

"So, what do you say, Carter?" Coop raises a brow in silent challenge. "You coming or what?"

The blonde looks me up and down. She quickly dismisses me with a giggle, apparently deciding I'm no threat. Fine by me. I have zero interest in Cooper DeLaurentis.

"I'll see you at practice on Monday." I force a little cheer into my words—we did just win our first game of the season, after all—despite the sour taste that lingers in my mouth.

Reid gives a curt nod, but says nothing and I watch, feet rooted to the ground, as he and the others retreat down the hall in search of food and festivities.

They might be good teammates, but that's where it ends.

It has to.

This little show proves they're exactly the kind of guys my mom always warned me about.

*Too much booze. Too much sex. Too few brain cells.*

Not exactly a winning combination—despite what the scoreboard said today—and I can't afford to get tangled up with a guy like that, one who's temporary at best.

No, I don't *want* to get tangled up with a guy like that.

Even if Reid's smile makes me want to throw caution to the wind and forget everything I know about football players. Even if Reid's touch makes me want to say yes to his offer, just this once, to see where the night could go.

# 17

# AUSTIN

GREEK ROW IS LIT up like a beacon for the young, dumb, and horny when we roll up on Sig Chi, surrounded by throngs of students looking for a good time. The house sits in the middle of the block, hedged in on either side by equally imposing, old-as-hell mansions that have witnessed generations of drunken debauchery.

Hell, it's a wonder some of these places are still standing.

From the outside the stone and brick behemoths look stately, a throwback to the good old days when the word *gentleman* carried weight. But inside? Whole different story. Sticky floors, missing doors—most doing double duty as beer pong tables—and enough sweaty bodies to send the fire marshal into a blind panic.

The party at Sig Chi is a rager, spilling out onto the front lawn with red plastic cups and tipsy girls who move in pairs across the manicured grass. There are a couple of guys sitting on the porch roof, their legs dangling over the front, welcoming newcomers.

The whole scene brings back memories of Spellman and the night he busted his leg.

I avert my eyes, the familiar guilt burning a hole in my chest.

Vaughn shakes his head, and I figure he's remembering it too, but before I can say anything, he breaks off from the group and makes a beeline for a solo drunk girl who's struggling with a busted heel and cursing a blue streak.

If it were anyone else, I'd be right behind him, but it's Vaughn, which means there are decent odds he'll bag the party and either walk the girl home or put her ass in an Uber and ride along to make sure she arrives safely.

I follow Coop up the narrow sidewalk, nodding at a few familiar faces.

If the entire town wasn't celebrating our first win of the season, campus police would probably shut this thing down. But we are celebrating our first win and as long as the shenanigans stay mostly aboveboard, the brothers will get a free pass tonight.

It doesn't hurt that Coop's a Sig Chi legacy.

It tends to make campus police look the other way, but it also helps ensure my guys stay out of trouble.

*As long as they keep their noses clean.*

The truth is, they busted their asses today and no one's going to raise an eyebrow if they want to throw back a few beers.

Not even Coach, thanks to his new on/off training policy.

We work hard during the week and keep our noses to the grindstone, then the training switch flips to the off position Saturday night, giving the team a chance to let loose and blow off steam. Monday morning, we'll be back to business as usual, but tonight, we're free to party and celebrate the win over Idaho.

Coop and I take the front steps two at a time, Parker and Smith right behind us, bypassing the kid collecting cash for cups. Sometimes being a football player does have its perks, one of them being that Coop will get us a decent beer and not the watered-down shit they're pumping through the keg.

The night's young. Plenty of time for that later.

Coop motions for us to stick close and shouts, "Follow me."

At least I think that's what he says. It's too damn loud to hear the words coming out of his mouth with house music blasting through the sound system. There are speakers set up in the living room and it's the usual scene. Bodies pressed together like they might start fucking any given second, beer pong tourney, and lots of small talk punctuated with erratic hand gestures.

We shuffle through the hall, the sea of bodies parting for Coop like he's the Second Coming.

He tends to have that effect on people, which comes in handy at times like this, when my mind is being pulled in a thousand different directions.

Or, more specifically, in one direction.

*Carter.*

I haven't been able to stop thinking about her. Her performance today, her reluctance to hang with us, the way she looked at me like maybe, just maybe the walls were coming down. At least, that's what I thought until she hit me with the bald-faced lie about studying.

Suffice it to say, I'm off my game.

Distracted. Stewing in frustration. Happy to let Coop run interference for the rest of us, doing most of the schmoozing, high-fiving, and fist-bumping as we make our way to the alcohol-stocked kitchen.

I'm not big on the party scene, outgrew it last year, which is why I don't live at the football house. But I need to be seen and chill with the guys, so here I am bumping elbows with sexy coeds and douchey frat guys that care more about tapping ass than delivering against their mission.

I probably shouldn't be so hard on Greek life. Coop says there are some decent guys here and I know for a fact he wouldn't tolerate any shady shit, but I've seen enough on Greek Row to be jaded.

Like the sloppy couple dry humping on the counter as I slide past, needing that drink more than ever.

"Party's lit," Parker says, rolling his shoulders as he scans the room.

Coop liberates four bottles of lager from the fridge and hands one to me.

"I've got some catching up to do." Parker reaches for the bottle Coop offers. "What've you got besides beer?"

"Now you're talking," Smith agrees, grabbing a beer. "Where do the brothers hide the good shit?"

*In their bedrooms, if they're smart.*

I watch in disbelief as Coop opens the bottom drawer of the stove and reveals a trove of liquor bottles. It speaks volumes about their lifestyle.

I twist the top off my beer, taking a long pull of the amber liquid.

"How about whiskey?" Coop holds up a bottle of Jim Beam.

There's a wicked gleam in his eye, and I suspect we aren't supposed to help ourselves, but I'm not about to intervene. It's our only night off and these are his brothers. He can sort it out himself if they get pissy about the missing alcohol.

Coop lines up a couple of red plastic cups and pours a generous shot into each. They've got to be at least doubles, but hey, we're big guys, and, fuck, maybe the liquor will take the edge off my nerves.

Coop raises his cup and we follow suit. "To Carter and her amazing fuckin' legs."

The asshole winks at me over the top of his cup, but I ignore the bait.

The last thing I want to do is shoot the shit about Carter's legs and he knows it.

The alcohol burns as it slides down my throat, warming my belly and giving immediate release to the tension coiled in my shoulders. I tell myself it's from the game, that I should see the trainer for a massage, but the lie falls flat.

"To Carter and her amazing fuckin' legs," Parker echoes, his appreciation for her legs apparent in his tone as he slaps his cup down on the counter.

"Show a little respect." My temper flares white-hot and the words are out before I can stop them, sounding more like a threat than a warning. "She's your teammate."

"Hey, man. No disrespect." A lazy grin spreads over Parker's face. "I'm thinking about asking her out. I'm kind of digging the hard-to-get vibe. I mean, I know she'd never go out with this asshole." He nods at Coop, who clutches his chest in mock injury. "But I figure I might have a shot."

*Like hell.* Carter needs a guy who—well, I don't actually know what she needs, which is half the problem, but I know Parker's not it.

I crumple my cup and toss it into the overflowing trash can. "Keep your dick in your pants unless you wanna ride the bench. Coach doesn't want any funny business."

Smith snorts and gives me the side-eye. "Who the fuck says 'funny business'?"

"You really think Coach would bench me for taking her out?" Parker asks, skepticism etched in the lines of his face.

"You wanna find out?" I take a pull of my beer, doing my best to look impassive despite the irritation roiling in my gut.

Parker and Carter? They're all wrong for each other. Anyone could see it.

"Dude, you guys are bringing me down." Coop pours another shot of whiskey and thrusts it into my hand. "This place is full of women dying to congratulate us on a hard-fought victory today. Can we please go enjoy the fruits of our labor and quit standing around with our dicks in our hands?"

Against my better judgment, I throw back the shot and follow the guys to the living room.

We're immediately swarmed with well-wishers who want to rehash the game. Smith and Parker slide in on the beer pong tourney, and it's not long before a smoking-hot brunette drags Coop upstairs, her barely there skirt giving him a preview of what's to come.

*What would Carter think of all this?*

Nothing good, that's for damn sure. I'm all for no-strings hookups, but I get the feeling she's not a fan of casual sex. The idea of bathroom BJs would probably offend her sensibilities and leave her fifty shades of embarrassed.

It has a totally different effect on me.

An image of Carter with her thighs backed up against the bathroom sink plants itself front and center in my brain.

It's easy to imagine cupping her ass and lifting her onto the vanity, her sexy legs parting to allow me access. She lifts her chin, revealing the long line of her neck as her hair tumbles over her shoulders. It's the sweetest damn sight I've ever seen. I'll bet she tastes like flowers and honey and sunshine and—*fuck*.

Why am I thinking about Carter?

She's off-limits. *Way* off-limits.

Hell, I'm pretty sure she doesn't even like me.

Okay, no big deal. It's been a few weeks since I've had sex and teammate or not, she's the woman I spend the most time with. It's only natural she'd appear in my fantasy, right?

Doesn't mean a thing. Except that I need to get laid.

I shake off all thoughts of Carter and grab another beer from the fridge.

Then I plaster a smile on my face as I field a million questions about our championship odds, bowl games, and what I'm doing later tonight. The night is young and there are women everywhere, plenty of whom are looking to score.

It's easy to tell which ones are DTF because they don't waste time on small talk and get right to the point. Sort of like Kendall, who's got my biceps in a vise grip as she rubs her perky tits against my chest. Her nipples stand at attention and she's licking her lips like she's remembering the taste of my cock in her mouth.

Six months ago—hell, six weeks ago—I would've jumped on the invitation.

But I'm not feeling it. Not even a flicker of interest from my cock.

*WTF.* I glance down at my beer, which is almost empty.

I've never experienced whiskey dick firsthand, but this must be it, because come on, no guy in his right mind could look at Kendall and not get hard. She's a knockout with shiny blonde hair, big brown eyes, and the kind of legs shaped by hours of spin classes.

"You played great today," she says, batting her lashes and giving me the standard line.

"Thanks."

Here's the thing, it's easy to tell the jersey chasers from the real fans because they know your stats and they want to actually talk about the game. In play-by-play detail. Kendall's cool, but I doubt she knows I threw for over two hundred yards today, because she doesn't know shit about football.

Hell, I doubt we have anything in common except a mutual interest in pleasure.

"Seeing anyone?" She practically purrs as she looks up at me, her seductive smile telling me everything I need to know.

Kendall's back in the game and looking to score.

"Nah." I drain my beer and nod a greeting to one of Coop's brothers. Poor bastard's eyeing Kendall like she's salvation, but he doesn't stand a chance. She's got a type and he's not it. "You know the drill. No time for commitments other than football."

Kendall laughs, her fingers loosening on my arm. "That's what I like about you, Reid. No bullshit."

"I try." I shrug and take the opportunity to disentangle myself from Kendall. We had a thing last year and it was fun while it lasted, but we went our separate ways when the no-strings sex had run its course. We parted on good terms, and last I heard she was seeing a guy on the baseball team. "What happened with you and McCoy?"

"Turns out I'm not cut out for monogamy." She tosses her hair over her shoulder and takes a sip of her beer. "I seem to recall you prefer it that way too."

"I did." The words hang between us a moment too long, and I realize my mistake. "I do," I amend, raking a hand through my hair. Maybe it's the alcohol that's messing with my head or maybe it's the way Kendall's eyeing me like a side of beef, but I need to bounce. "I'm going to grab another beer. I'll catch up with you later."

I turn and push through the crowd, not giving her a chance to protest. I should've offered to get her another drink too, but the truth is, I don't need another beer. I need to get out of here. Away from this whole scene and these people with their impossible expectations of who and what I am.

What I need tonight is someone who doesn't expect much of me at all.

## 18

# KENNEDY

"ARE you sure you don't want to come with?" Becca calls from the hall bathroom, where she's spent the last hour perfecting her hair and makeup. "The team would love to see you."

*Yeah, right.* I've got a couple Snapchat messages that suggest otherwise.

Not all the women on the team were as understanding as Becca about my choice to drop soccer for a football scholarship. The fallout hasn't exactly been nuclear, but that doesn't mean I'm about to crash their girls' night out.

Not while the wounds are still fresh, anyway.

"No, thanks." I glance up from my laptop just in time to see her head peek around the bedroom door. "I have a lot of work to do on this proposal for the ACME design competition."

Technically, I have a few more weeks to get my proposal approved, but since I'm entering solo, I'll need every spare minute to prepare. The ACME design competition is *the* competition for mechanical engineering students, and I can't afford to blow it.

Not if I want to land a decent job after graduation.

"*Bor-ing.*" Becca rolls her eyes and pushes the door open the rest of the way. "I thought a full-ride would give you more time to, I don't know, *have a life*." She plants her hands on her hips and narrows her eyes like she can see right through my bullshit. "I mean, shouldn't you be out celebrating with the football team tonight?" She pauses, her next words very deliberate, although I can hear the suspicion in them. "Are you holding out on me?"

"Of course not." I toy with a loose thread on my comforter. Here's the thing: Becca's not going to understand turning down an invite to party with the football team. Where I see danger, she sees man candy. "You know how I feel about football players."

This earns me another eye roll, even more dramatic than the last. "Sweetie, I know your dad is an asshole—I get it; mine is, too—but you can't assume all football players are the same."

"Why not?" I tease, trying to lighten the mood.

After all, Becca's going out to cut loose.

The last thing she needs is depressing talk about my daddy issues.

"Because if there's even one nice guy in that bunch of hotties, it would totally be worth the risk." Spoken like a woman who's never had her heart broken. It's not a risk I'm willing to take, not after years of watching my mom try to change my father—and failing. "Oh, and speaking of things that are hot, I put a new book in your bag for next week's away game." She gives me a devious smile. "It's a scorcher, so try not to blush."

Becca and I have a shared love of romance novels, but she leans toward books with a heat level that are best read in private, while I prefer a nice slow burn. She's always slipping me books she thinks will expand my sexual horizons...whatever that means.

"What is it this time?" I ask, curiosity getting the better of me. "Bikers? MMA fighters? Tattoo artist?"

She wiggles her brows. "You'll have to read it to find out!

Anyway, text me if you change your mind about coming out, 'kay?"

I smile and nod as Becca retreats into the hall, although I know deep down it won't happen. I really do need to work on this proposal, and I've already made up my mind. I just need to stay the course, even if it means spending my night off trapped in the apartment with no one but Baxter, Becca's Labradoodle, to keep me company.

A few minutes later, the front door closes with a soft bang.

"Three, two, one." Baxter thrusts his head through the door and struts over to the bed like he owns the place. I lower my hand and he nuzzles against it, his golden curls soft and silky. "It's just you and me tonight."

He gives a small yip of approval and flops down on the floor, using my discarded Waverly sweatshirt as a pillow.

I manage to lose myself in the project for a couple of hours, nailing down the overall concept for my design, while Baxter snores softly next to me.

My phone rings and I grab it off the nightstand, surprised to discover it's after eleven.

Mom's smiling picture flashes on the screen, and I swipe right.

"Hey, sweetie," she says, not even waiting for me to say hello. "I'm on a break, so I've only got a minute, but I wanted to call and congratulate you on the win today. I'm working a double, but I heard most of the game on the radio."

"Thanks, Mom." There's a surge of warmth in my chest at her words. I know she's proud of me, she always is, but I also know that congratulating me on a football win takes some real effort on her part. "It was...wild. I was a little worried I might actually shank it."

"Listen to you," she says, a note of sadness in her voice. "Talking like one of the guys."

"Ha," I scoff, telling myself it couldn't be further from the truth. "Football terminology does not a football player make." That's true enough. It's not the lingo that's made me a player, it's the countless hours I've spent on the practice fields perfecting my technique. "How're things at the hospital?"

"Busy." I know that's my cue to wrap it up, that they've just done shift change and she's needed on the floor, but I'm not quite ready to let go. "You know how it is, always shorthanded."

I hate that she tries to make light of it, that her hours are so long, but I hate myself even more for what comes out of my mouth next. "Do you think you'll be able to make it to a game once your hours get cut back?"

There's a long pause, but eventually she promises to come see me play. "Of course, sweetie, but I have to get back to work now. Have a good night, okay? I love you."

"Love you too."

I stare at the phone for a while after I hang up, feeling empty.

Maybe I shouldn't have asked her to come, to watch me play like she's probably watched my dad do a hundred times before.

My stomach growls.

*Or maybe I just need a snack.*

I climb off the bed and tuck my phone in my pocket, determined to find something bingeworthy in our barely passable kitchen.

The thing is, neither Becca nor I can cook, so we gave up trying.

Which is probably for the best since she once caught a towel on fire when using it as an oven mitt. To avoid such disasters (and eviction), we mostly subsist on cafeteria food and frozen meals. Case in point, the stir-fry dinner that barely put a dent in my appetite.

I scavenge through the cabinets and find a box of popcorn. I toss a bag in the microwave, refill Baxter's water bowl, and lean against the counter to wait.

The kernels explode rapid fire as the bag makes its revolutions behind the glass door.

*You should've accepted Reid's dinner invitation.*

It was probably a shit move to decline. It was just burgers and shakes, after all, not a team orgy.

*Mmm.* What I wouldn't give for a chocolate milkshake right now.

But no, burgers and shakes is how it starts. The moment I stop seeing Reid for the good-time guy he is, that's the moment I'll lose all conviction. Right?

The microwave dings and I grab the popcorn, careful not to burn my fingers on the steam leaking from the bag. I dump the contents in a bowl, grab a bottle of water from the fridge, and grant myself the rest of the night off. I played a good game today and made decent progress on my design proposal.

Time to veg out and catch up with my favorite TV couple.

I'm curled up on the couch, doing my best not to think about football—no small feat since every time Red flashes his washboard abs, I find myself comparing them to Reid, who wins hands down every time—when there's a knock on the door.

It's so freaking loud I nearly jump out of my skin.

Popcorn spills on the floor, but I stay frozen on the couch. It's kind of late for company and I'm not expecting anyone. The practical part of my brain says it's probably just some drunk knocking on the wrong door.

Maybe if I wait it out, they'll go away.

*Thump! Thump! Thump!*

Or not. The idiot actually knocks louder this time.

I sigh and climb out of my blanket fortress.

Probably just a drunk neighbor, but I'm a safety girl, so I

grab the Taser from my purse and tiptoe toward the door, the thick carpet muffling my steps.

Now, I've seen a lot in my three years at Waverly. Naked guys streaking across campus, tipsy girls railing Gloria Gaynor as they dance on their front porches, and even professors LARPing in the Quad, but none of that has prepared me for what I see when I look through the peephole.

*What the hell is Austin Reid doing on my doorstep?*

# 19

# AUSTIN

THIS WAS PROBABLY A STUPID IDEA, but my whiskey-addled brain can't decide if the bad idea was consuming copious amounts of liquor or showing up at Carter's apartment uninvited.

*Both, asshole.*

Whatever. I raise my knuckles and rap on the door once more.

If she doesn't answer this time, I'll go.

Probably.

*Fuck.* I shouldn't be here.

It's wrong on so many levels, not the least of which was telling one of my best friends to back off—like I have any claim over Carter—but I can't get her out of my head. The way she isn't impressed by the swagger and stats. The way her eyes sparkle when she's being a smart-ass. The way she gives as good as she gets with that tart little mouth of hers.

She doesn't preen, and she sure as shit doesn't want anything from me.

*Unlike most people in my life.*

I know I'm lucky to be following in my father's footsteps, that I'm blessed with talent and living a life most people only dream of, but it took a hell of a lot of hard work to get where I am and sometimes the pressure feels like it'll crush me. I don't want to sound like a whiny little bitch, but the truth is, most people in my life are angling for something.

Sex. Parties. Tickets. Autographs.

Listening to all those people at the party talk about how I'm going to win Waverly a national title and get drafted in the first round?

It's exhausting.

I just want to be somewhere that I can be myself, with someone I know doesn't give a shit about the Austin Reid legacy or what I can do for them. And that's the crux of the matter, isn't it?

Everyone wants a piece of me, expects great things from me.

*Except Carter.*

With her, I can be myself.

It's funny, actually. I thought that leg of hers would be my saving grace. Turns out it's just...her. The indifference she wears like battle armor is a salve to the pressure that's always burning, slow and steady, just below the surface.

The weakness I can't show anyone.

Not even my own father.

I raise my hand to knock again, but the door swings open and there stands Carter, looking more tempting than a midnight snack.

My gaze drifts over her, drinking in every detail from the way her hair falls in loose waves over her bare shoulders to the look of surprise that makes her dark eyes appear so damn innocent. She's wearing a pink tank top—no bra—and I can see the faint outline of her nipples through the thin fabric, which skims the waistband of her shorts.

I shouldn't look, but I'm only human, for fuck's sake, and I can't tear my eyes away from the tiny sleep shorts that showcase her gorgeous legs.

Carter clears her throat and I raise my eyes to meet hers, flashing the cocky grin that drives her nuts.

"What are you doing here?" she huffs, feigning annoyance.

She's a terrible actress. Her body language totally gives her away as she leans toward me, closing the distance between our bodies. Plus, she doesn't slam the door in my face, so that's got to be a good sign, right?

"You know, where I come from, it's considered good manners to invite a guest in, maybe offer them a cold beverage, before the inquisition."

She gives a sexy little snort and juts out her hip. "Funny, where I come from, it's considered good manners not to show up in the middle of the night uninvited. You do realize I'm not one of the jersey-chasing fangirls who are enamored by your ability to throw a ball, right?"

"Trust me, Carter. I would never mistake you for the kind of woman who would be impressed by my amazing athleticism." I raise an arm over my head, resting it against the doorjamb, my bicep inches from her face.

She'd never admit it, but I saw her checking me out in the locker room, and I have a feeling I'm not the only one here having NC17 thoughts about my teammate.

This time she rolls her eyes, but there's a hint of a smile on her lips.

*I'm totally wearing her down.*

"You're lucky I didn't tase you." She waves a little black flashlight in the air and at the press of a button, a bolt of electricity crackles to life.

*Holy shit*. She's serious. "You were going to tase me?"

She shrugs and opens the door wider, a sly grin spreading across her face. It's sexy as hell and a thrill races up my spine.

"Still might, but you're welcome to come in and take your chances."

There's a tiny voice in the back of my head telling me there's no way Carter's going to tase me, so I latch on to it like a frat boy to a keg and follow her inside. Besides, the knowledge that Carter can take care of herself is kind of hot. Damn right she should tase any prick who hassles her—*twice*.

The apartment is smaller than my town house, but has the same basic furnishings since—surprise, surprise—we live in the same complex. But where my apartment is decorated with Wildcat gear, pizza boxes, and discarded athletic shoes, Carter's feels like an actual home.

Hell, she's even got real curtains on the front window.

Here's the thing. I've been inside my fair share of women's apartments and I've learned to expect certain things. The same mix of bookstore art prints, an abundance of candles, and at least one tapestry hanging on the wall or over a window.

Carter's place is different.

There's an abstract painting over the couch, something with actual character, the splashes of color bold and provocative. There's a candle burning on the coffee table (is no woman immune to this basic need to burn shit?), and there are a handful of pictures displayed throughout the room. Most are of Carter and a blonde who looks like she's got pep for days.

*Probably her roommate.*

Although I want to take a closer look, I resist the urge. It seems too personal and something tells me she wouldn't approve of me touching her stuff.

Plus, she still has the Taser.

"How did you know where I live?" Carter crosses her arms over her chest as if she's just realized the tank top might not be concealing all the goods.

"Student directory. You should really think about removing

your address." I flop down on the couch, right next to the spot with her blanket and popcorn. "The last thing you want is unscrupulous fans or reporters showing up at your door at all hours of the night."

"The same could be said of cocky quarterbacks." She eyes her vacant spot on the couch, probably trying to decide if I'm invading her space on purpose (spoiler alert: I am). It's not until I dig into her popcorn that her stubborn pride kicks in. She puts the Taser on the end table and curls up on the cushion next to me, body turned toward mine, knee pressed against my thigh. "Are you drunk?"

I do my best to look incredulous because I'm definitely not drunk.

At least, I'm pretty sure I'm not.

"I'm the captain of the football team. It would be irresponsible to drink to excess. It's my job to set a good example, remember?"

She arches a brow. "Really?"

"Really, really," I say, quoting my favorite ogre.

Carter shakes her head and laughs, bringing her hand up to cover her mouth. "Then why do you smell like my grandpa's liquor cabinet?"

"Dunno." I roll my shoulders and settle back into the couch. Turns out, they may look the same, but hers is way more comfortable than the one in our town house. "For what it's worth, I'm pretty sure I haven't been drunk since sophomore year."

"Somehow, I doubt that." Her words may be snarky, but her tone is playful. I'm digging it. "You go to parties all the time."

"I don't need to be drunk to have a good time. In fact, some things are better sober."

I might be a little buzzed, but it's the truth.

Liquid courage is a cop-out for guys who don't have the balls to talk to women.

That's never been an issue for me because I know what women like.

Not because I'm some kind of sexual savant—although I kind of am—but because I pay attention. It's that simple. When I'm with a woman, I give her my undivided attention, my respect, and I always make sure she comes first.

Preferably on my tongue.

"Take football, for example." I slide my arm across the back of the couch, careful not to touch Carter. Her knee is still pressed to my thigh and it's enough contact. For now. "When I'm on the field, I want to feel every sweaty, pulse-pounding play. I want to pump everything I've got into being the best, into scoring a goal. For my teammates and myself." My voice is low and gravelly and I swear to Christ you could cut the tension with a knife. "Even if I have to grind it out inch. By. Inch."

I reach out and twist a strand of Carter's hair between my fingers. It's soft and silky, just like I imagined. I brush it back from her face, the rough pads of my fingertips scraping across her cheek. Her breath hitches and for a moment, I think she's going to turn away, but her eyes remain locked on mine. Like maybe she's as into this analogy as I am.

"Inch by inch?" she asks, her voice rising an octave.

"There's no greater satisfaction."

She bites her bottom lip, teeth digging into the plump flesh and driving me wild.

I'd like nothing more than to nibble on those pouty lips myself, but when she finally speaks, she blurts out the last thing I'm expecting.

"You must be hungry. I mean, you should probably eat. To help you sober up. I think I've got a sandwich from the café in the fridge."

Oh, I'm hungry, but I doubt a sandwich is going to satisfy this craving.

I reach for her arm, but she bolts off the couch like her hair's on fire. "I told you I'm not—"

The word *drunk* dies on my tongue because Carter's shorts? They barely cover her ass.

The curve and swell of her flesh is on full display and my cock is suddenly ravenous, straining painfully against the zipper of my jeans.

I subtly adjust myself as Carter flits around the kitchen, but the sight of her perky backside is making it impossible to concentrate. I close my eyes and try thinking of the usual boner killers—football stats, Pittsburgh, the draft—but it's pointless.

Her tight little ass is imprinted on the inside of my eyelids.

*Get it together, asshole.*

The last thing I want is for Carter to throw me out for being a perv, but I can't help it if my dick wants to play man-to-man.

"Here you go." She nudges my foot.

When I open my eyes, she's studying me like she's afraid I'm going to pass out on her couch.

"Thanks." I accept the bottle of water and plate she's offering, resolved to sate my appetite with the sandwich and chips. "Don't look so worried. I'm not going to pass out on your couch. If anything, I'm tired from today's game. I didn't get a lot of sleep last night. I was up late reviewing plays."

She nods and takes her spot on the couch, folding her legs beneath her.

Warmth spreads up my leg and straight to my cock as her knee brushes mine, but I keep my attention focused on the TV, where there's a dude with big-ass horns and tree branches sticking out of his back like wings. "What the hell are we watching?"

Carter throws her head back and a throaty laugh I've never

heard before bubbles out of her. “Only the greatest show on TV.”

She spends the next ten minutes explaining the teen drama to me and despite all odds, I’m kind of intrigued by the dark, vampy feel, so I settle in to watch as I chug down the last of my water.

“Who’s that?” I ask when a skinny, dark-haired emo dude starts pounding away on his laptop.

“Only the best half of Bughead.” Her whole face lights up, triggering a pang of jealousy low in my gut. Great. Now I’m jealous of a guy on a fucking TV show? That’s stupid, right? “They’re my favorite ship.”

I don’t even ask. I’m pretty sure it’s short for *relationship*, but hell if I know.

More importantly, I can’t help but notice the guy’s wearing a black and red T-shirt. Just like the one Carter was wearing earlier. Makes perfect sense now.

“That’s the kind of guy you’re into?” I jerk my head toward the screen and turn my body toward hers, encroaching on her cushion so our legs are fully pressed together now. “You can’t be serious.”

“What?” She squares her shoulders and lifts her chin. “He’s actually kind of badass, but he also happens to be a nice guy.”

I snort, my breath coming hot and fevered. “Nice?”

“There’s nothing wrong with being attracted to nice guys.” Her nostrils flare just a tiny bit, and I know I’m getting under her skin in more ways than one. Is it possible she’s feeling the same undeniable pull of attraction? “They’re...*safe*.”

I get it. She thinks I’m a man-whoring asshole. It fits the played-out baller narrative.

I should be glad of it for about a million different reasons.

Problem is, I’m having trouble remembering those reasons

when she's looking at me with fire in her eyes, chest rising and falling with labored breaths.

"Safe is boring."

I don't give her a chance to protest. I slide a hand around the back of her neck, relishing the pleasure of skin-to-skin contact—hers smooth and silky, mine rough and calloused—before I tangle my fingers in her hair and pull her close, stopping when our lips are a breath apart.

I shouldn't be doing this.

*We* shouldn't be doing this.

But she doesn't pull away, just keeps those big brown eyes fixed on mine, and it's so fucking hot I know safe is the last thing she wants, even if she'll never admit it.

*Just one kiss. One taste of the forbidden fruit.*

We'll get it out of our systems and move on.

The air is practically humming with electricity as I bring my other hand up to cup her cheek. I close the gap between us, brushing my lips against hers. I expect the kiss to be slow and gentle, but when she parts her lips, a small sigh escapes, and my control slips.

The kiss explodes like wildfire, a desperate mating of tongues and desire as her lips incinerate the last of my restraint.

Carter's mouth is soft and welcoming, and every nerve in my body is screaming for more.

I don't know how long we go on like that, mouths searching for sweet salvation. It could be minutes; it could be hours. But when she finally pulls away, her lips red, swollen, and thoroughly kissed, reality comes roaring back into focus and I know I'm fucked.

One taste of Carter will never be enough.

## 20

## KENNEDY

"RISE AND SHINE." The insistent whisper-hiss is followed by a not-so-gentle shake. I give a tug on the comforter and bat aimlessly at the hand clutching my shoulder. It's my only day to sleep in. I am so not getting out of this bed. "What is Austin Reid doing on our couch?"

*Shit.*

Panic slams through me as I try to think of a good explanation. Truth is, there's no good explanation for making out with Reid on the couch, so I stall, taking the time to wipe the sleep from my eyes. Part of me had hoped he'd just sort of shuffle out in the morning and we could avoid this whole awkward morning-after disaster.

Clearly that was wishful thinking.

Becca's watching me expectantly, a devious grin on her face as she waits for details.

*Best to stick with the truth.*

Just maybe not the whole truth.

Yes, I'm a hypocrite. But it was a onetime thing. No repeat performances.

And definitely no post-kiss obsessing with my bestie.

When I finally meet her eyes, Becca's practically vibrating with excitement.

"I can't believe Austin Reid is on our couch. God, he's so hot. Even when he's sleeping. Wait. Did you hook up with him last night? Please tell me you hooked up with him. Was it amazing?"

As a matter of fact, it was.

The guy damn near set my panties on fire—with just his mouth—and it was all I could do not to rip his shirt off and lick each and every one of those perfectly sculpted muscles.

But I can't say that, so I stuff the guilt down deep and gesture to my fully clothed self, then at the empty bed. "Does it look like we hooked up?"

Not exactly a lie, but not the whole truth either.

"I knew it was too much to hope for." Becca sighs dramatically and inches back toward the door, sneaking a peek down the hall. I'm not sure if she's checking to make sure he's still asleep or if she's just plain old checking him out. I bite the inside of my cheek. *Probably the latter.* "Only you could have that sexy man beast over and not make a move. So, what's he doing here then?"

I climb out of bed and grab a sweater off the back of my desk chair.

Reid's not getting another free pass to the peep show. Even if he is the world's best kisser.

Is it any wonder the women on campus are lining up for a taste?

Just the memory of his lips on mine brings a rush of heat to my cheeks.

I turn from Becca, hoping she won't notice my telltale blush. "He stopped over last night. We watched some TV and he fell asleep. No biggie."

"He just stopped over on Saturday night to watch some TV?"

Okay. I totally get why she sounds skeptical. It does seem

unlikely given he's one of the hottest guys at Waverly. Toss in my aversion to football players, and my story's like a house of cards.

"And then y'all decided to have a sleepover?" she asks, pointing from me to the general direction of the living room.

The smirk on her face says she's not buying.

I shrug and wrap my sweater around my body, making sure there's no nip action. "I got up to use the bathroom and when I came back, he was asleep. Maybe he passed out."

Even as the words leave my mouth, I know they're bullshit.

Reid wasn't drunk. And I may have been in the bathroom longer than I thought, having a mini-meltdown, because, seriously, what was I thinking letting him kiss me?

Or, okay—real talk—kissing him back?

"I cannot believe Austin-*freaking*-Reid is sleeping on our couch!"

Becca's squealing now and if I don't calm her down, she's going to wake him up.

Which would probably be fine except for the part where we sound like unhinged fangirls.

Or fangirl, I guess, since it's just Becca.

Whatever. I just need her to bring it down a notch.

"Shh! He's going to hear you." I gesture for her to lower her voice. "You cannot tell anyone about this. They'll get the wrong idea and I do not need that kind of drama. The media is already a circus and Coach will kick me off the team if he thinks I'm distracting his star player." I sigh and rake a hand through my hair. "Plus, my mom would kill me."

Becca laughs it off, but my mom would flip her shit if she knew a football player spent the night in my apartment. I can't deal with that right now. I've got enough on my plate without adding her disappointment.

"My lips are sealed." She presses her lips flat, but it only lasts for maybe half a second. "But, um, what do we do now?"

"I guess we go wake him up."

I gesture for her to lead the way, but when we get to the living room, it turns out Baxter's taken it upon himself to rouse our guest, giving Reid an up-close-and-personal wakeup call. The dog is giving him a total tongue bath, but Reid takes it in stride, stroking Baxter's head before sitting up and moving out of his reach.

Sometime during the night he must've stripped off his button up, leaving only a tight white T-shirt that shows *all* the muscles. My pulse thrums at the sight of all that masculinity and puppy-loving goodness and I hope like hell my roommate can't hear it.

"He's a dog lover," Becca whispers. "Could he be more perfect?"

I don't answer. I can't. Because seeing Reid all sleep rumpled and adorable?

It's almost more than my ovaries can handle.

He spots us hovering in the hall and rubs the back of his neck, completely oblivious to the fact that his hair is sticking up at odd angles. "Who's the little guy?"

"Oh, that's Baxter." Becca flounces across the room to scoop the puppy up. The little guy was asleep in my room when Reid showed up last night, proving he has zero future as a guard dog. "You'll have to excuse him. He's not used to male company. It's been *ages* since Kennedy's brought a guy home."

*What the hell?*

Heat blazes up the back of my neck and fans out across my chest. I give my best friend the side-eye—I'm so going to kill her—but she ignores me. No doubt thinking she's being helpful by making it painfully obvious I'm single. And have been since New Year's when I called it quits with Two-Minute Mitch, unable to bear the thought of even one more sloppy gropefest.

Don't get me wrong, he was a nice guy, but the sex? It was like getting humped by a dog.

My gaze slides back to Reid. What would sex be like with him?

Judging by the way he kisses, incredible.

I resist the urge to touch my lips, remembering the way his kisses felt like being at the center of a supernova, white-hot and explosive.

"So what did you two crazy kids get into last night?" Becca looks from me to Reid, the picture of innocence, although there's a spark of amusement in her eyes.

*Traitor.*

"We just watched some TV," Reid says casually, the words falling from his lips smooth as silk. He steals a glance my way and when he smiles like we're sharing a private joke? I swear my stupid heart skips a beat. Not good. *Time to wrap this up.* "Hey, did you notice Baxter and Coop have the same smile?"

His question is so unexpected, I laugh out loud. It feels good, like a release valve for the tension that permeates the air.

"Right? I had the same thought the first time I met Coop."

Reid stands and slips on his shoes. "I should probably go and let you ladies get on with your day. Thanks for letting me crash on your couch."

Before I can formulate a response, Becca's given him an open invitation to return. "You're welcome anytime."

I've got to give Reid credit; he seems to be taking Becca's antics in stride. This sort of thing probably happens to him all the time, because he just shakes his head and gives a half-smile. Then he moves to let himself out and I follow.

So I can lock the door, not because I'm checking out his ass.

*Obviously.*

He turns and stuffs his hands in his pockets. "I guess I'll see you at practice."

"Sure. Practice." Okay. This isn't awkward at all.

Are we just going to act like the kiss was no big deal? Or maybe he was so drunk he doesn't remember it?

But no, he wasn't drunk. Pretending he was would be an easy excuse, a way to explain our actions, but it would be bullshit and I'm not in the habit of lying to myself.

He opens his mouth, and for a second I think he's going to bring up the kiss, but he just says, "Until tomorrow then."

"Until tomorrow," I echo as he turns to go.

Maybe I'm overthinking it. It *has* been a while since I've been with a guy and it *was* just a kiss. A super-hot, panty-melting kiss, but a kiss just the same.

I should be glad he doesn't want to talk it out.

It proves we're on the same page, that it was a onetime thing, right?

# 21

# AUSTIN

I RESET the game tape and settle in to watch the footage of last week's Pitt game. I've already watched it twice, and most of the guys have called it a day, but Pitt beat us last year. There's no way in hell I'm going to let it happen again.

They aren't even in our conference.

I press play and the players on the screen leap into motion.

It'll be a tough game and Coach has reminded me every damn day that there will be scouts present—like I could possibly forget. I just need to get my head in a good place. Half the game is mental, but knowing that doesn't make it any easier. I'll be useless to the team if I can't learn from last year's mistakes.

I'm watching Pitt execute a perfect zone blitz when the door clangs shut.

I turn in my seat and spot Carter at the back of the dark auditorium.

"Sorry to interrupt." She wrings her hands in a very un-Carter-like gesture. "I thought Coach might be in here watching game tape."

"I'm the only one left." I point the remote at the projector and pause the film. "Coach took off a while ago and most of the guys were right behind him."

"But not you?" She tucks her hands in the back pockets of her jeans and walks down the aisle, still looking unsure of herself, which makes no sense since she's been killing it on the field and at practice.

A fact I only know because I check in with the other kickers regularly.

"Nah, I've got to be sharp for Saturday's game. I can't afford to make mistakes against Pitt. Not unless we want a repeat of last year."

Carter stops a few seats away and drops down into one of the empty chairs.

"What about the rest of the team?" She makes a show of looking around. "I don't see them in here watching endless hours of game tape."

I shrug and tap my pencil on the desktop. It's the first time we've been alone since the kiss two weeks ago and even now, three seats away, I can feel Carter's pull. The urge to drag her onto my lap and show her what she does to me is nearly impossible to ignore.

It's fucking distracting.

"Yeah, well, they're not the offspring of the great Derrick Reid. Every move I make is news and every misstep is analyzed to death. I can't afford to make mistakes."

She laughs, but there's no mirth in it. "Sounds exhausting."

"You have no idea." My phone's been blowing up this week with jersey chasers who want to party, but all I can think about is Carter. She's the only distraction I've allowed myself and the one distraction I can't afford. And not just because Coach forbade it. "The last thing I want to do is let my father, or the fans, down. Everyone thinks being a football legacy is a gift, but the reality is there's a lot of pressure to be as good as my old man. Otherwise, I'm nothing but a failure."

Carter's brows flatten and a tiny wrinkle forms in the crease between them. "I guess I never thought of it that way before."

I stretch my legs, trying to look unaffected by her empathy. I refuse to think of it as sympathy because I do not need Carter feeling bad for me. Why the fuck am I telling her these things anyway?

Sure, I think them all the time, but I've never voiced them aloud.

Certainly not to my teammates.

Still, I can't seem to shut the hell up. "You know that old saying, walk a mile in someone else's shoes?"

"My mom used to say it all the time when I was a kid." A smile tugs at her lips. "Usually when she thought I was being ungrateful."

"Let's just say it never sounded like a bad thing to me. Hell, I would've given anything to walk in someone else's shoes as a kid." She tilts her head as if she's trying to put it all together and I realize I'm fucking it up. Maybe this is why I've never been stupid enough to voice my thoughts aloud. "Don't get me wrong. I love the game, but it always comes first in my family. I used to be jealous of kids whose lives weren't defined by football."

"Meanwhile, I'll bet every kid on your team wished they had your life. After all, who wouldn't want an NFL star for a father, right?" Carter laughs, but it rings hollow, and I can't help but think we aren't talking about me anymore.

"You." I'm not sure exactly what she's trying to tell me, but everything I know about her tells me it's true.

She shrugs. "You got me. My dad was a football player. I'll see your future Hall of Famer and raise you a washout."

There's a note of sadness in her voice, and it strikes me like a late hit.

I want to move closer—to take her hand in mine—but I'm frozen in my seat.

This...baring of souls is the closest we've ever come to a real conversation, and I don't want to upset the delicate balance.

Carter offers me a wry smile and I give silent thanks for the dim lighting.

Our secrets aren't the kind you share in the light of day.

"My dad was the worst kind of washout. The kind who couldn't accept it and spent his best years chasing a life that wasn't meant to be."

She doesn't say it—doesn't have to—but I can see it in her eyes, hear it in her voice. There's a deep-rooted sadness that confirms her father is the one who shaped her perception of football players. The drinking. The partying. The women. He sounds like a real prick, and I want to say as much, but I bite my tongue.

She already knows he's a bastard. She doesn't need to hear it from me.

"We're not all like him, Carter." It's true. Sure, some football players are dicks, but not all of us. The same could be said of the whole male population. I'd hate to see her spend the rest of the season closing herself off from the team—and, okay, me—because of her father's mistakes. "I'm not like him."

"Doesn't matter." *The hell it doesn't.* She hops to her feet and I follow her lead, noticing the way she seems to straighten her spine and pull herself up to her full height, as if she's fortifying herself against this quiet moment, against me. When she speaks, there's steel in her voice. "That kiss? It was a onetime deal, okay? It can't happen again."

She doesn't wait for my reply, just turns on her heel and hurries up the aisle like she can't get away fast enough.

Part of me knows it's just as well. We're teammates and

nothing good can come of it. Not when I've got a job to do, a team to lead, a championship to win.

But another part of me? The part that's sick of always doing what's expected?

It says *fuck that.*

We've got the kind of chemistry that could burn up the sheets.

Saturday night proved it.

Now that I've had a taste of Carter? I want more.

More of the fiery passion that keeps me jerking off to the memory of her lips on mine, the only cure for the near constant hard-on I've battled since Saturday night.

There's something worth exploring between us, and I'm not about to walk away.

I'll put in the work to show her not all football players are assholes. The next time I kiss Carter? It'll be because she wants it.

*Because she's begging for it.*

"Hey, Carter." She freezes, but doesn't turn to look at me. That's okay. My ego can handle it, because I know this thing between us is far from over. Hell, we're just getting started. "You can try to shut me out, but the thing is, I'm an offensive player. There's no one better at reading—and bypassing—a defensive move than me."

## 22

# KENNEDY

"I CAN ONLY TALK FOR A MINUTE." I glance at the clock in the makeshift dressing room. It's the office of one of the Nebraska assistant coaches, but I don't mind. It's private and smells better than a lot of the locker rooms I've had the misfortune of using for away games.

"I won't keep you long," Mom says, her voice crystal clear, despite the miles separating us. "Just wanted to say good luck today, since we didn't get to talk yesterday." Her hours have been cut back, but not as much as either of us would like. Apparently there's a nursing shortage—*again*. "How'd your proposal for the ACME competition go?"

I'm about to step on the field to play Big Ten football and my mom's more concerned with my academics. If I could reach through the phone and hug her, I would.

"My advisor loved the concept, though he's concerned about the complexity. He thinks I won't be able to finish on time, but I'll prove him wrong."

Without work study, I'll be much better positioned to work on this year's design, even if it is far more complex than anything I've attempted in the past.

"Are you sure you won't need help?" Her tone is cautious, like she knows how much I'll hate this question. After all, she's the one who raised me to be self-sufficient. "Maybe you should consider a partner this year."

Yeah, right. And put my chances of success in someone else's hands?

*So not happening.*

It's a national competition, and the top finishers are pretty much guaranteed the best job offers. The company sponsoring this year's competition has locations in a half-dozen major cities and career tracks with sweet starting salaries. Plus, they'd pay for my master's degree.

"Don't worry. I've got everything under control."

*Mostly.*

She clears her throat. "Speaking of control, how're those boys on the team treating you?"

"Everything's fine, Mom. Stop worrying." No way I'm telling her I kissed one of them or that I can't stop thinking about him. The thought of Reid's lips crashing against my own sends a flash of desire straight to my core, and just like that, I'm thinking about what it would be like to have his chiseled body pressed to mine. *Damn Reid and his kissable lips.* "Team's on a winning streak. We're five and oh. Soon to be six. Everything's great, but I need to get over to the locker room for Coach's pregame huddle. Talk soon, okay?"

She barely gets out her goodbye before I disconnect.

*Real smooth, Kennedy. I'm sure she won't suspect a thing.*

My phone vibrates and a text pops up on the screen.

At first I think it'll be a message from my mom, the "I love you" I cut off with my hasty disconnect. I couldn't be more wrong.

*Hey Kenny. Let me know when you're free for lunch. I need to see you.*

Red-hot fury coils low in my belly, incinerating all thoughts of Reid's nibblicious lips.

I hate it when my dad calls me Kenny. It just reinforces the knowledge that if I'd been born with a penis—if he thought we had anything in common—he might've taken more interest.

I shove the phone in my bag without responding. I have no idea why he wants to see me now, or why he assumes I'd want to see him. We haven't spoken in months, so why now?

The answer is so painfully obvious, I almost laugh.

He saw my picture in the press and he wants something.

I try to stuff my anger down, to ignore the pain that comes with it. So, my father's an asshole. It's not new news. And still, the knowledge finds the cracks in my armor, wedging itself into the dark corners of my heart I'd thought long hardened to his machinations. I hate that I care so much when he cares so little.

It's not fair.

*Yeah, well, life's not fair. If you haven't figured it out yet, let this be a reminder.*

I suck in a breath, the air slicing through my lungs like razor-tipped wire.

It doesn't matter. This is hardly the time to reflect on my father's shitty parenting skills. I've got a game to play and the team's counting on me.

I grab my helmet and head for the team locker room on shaky legs.

Four hours later, I return to the tiny office/dressing room, secure in the knowledge I lost my team the game. What should've been a 6-0 record is now 5-1. I kick off my cleats and then strip off my jersey and pads, tossing them unceremoniously on the floor.

I never should've looked at my stupid phone before the game.

My father got in my head and it cost me.

*Cost the team.*

It might even cost them their title run.

I shimmy out of my pants and trade them for a black skirt that falls to midthigh. I should've made that field goal. I've been hitting seventy-nine percent of my long-range kicks. Forty-five yards is completely doable, especially with ideal conditions.

"*ARGH!*" I roar, frustration getting the better of me as I wriggle out of my sports bra and fling it over the arm of a chair.

*Relax. It isn't like they're going to revoke your scholarship over one missed field goal.*

That's the most important thing, right?

Right.

Except... I let the team down. No one will come out and say it, but I know it's on me. They were counting on me to deliver today, and I screwed up. I may have a full set of baggage when it comes to football, but I'm no stranger to being on a team, and it grates that I didn't give it one hundred percent today.

I'm better than that.

I slip on my lace bra and white blouse, fumbling with the tiny buttons. It takes twice as long as it should to button the damn shirt in my irritated state.

There's a knock at the door, but the last thing I need right now is company.

I doubt it's for me anyway. Probably just someone looking for the coach whose office I've been assigned. I glance down, confirming I'm presentable, and open the door to find the last person I expect.

"Hey." Reid's still wearing his uniform, the jersey covered in grass and mud, a testament to the hard-fought battle. He gestures to the tiny office at my back. "Can I come in?"

"Sure." I step aside to let him enter. Should I close the door or leave it open? Closing it would give us more privacy for whatever it is he's come to say, but the last thing I need is to be alone with Reid. It's been almost three weeks since our chat in the team meeting room, and I haven't forgotten his...declaration. Still, I don't want him to think I'm afraid to be alone with him, like I can't control my hormones, so I leave the door cracked, giving us a modicum of privacy. "What's up?"

"I thought maybe you could use a friend." Reid leans against the wooden desk, arms crossed over his chest, relaxed as you please. Even with the bulky pads, his body is long and lean, a veritable powerhouse. His voice is like gravel when he finally speaks again. "That was a tough game."

"You think?" I regret the snarky reply immediately. Just because I'm pissed at myself doesn't mean I can take it out on Reid. That would be a bitch move. "Sorry." I toy with the end of my braid so I don't have to look him in the eye. "It's just...I should've made that kick. I've made it a hundred times in practice, but I let myself get distracted."

"Distracted?" His face is open and warm, and I can tell his interest is sincere, but no way in hell am I telling him about my dad's text. I've already said too much—revealed too much—about myself. When I don't answer, Reid continues. "Yeah, well, if I'd been on my game, you never would have been in that position in the first place."

The snort is out of my mouth before I can think better of it. "What? Because you're Austin-*freaking*-Reid? Like you're a one-man show?"

I narrow my eyes at him until I'm sure they're just little slits, but he doesn't even flinch. Just gives an almost imperceptible shrug as if to say, *If the shoe fits.*

"Oh my God. You really believe that crap, don't you?" I throw my head back and laugh, although in truth, it's anything but funny. Most people would crumble under that kind of pressure. For the first time, I truly understand what it must've been like growing up in his father's shadow. "Shit. That must be some burden to carry...the weight of the entire team." I drop down into one of the chairs opposite him and give what I hope is a teasing smile. "Pro tip: I don't need you to save me or shoulder the burden or whatever it is you think you're doing. Neither does the rest of the team. We're all adults here."

He arches a brow, a grin tugging at the corner of his mouth. "Is that so?"

I nod vigorously, refusing to be distracted by that adorable, kissable dimple. "Definitely. You can't take all the credit for our mistakes any more than you'd try to take credit for our success."

"I'd never do that." He sits up straighter, cheeks flushed with indignation.

His dark hair falls over his left eye, giving him a dangerous edge, and despite the fact that he's sweat stained and dirty, he's hot as hell.

*Who knew the man could wear outrage so well?*

"Exactly." I shift in my seat, crossing my legs. Because I'm wearing a skirt and it's ladylike, not because I'm getting hot for him and crave the friction. And I'm definitely not thinking about what it would be like for him to bend me over the desk and do a quarterback sneak.

That would just be fifty shades of wrong.

He pushes off the desk so only inches remain between our bodies.

Which is slightly awkward since now I'm face-to-face with his package.

His rather large package.

Heat floods my body, pooling low in my belly.

God, what is wrong with me? I should not be thinking about Reid's—

"You're probably right."

*Crap. What was I right about?*

Oh yeah. Teamwork. Shared responsibility.

"I know." I force myself to focus on the issue at hand, despite my raging hormones. "I made mistakes today and so did the defense. You don't get to take all the blame when there's plenty to go around. It's like you said, we have to learn from our mistakes." Which is exactly what I should be doing, so I stand, which turns out to be the wrong move, because now my breasts are practically skimming his chest. "Also, why am I now consoling you? I thought you were here to cheer me up?"

Humor sparks in his eyes. "I'd be happy to cheer you up. Just say the word."

*Nopenopenope.*

I've got to put a stop to this, whatever *this* is

We're too close, the chemistry between us a dangerous, unwieldy thing with a mind of its own.

"You should probably go shower. The bus will be leaving soon."

"I'll go, but first you have to make me a promise." His voice is like a caress, soft and gentle, as his hot breath skates across my cheek. He's got me and he knows it, judging by the self-satisfied smirk on his face. I'll agree to anything just to get rid of him and put some space between us. "Join the team for the homecoming activities next weekend. I promise you won't regret it."

## 23

# AUSTIN

THE HOMECOMING PARADE is a total circus. In all my years at Waverly, I can't remember the crowds ever being so large. Or rowdy. Rumor has it there are six degrees of separation between all Wildcat fans and it seems like they all turned out, determined to cheer us to victory over Ohio tomorrow.

It'll be a tough game.

Especially with the week six loss hanging over the team like a dark fucking cloud.

It doesn't help that the press has been brutal. They're already speculating about the impact on my draft stock because, like I told Carter, that shit's on me. Every mistake I made has been analyzed six ways from Sunday as the talking heads look for weaknesses in my game.

I suck in a sharp breath, the cool air whistling between my teeth.

*Doesn't matter.*

If we run the table from here on out, we've still got a shot at the championship game.

We just need to stay focused and take it one game at a time.

Despite the pressure, it's impossible not to get swept up in the excitement of the parade.

There's music, dancing, and more open containers than the police can possibly confiscate.

I steal a glance at Carter, mainly to reassure myself she's having a good time. I did promise, after all, and I'm a man of my word. She's laughing at something Coop said, and even though I know there's nothing between them, the sting of jealousy is sharp.

She looks great today, and I'd have to be oblivious not to appreciate it.

Since she's distracted, I take the opportunity to look my fill. Her hair is tied back in a ponytail and she's wearing makeup. It's not dramatic enough to change her girl-next-door vibe, but it sure as hell complements it, her face glowing under the old-fashioned streetlights.

Like the rest of the team, she's wearing jeans and her jersey.

But unlike the rest of us, her jeans hug the soft curve of her ass and her tits bounce gently with each step.

I've never been one to share my jersey, but a lot of guys on the team swear there's nothing sexier than a woman wearing their numbers. They've got it all wrong. Looking at Carter, I'm certain there's nothing sexier than a woman wearing her own numbers.

I can easily picture her prancing around my bedroom in that jersey and nothing else, her golden legs leading straight to the end zone.

My cock twitches at the thought.

*Get a grip. Much more of this and you'll be walking the parade route with a hard-on.*

Not exactly the kind of press I need heading into the big game.

Ohio's playing well and they're currently leading us in the

rankings, but I don't put much stock in those numbers. We're just breaking into our conference schedule and if we play well, we'll improve our position.

Just like I've improved my position with Carter, although not half as much as I'd like.

Hell, I should just be glad she's walking the parade route with me and my roommates where I can keep an eye out for her. Not that it should be any great surprise. I don't get the feeling she's particularly close to the guys on Special Teams, and let's be honest, none of them are willing to put in the work. It took a hell of a lot of persistence on my part to get her to hang with the us this week, but it was worth it.

Especially when Carter won a pink unicorn at the carnival and gave it to Coop, because only a guy who preens as much as he does could appreciate such a beautiful creature. The guys ate that shit up and the unicorn has sort of become the unofficial mascot of the week. It's taken longer than I would've liked, but Carter's finally finding her place on the team. The guys are starting to trust her and vice versa.

Not that I'm patting myself on the back or anything.

It's part of my job as captain to ensure the team gels.

Sure, there's a little voice in the back of my mind that says my interest in Carter exceeds my obligations as team captain, but I ignore the fucker.

Carter turns from Coop and catches me staring. She lifts a brow but says nothing, just continues waving to the fans that line College Ave. There's a flush in her cheeks that could be from exertion, but I prefer to think it's proof she's as hot for me as I am for her. Carter's doing her damnedest to pretend that kiss didn't happen, but I've never shied away from a challenge, and I'm not about to give up on the heat between us.

After all, what Coach doesn't know won't hurt him.

"Having fun?" I ask, waving to a group of pint-size fans.

She bites her lower lip and my balls tighten.

Does she do that shit on purpose, just to torture me?

*Probably.*

"Who doesn't like a parade?"

I snort. "Would it be so hard for you to admit I was right?"

"Just doing my part to keep that ginormous ego of yours in check."

"Whatever. Nobody's got a bigger ego than DeLaurentis and I don't see you busting his ba—chops." I nudge her with my elbow. "Don't worry. Your secret's safe with me. I won't tell anyone you had actual fun with the football team."

She wipes her brow. "*Phew!* For a minute there, I was worried about my reputation."

"You know, if I'd known you were going to be such a smart-ass, I might not have asked you to try out."

"Liar. You totally would've asked. You were desperate. I could smell it on you like cheap cologne." There's a wicked gleam in her eye and it's sexy as hell.

Most of the women I hook up with will say and do anything to make me happy. They wouldn't dream of giving me the kind of lip Carter does, but it's one of the things that sets her apart.

I fucking love it.

"Are you sure that wasn't Coop?" I frown, feigning confusion. "He wears more body spray than a teenage boy."

"There's nothing wrong with my cologne," Coop protests, slinging an arm around Carter's shoulders. Why the fuck is he always touching her? It's like he can't keep his paws to himself lately. "I've never gotten a single complaint from the female population." He pauses and winks at Carter. "Of course, it could be due to the fact that I give such good orgasms they're usually left speechless."

"You're such a pig." Carter rolls her eyes and shrugs off his touch.

"You say pig, I say generous lover." Coop shrugs. "Potayto, potahto."

"Incoming," I say, thankful for the interruption.

If Coop lays it on any thicker, I'm going to lose my lunch. Or knock out my best friend.

Coop peels off as two little girls in Waverly jerseys approach, pens in hand.

"Can we have your autograph?" they ask in unison.

"Sure." I stop and reach for one of the pens. "What're your names?"

The girl snatches her hand back.

"Not you. Kennedy." She swivels from me to Carter, a look of pure adoration on her face.

Well, fuck me. Maybe Carter was right about my ego.

"It's so cool that you're playing football with the boys. I want to play football next year too! Just like you."

"Oh." Carter's eyes widen, as if it never occurred to her that someone might take inspiration from her story or ask for her autograph. "Um, who should I make it out to?"

"Beth, please." The girl holds out her pen and Carter accepts.

"And Maggie. Is it true you used to play soccer?" the smaller one asks, hope shining in her eyes. "I play soccer too!"

"That's awesome." Carter scrawls her name on the team photo. "What position?"

"I'm a striker." She points to Beth, the girl who checked my ego. "My sister's a goalie."

"Two vital positions that require speed and strength." Carter smiles and hands the pen and signed picture back. "Both good skills for a kicker."

"Thanks!" The girls squeal, each grasping a corner of the photo. "This is so cool. Wait until I tell my friends at school I met you."

"She's a great kicker. We're really lucky to have her on the team," I say, figuring Carter might need an assist wrapping this up since it seems like her first time signing autographs. "I'll bet if you keep practicing, you can be just as good as her and play for Waverly one day."

"Totally!" Carter agrees, giving the girls a small wave as they race back to the curb where their parents wait.

We rejoin the team, now bringing up the rear of the procession.

"Does that happen to you often?" Carter asks, keeping her gaze fixed ahead.

"Often enough." I shrug, trying to match her energy. "Pretty cool, huh?"

She wrinkles her nose. "What? Getting my ego stroked?"

"No, inspiring the next generation." I wave to a group of fans doing the Waverly cheer as we pass by. "I remember the first time I met Peyton Manning. Damn near pissed myself, I was so excited."

She does a double take. "You were a Peyton Manning fanboy?"

"Hell, yeah. Still am," I say, ignoring the half-hearted fanboy dig. "The guy's a legend. Meeting your idol can be a real motivator. To those little girls, you're a hero, someone who's breaking down barriers and showing them anything is possible."

Carter stops, a thoughtful look replacing her prior distaste.

"I'd rather inspire them with my brain than my ability to kick a ball." Her bottom lip juts out like an invitation. One I'd greedily accept if it weren't for the horde of onlookers. The urge to take her in my arms and suck that bottom lip until she's begging for more nearly obliterates all rational thought. "Girls are always shortchanged when it comes to STEM."

"Who says you can't do both?" I stuff my hands in my pockets. It doesn't eliminate my desire to touch her, but it damn sure makes it impossible to act on the impulse. An impulse that's getting harder to resist each day. "Change the narrative."

"It's not that simple. Not with all the hoopla surrounding my role on the team."

"Nothing worth having comes easy."

I don't need to look her in the eye to know she gets my meaning.

The air around us hums with electricity that has nothing to do with the crowds and everything to do with the pull between us.

Maybe we aren't relationship goals, but fuck, doesn't she want to sweat this thing out between the sheets as badly as I do?

Carter clears her throat. "Your poker face is shit, you know that, right?"

I turn to look at her, but she keeps her eyes straight ahead, smile frozen in place.

"I'm confident enough that I don't mind showing my hand." Carter can deny it until my balls turn blue and shrivel off, but the way she kissed me? I know she feels the spark between us, even if she thinks acting on it's a bad idea. Hell, I can't disagree, but I'm a risk taker by nature and I'm not about to let the knowledge hold me back. "I've learned to take pleasure in the game. To appreciate the slow burn of a well-executed play. Because that constant ache of desire? It makes the victory dance that much sweeter."

# 24

# KENNEDY

HOLY SHIT. This homecoming game is no joke. The stadium's packed, and I'm pretty sure the announcer said it's a record crowd, but it's nearly impossible to hear anything over the roar of the fans.

It's one of Waverly's famous whiteout games and the stadium is awash in white. There isn't an Ohio fan to be found, and the band is bringing down the house with something peppy and upbeat as the offense drives down the field.

Reid's on his game and the O-line is playing well, but we're down by three and it's starting to look like this thing might go down to the wire.

My stomach churns with nervous energy, and there's a real possibility I might hurl.

I can't stop thinking about the week six game and the forty-six-yard field goal I missed.

*That cannot happen today.*

It would end Waverly's shot at the national title. But even more importantly, I'd probably be tarred and feathered by the fans before I could escape the stadium, and I have zero interest in killing the homecoming spirit that's taken over the entire town.

Hell, Wildcat Nation.

So, yeah. I'm only half watching the game as I practice kicking into the net.

My leg is loose and my form is good. Conditions are optimal. What more could I ask for?

*Other than a gimme?*

*Ha!* There's no such thing as a gimme in football.

Even a twenty yarder can be blocked.

I steal a glance at the scoreboard. Reid's third and long.

If he doesn't convert on this drive, Jackson will be calling for me. I close my eyes and draw a deep breath, doing my best to push out the noise of the crowd.

Turns out, it's impossible.

I give up and turn my attention to the field just in time to see Reid get sacked at the twenty-two.

"Carter! You're up!" Jackson bellows, adjusting the visor on his hat, a sure sign he's sweating this kick. He always fidgets when he's nervous.

*Thanks for the vote of confidence, dude.*

"You've got this," he says as I slide past him. "No wind. Get it up quick!"

I give him a curt nod and jog onto the field.

The stadium noise begins to die down as I walk off my steps and line my body up with the upright.

*Thirty-nine yards.*

Just thirty-nine yards and I can haul ass back to the sideline and lose myself in the anonymity of the team. Piece of cake.

The ball is snapped, but it's short. James has to reach for it and loses his footing.

*Shit. Shit. Shit.*

Panic beats a staccato rhythm through my veins as he struggles to plant the ball. There's no time. Laces out or not, I've got to move if we want to have any shot of making this thing.

I take one short step, followed by two longer ones and swing my foot, the cleat connecting with a loud *thwump* as the ball takes flight.

It sails through the air and I watch, not daring to breathe.

It's leaning right, but there's a chance...

*Yes!*

Tie game. I punch my fist in the air as the refs raise their arms to signal a field goal.

The crowd goes nuts, the screaming and stomping so loud it's a wonder the ancient stadium doesn't come crashing down around us.

I jog over to James and praise his solid recovery. The guy's got insanely fast hands and he totally saved my ass out there. No way I could've salvaged that ball if our positions were reversed. He blushes a bit, but I can tell he's pleased with the compliment.

When I return to the sideline, I'm met with high fives, fist bumps, and a few slaps on the ass, which I interpret to mean good work. I grab a drink of water and settle in to watch some more football.

Ohio's three and out deep in their own territory.

I do a mental happy dance when they're forced to punt and before I know it, Reid's back on the field.

The game goes on like this for a while, neither side scoring, but both delivering a lot of blows. I see more blood, sweat, and grass stains than usual with neither team yielding ground. The clock's running out. Only two minutes to go when Waverly gets the ball back and now I'm hovering on the sideline with the rest of the team, hoping, praying, cheering for Reid and the offense to find the end zone.

Reid completes a pass to Coop for a first down, but he's tackled almost immediately.

They run the ball on the next play, followed by another pass.

Then it's first and goal and I'm biting my damn nails as the play clock runs down.

Ohio's defense rallies and they crush our offense.

Same result on second and goal.

Reid passes on the next play, but Coop is tackled short of the goal line.

It's forth and inches now with only seconds to go, and I swear I'm going to crawl out of my skin. The stadium has once again reached fever pitch. I don't know how Reid could possibly call a play over this kind of noise.

Not that it matters. Everyone knows it's going to be a running play.

Ohio's defense piles up on the center, but Reid tucks the ball under his arm and punches it through to score the game-winning touchdown.

Up until this point, it's been the crowd going wild, but when Reid puts up six points, the team goes crazy on the sideline. The clock's run out and the extra point isn't required, so the team rushes the field. Someone grabs my arm, sweeping me up in the frenzy. The team gathers near the end zone, congratulating Reid and celebrating a much-needed victory over one of our conference rivals.

I find myself floating through the sea of bodies, exchanging celebratory hugs and fist bumps with my teammates and coaches. The thrill of victory is like a drug, working its way through my system with enough endorphins to guarantee I won't be sleeping tonight. I could never tell Becca, but the rush is even better than winning a soccer game.

When I reach the center of the crowd, I'm face-to-face with Reid. His helmet is tucked under his right arm, locked in place by the glistening muscles that helped deliver the game-winning touchdown. His sweat-dampened hair sticks to his forehead, but his eyes shine with victory and when he gives me that cocky grin of his, I swear no man has ever been sexier.

Not Chris Hemsworth. Not Ross Butler. Not Cole Sprouse.

Which I definitely should *not* be thinking.

Our eyes meet and it's as if the crowd and the noise fall away.

For an instant, it's just me and Reid.

And judging by the look on his face, he's thinking about that victory dance.

Desire curls low in my gut, and I'm not sure whether to hug him or...

Well, none of those other options would be acceptable, so I just give him a nod and tell him good game, because, hey, I'm super awkward like that and climbing your teammate like a tree tends to be frowned upon. Even if he's made it clear he'd welcome the experience.

Besides, the night is young. There's still plenty of time for victory dances and bad decisions.

## 25

# AUSTIN

I'M FLYING high after the win over Ohio, the rush of victory pumping through my veins as we wade into the Wildcat's Den. It's one of the hottest bars in town and with a homecoming victory to celebrate, the place is at max capacity. Not like the bouncer would turn us away though since we're basically the guests of honor.

The celebration is in full swing when we arrive and I follow Coop as he weaves his way through the swell of bodies, sweaty flesh pressing in on us from all sides as we snake past the dance floor. Several people slap me on the back and there's a Wildcats chant picking up momentum, but I don't stop.

The bar is crowded as fuck and I don't want to lose my roommates.

We won a big game today. The team's killing it, and I'm more confident than ever we're poised for a championship run, despite the week six loss. We just have to keep the wheels on the wagon.

*No distractions.*

My phone vibrates in my pocket, but I ignore it. It's been blowing up all night with offers to party. I've ignored most of them, only responding to messages from close friends and family. Tonight's about the team and I want to hang with the guys.

*And Carter.*

Shit. I know I should be thinking of Carter as one of the guys, especially given the whole no-distractions thing, but come on. After that kiss? Impossible.

We find a high-top table in the back and order a round of beers. The server tells us they're on the house, thanks for a job well done. When she shows up a few minutes later with a round of shots, we aren't about to turn them away.

It would be a dick move to decline them, so I smile and say thanks, making a mental note to call and thank the owner personally next week.

We're on our second round of beers when the server, who's been flirting nonstop with Coop, asks why Carter isn't with us.

*Great fucking question.*

I drain my glass and slam it down on the table harder than necessary. She better not bail. She promised she'd be here, and I thought—

*Holy. Shit.*

Is that Carter?

My dick comes to attention, and I do a double take.

Carter sidles up to the table, tugging at the hem of a black skirt that was clearly made for someone six—hell, maybe eight—inches shorter. She's wearing a slinky red tank top, and her dark hair's been straightened so it falls over her bare shoulders in a silky curtain. Her lips are painted the same shade of red as her shirt, and her eyes are rimmed with a smoky shadow. But it's the shoes that do me in. They're black, strappy, and sky-high.

It doesn't take much effort to imagine those heels digging into my ass as I bury myself between her thighs.

"Looking good, Carter," Coop says, giving her an appreciative once-over.

"Thanks." She flashes an uncertain smile and tugs at her skirt again. "My roommate's handiwork."

"Never would've guessed."

"Liar." Carter laughs as he pours her a beer, forgetting about the über-short hemline for a minute. "But I appreciate the effort."

Coop visibly inflates, and for some reason it annoys the shit out of me.

I grit my teeth and smile, feeling like an asshole for not complimenting Carter myself.

*Too late now*. I'll just sound like a pandering douche.

Parker turns to Carter and drapes an arm across her shoulders as she slides onto the stool next to him. "It's about time you joined us for post-game libations. I was starting to get a complex."

"I doubt that." She rolls her eyes and takes a sip of her beer. Her tongue darts out to lick the foam from the corner of her lips, and I'm reminded of the white-hot passion that simmers just below the surface.

"Trust me, Parker could stand to get a complex," Vaughn says, lifting his chin in greeting. "You'd be doing us all a favor."

Carter throws her head back and laughs, that sexy, throaty laugh that makes my cock swell in anticipation.

Parker flips him the bird and raises his glass. "To Carter, for sending those Ohio pricks home with their tails between their legs."

"I'll drink to that," Vaughn agrees, raising his own glass.

I follow suit, frustration stirring in my gut.

*What the fuck is wrong with me?*

I'm totally off my game.

It should be me drawing that sexy sound from Carter. Me toasting her amazing fucking leg.

And not just because I'm the team captain.

There's something between us and I can't ignore it any more than I could ignore a pass rush at the line of scrimmage.

We talk about football for a while and a steady stream of our teammates trickle past. Everyone's feeling bullish about the upcoming game against Wisconsin, and by the time the server brings a fourth round of drinks, rubbing up against Coop with all the subtlety of bulldozer, it's clear he's done shooting the shit.

"Time to break up this sausage fest." He turns to Carter with a flirtatious grin. "No offense."

She shakes her head and throws up a hand. "None taken."

And just like that, Coop disappears into the writhing crowd on the dancefloor.

No sooner has he vacated his seat than a guy wearing Greek letters slides into it. I've seen him around on Greek Row. I don't know his name, but I know he's got too much product in his hair, an arrogant grin I'd like to wipe off his face, and a reputation for being a player.

I don't like the way he's looking at Carter.

"Hey." The creep directs the greeting to her like the rest of us are invisible. He's got balls, I'll give him that much. "You're Kennedy, right? I think we had a class together last spring."

*Bullshit. If this guy's an engineering major, I'll eat my helmet.*

Kennedy scrunches her brow like she's trying to place him. "I'm sorry. I don't remember."

Probably because it's a lame-ass pickup line.

"Landon," he says, flashing that shit-eating grin again.

"That seat's taken." I level him with my eyes. "*Landon.*"

He puffs out his chest like those Greek letters mean shit. "Looked empty to me."

"Honest mistake." Parker shrugs and shifts in his seat,

crowding the newcomer with his massive body. "You should probably move along before our buddy comes back. He gets a little short-tempered when he's been drinking."

Total lie. The only thing Coop gets when he's been drinking is horny.

Landon's gaze slides from Parker to me. "No worries, man. I just wanted to catch up with Kennedy. I'll see you around."

He abandons the chair and gives her a curt nod before returning to his friends a few tables over. They break out in raucous laughter, slapping him on the back and throwing bottle caps at him, probably assuming Carter shot him down.

"What the hell was that?" Carter demands, glaring at me.

She's pissed. And I get it—sort of—but no way was I letting that douchebag get within a mile of her.

"Just looking out for you." Parker drums his fingers on the table. "We're good teammates like that."

Carter rolls her eyes. "I didn't see you pulling that shit on Coop."

"Yeah, well, that's Coop." It sounds like a double standard, even to my own ears, but Coop plays it straight with his hookups. There's no chance of him getting hurt. "Besides, I wouldn't let my sister near that guy."

Her eyes widen. "You have a sister?"

"No, but if I did—"

"You're all being ridiculous." Carter throws up her hands. "He probably just wanted to ask me to dance."

Yeah, right. The horizontal mambo. "You can thank me later. The guy's a douchebag."

She smiles sweetly, and I know I'm about to get a dose of sexy-as-hell sarcasm. "And what do you call chasing off the only guy with the nerve to come over and talk to me?"

Before I can come up with a witty reply, Vaughn cuts in. "I'm pretty sure Landon's dating a Tri-Delt. Better not to get mixed up with a guy like that. I doubt he knows the meaning of the word 'respect.'"

"Exactly." I cross my arms over my chest and lean back in my chair, admiring the flush in Carter's cheeks.

I've never enjoyed getting under a woman's skin as much as I enjoy getting under hers.

"Well, this has been fun." Parker stands and drains his glass. "But I gotta see about a girl."

He slips into the crowd, leaving Vaughn and I alone at the table with Carter.

"Do you dance?" Carter asks, careful to direct the question to Vaughn.

She's been doing that all night. Avoiding my gaze. Not talking to me directly if she can help it.

It's driving me fucking crazy.

"Nah." Vaughn gives a casual shrug, his face unreadable. "Not really my thing, but don't let that stop you. I'll probably cut out soon anyway."

Carter snorts. "I'm sitting at a table with two big-ass dudes—who've already chased off my only prospect like a bunch of overprotective cockblockers—so I'm pretty sure that ship has sailed."

She cuts her eyes at me when she says *cockblockers* because apparently I'm doing a shit job hiding my intentions. Doesn't matter. She's just given me an opening. If I know anything about Carter, she won't back down from a challenge.

"You wanna dance? I'll dance with you."

She freezes, probably hoping like hell she misheard.

"I'm a pretty good dancer." I flash her a cocky grin like this is the best idea I've had all day. And let's be honest, it kind of is. "Ask Vaughn."

She looks at him warily, realizing too late she's backed herself into a corner. There was no scenario where I wasn't going to call her bluff. She'll have to put up or shut up.

"He's a regular twinkle toes," Vaughn deadpans. He lifts his beer and empties the glass in one long chug. "Might as well. I'm heading out anyway."

Panic flashes in Carter's eyes. "So soon?"

"Got a paper to write tomorrow." Vaughn climbs to his feet and slaps a few bills down on the table. "See y'all at practice."

When Vaughn's gone, I fix my gaze on Carter. "What do you say? You up for it?"

She huffs and flips her hair over her shoulder. "Just try not to step on my toes."

# 26

# KENNEDY

WHY DID I say I wanted to dance? And, more importantly, why did I let Becca talk me into this stupid tank top? The back plunges nearly to the waistband of my skirt, leaving a long column of skin exposed. I can feel Reid's eyes on my bare flesh as he guides me to a dark corner of the dance floor, hand pressed gently to my lower back. Warmth radiates from his body and I want nothing more than to feel his fingers skimming down my spine so I can soak up their heat.

Which makes no sense, because, hello, it's Reid.

*Totally. Off. Limits.*

Dammit. This was a terrible idea. I never should've brought up dancing.

Of course Reid called my bluff. Now I'm stuck with him for at least one song.

No way I'm backing down.

Because of the stunt he pulled with the frat dude, not because I actually need to feel his body pressed to mine.

*Obviously.*

The opening chords of "Pour Some Sugar on Me" blast through the sound system, and I throw my arms up and do a little shimmy. Becca's tiny skirt rides up on my hips, revealing even more of my thighs than before. I should pull the skirt back down—it's getting downright scandalous—but when I glance over my shoulder at Reid, he's staring at my legs like they might be the death of him.

*Good. Serves him right for being a controlling ass!*

Encouraged by his reaction, I do the shimmy again and sway to the music, tossing my hair over my shoulder. I start to move in time with the beat, keeping my back to Reid as I sway my hips seductively, inviting him closer.

If we're going to continue this battle of wills, you can bet your ass I'm playing to win.

Apparently, so is Reid.

The song's half over before his restraint cracks.

He steps up behind me, matching the lazy rhythm of my hips as he molds his body to mine. I stiffen instinctively at the closeness, but relax after a beat, melding my back to his chest. His cock is flush against my ass, and I give another slow sweep of my hips, enjoying the feel of his hard length against my backside.

This is wrong on about twelve freaking levels, but in the dark with the happy glow of alcohol buzzing through my system, it feels right.

Why shouldn't I dance with Reid? It doesn't mean anything, and he did scare the frat guy off.

Not that I was into him, but still.

I raise my arms over my head, letting the beat of the music drive my movements as the heavy bass reverberates through my body. I've always loved dancing, that feel of letting go of everything and connecting with something bigger than yourself.

The hem of my tank inches skyward, exposing the flesh beneath. Before I can cover it up, Reid skims calloused fingers over the curve of my hip, leaving a trail of scorched skin and unfettered desire in his wake.

*I'm so screwed.*

We lose ourselves in the beat of the music, sweaty bodies saying everything our mouths can't or shouldn't. As one song bleeds into another, our limbs moving in harmony, I forget about all the reasons this is a bad idea.

All the reasons Reid's off-limits.

All the reasons I shouldn't want him.

When the DJ slows it down, I turn to Reid, ready to suggest we take a break, but he reaches for me, offering me his hand. There's a challenge in the arch of his brow and the slant of his lips.

*He thinks I'll say no.*

I clasp my fingers with his and allow him to pull me close. Then I wrap my arms around his neck, my breasts pressed to the hard muscles of his chest like it's no big deal—even though it so is—as we sway to the music.

"You weren't kidding." I look up at him from under my lashes, taking the opportunity to study his face. His cheeks are flushed and there's a fine stubble lining his jaw, but it does little to detract from the fullness of his lips or the dimple I can't stop thinking about. "About being a good dancer, I mean."

"Parents made me take dance until I was twelve," he admits, his breath hot against my cheek.

"You did not." Although as soon as I say it, I remember Vaughn's nickname: Twinkle Toes.

"Would I joke about wearing a leotard?" He wiggles his brows. "Trust me. There's nothing more awkward than a twelve-year-old boy with raging hormones and a pair of ill-fitting tights."

I laugh in spite of myself. "You probably loved it because it gave you a chance to show off your giant package." Heat floods my cheeks, and I take a step back, dropping my hands to my sides. I cannot believe those words just came out of my mouth. "I didn't mean that. I meant—"

"Oh, no you don't." He smirks and pulls me back into his arms, locking them around my waist. "I want to hear more about this giant package."

"Yes, well, I actually meant to say giant ego."

God, I suck at lying. He can probably see right through me.

"*Riiiight.* You know, if you want to see my package, all you have to do is ask." My nostrils flare, and I'm sure he knows I'm thinking about his giant cock—how could I not after that statement?—so he pushes the advantage. "I promised myself the next time we kissed, it would be because you were begging for it. But I've realized something. A real man doesn't need a woman to beg. Hell, I should be groveling at your feet for another taste of sweet salvation."

*Sweet salvation.*

Reid's words land like a firestorm, obliterating all rational thought and melting my defenses.

He's the last guy I should want. Problem is, he's the only guy my ovaries crave.

I haven't forgotten the way his lips worshipped mine or the feel of his thick arms wrapped around me, holding me tight. And all this dancing—if you can even call it that—has only increased the need to feel his mouth on mine, his tongue promising exquisite pleasure if I could just give myself over to the base instincts that connect us.

He watches me, eyes burning like a blue flame.

I should walk away. It would be the smart thing to do.

But my feet are glued to the floor, making it impossible to move.

I could blame it on spilled beer, but the truth is, I want this as badly as he does.

Maybe more.

The way he pressed his body to mine while we danced? I felt a hell of a lot more than the chiseled muscles of his abs. And I'd only be lying to myself if I said I didn't enjoy the length of his cock snug against the curve of my ass.

"Reid." His name is barely a whisper on my lips, but it's enough.

I'm not sure which of us moves first. Maybe we move at the same time.

It doesn't matter, because our lips are crashing together and he's stroking my back, his fingertips sending a thrill up my spine as the rough pads skate over my bare flesh.

Reid's mouth is hot and greedy, slanting over mine possessively as his tongue darts in and out, sweeping across my own like a man without control. I tangle my fingers in his hair, losing myself in the pool of desire that wells up from deep in my belly.

When I finally pull back, gasping for breath, Reid brushes kisses across my cheek, along my jawline, and down my neck. I melt in his embrace, and it's all I can do not to grind my pelvis against his, seeking relief for the rising tension between my legs.

We should stop. There are hundreds of people in the bar, including our teammates, but it's dark as hell and I can't bring myself to care.

Not when Reid's kissing me like this.

He captures my mouth again and our teeth grind together at the force of it. I've never been kissed like this and I know without a doubt that sex with Reid will be like nothing I've ever experienced before either.

He's brimming with passion and while our kisses are frantic, there's nothing sloppy about the way his mouth moves over my body or the way his fingers lace with mine as he raises our joined hands and presses a kiss to my inner wrist. My skin is on fire and there's a bead of sweat between my breasts that wasn't there when we were dancing.

"Let's get out of here," he says, pitching his voice low so only I can hear the words he whispers in my ear. His cool confidence rattles me and I freeze, certain *let's get out of here* is code for *let's fuck*. After all, hadn't I just been thinking the same thing? "I want you on your back screaming my name, Carter. And I think you want it too. The only question is, how long are you going to fight the chemistry between us?"

## 27

# AUSTIN

THE FIVE-MINUTE RIDE to the apartment complex feels like fifty with Carter sitting next to me in that tiny fucking skirt. Hell, I'm surprised she agreed to leave with me. I figured she'd bolt, but when she suggested we go back to her place, I wasn't about to argue.

For once we're on the same page.

I glance over at her. We're sitting at a red light and she's staring out the window, unusually quiet.

*Is she having second thoughts?*

Wouldn't that be a kick in the balls.

I reach across the console and lay a hand on her thigh, caressing the lean muscles that drive me wild. "What's on your mind?"

Carter glances over, a mischievous smile curving the corners of her heart-shaped lips. She spreads her legs just a tiny bit wider. "I've always wondered what it would be like to have sex in a car."

*Fuuuck.*

I'm so hot for her my dick will probably have a zipper imprint for the next week.

A woman who knows what she wants is sexy as hell, and the last thing I want to do is deny Carter, but it's not gonna happen.

"Our first time isn't going to be in the Jeep." I slide my hand higher, fingers scraping her inner thigh. "But there are plenty of other things we can do."

The light changes and I press down on the accelerator as I slip my hand under her skirt. My knuckles slide across her center and Carter gives a small gasp of pleasure.

She's ready to go.

Me? I'm about to lose it in my pants.

I shift in my seat, trying to adjust myself as I trace a line down the damp fabric of her panties with my finger. When Carter leans her head back and moans, I take it as an invitation to continue, sliding her underwear to the side and dipping my fingers between her slick folds.

*Christ, she's wet.*

I start off with slow, lazy strokes, but by the time I sweep my thumb across her clit and plunge my fingers inside, her hips are bucking against the leather upholstery and the seat belt is the only thing keeping her body fixed in place. I increase the pace—we're almost to her apartment—and watch as she comes, head back, eyes closed, with a white-knuckled grip on the door handle.

She's fucking beautiful and her soft moans nearly undo me.

It's the first time Carter's allowed herself to be vulnerable.

The realization tugs at something in my chest, and I swear she won't regret it.

Her eyes are still closed when I withdraw my hand and throw the Jeep in park in front of the apartment complex. "That was..."

"Foreplay," I say, unbuckling both our seat belts. Then I hop out of the Jeep and jog around to the other side, opening the door to help her out. I grab a sleeve of condoms from the glove box before I shut the door. Carter eyes the gold wrappers and straightens her spine. With the heels, we're nearly at eye level. She's got this blissed-out look and her pupils have grown so wide they blend into the coffee-colored irises. I lean forward and plant my hands on the Jeep, trapping her between my forearms. "You sure about this?"

Carter sparks like a lit fuse, launching herself forward and capturing my mouth with her own. Her soft lips crash against mine with vigor and she grabs my cock, cupping it over the thick denim. A jolt of electricity goes straight to the base of my spine and I groan, unable to stop myself. My balls are drawn up so tight I swear they might explode at even the slightest touch.

"We should probably move this inside before you get a ticket for indecent exposure." She releases my dick and gives me a playful shove. "Wouldn't want that on the front page of *The Collegian*, would we?"

*Among other things.*

I follow her to the apartment, admiring the view of her perky ass as we climb the stairs.

When she turns the key in the lock, all bets are off. I snake an arm around her waist and lift her off her feet, pressing her back to the wall even as she wraps her legs around my waist. I think I hear the sound of fabric ripping, but I can't bring myself to give a fuck because she drags my mouth to hers and plunges her tongue inside with renewed enthusiasm. Carter rocks her hips against my cock with desperate motions that mirror my own.

I need to get this woman naked.

With my hands clasped on her ass, I turn toward the hall.

We've barely made it three steps when Carter freezes, her eyes growing round.

"Shit!" She pushes away from me, and I let go as her feet drop to the floor. I watch in fascination as she tiptoes down the hall with her left ass cheek hanging out, and looks in one of the bedrooms. Now that I'm not so distracted with thoughts of Carter riding my cock, I can hear the sounds of...*a rainforest?* Must be one of those sound machines. All the better for masking Carter's sexy little moans. She shuts the door and whispers, "Becca's home."

"So we'll just have to be quiet." I close the distance between us and trail my fingers down her arm. "Think you can manage?"

Carter lifts her chin. "I can manage if you can."

*That's my girl.*

I discard the thought as soon as it crosses my mind.

Carter's not my girl. She never will be. This thing is purely physical.

Hell, once we get it out of our systems, it'll be business as usual.

She grabs my hand and drags me down the hall. Like an asshole, I stumble over my own two feet and she giggles. It's light and flirty. Definitely not the kind of sound I associate with Carter, but I'm digging it.

No sooner has she closed the door than she's pushing me down on the bed, climbing astride as she yanks her tank top over her head. The room is dark, but a shaft of moonlight slants across the bed, bathing Carter in its soft glow. My gaze goes straight to her tits, which are fucking perfect.

They're full and round with rosy nipples that are just begging to be sucked.

I cup the soft flesh in my hands, massaging her breasts as I take them in my mouth. First the right, then the left, using my tongue to stimulate the tender peaks before biting them gently. She throws her head back and moans, arching her back and begging for more. I'm lavishing kisses on her collarbone when she starts rolling her hips, creating the kind of friction that's liable to make my cock go off like a rocket.

I want to take things slow and give her the pleasure she deserves, but fuck.

I didn't expect this side of Carter.

She's ravenous, and there's no way I can slow things down.

I grab her hips and roll us over, so I'm pinning her to the mattress. I don't mind giving up control once in a while, but if I don't wrest it from her now, this whole thing will be over in two minutes.

*Unacceptable.*

After weeks of foreplay, I fully intend to give Carter the best goddamn orgasm of her life.

I don't care if it's a bad idea or if Coach forbade it.

There's nothing I want more than to claim Carter.

Her mouth, her breasts, those beautiful fucking legs.

The image of them wrapped around my hips while I'm buried in her tight little pussy has inspired more than one of my fantasies, and now that it's finally going to happen, I intend to enjoy every second of it.

With her hair splayed out around her head and her full breasts on display, she's the epitome of temptation. I pepper kisses down the column of her neck, across her breasts and over her belly. She strokes the back of my head, sending a shiver down my spine as I make my way toward the tiny skirt.

The damn thing needs to go, but I can't find the zipper.

Carter reaches behind her and I hear the slow drag of metal as the skirt loosens around her waist. I tug the skirt down, taking the black lace underwear with it. Then I stand at the foot of the bed and pull my T-shirt over my head as Carter watches with heavy-lidded anticipation. She must like what she sees, because her bottom wriggles and she rubs her knees together.

I know the feeling. I've never been so desperate for a woman in my life.

I want to touch every part of her body, learn every curve, and explore every inch of it with my mouth until I know it better than I know my own.

"Don't worry, gorgeous. I promise to make it worth the wait." I unzip my jeans and free my cock, gripping the base in my hand so Carter can get a good look at what she does to me.

"I guess now I know what all the fuss was about."

"Damn right."

I grab a condom and tear it open, rolling it on as I step out of my jeans. Then I climb onto the bed and settle between her thighs, my cock nudging at her entrance.

"Um, it's been a while," she says, not meeting my eyes. Her limbs stiffen beneath me. "Since I've had sex, I mean."

The admission awakens my inner caveman, and I want to pound my chest, simultaneously thrilled she's chosen me and determined to protect her. I have to be sure she isn't going to regret this later.

Even if it means a week's worth of cold showers and selfie time.

"It's been a while for me too." I press a finger to her chin and turn her face to mine. "I haven't been with anyone else since before training camp."

"Two months? That's your definition of a dry spell?" She rolls her eyes, clearly not appreciating what a big deal it is. "I haven't had sex in—"

"Hey." I stroke her cheek. "It doesn't matter if it's been a few weeks or a few months. None of that matters. We've been on a collision course since you told me you'd rather streak across campus than play ball with me."

She laughs at this, the tension melting from her shoulders. Her face softens, and I lower my mouth to hers, claiming it the way I've wanted to since the first day she tempted me with those sassy lips.

The kiss starts slow and gentle, but when she opens her mouth and body to me, a silent invitation, it's all I can do not to sink into her with one hard thrust. But I've waited weeks for this; I can wait a few more seconds.

"I probably shouldn't admit this, but I've imagined this moment so many times."

"You're not the only one." She spreads her thighs and hooks her ankles around my back. "Fuck me, Reid."

I ease in slowly, savoring the feel of her hot, wet pussy gripping my cock. When I'm seated to the hilt, she lets out a breathy moan that nearly snaps my restraint.

"*Ooooh.*"

She's so fucking tight it's torture not to move, but I hold steady, giving her a chance to adjust to my size. When she rotates her hips, I drop my forehead to hers and match the pace she's set, sealing our bodies together. She skims her hands over my shoulders and rakes her nails down my back, digging them in and pulling me closer, like she can't get enough.

The feeling's mutual.

Sex with Carter is so much better than the fantasy.

I roll my hips and she moans. I do it again and press my lips to hers, swallowing the sexy noises she's making.

"You feel so fucking good, Kennedy."

She freezes, and I get another glimpse of the vulnerability she hides behind her quick wit and cool exterior. I pause and sweep a strand of hair from her damp forehead.

"What is it?"

"That's the first time you've called me Kennedy." She bites her lower lip, the flesh plumping under her teeth. "I kind of like the sound of my name on your lips...*Austin.*"

When she says my name, the tension at the base of my spine

becomes almost unbearable and I know I won't be able to hold out much longer. I take her mouth in mine, pouring weeks of pent-up frustration and raw desire into the kiss, and push us both toward oblivion. My hips crash against hers, and I sink into her warmth with renewed fervor. When Carter's back bows off the bed, my name on her lips, I come, spiraling right over the edge with her.

# 28

# KENNEDY

THE EARLY MORNING sun cascades over the bed, but I squeeze my eyes tight and snuggle down under the covers. I'm warm and cozy and content, and honestly, who needs sunshine when there's sleep to be had? Not me.

It's my day off and nothing is getting me out of this bed.

I stifle a yawn and roll onto my side, which takes some effort because there's a heavy weight across my midsection. It takes my groggy, caffeine-deprived brain a few seconds to catch up with my body, but when it does? I kind of want to slink back into blissful ignorance.

Austin. Sex. Multiple orgasms.

Everything comes rushing back to me in the harsh light of day, panic rising in my chest.

Okay, no need to freak out. It was probably just a dream.

*One that needs repeating every freaking night.*

I slowly open my right eye and find myself face-to-face with Waverly's golden boy. I squeeze my eye shut again, lowering the lid in swift denial.

Big mistake.

Shutting out the world only brings my night with Austin into sharper focus, my brain replaying our time together like a highlight reel.

I had sex with Austin Reid. A football player. And it was the best sex of my life.

Maybe there was something to be said for experience after all.

But no, that wasn't it.

Austin was a generous lover, practically a unicorn on this campus. He paid attention to what curled my toes and wrung those embarrassing moans from deep in my throat. He'd dedicated himself to my orgasms with the same vigor he gave the game. It was something I hadn't expected, hadn't known I craved, but now that I've had a taste—

No. Just no. This was a onetime lapse in judgment. It can't happen again.

I promised my mom and that means something.

God knows she hasn't asked much of me over the years.

Besides, Coach would have our asses.

There's a muffled thump from down the hall, followed by a low yip from Baxter.

*Becca.*

Just my luck. The one time I have a secret hookup, she comes home early.

She wasn't even supposed to be here last night. Not that it matters now. She's here and she's up at… I turn and squint at the bedside clock, unable to make out the numbers without my contacts. *Whatever*. It has to be early because I'm tired as hell.

Of course, that could be the result of last night's sex marathon.

I sneak another peek at Austin. His chest rises slow and steady, confirming he's sound asleep with his muscular arm draped possessively across my hips. There's something intimate about seeing him this way, his handsome features more relaxed and innocent than I've ever seen them.

Gone is the swaggering BMOC with the cocky grin. In his place is the man who made me laugh during sex, taking the time to ease my nerves before he worshipped my body. All. Night. Long.

*With the world's best orgasms.*

Come to think of it, he should probably trademark those moves because just the memory has my pussy desperate for an encore.

"Austin," I whisper, giving his shoulder a not-so-gentle shake. *Please don't let him be a deep sleeper.* We so don't have time for that right now. "Wake up. You have to go."

His lips curve into a smile, and when he opens his eyes, there's a wicked gleam that almost makes me reconsider my position on morning sex. Because, world's best orgasms. But, no. I have to stay strong.

One night with the guy isn't going to turn me into some sex-addled nympho.

I do have some self-control.

*Just keep telling yourself that.*

"Hey, beautiful."

"Hey, yourself."

I roll out of bed—determined to prove sex with the cocky QB hasn't short-circuited my brain—and grab a pair of pajamas from my dresser. I tug the shorts on before pulling the tank top over my head.

*No time to worry about bed head or bad breath.*

I've got to get him out of here before Becca sees him.

When I turn around, Austin's still lying in bed, the sheet covering all his best parts.

*Bummer*. "Let's go, Sleeping Beauty. Time to rise and shine or whatever it is you normally do on a Sunday morning."

"I like to sleep in." He locks his hands behind his head, looking way too comfortable. "Maybe spend the day in bed."

"So not happening." I shoot him a dark look. "Unless you want the whole campus knowing what happened last night, you need to get up and get out of here before Becca sees you."

That gets his attention. He sits up, dropping his feet to the floor with a leisurely grace I will forever associate with ballet lessons.

"You can go out the window or you can go out the door, but you have to go now."

"One small problem."

One? More like half a dozen, but who's counting?

There's another thump from Becca's room. I crack the door to the hall, relief flooding my veins. The coast is clear—for now.

When I turn around, Austin's just standing there in his boxer briefs—which leave little to the imagination—staring at me with a bemused expression and a wicked case of bed head. Or maybe it's sex hair. I seem to remember running my fingers through it last night.

Either way, one thing's clear. He's not budging.

He hooks a thumb toward the window, cocky grin securely back in place. "We're on the second floor."

"Good point." I scoop up his clothes from the foot of the bed and thrust them into his arms. "Front door it is," I whisper, grabbing his arm and dragging him into the hall.

He's still not moving fast enough for my liking, so I slip around behind him and give him a little shove, scooting him toward the front door even as he protests.

Funny thing about whispered protests: they're ineffective.

Mostly.

"I'm just saying, this gives new meaning to the walk of

shame." He turns and leans in close, grabbing a strand of my hair and twisting it around his fingers. "I feel so used."

"I seriously doubt that."

Guilt rears its ugly head, but I shut that bitch down.

Becca cannot find Reid in the apartment again. Especially half-naked.

She will never believe the old "nothing happened" lie and even though I'm ninety-nine and a half percent sure she'd never spill the tea, it's a chance I can't take. Coach would have a shit fit if he caught wind of this, and I don't even want to think about my mom's reaction because I'm pretty sure only cockroaches could survive the fallout.

Which is why Austin's got to go.

I can cross the living room in ten steps when I'm late for class (which is often), but with my one-night stand dragging his heels, it feels like twenty. If I didn't know better, I'd think he wants to get caught. When we finally reach the door, I release the deadbolt, wincing at the loud *thwack!*

I glance back to confirm Becca's nowhere in sight; then I open the door and gesture for him to hurry up.

"What? No goodbye kiss?" he teases, stepping out onto the cement walkway that connects all the second-floor apartments.

I blow him a kiss and shut the door without another word, anxiety swirling in my gut.

The sun is shining and there are birds singing somewhere nearby, but it's the sound of Austin's low chuckle that pierces my concentration as I count to ten.

Once I'm sure we're in the clear, I climb onto the couch and peek out the front window.

Austin hasn't bothered to put his clothes on, so I've got a nice view of his ass.

Apparently when you've got a giant package, walking around the complex in your underwear is no big deal. Two girls approach from the opposite direction, giggling as they pass him by. His steps don't falter and even though his back is to me, I know he's giving them that cocky QB grin, because only Austin Reid could pull off the walk of shame in his underwear.

*Not that it matters since last night's hookup was a onetime deal.*

# 29

## AUSTIN

I BARELY MAKE it to study hall on time, not that anyone's taking attendance. Still, I'm the team captain, and it doesn't look good to be sliding in late. Football players get plenty of exceptions on campus, but gaming the system isn't my style.

It's not the kind of example I want to set for the guys.

When I drop my bag at the table next to Coop, I scan the room, trying to be subtle as I search for Kennedy. She's been avoiding me since our hookup.

Which makes no sense.

The sex was incredible. No way she wasn't satisfied.

Hell, she came four times.

Granted, she was pretty freaked out about the sleepover. Can't say I blame her there. I've never spent the night with a woman before, but it's no big deal. We're both mature adults. And I sure as hell didn't hate falling asleep with her curves tucked against my body.

"Did you bring food?" Parker pats his stomach. "I'm starving."

"No. I had a mandatory meeting with my advisor." The uptight dick is one of the few profs on campus who isn't exactly falling all over himself to accommodate the football program. I'm pretty sure he purposely assigned me a meeting time that would conflict with football practice. When I asked for a different time slot, he refused. But the guys don't need to know my advisor's a prick or that I missed dinner. They've got their own shit to deal with. "No time to stop."

"First Carter blows us off." Coop tips his chair back on two legs, arms crossed over his chest. "And now you forget the snacks. I'm not really feeling the love, brother."

"Feel this." I give him the one-finger salute. "I'm your captain, not your nanny."

"Kind of the same thing, don't you think?"

Parker snickers, but I ignore him and unpack my bag.

I toss a few notebooks on the table and find a slightly bruised apple buried at the bottom of my bag.

*Thank Christ.* I'm starving.

I take my seat and devour the apple in a half-dozen bites as I flip through my notes for this week's sports marketing midterm. I last a whole thirty minutes before I give up.

What's the point of midterms anyway? We're going to see all the same material on the final in six weeks. Talk about redundant. It doesn't help that I can't stop thinking about the other night with Kennedy. She's totally messing with my head.

It's a distraction I can't afford. On the field or in the classroom.

I slap my notebook closed and roll my shoulders.

I'll take a break and try again. Maybe I just need to stretch my legs.

Or maybe I just need to talk to Kennedy, who's racing out the door like her hair's on fire, bag slung over her shoulder.

"Be right back." I climb to my feet and head for the door, forcing myself to keep a leisurely pace, eyes pinned to her back.

I follow her down the steps and finally catch up with her on the first floor.

"You've been avoiding me," I say, matching her stride and falling in step with her.

"I don't know what you're talking about." She adjusts her bag and looks around, guilt plain as day on her face. "I'm just busy with practice and midterms and...stuff."

"Stuff? Is that a technical term?" I grab her elbow and steer her toward an empty stack.

"Football players." She huffs out a breath. "Should've known you'd go all caveman if I ignored you."

I smirk. "So you admit you've been ignoring me?"

"What do you want, Austin?"

She says my name like it's a blessing and a curse, and I gotta admit it's a huge fucking turn-on. "I just want to talk."

"What is there to talk about?" She tucks a strand of hair behind her ear. "We had sex. It was nice. It can never happen again."

"Nice?" Not gonna lie. I don't hear anything she says after the word *nice*. "Flowers are nice. The weather is nice." I take a step closer. We're toe to toe now. It wouldn't take much to sweep her into my arms, those perky tits pressed against me as I erase the word *nice* from her vocabulary with my mouth. My heart thunders in my chest, but I can't tell if it's from her dismissive attitude or the closeness of our bodies. "What we had? There was nothing nice about it. It was hot and dirty and explosive."

She swallows and her throat bobs delicately.

"I think you're missing the point here." She does one of those sexy little eye rolls and her lips tilt down at the corners. Damn if I don't want to kiss them. "Coach forbade it. And you know how I feel about football players. It's a bad freaking idea all around. Just no."

She's not wrong.

There are a lot of people counting on us.

If it goes to shit, it could impact the team, and there's no way in hell I'd do anything that could damage the team's playoff hopes or my own career. I've worked too hard for too long.

Hell, Coach would have my ass if he knew I was sleeping with Kennedy.

But here's the thing. I've dedicated my whole life to football.

I play by the rules. I'm a good role model. A good teammate. I bust my ass day in and day out. So why can't I have this one thing?

"Just hear me out." I stuff my hands into my pockets. One, because I don't know what to do with them. Two, to hide the chub that's growing in my pants. "I know you aren't into ball players, and let's be honest, we'd be a terrible match." The words feel like ash on my tongue, but I can't take them back now. The insinuation that she's not my type seems to have captured her attention. There's fire sparking in her eyes, and I'm not above using it to my advantage. "We have blistering chemistry, so why shouldn't we take what we need from each other?"

She wrinkles her brow. "I don't—" She pauses. "What are you suggesting?"

"I'm suggesting neither of us has the time or interest in a romantic relationship, but we both have needs. Think about it." I pitch my voice low, my proposal for her alone. "No strings. Lots of chemistry. Matching schedules. Totally convenient."

She tilts her head to the side, her expression giving nothing away.

I can't tell if she's considering my offer or if she's thinking about kicking me in the balls for even suggesting it.

*Doesn't matter.*

Now that I've had a taste of her—of the fiery passion behind all the snark and sarcasm—there's no going back.

"You're serious, aren't you?"

"Yes." Sometimes less is more, even though I'd grovel at her feet right now if it meant getting back into her bed.

She chews her bottom lip, thinking it over.

Her lids become heavy and my cock does a victory dance. Ten to one she's thinking about Saturday night and the four orgasms I gave her. Probably a first. Most guys don't have that kind of stamina.

*Just one more perk of being a hard-bodied athletic specimen.*

"And this will stay between you and me? Coach can't find out."

"Naturally. No one can know."

"And nothing else changes between us? I'm just one of the guys, and we call it quits at the end of the season or when one of us gets tired of the arrangement?"

Like that's gonna happen. "Exactly."

"If we do this, there can't be anyone else." She twists a strand of hair around her finger. "If you want to hook up with some jersey chaser—"

"Kennedy." I hook a finger under her chin and force her to look up at me. "It goes without saying that if we're sleeping together, there won't be anyone else."

I don't add that the idea of her getting naked with another guy makes me want to throttle something.

"Okay." She shakes her head. "I can't believe I'm agreeing to this, but yeah. Let's do it."

My dick takes the invitation literally, rising to full mast, and an idea takes hold. "You know, I could drive you home tonight. I've got the Jeep."

She sighs. "Sex only, remember? Just one of the—" I can see it the moment she realizes I'm offering to make her fantasy come true, because a slow smile spreads over her face and her pupils dilate despite the bright lights of the library. "You know, come to think of it, I could use a ride."

# 30

## KENNEDY

*Dammit*. I glare at my laptop, frustration taking root. Why isn't this stupid equation balancing?

I must be missing something. I pinch the bridge of my nose and blow out a breath.

Getting pissed isn't going to solve the problem, but it might get me kicked out of study hall. I'll just have to go back to the beginning and check my figures. I must've made a mistake somewhere along the way.

Maybe I miskeyed one of the numbers.

God knows I've been distracted.

This whole teammates-with-benefits arrangement Austin proposed is equal parts guilt and pleasure. I peek up at him from under my lashes. A backward ball cap covers his dark hair, and he's wearing a navy Waverly tee that hugs his broad shoulders. He taps his pencil on a notebook, and I watch with rapt attention as the muscles in his biceps jump.

The man oozes sex, and I find myself counting down the minutes until our next hookup.

Desire heats my cheeks and I tear my gaze from the sexy QB, forcing myself to look down at my notes even as the numbers swim before my eyes. Because, yeah, sex with Austin really is that good. It doesn't help that I'm new to this whole casual-sex thing and still figuring out the rules.

Like, no staring at the man candy during study hall.

I'm no prude, but I was in committed relationships with both of the guys I slept with in the past.

*And look how well that turned out.*

Still, I hate lying to Becca and my mom, even if it's a lie of omission. But at least I'm keeping my promise not to get involved with a football player. Because what Austin and I have?

It's purely physical. No hearts and no heartache. Just sex.

*The hot, sweaty, pulse-pounding kind.*

I don't expect anything from him. Aside from mind-blowing orgasms, anyway.

Who knew having a dirty little secret could be such a turn-on?

Just the thought of Austin's touch sends a thrill pulsing through my veins. Which is probably why I can't balance this equation.

I push all thoughts of Austin from my brain and redouble my efforts to find the mistake in my work. I need to finish top three in the ACME competition, which will be impossible if my calculations are crap.

I'm halfway through the validation process when my phone starts vibrating. I know without looking that it's distraction number two: my dad. He's been texting me around this time every night for the last three days.

What part of *I don't want to see you* doesn't he understand?

I grab a pencil and scratch out some notes, feeling like an asshole for ignoring him. I mean, I know he's the asshole, but apparently there's still some small part of me that holds out hope.

*Things would be so much easier if he'd just fade to black.*

After all, that's been his MO for the last twenty-one years.

The phone buzzes again and the pencil in my hand snaps in half.

*Fan-fucking-tastic.*

I rifle through my bag for another and come up empty. Before I can ask one of the guys for a spare, Austin reaches across the table and offers me his.

"Need some help?" he asks, giving me that infuriatingly sexy smirk as he gestures to the problem I've been working on for the last fifteen minutes.

"Nope. I've got it covered." I snatch the pencil from his hand. "Unless, of course, you're an expert in differential equations?"

"Who says I'm not?" He arches a brow in mock indignation. "I'm more than just a pretty face, you know."

I roll my eyes, but the guys burst out laughing, drawing the ire of the study group at the next table. If looks could kill, Waverly's starting lineup would be short two All-Americans, one Heisman contender, and one genuinely nice guy.

"Dude, you've been spending too much time with Coop," Vaughn says, slapping him on the back. "You might want to tone it down before Media Day or Coach'll have an aneurism."

Austin shrugs, his eyes locked on mine. "Figured maybe you could use some help."

I smile, although it feels tight and awkward. "Just because we're"—I catch myself before the words *sleeping together* pop out—"*on the same team*, doesn't mean you get to stick your nose in my business."

"Wouldn't dream of it." He leans back and crosses his arms over his chest. "And you're right. I'm no expert on differential equations, but I know someone who is. If you'd like a second pair of eyes to look over that before you make yourself nuts."

He nods toward the hot mess that is my notes.

I sigh. "Is it that obvious I'm about to go full Hulk?"

He ignores the question—smart guy—and counters with one of his own. "Is that a yes?"

"Sure." I flop back in my chair and toss the pencil on the table.

I've still got a crap ton of work to do. No sense letting my pride stand in the way of solving one stupid equation, even if it grates.

Austin's eyes remain fixed on me as he calls over his shoulder, "Hey, Gonzalez, got a minute?"

My gaze shoots a few tables over, where a guy I don't know but recognize from practice springs to his feet, apparently too happy to do the captain's bidding. My phone buzzes again and I shut it off.

*One distraction at a time.*

Gonzalez's eyes sweep the table as he approaches, hands tucked into his pockets. He's got a dark, serious vibe and lacks the swagger the other guys wear like war paint.

I like him instantly.

"Enzo." Austin offers his hands and they do one of those complicated dude handshakes.

I can't help but feel he used Enzo's first name for my benefit. It irks me that he knows me so well. It feels like a weakness, but the truth is, I don't practice with the team most days and I haven't had the opportunity to learn the names and faces of all one hundred and thirteen players.

Austin turns back to me. "Have you met my man Enzo? This kid's wicked smart and he's a mechanical engineering major too."

I hesitate. I don't think we've met. Any familiarity is probably just from football.

Enzo smiles, revealing a row of bright, even teeth. "We haven't been officially introduced," he says, "but we were in Beck's class last spring. You probably didn't notice me because I always sit in the back."

"Nice to meet you." I lean forward and rest my elbows on the table. "Beck, huh? That class was brutal."

I got a B, but just barely. The man gave new meaning to the phrase *anal retentive*. Rumor has it ME students complain about his unfair policies every semester, but the complaints fall on deaf ears. And since the only path to graduation is through him, we all earn our battle scars one lecture at a time.

Enzo rubs the back of his neck. "Toughest SOB on campus as far as I'm concerned, but I managed to squeak out an A."

My jaw nearly hits the table. *An A? From Beck?* It's unheard of.

Enzo chuckles. "I also got a severe case of anxiety. Glad I didn't have him during the season."

"You and me both." I shake my head in wonder.

Austin was right. Enzo's a smart guy. But he's obviously busy with his own course load, judging by the stack of thick textbooks on his table. I don't want to impose, but maybe it wouldn't hurt to feel him out. I could use another pair of eyes on this stupid equation because I am about one step short of crazytown.

"I can't imagine dealing with Beck on top of the ACME design." I gesture to my work and give him a wry grin. "I've been working on this equation half the night and can't find my mistake."

"I'd be happy to take a look. If you want?"

"That would be great. I'll owe you one."

Truth. I've gone over the numbers so many times I doubt I could find the mistake at this point, even if it were highlighted.

He waves me off. "We're teammates. This is study hall. No biggie."

Enzo pulls a chair up next to mine and I slide my laptop over so he can take a look. While he's checking my calculations, I turn on my phone and steel myself against my dad's latest barrage of text messages.

I scroll through them quickly, although the urge to swipe delete is tempting.

*Dad: You can't ignore me forever. I'm your father.*

*Dad: I know your mom raised you better than this, Kennedy.*

*Dad: Please call me back. I miss you.*

The last one steals the air from my lungs. I sit frozen, staring at the message for a long time.

How can he claim to miss me when he's been MIA most of my life? That was his choice, not mine. And where does he get off acting so self-righteous? Self-absorbed would be a more fitting role. I can't even begin to count the number of times he's let me down. All the times he's shattered my heart with his stupid, selfish—

"Carter?"

I glance up, realizing too late it's not the first time Enzo's said my name.

All the guys are staring at me as I stuff the phone in my bag and force a smile. It feels brittle, but it holds. "Any luck?"

"Yeah, I think I found the issue." He points to the screen, tapping one of the calculations. "The numbers were transposed. Should be twenty-three, not thirty-two."

I give myself a mental facepalm because, data-entry error. "Thanks. You're a lifesaver."

Enzo shrugs. "Truth be told, I'm kind of jealous you're competing. I couldn't find a team to work around my football schedule. You're lucky."

I snort. Hardly. Going it alone is probably closer to insanity. Even my advisor thinks so.

At first I thought he was just citing the rules, but the further I go down this rabbit hole, the more I'm sweating the scope of work required. Problem is, I'm used to doing things on my own. It's how I was raised and the idea of needing help rankles.

Having a teammate means giving up control, and I'm not a fan of putting my fate in someone else's hands.

I watch as Enzo stands and turns back toward his own table, shoulders slumped.

He got an A from Beck, which means he's meticulous.

And he found the error in my calculations in just a matter of minutes.

Still, the competition is important. Placing in the top three guarantees interviews with some of the top engineering companies in the country.

*And not finishing on time guarantees you won't place at all.*

"Hey, Enzo?" The words tumble out before I have time to change my mind. "I entered solo, but it's not too late to add a partner." I pause, and he looks at me in surprise. "I—I have a design concept, but there's still a lot of work to do on the final prototype. I could really use a sharp pair of eyes for validation and drafting the report. If you're interested."

"Yeah?" he says, flashing me a giant grin as he sits back down at the table.

"Yeah." There's a nervous flutter in my belly.

*Please don't let this be a mistake.*

I have so much riding on this competition. I steal a glance at Austin, who's pretending not to eavesdrop, although he hasn't turned the page in his book since I opened my mouth. Then it hits me. This must be what he feels like on a daily basis, shouldering the burdens of the team, and the expectations of his family and fans, every decision feeling like it's make-or-break under that kind of pressure.

I shake off the thought.

What Austin and I have isn't about empathy or shared experiences.

I don't need—or want—to get in his head.

No, the only brain I need to pick is my new partner's.

Enzo and I spend the rest of the study hall reviewing my design, and when I meet Austin in the parking lot an hour later, I'm not thinking about my dad or the design competition. The only thing on my mind is pleasure, something I know Austin can deliver.

## 31

## AUSTIN

THE MINUTE I step foot inside the football house, I know I've fucked up. Pizza boxes and empty beer cans litter the living room, covering every flat surface. There are a couple dozen guys, including Johnson and Smith, shouting at the TV where Bama is giving Ole Miss a beating they won't soon forget. The music's so fuckin' loud, it's a wonder the neighbors haven't called campus police...yet.

That's not even the worst of it.

One of the freshman recruits is puking his guts out in a trash can, and there are a half-dozen jersey chasers in various stages of undress because they're in the middle of a goddamn strip game. I scrub a hand over my face and try not to think about what's going on in the rest of the house.

I'm probably better off not knowing.

My temper flares, a hot flush streaking up the back of my neck. I'm not sure who I'm more pissed at, Johnson or myself.

"What the fuck?" I shout, slamming the front door.

God forbid someone roll past and get a look at this shit show. It's a bye week and Coach asked me to show a few high school recruits around campus, which I agreed to do, despite being dead-ass tired and up to my eyeballs in...everything.

It's not like I could say no. I'm the team captain and it's my duty to host potential talent.

It's important to give these kids face time with the team and a taste of life on campus. It can make a real difference when it comes time to sign their letters of intent. Which is why I met them at eight and took them on a tour of the football facilities, the stadium, and the best parts of campus. We even went to lunch at the Diner, so they could check out the social scene downtown.

My mistake? Leaving the recruits with Johnson for a few hours while I met with my study group. *Two fucking hours*. He was supposed to take them for dinner at the dining hall and get ice cream, not get them wasted.

I should've skipped study group. The thing is, I've got a paper due for career management next week, and I needed the extra help. I didn't do great on the midterm, and I need an A on my paper to offset it.

"Relax, we're just watching the game." Johnson gestures toward the TV with his beer. He's slouched in a recliner, and Kendall's sitting on his lap. Neither of them is wearing a shirt. "It's not like we took them to the End Zone."

The local strip club. Thank Christ for that.

"They're underage, asshole." I point at the kid who just puked in the trash can. "Do you have any idea what happens if we get a UAD during a recruitment visit?"

Johnson gives me a blank stare. I can't tell if it's because he's wasted or if he really doesn't understand what a big fucking risk this is to the program. To our shot at a national title.

*To our futures.*

I cross the room in a few easy strides and shut off the TV and the music. "Party's over."

There's a collective groan, and the puker heaves into the trash can again.

I close my eyes and count to ten, ready to be done with this day.

The whole place is starting to smell sour, a putrid mix of sweat, beer, and vomit. If this is the kind of shit they can get into in just a few hours, I don't want to think about what might have happened if I'd been gone any longer.

"If you don't live here, get dressed and get out."

Several of the guests file out. I hope like hell they won't be lighting up social media with pics of our drunken recruits. Kendall stops on her way to the door, brushing her fingertips down my biceps the way a kid might stroke a favorite pet. My muscles tense at the unwelcome contact.

"I never took you for a buzzkill, Reid."

I ignore the cheap shot—Kendall's the least of my problems—because there are fucking baseball players in the house. Talk about courting trouble. There's no love lost between the two teams, so what the hell are they doing here?

Kendall tracks my gaze and flashes a thousand-watt smile.

*Mystery solved.*

I grit my teeth. "Never took you for the kind to stir shit up."

"You haven't been returning my calls." She shrugs. "I got bored."

*Un-fucking-believable.*

"What a bunch of pussies," McCoy says, slinging his arm around Kendall's shoulders. His buddies laugh, and I curl my fists so I don't do anything stupid. "Told you we should've gone downtown to the watch the game."

The shortstop snorts and takes a pull on his beer. "Wha'd'ya expect? They've got a girl on the team." He pauses and looks me dead in the eye. "She's kind of hot though. I'd fuck her."

This asshole thinks he can come up in our house and talk shit?

*Fuck. That.*

I get right up in his face, close enough to see the peach fuzz on his cheeks. He's lit. I can see it in his eyes, but that doesn't mean I'm going to stand here and let him disrespect Kennedy.

"I suggest you shut your fucking mouth and take a walk."

"Or what?"

Silence falls over the room, and even though I'd like nothing more than to knock the smirk off his face with my fist, it's not an option.

Not today, anyway. That shit would get me benched for sure.

I crack my knuckles and turn to McCoy, anger pulsing through my veins like molten steel. "Get your boy out of here before I throw him out."

McCoy gives his buddy a shove. "Let's go."

The asshole takes a few steps toward the door, then turns back to me. "Must be some good pussy to get your hackles up like that. Tell me, Reid. Does she give all the guys a taste or just you?"

White light explodes behind my eyes and I lunge forward, prepared to beat an apology from his dumb ass. He stumbles backward, just out of reach, and a pair of strong arms lock around my waist, holding me back.

"He's not worth it!" Smith yells. "He's not worth our season, man! He ain't shit."

The stupid fucker actually steps forward and tries to take a swing at me before McCoy grabs his collar and jerks him back.

"All right! Break it up!"

When I look up, campus police stand in the foyer.

*Fuck.*

Fuck. Fuck. Fuck. Could this day get any worse?

All the fight leaves my body, and Smith relaxes his grip.

I straighten my shirt, praying the cop doesn't ask for IDs. "Can I help you, sir?"

"We had a noise complaint." He rests his hands on his belt as he surveys the scene. "But it looks like you've already taken care of the music, so I'm going to let you off with a warning. We get another call, I'm going to need names and IDs. Understand?"

"Yes, sir," McCoy and I say in unison.

Rivalry or not, neither of us can afford to see our guys facing charges.

The cop looks me over. "Good game against Ohio, son. Best damn game I've seen in ages."

"Thank you, sir."

He wishes us luck against Wisconsin, and the baseball players follow him out when he leaves. Kendall brings up the rear, sauntering out the door with Johnson's eyes glued to her ass.

I heave a massive sigh of relief. That was too fucking close.

The door slams and I do a quick head count, verifying all the recruits are present. Then I turn to Johnson.

"What the hell were you thinking?" It's a rhetorical question, but his half-assed shrug has me seeing red, fury making my chest heave like I've just run the forty-yard dash. "You want to be captain next year? Being captain isn't about being everyone's drinking buddy. It's about being a leader and setting a good fucking example!"

This time, he at least has the decency to look chagrined.

Coach'll cut off my nuts if word of this gets out.

This is the kind of shit that ruins reputations and gets teams put on probation. This is not what Waverly football is about, and it's sure as shit not how we recruit.

I can't believe Johnson could be this irresponsible, but I'm even more pissed at myself for not realizing it ahead of time.

These kids are my responsibility. I've let them down, even if they're too fucked up to realize it at the moment.

"Dude, *chillllax*. We're just having a little *fuuun*," says one of the recruits, slurring his words. I narrow my eyes at him. Hawkins, from Maryland. The kid may be quick on his feet, but I'm not in the mood for excuses. Especially not from a shit-faced high school punk who can barely string two words together. "No harm, *noooo* foul."

I'm about to unleash some next level heat on the kid when Tate, one of Johnson's roommates, wanders down the stairs with his girlfriend close on his heels.

"You were part of this too?" I ask, unable to believe Tate could be this stupid.

He steals a glance at the kid hugging the trash can and holds up his palms. "Hey, man. I thought it was just going to be a few beers."

"Just a few beers?" My voice comes low and calm despite the anger roiling in my gut. This is exactly the kind of juvenile bullshit that gives football players a bad rep. "We aren't going to win a national title drinking and partying like a bunch of overindulgent assholes. It's going to take discipline. Respect for the team. Respect for each other," I say, glaring at Johnson, Smith, and Tate in turn.

The hypocrisy of my words isn't lost on me—I am, after all, sneaking around with Carter—but I'm too pissed to think clearly at the moment.

I glare at a few of the recruits for good measure.

Most drop their eyes.

"There's some real talent in this recruiting class, but if this is how you conduct yourselves, well, I guess it won't much matter if we win the championship or not because you won't stand a chance in hell of defending it."

I turn back to Tate, the only sober one of the group.

"Get your keys and help me get these guys back to the hotel." I pause, sweeping the room with my gaze. "The puker rides with you."

I have enough shit to deal with. I don't have time to scrub vomit out of the floor mats.

It takes us an hour to get the recruits settled at the hotel with enough water to keep them hydrated and I'm in a foul-ass mood as I drive home.

My cell phone vibrates in the cupholder and my father's name appears on the in-dash screen. I'm still feeling raw about the day's events. The last thing I want to do is shoot the shit with my old man. I consider letting the call roll to voice mail but answer on the third ring.

No point delaying the inevitable.

"Hey, Dad."

"I just got off the phone with John Hays," he says, skipping the greeting and diving right into business. "He'll be in town for the Michigan game in three weeks. He wants to meet."

A familiar tightness grips my chest and crawls up the back of my throat. Hays is an old friend of the family. He's also a scout in Pittsburgh. "Shouldn't we wait until the end of the season, when my eligibility expires?"

My father makes a dismissive sound. "The NCAA doesn't forbid us from having lunch with an old family friend. Hays has already spoken with Coach Collins. Practices will be open that week. I doubt Pittsburgh will be the only one watching, so make sure you're on your A game. The more interest you generate, the more valuable you are to the franchise."

I tighten my grip on the steering wheel. Like I need to be told to make a good show for the scouts. It's my future on the line and I've trained for this nearly every day of my life.

"When's the meeting?" If my dad notices the hard edge to my words, he doesn't mention it.

I blow out a breath, reaching for whatever patience I have left.

"Friday at two. Should work for your schedule." He pauses, but it goes without saying we'll be meeting at his favorite College Park steak house. "Make sure you put it on your calendar. I know how busy you are, son."

"I'll take care of it when I get home." I tap my blinker and turn left onto University Drive. "I'm heading there now."

"Good. I'm glad to hear you aren't out partying." *If he only knew.* "You need to rest up this week. Wisconsin is looking good."

He's not wrong. Their defense is on fire. It's going to be a hard-hitting game.

"We'll be ready for them. You coming to the game?"

"Wouldn't miss it," he says, and I can hear the pride in his voice.

I may not share my dad's love of Pittsburgh, but I know he just wants what's best for me.

Or what he thinks is best.

The pressure is like a vise, but I can't bring myself to tell him the truth. That I don't want what he wants. That meeting with Hays in a professional capacity makes me want to gouge my eyes out.

That I need a release from the constant pressure of school and football.

A release only Kennedy seems able to provide with her quick wit, lush curves, and low expectations. Some days it feels like she's the only person in my life who doesn't want something from me.

Or at least, not something I'm unwilling to give.

Our relationship is all about give-and-take, the push and pull of fire and ice, pleasure so intense it sometimes borders on pain. But damn if I don't crave it at times like this, when it feels like I'll explode if I can't slip out of my own skin, if only for a few hours.

It's a weakness I can't show anyone. Especially not my father.

He thrived under the pressure. He'll accept no less from his only son.

"And Austin? Make sure you write down the meeting with Hays."

# 32

# KENNEDY

Enzo and I are three hours into design tweaks for the ACME competition when Austin texts me.

*Austin: You free tonight?*

The obvious answer is yes. My roommate is away. I'm horny as hell. And I've had enough orgasms...*said no woman ever.*

But then I glance at Enzo, who's got his nose buried in a textbook.

*I can't very well kick him out for a hookup. Can I?*

No. Definitely not. He's a good guy, and he's doing me a huge favor by partnering. Although a horny little voice in the back of my head reminds me I'm doing him a favor as well, since he couldn't find a team to work with his crazy-pants schedule. Still, it's a new partnership, and I don't want to do anything to screw it up.

Besides, it was my brilliant idea to spend our Saturday night working.

*Me: I wish. Enzo's here. Working.*

Enzo glances up, and I drop my phone into my lap.

I don't want him to see Austin's messages any more than I want him to think I'm slacking. I turn my attention back to my open laptop and the design schematics that are nearly complete. Turns out, Enzo is the partner I never knew I needed. He's the perfect balance of helpful and constructive, not hesitating to challenge my design while also helping with some of the legwork and data validation that was slowing me down.

I'm thrilled with today's progress, but there's no shortage of work to be done.

My phone buzzes again and I glance down.

*Austin: Come on. I just got off babysitting duty and I'm ready for some adult time.*

Apparently, so are my ovaries, but I have to be strong.

*Me: No deal. This project is important.*

I try to focus on my design. I really do. But it's impossible to concentrate when the phone keeps buzzing. I can feel Enzo's gaze on me, although I keep my eyes trained on the laptop screen, determined to ignore the messages coming in.

I last all of three seconds.

*Austin: New deal. I'll bring dinner AND dessert if you wrap things up in the next thirty minutes.*

My stomach rumbles as if on cue.

*No, no, no.* I will not be ruled by my stomach. Or my hormones.

Maybe I can rustle up some snacks in the kitchen.

I start to get up, but sigh and flop back into my chair. Tomorrow is grocery day, which is pretty much the only day there's actual food in the kitchen of a student athlete.

"Man, I didn't realize how late it was getting." Enzo stretches, suppressing a yawn. "You want to call it a night? I'm starving."

*Best. Partner. Ever.*

I grin, a real honest-to-God smile with teeth and all. "You totally heard my stomach, didn't you?"

He shrugs, but the corners of his lips twitch. I should probably be embarrassed, but I'm not. Maybe his chill vibe is rubbing off on me.

"It's cool. My girlfriend is always hungry too. I swear there are days the woman eats more than I do, even though she's half my size."

Most people would probably latch onto the fact that he basically just called his girl a human garbage disposal, but not me.

"You have a girlfriend?" It's hard to keep the surprise from my voice.

Enzo arches a brow. *Crap*. I probably offended him.

"Emma and I have been dating since freshman year." He pulls out his phone and shows me a picture of a lovely girl with dark hair, dark eyes, and a sweet smile.

"She's pretty." I tilt my head for a better look. "Must be pretty understanding too, given all the groupies."

Enzo laughs. "Just because I play football doesn't mean I'm into the party scene. You think I got an A in Beck's class by spending my free time drinking my face off and hooking up?"

Fair point. "No, I suppose not."

I'm starting to wonder if I've got the whole football-player narrative wrong.

Sure, there are plenty of guys on the team who spend more time chasing skirts than studying, but not all of them.

"Naw, Emma keeps me grounded. I love the game, but I'm a realist. I won't be playing pro ball after college. I need my degree." He pauses and rubs the back of his neck. "I'll be the first one in my family to graduate from college and football's given me the discipline to manage my time and my studies. Plus, it looks good on a resume." He laughs. "Lots of companies who want to support the blue and white, you know?"

"Preach."

Enzo wouldn't be the first graduate counting on the Waverly network to help him land a job after graduation. But I can't afford to hope some random alum will take an interest. I need this competition. I don't have a lot of connections, and networking isn't my strong suit.

I've always been too busy with work and school.

I close my laptop and rub the back of my neck, trying to ease the tension that's settled between my shoulder blades. We made good progress today and if we finalize the design this week, we can start working on the prototype next weekend.

Enzo stands and slings his bag over his shoulder. I follow his lead and tuck my buzzing phone in my pocket as I walk him to the door.

When he's gone, I pull out my phone and glance at the screen, the earlier spark of desire catching fire.

*Austin: You're killing me, gorgeous. Don't make me beg.*

He thinks I'm playing hard to get. If he only knew...

*Me: You had me at dessert. What's on the menu?*

*Austin: YOU.*

That one word goes straight to my core. I clench my thighs together, desire slamming through me like water from a burst dam.

*Three little letters. Lots of promise.*

If I hurry, I can squeeze in a quick shower before he arrives.

I race like the wind, but it's still not fast enough. There's a knock on the door as I'm towel drying my hair. I toss on a pair of boxers and a cami and pad out to the living room barefoot.

When I open the door, Austin's leaning against the doorjamb with a white bag dangling from his right hand. He's wearing a fitted black T-shirt and his jeans hang low on his hips, revealing a swath of bare skin and hardened muscle that makes my ovaries do a happy dance.

*Mmm.*

I swear the man looks good enough to eat, but apparently my stomach didn't get the message, because it growls again.

"I take it we're eating first." Austin's words are wrought with amusement, but there's hunger too. And not the kind that can be satisfied with a mere sandwich. "A woman after my own heart."

It's meant to be a joke, but the way he says it? All low and husky? The words skate across my skin, leaving a trail of goose bumps in their wake. I don't like it one bit. Our hearts have nothing to do with this arrangement.

I snatch the bag from his hand and flounce into the kitchen, determined to focus on our most basic needs: food and sex.

That's the deal, after all.

Once I've unpacked the sandwiches and put them on plates, I toss Austin a bottle of water and join him at the table, which is still covered with the remnants of my design project. I sit down and pluck a fry off my turkey and cheese sandwich as Austin's gaze sweeps across the table.

I chew slowly, realizing it probably looks like a total mess to the casual observer.

Austin leans back in his chair, massive sandwich untouched. "So what's the deal with this competition anyway?"

"The American Coalition of Mechanical Engineers design competition is *the* competition for mechanical engineering majors." I pause and take a sip of my water. "Think of it as the championship game. The winners are pretty much guaranteed job interviews with the top engineering companies in the country."

"I take it you're planning to claim one of those top spots."

I grin. "Why enter if not to win? I need every advantage I can get when it comes to job placement." I pop another fry in my mouth, savoring the greasy, starchy goodness. "I'll be paying off my student loans until the end of time."

The muscles in Austin's jaw tense, but he nods in understanding before turning his attention to his sandwich. We eat in silence for a while, but it's surprisingly comfortable. When he finishes eating, he turns his attention back to the mess that surrounds us.

"So what exactly are you designing?" He picks up one of the sketches from the table, and I cringe. It's pretty rough. Definitely not my best work. "Is this a robot?"

He holds up the drawing, interest flaring in his eyes.

"Yeah." I tear a piece of crusty Italian bread from my sandwich and mayo drips over the edge of the paper wrapper. Leave it to Austin to hit up the one place in town that serves a Pittsburgh-style sandwich, complete with coleslaw and French fries. There's no way I'll be able to eat the whole thing. "This year's contest is a Pick and Place race. The challenge is to design a robot capable of picking various size balls from tall plastic platforms and depositing them in a collection bin."

It's a quick and dirty description, but I doubt he wants all the boring details.

Austin arches a brow, and I catch a flash of his dimple before he speaks. "I'm guessing it's a little more complicated than it sounds."

"Little bit." I pinch my fingers together so that only a small gap remains between them. "There's a lot of work that goes into the design and construction phases. Plus a written paper and presentation that detail the engineering principles the team used to build the bot."

"Does it include lots of differential equations and advanced calculations that would be too complex for a jock like me?"

He laughs, the sound scraping over my skin like gravel. It's sexy as hell, but I refuse to take the bait. I never said football players were dumb. Just that they have a tendency to think with the little head.

Austin grabs the edge of my chair and drags it closer to his own. Our knees are touching and he's looking at me like I might be next up on the menu. A bolt of desire goes straight to my belly.

I'm going to have sex with Austin-*freaking*-Reid.

It's not the first time or even the second, but I swear, the thrill of it never wears off.

"You know," he says. "I kind of like it when you talk nerdy to me."

I swallow, my brain instantly short-circuited by the press of his body against mine.

And then I'm reciting the principles of robotics and offering him a tutorial on CAD. Like he wants to see how a technical drawing is built. Then again, maybe he does.

He did just say nerd-talk was hot.

*Stupid nerves. You've had sex with this man before. Get a grip!*

But then it's not just my knee he's touching. He leans forward and pulls me onto his lap like I weigh no more than a paper doll, my legs straddling his hips. I can feel the hard ridge of his erection pressed against me, and it's all I can do not to rock my hips as he strokes my cheek, brushing the damp hair from my face.

His voice is low and husky when he speaks again, sounding like sex personified. "That's better."

"Much better," I agree, meeting his eyes as I rotate my bottom, giving sweet relief to the growing ache between my legs. *So much for self-control.* "Remind me again whose idea it was to eat first?"

He laughs and grips my hips, his strong hands pulling my body flush to his before crushing his lips to mine. Our tongues collide fiercely and a deep moan shatters the silence.

*Shit. Was that me?*

Doesn't matter. Austin's hands slide gracefully over my back and then they're tangled in my hair, twisting it around his fingers as he tilts my head, baring my throat. He trails openmouthed kisses down my chin and neck, sucking and biting as he makes his way across my collarbone.

Another breathy moan rolls off my lips, but I'm beyond caring.

My skin ignites like wildfire at the brush of his lips. I'm burning up from the inside out, desperate for more. His fingers are everywhere at once, moving hungrily over my heated flesh and leaving a trail of desire in their wake. It's too much and yet... it's not enough.

*It will never be enough with Austin.*

I grab the hem of his shirt and pull it over his head, revealing the chiseled muscles I've spent countless hours worshipping. In the back seat of his Jeep, in the visiting team locker room, against his bedroom door, and once in the library bathroom.

Although, to be fair, that only took a few minutes.

*A few glorious minutes.*

I trail my fingers over his pecs, savoring the smooth, firm skin that covers every dip and ridge. There's a fading bruise on his right side where the flesh is a mottled shade of purple. A reminder of the hard-hitting game against Ohio.

I skim my fingers over the lingering injury and Austin shivers at my touch, lowering his forehead to mine. Our eyes lock, and I wrap my legs around his waist as he stands and carries me to the couch. He lays me on my back, his weight pressing me into the cushions as his hips rock against mine, his cock grinding against my core with tantalizing precision. I wriggle and arch my back, trying desperately to get closer to him, to meld my body to his.

An impossible feat when he's wearing jeans.

*They need to go.*

Like, right now.

I grab for his belt, shaky hands fumbling with the buckle. Austin seals his lips to mine, a hot brand that confirms I'm not the only one anxious to get to O-town. I manage to unclasp his belt and flick open the button on his jeans. He climbs to his feet and I gasp at the loss of contact, my swollen lips abandoned as he unzips his fly and shoves his pants to the floor, revealing the long, thick cock that's left me blissed-out more nights than not since we made our little deal.

I swear it's the stuff of fantasies. Or romance novels.

Best of all, he knows how to use it.

Which is why tonight, I want to do something for him.

I sit up and take his cock in my hand. With a firm grip, I stroke him from root to tip, relishing the feel of his silky skin against my palm. Austin's eyelids droop and he sighs.

The sound is rough and jagged and full of unspoken need.

My body clenches in response, urging me on. There's a bead of moisture on the head of his cock and I lick it off, my tongue darting out to tease the unflappable QB. He throws his head back and groans, sending a thrill up my spine.

There's something empowering about having this hulk of a man surrender to my touch, giving up control in exchange for the pleasure I offer. It feels...right. And I know that when the time comes, my own orgasm will be explosive, so I take him in my mouth, working him with my tongue as he tangles his fingers in my hair, guiding me. I lose myself in Austin, licking and sucking and teasing as he chants my name like a prayer.

"*Fuuuck.*" He abruptly pulls me to my feet.

*Shit. Did I do something wrong?*

But no, he's reaching for my tank top, dragging it over my head and freeing my breasts. He cups them in his large palms, stroking lazy circles around my hardened nipples as I shimmy out of my shorts. When I stand naked before him, he rolls on a condom and tugs me down on the couch, so I'm straddling him.

His normally bright eyes are dark with lust, and when he

looks at me like there's no one else who could make him feel this way, I can't deny the swell of pride that expands in my chest.

*I've done this to him.*

Brought him to the edge of madness with my touch.

He strokes my cheek, the calloused pads of his fingers a sharp contrast to my own soft skin. "I need to come inside you. I want to feel you come on my dick."

He doesn't have to ask twice.

I lower myself without hesitation, moaning as Austin is fully seated, filling me completely.

We move in unison, our sweat-slick bodies coming together as we push one another higher and higher, soaring toward release. When I feel his body tense under mine, his hips bucking off the couch as though he's lost all sense of control, I fly over the edge with him, my own orgasm spiraling through me with such intensity I cry out his name before his lips clamp over mine.

The kiss is deep and sweaty and utterly perfect.

When we finally break apart, I climb to my feet on shaky legs. I gather my clothes and get dressed as Austin does the same. Then he grabs the remote and flops down on the couch, arm draped across the back.

"What are you doing?" I ask, narrowing my eyes.

He looks way too comfortable on my couch.

"It's early." He shrugs. "I figured we could watch a movie if you're up for it?"

I worry my bottom lip between my teeth. Aren't hookups supposed to, I don't know, *leave* afterward? This is new territory for us, but... It's early and Becca's gone for the weekend.

And it's not like he's planning to sleep over.

I'm probably making a big deal out of nothing.

"Relax." He pats the spot next to him on the couch. "It's not like we're going to watch *The Notebook* and talk about our feelings." The color drains from his face and his eyes go wide. The guy's faced down three-hundred-pound linemen, but it's the first time I've seen real fear in his eyes. "Are we?"

I can't help it. I burst out laughing, doubling over as the laughter shakes my body from the inside out. The look on his face is priceless. I'm half tempted to grab the DVD from Becca's room just to see what he'll do, but in the end, I take pity on him.

After all, he did just wring the tension from my body with that gifted cock of his.

We agree on a Ryan Reynolds action flick neither of us has seen, but halfway through the movie Austin starts massaging my thigh. His fingers march north, kneading the muscles just below the hem of my tiny shorts. A ripple of desire pulses through me, and I forget all about the movie.

I forget my own name when his roving hand snakes under my shirt, the rough pads of his fingers gliding over my belly, tracing a path to the hardened nipples that strain against my tank top. Then his lips are moving over mine, the firm weight of his body descending on me with such perfection I give myself over to him with total abandon, letting him set the pace for the pleasure I know will follow.

Because his mouth, his hands, his body? They're exquisite.

As if they were made for pleasure. As if they were made just for me.

And that kind of perfection? It won't be easy to give up at the end of the season.

# 33

# AUSTIN

SOMETHING'S UP. I feel it the instant I step onto the practice field. It's deadly quiet. No jokes. No complaints. No warm-ups.

Coach glares at us as we take the field—eyes narrow, brows flat—like he's just waiting to unleash the beast. The rest of the coaching staff stands behind him, arms crossed, faces blank, as we line up, forming a loose semi-circle.

The day is cold and gray, the sun nonexistent.

*Perfect for a good ass chewing.*

The only question is whether it'll be worse than the tongue lashing we got after Spellman busted his leg.

*Fuck. Did he hear about the recruits getting wasted?*

Fear grips my chest like a vise. That would definitely be a whole other level of shit. One we can't afford with the Badgers on the schedule this week.

They're playing well and we need our best guys on the field.

We also need them focused on the game.

I take my place at the front of the group, Coop at my side, and resist the urge to look at Johnson. Whatever's coming, we're all in it together. Otherwise, Coach would've called the offenders into his office.

Whatever he's got to say, it's for the whole team.

A bead of sweat trickles down my right temple despite the October chill.

Kennedy catches my eye and lifts a brow, but I don't acknowledge her. Not even to give the slightest shake of my head. Coach's red-hot glare is fixed on me, and for now, that's where it needs to stay.

*Just another perk of being team captain.*

Coach grunts and the mass of tension-filled bodies surrounding me stand up even straighter.

"Imagine my surprise when I got a call from campus PD," Coach says, each word landing like a blow to my solar plexus, "informing me that a few of my guys were caught tussling with the baseball team Saturday night."

A murmur of surprise rises from the back of the group. Proof that word of the scene with McCoy and his boys hasn't spread far and wide...*yet.*

Heart racing, I will Johnson to keep his mouth shut as Coach's gaze swings his way. Lucky for Johnson, it doesn't hold. Coach's eyes pivot, slamming into me with the force of a defensive end.

"You were supposed to be babysitting recruits, so what the fuck were y'all doing messing with the baseball team?" he demands. I bite my tongue, hoping it's a rhetorical question. "Well?"

*Fuck.* He actually expects an answer.

I take a steadying breath and force myself to look him in the eye. It's moments like these when being the team captain really blows.

"A few of the guys were watching the Bama game and things got a little tense, but it was no big deal."

"No big deal?" Coach snorts. "The way I hear it, Reid, you went after one of their guys, so I ask you again, what the fuck happened?"

I grit my teeth, careful not to look at Kennedy. No need to drag her into this mess.

"One of their guys had a little too much to drink and disrespected the team." I shrug, doing my best to downplay the whole incident. It's not like it was a legit fight. The cop was there for a noise complaint, a fact I'm sure Coach knows. Just like he knows there's bad blood between the two teams. "I told them to leave."

"Was that before or after you took a swing at him?"

Anger stirs in my gut at the memory of the shortstop's words and the way he disrespected Kennedy, but I tamp it down.

Smith was right. Rearranging his face might have felt good, but it wasn't worth our season.

"Before, sir."

Johnson and Tate turn their attention to Kennedy. I silently curse them for being assholes.

Might as well have pointed at her and declared it was all her fault.

Coach follows their line of sight, and I swear his face gets two shades darker. He stomps over to Kennedy, so they're nearly toe to toe. "And what was your role in all this, Carter?"

"Me?" She scrunches up her nose. There's a hint of annoyance in her tone. Can't blame her given she's totally innocent. "I wasn't even there."

Coach cuts his eyes at her, and I jump in before either of them says something we'll all regret. "It's true, Coach. It was just a few of the guys."

And the underage recruits, but if he doesn't already know they were drinking, I'm not about to volunteer the information. We're in enough trouble thanks to Johnson and his boneheaded roommates.

"What the hell is wrong with y'all?" Coach spins on his heel and returns to the front of the group, looking even less pleased than when we arrived. "We're six and one, and you're throwing parties and getting into fights?"

"It wasn't a party, sir. Just a few friends is all."

*Fuckin' Johnson.* It's bad enough he was hanging with the baseball team. Now he's trying to justify it?

"Johnson, I don't give a shit if it was Bible study." Coach points a meaty finger at him. "Campus PD shows up at your door again, your ass will be riding the bench. You got me?"

Johnson pales, finally grasping the seriousness of the situation. "Yes, sir."

Coach turns his attention to the rest of us, lips pressed into a flat line as he marches from one end of the group to the other, glaring at us. "Do y'all wanna win a national title or not?"

The question is met with a resounding, "Yes, sir."

"Yeah? Then you're going to have to be smarter. Use your goddamn heads once in a while. First Spellman. Now this?" He shakes his head. He's getting really worked up now, his words coming fast and loud. "The next person on this team to step one goddamn toe out of line will be riding the bench." His gaze pans the group, making it clear he's not playing. "I mean it. One toe out of line and I will bench your ass. I don't care who you are. We haven't worked this hard to piss it all away because some asshole on the baseball team hurt your feelings!"

He says the last part with disgust and shame washes over me.

I risked everything taking a swing at that kid, and for what? Because he was talking shit? Those taunts were nothing compared to the press I'd get for assault charges. Not to mention the team supplying alcohol to minors.

Coach is right. We've only got a few games left.

I need to keep the team focused and out of trouble. For the title and my reputation.

No one wants to draft a troublemaker. I've worked hard to keep my nose clean. I'm not about to throw it all away now.

Not when everything I've ever wanted is within my grasp.

Coach Collins turns to the rest of the coaching staff. "These boys have energy to burn, so let's work 'em hard. I want 'em too tired to make trouble when they leave this field today."

There's a rumble of dissent, but one scathing look from Coach squashes it.

We line up for warm-ups, and the staff puts us through the wringer.

It's the hardest workout of the year. By the time the practice is over, my muscles feel like Jell-O. I couldn't do another burpee if I tried and sweat is pouring off me like a waterfall.

All I want to do is hit the showers, but when the team is dismissed, Kennedy hangs back. The weight of her gaze is crushing, making it clear she wants to talk. Probably about the incident at the football house.

*So much for the brutal workout squashing her curiosity.*

I drag the back of my hand across my forehead and make my way to the thirty-yard line where she stands, helmet wedged against her hip, waiting expectantly. There's a light breeze and despite the chill, it feels like heaven against my sweat-soaked skin.

The wind catches the end of Kennedy's ponytail, making it flutter around her head like a halo. Fitting, I suppose, since even sweat slicked and exhausted, she looks like an angel.

*My angel.*

For now anyway. We'll see how long that lasts when she hears what went down at the football house. Something tells me she didn't like being singled out by Coach today and there's going to be hell to pay.

## 34

## KENNEDY

"What happened Saturday night?" Judging by the way Johnson and Tate gave me the side-eye at practice, it has something to do with me, which just figures. You know, since I wasn't even there.

The last thing I need is Coach breathing down my neck.

I haven't forgotten his threat to bounce me out on my ass if I cause trouble.

Given the way he came down on me during practice, he's more than happy to make good on the promise.

Austin scrubs a hand over his face and wipes it on his jersey. Desire stirs low in my belly, spreading through my limbs like a current. The man is dripping sweat, and I know I should be grossed out, but I'm so not. It's possible he's never looked sexier than he does in this moment, with glistening muscles and ruddy cheeks.

I'm tempted to scrap this whole discussion and invite him back to my place.

Which is exactly why I need to focus on the matter at hand.

"Nothing to worry about." He smiles, but it doesn't quite reach his eyes. Which means he's shutting me out or he's falling back on his captain's laurels, assuming it's his job to shoulder all the hard stuff. "Just guy stuff."

"Guy stuff?" I snort. He can't actually expect me to buy the half-assed lie. The wind howls around us, and dried leaves cart-wheel across the empty practice field. "Try again, Reid, because I'm not buying it. Why did Johnson and Tate stare me down when you said the baseball team was talking shit?"

Frustration flashes in his eyes and he crosses his arms over his chest, helmet dangling from his right hand.

"Oh, for crying out loud. Can we not do the whole strong and silent thing? I have a right to know." And I'll be damned if I'm going to let him stonewall me. "Coach just singled me out in front of the entire team, and he's made it clear he'd be more than happy to give me the boot if I don't walk the line."

Austin raises a brow, the corner of his mouth inching skyward. "Coach isn't going to bench you because I took a swing at some asshole from the baseball team. Our rivalry predates you joining the team."

It sounds so reasonable when he says it, but I haven't forgotten Coach's hot breath on my face or his prior warnings.

"Yeah, well, forgive me if I'm not willing to stake my scholar-ship on your word. Stop deflecting and tell me what happened."

He gives a long-suffering sigh.

I can't tell if it's in reaction to my persistence or the story he's about to tell.

"Johnson and a couple of the guys were supposed to be keeping an eye on the recruits while I was at study group. Instead, they got them wasted and decided to chill with our rivals. It was a total cluster. Campus police showed up right after one of their guys made a derogatory remark about you."

I frown, fighting the urge to ask exactly what was said.

It doesn't matter, and I doubt Austin would tell me anyway.

I can't decide if I'm touched he had my back or annoyed I've become exactly the kind of distraction Coach Collins was worried about. Assault charges against Waverly's golden boy would've put an end to the season. No way I want that kind of guilt hanging over my head.

"You're not my boyfriend. I don't need you going all territorial, and I don't need you to fight my battles." I poke him in the chest to emphasize my point.

Fat lot of good it does because, *shoulder pads.*

"I know you don't need me to fight your battles, but I wasn't going to stand there and let some douchebag disrespect you." He presses his lips flat, the hard set of his jaw like granite. "Or the team."

"I doubt you would've reacted so strongly if he'd been talking about Coop. Or Vaughn. Or basically anyone else on the team."

His silence confirms my suspicions.

Because despite the rules we've set, I'm not just one of the guys. And neither is he.

I start to reach for him and catch myself, my hand freezing in midair.

"This is exactly what I didn't want. What Coach didn't want. Maybe we should call it quits." I pull my hand back and rake it through my hair, tucking loose strands behind my ear. "I know we said the end of the season, but if Saturday night is any indication, things between us are already getting too messy. Neither of us can afford the distraction, and I don't want to be responsible for screwing up your season."

"Fuck that." He takes a breath and closes his eyes, gathering his composure before he speaks again. "We aren't hurting anyone, and the situation Saturday night was a onetime deal. It changes nothing between us."

"Doesn't it? You took a swing at some guy because you didn't like what he said about me. Pretty sure that's a game changer."

It's sweet that Austin wanted to defend my honor, but it doesn't change the fact that maybe we're getting in too deep.

"It won't happen again." His blue eyes flare with determination and I steel my resolve. "I was upset about the guys getting the recruits drunk. I let my temper get the best of me."

"I don't know. Seeing Coach fired up today..." I bite my lip. "We're taking a big risk."

"Trust me, today was nothing." He traces a finger along my jawline. There's a tenderness in his eyes, in the way he studies my face, that I haven't noticed before. My pulse leaps in response, and I curse my traitorous mind for imagining meaning that isn't there. "It's not that big a risk. We aren't breaking NCAA rules." He lifts my chin, forcing me to meet his smoldering gaze. "I'm not ready to give you up yet, and I don't think you're ready to give me up either. The way you scream my name? There isn't another man on campus who can give you that kind of pleasure. And I think you know it, don't you, gorgeous?"

"Yes," I admit, hating the breathless sound of my voice. Problem is, he's right. I'm not ready to go back to the way things were. Not yet, anyway. My body is already protesting at the mere suggestion. "But we have to be more careful. No more unnecessary risks."

Austin grins down at me, his dimple sending my racing heart into overdrive.

"You worry too much. We aren't going to get caught."

# 35

# AUSTIN

"REID. MY OFFICE. TEN MINUTES." Coach barks the order and turns on his heel without waiting for a reply.

*Fuuuck.* What now?

I had a good practice. The team's looking solid, and everyone's well rested coming off the bye week. The team's been on virtual lockdown since Monday's practice. No way have any of the guys had time to get into trouble. Even if they had, he wouldn't give me ten minutes to clean up if he was really pissed. And he probably would've made practice a living hell.

Sure, it was rough, but no worse than usual.

I strip off my pads and notice Coop eyeing the bruise on my right side. It's nearly faded, but it's ugly as sin.

"Still a lot of games to play." Coop slides his helmet into his locker. His tone is neutral, but we've been friends long enough I can read the tension in his shoulders and in the pinched corners of his mouth. Something's bothering him. "Maybe do the rest of us a favor and get rid of the ball next time. Better to lose a down than a QB."

I grit my teeth. It was a late hit and he knows it, but that isn't the point.

Even if the refs had called it, I'd still be banged up. I know he's right. Smart players don't take unnecessary risks, not when it could blow the whole season. Problem is, when I'm on the field and the adrenaline's pumping, I have to be the best. There's no other option. Sometimes that means making the play, the hell with the risk.

This time, it paid off. We won the game. No point sweating what-ifs.

But I can't say that to Coop.

It wouldn't be very captainly and I sure as shit wouldn't accept that answer from one of my guys.

"Duly noted."

He just nods, and I head for the shower. Clock's ticking, and Coach won't tolerate lateness. Especially from me.

I make it to his office without a minute to spare.

He's sitting behind his desk, flipping through the grade book. I didn't do as well as I should have on my midterms, but my grades are decent. Doesn't stop a sheen of sweat from rising on my forehead.

"Coach."

He closes the grade book and leans back in his chair, crossing his arms over his chest and giving nothing away. I wait him out. If one of my guys is about to get benched for grades, I'll know it soon enough.

"I've been getting a lot of calls from scouts this week. You played a hell of a game against Ohio." He pauses. "There are a lot of guys who want to come out and see you play. Including Chicago."

*Chicago.*

My pulse quickens. I have a million questions, but I do my best to remain impassive. No sense getting myself or Coach excited.

Coach grunts. "Lot of guys in this senior class getting looks, so I'm going to open practice the week of the Michigan game."

I should've seen this coming. It's the same week Hays is coming out. Talk about a full house.

Did my old man already talk to Coach about my prospects? If he has, Coach hasn't mentioned it, but I doubt he would. The man's a closed book when he's not busting my balls.

"Have you given any additional thought to what we talked about?" he asks.

He's referring to Chicago, to blazing my own trail and finding a team that's a good fit for my style and skill. I play dumb. "Sir?"

Coach shakes his head. He's not buying.

No surprise there. I've always been shit at lying, especially when it comes to authority figures.

"Son, I think you need to be a realist here. Based on their current rank, Chicago could very well have the number one draft pick and they're in desperate need of a QB to build the program. I'd be lyin' if I said I didn't think your name was on the short list. Hell, the scout said as much."

I shrug, reaching for indifference. "No sense wasting his time or mine. I told you, Coach. It's not in the cards."

"Be that as it may, it wouldn't hurt to show them what you can do. Let them know you're open to a conversation at the NFL Combine in the spring." He pauses, leaning forward to rest his elbows on the edge of the cluttered desk. "I'm also going to schedule an optional practice for Sunday. Mainly drills. It'll be a good opportunity for some of the juniors and seniors who don't get as much press to showcase their skills. I'd like you to consider attending."

He doesn't have to say the Chicago scout will be there. It's implied.

Coach has to walk a fine line, remaining impartial while also advising players he's coached for years, many of whom have nowhere else to turn for career advice and view him as a father figure.

The hard-ass kind that doesn't take any lip or no for an answer.

If Coach can sense how bad I want to meet with Chicago, he doesn't let on. Neither can I. My old man would flip the fuck out if he knew I expressed interest in a team other than Pittsburgh. Which is why there's no point shining Chicago—or myself—on.

It'll just make it harder when the Steel City calls my name in April.

The sooner I accept the path that's been laid out for me—the one I've chosen—the easier all of this will be. I start making noise, things could go sideways and the next thing you know, my old man's telling the owners I'll sit out a year before I play for the wrong team.

Not exactly how I want to start my career in the NFL.

"What do you say?" Coach rubs his chin. "Can I count on you for Sunday? If I tell the scouts you're participating, it could help some of the other guys get a look."

Shrewd bastard. He thinks I won't say no if it's for the benefit of the team.

"I'll think about it."

## 36

## KENNEDY

"We should do that again." I curl into Austin, shamelessly rubbing against him so I can soak up his body heat. We're tangled in the sheets, my head resting on his chest, and despite the workout he just gave me, I'm freezing. Probably because Becca and I agreed not to turn the heat on before November.

We're holding out to keep the electricity bill down, but it's just as well because having Austin around is like having my own personal heater. The man is always hot, not just when we're burning up the sheets. I wouldn't be surprised if he's one of those dudes who wears shorts all winter.

Austin chuckles, his warm breath rustling the hair on the top of my head. "Give me twenty, and I'll give you a repeat performance."

"And you call yourself an athlete." I scoff and poke him in the ribs, tilting my chin to look up at him. With a strong jaw and eyes like Caribbean waters, he really is beautiful. Although I suspect he'd prefer the word handsome. *Too bad.* My brain, my label. "Aren't you guys supposed to have stamina?"

He gives me a lazy grin, revealing the sexy little dimple that melts my marshmallow heart. "You do know I played three hours and twenty-six minutes of Big Ten football today, right?"

I snort-laugh and clamp a hand over my mouth. "You didn't play the *whole* time."

"You want to see stamina?" A mischievous grin spreads over his face, and I know I'm in trouble. "I'll show you stamina."

I roll out of his arms, but it's a half-hearted escape attempt. He's too fast, and let's be honest, I kind of want to be caught. He grabs me around the waist and turns me over, pinning me to the bed, his muscular thighs straddling my hips.

The view's not half bad, so I don't resist when he raises my arms over my head, binding my wrists together with one hand. If he wants to prove he's got stamina, who am I to argue, especially when it involves orgasms?

Austin leans forward, lowering his soft lips to mine. The stubble on his chin scratches my face in the best way as he parts my lips with his tongue and plunders my mouth like a pirate in search of booty.

*Pirate? Booty?*

I giggle. Might be time to lay off the pirate romance novels.

Austin pulls back. "Oh, that's funny, is it?"

He caresses my side with his free hand, his touch sending a shiver up my spine as visions of orgasms dance in my head. Unfortunately, he's got something else in mind, and my fantasy grinds to a halt when he starts tickling me.

I squeal and thrash, trying to free myself from his grip, but it's no use.

It's like fighting a wall of sexy man muscle.

He keeps at it until tears leak down my cheeks and my right side is aching from the laughter. Then the cocky bastard flops down next to me, head propped up on his hand, looking quite pleased with himself.

"For the record," I huff, blowing a strand of hair out of my face. "That did nothing to improve my opinion of your stamina."

"Yeah, but it was fun."

He wiggles his brows and for a second, I think he might tickle me again.

"Don't even think about it." I narrow my eyes and pull the sheet up over my breasts. "If you want fun, you can always grab your toga and head over to Sig Chi. I'm sure Coop and his entourage would be happy to provide plenty of entertainment."

"Yeah, no." He rolls his eyes. "I've been to enough drunken Halloween parties to last a lifetime, thanks."

"But you're missing out on all those *ah*-mazing Halloween costumes." I bat my eyelashes for good measure.

Honestly, I still can't believe he bagged a Halloween party to hang out with me at the apartment. Then again, he is getting sex out of the deal, in a bed nonetheless, so maybe it makes sense after all.

"I only have eyes for one woman and I kind of prefer her naked." A flush crawls over my skin at the compliment. I happen to like him naked too, but I'm pretty sure I'm getting the better end of the deal, because, hello, muscles. "Besides, there are only a few weeks left in the season." *Ugh. Don't remind me.* I've gotten so spoiled by regular orgasms, I don't know how I'm going to survive the spring semester with just my vibe now that I know what I'll be missing. "I need to stay focused on my future."

"I thought you had it all figured out. National championship, NFL draft, football god," I tease, trying to lighten the mood.

He's always so serious. And I get it, I do. But he deserves a night off.

Even when I was at my worst, spread thin by school, work, and soccer, I always carved out a few hours for myself.

As far as I can tell, Austin never cuts himself any slack.

"I wish it were that easy." He scrubs a hand over his face and

I notice for the first time the lines of tension around his eyes. "Officially, the draft will decide where I play pro ball, but there are a lot of dealmakers in the background, so..."

It's clear he has more to say, even if he can't find the words, so I stay quiet. Something tells me he doesn't talk about his future much, although it's the second time he's brought it up to me. Maybe because I'm a step removed from his world, someone who plays the game but doesn't live and breathe it.

"Coach called me into his office yesterday. Told me there's a scout for Chicago who's got his eye on me. Asked me to do an extra workout with some of the guys when he's in town, but I don't think I'm going to do it."

"Why not?" I ask, curiosity nibbling at me. I mean, Austin's a great player. He's sure to be a top draft pick, so what's he got to lose? "You wouldn't want to play in Chicago?"

"No, it's not that." He tugs on a strand of my hair, twisting the loose wave around his finger. "I'd love to play ball in Chicago, but there's no point wasting his time or mine. My parents have always wanted me to play ball in Pittsburgh, so that's where I'll go."

I scrunch up my nose. "But you just said the draft will determine where you play. I'm no expert, but how can you be so sure you'll end up in Pittsburgh?"

He smiles, but it's devoid of actual happiness. It looks a hell of a lot like defeat, although I can't be sure since I've never seen Austin give up on anything.

Not me. Not a play. Not the team.

"Politics, remember?"

I arch a brow but say nothing. Turns out, it's the right move.

"Pittsburgh is going to need a new franchise quarterback, and while they're in no danger of getting the number one pick, they can trade their way up the draft if there's a player they want badly enough. My old man is a legend in Pittsburgh, and the organization has shown interest. It's just a matter of time until they work out the logistics."

"But can't you, I don't know, trade teams later? You're not obligated to spend your whole career there just because your father did."

He sighs. "It's complicated."

*Bullshit.* "So is engineering, but hey, there's always a solution if you want to find it badly enough." I know my tone is flippant, but he acts like he's staring down a death sentence. Which is ridiculous since most of the guys on the team would probably trade their man card for a shot at the NFL. "If you don't like the choices you're being offered, why not consider alternatives?"

His lips are pressed into a flat line. I've hit a sore spot.

The last thing I want to do is pick at old wounds, but he's the one who brought it up. He obviously wants to talk about it, which means I owe it to him to be honest, to not pull any punches.

He'd expect nothing less.

"Everything I've done has been to make my parents proud. They've always dreamed of me wearing the black and gold in Pittsburgh, just like my old man. I can't disappoint them by turning my back on the dream."

"Austin." I caress his arm, stroking his biceps with gentle fingers. "It's your life. What they probably want more than anything is for you to be happy. That's what my mom always says, anyway."

Usually when she's railing about football players being unreliable losers, but no need to mention that part.

"Clearly, our parents have different priorities." He rolls onto his back, staring at the ceiling. "Mine have been planning my life since before I was born."

"And you always do what they say?"

I want to call bullshit again, because, come on. All kids rebel at some point. Even little ol' me. Case in point, there's a naked QB in my bed.

One who needs a friend to listen.

And whatever else Austin and I are to each other, we are friends.

A few months ago, I never would've thought it possible, but somewhere along the way, between snarky exchanges, grueling practices, and secret hookups, I've come to count Austin as a friend.

"I don't want to let them down. Especially my mom." He swallows. "She was diagnosed with breast cancer when I was fourteen. She died the following year."

"I'm so sorry, Austin."

If anything happened to my mom... I can't even think about it.

His eyes remain fixed on the ceiling, but in the moonlight, I can see their glassy sheen and my heart breaks for him. Cracks wide open for the boy who lost his mother at such a young age and the man who would do anything to make her proud.

"My mom was my biggest fan. She had a lot of spirit, always yelling at the refs and raising hell on the sideline. And she was always the first to call me on my bullshit." He pauses, a faraway look in his eyes. "You would've liked her."

"She does sound like my kind of woman."

I brush a strand of sweat-slick hair back from his forehead, and he turns to face me, so I'm cupping his cheek in my hand. Austin doesn't need my pity. He needs understanding. He needs acceptance.

The kind that doesn't come with strings and conditions.

"Even when she was at her worst and could barely get out of bed, she never missed a game." He clears his throat, for all the good it does. His voice is a low rasp when he continues, and I know he's fighting for control. "The last thing she said to me was that she was proud of the man I was becoming and her greatest regret was that she wouldn't be there to cheer me on the first time I came running out of the tunnel as an NFL quarterback."

My eyes sting, and I'm afraid if I speak, the sob I'm holding back will be wrenched from my throat.

How can I make him understand that her words don't make playing somewhere other than Pittsburgh a failure? Is it even my place to try?

I don't know his mom, but if she's even half the woman he's described—and I know in my bones she is—she'd be proud as hell of all he's accomplished, regardless of where he plays professional ball.

I scoot closer to Austin and wrap my arms around him, holding him tight in my embrace.

When I can finally trust myself to speak, I choose my words carefully.

"It sounds like your mom loved you very much." I don't believe for a minute his mom would be disappointed in him, but what I think doesn't matter. Only Austin's opinion matters. He's the one who has to believe it. "It's hard to imagine she could ever be disappointed in you. I think she'd want you to be happy—whether that's in Pittsburgh or Chicago—but what does *your* heart say?"

## 37

# AUSTIN

"I'm about to own your sorry ass," Parker taunts, eyes glued to the TV as his on-screen running back does a touchdown celebration.

I bite my tongue and roll my shoulders.

He's not wrong. My head's not in the game.

Problem is, I can't seem to focus on shit today.

I can't stop thinking about Kennedy's question. Would my mom have understood if I'd said I didn't want to play in Pittsburgh? I'm not sure. My old man sure as hell wouldn't understand.

He can't imagine a world where I wouldn't want to follow in his footsteps.

I get it. He had an amazing career in Pittsburgh, the fans love him, and the franchise treated him well. Doesn't mean I want to live in his shadow, listening to the talking heads compare me to my old man week in and week out.

"I'm out." Parker tosses his controller on the coffee table. "Shit's no fun when you're not even trying." He turns to face me and there's real concern in his eyes. "You want to talk about it?"

I snort. "Fuck no."

Even if I wanted to talk about it, I couldn't. Not really.

Parker's one of my best friends, but we don't exactly sit around braiding each other's hair and talking about our feelings. I've been lying to the guys for weeks about my hookups with Kennedy, making excuses for my late nights and not carpooling to study hall. Plus, there's the fact that she'd kill me if word got out that we'd been hooking up.

Assuming Coach didn't get his hands on me first.

Parker shrugs, a shit-eating grin on his face. "I had a feeling you'd say that."

"So, you offered hoping I'd say no?"

"It's actions that matter, not intentions."

"You're a real piece of work, you know that?" I throw an empty water bottle at him. He deflects it with his right arm and it lands on the floor, rolling under the coffee table. "What if I would've said yes?"

"Then I would've listened," he says, wiggling his fingers, "and rubbed your back."

I'm about to tell him what he can do with his back rub when the front door bangs open and Coop rolls in, expression unreadable. He ignores Parker and tosses a rolled-up newspaper at me without saying a word. It lands in my lap.

"What's with the theatrics?"

I scoop up the paper and unroll it.

My heart stutters when I read the headline, and a cold sweat breaks out on my brow. *Waverly's Newest Couple?* Below it there's a picture of Kennedy and I kissing in the library.

It's a good shot. You can see both our faces. And my tongue shoved down her throat.

*FUCK.*

This is bad. Real bad.

I take a deep breath before looking up to meet Coop's stare. "What do you know about this?"

Parker leaps out of his seat and snatches the paper from me. His eyes go wide when he sees the headline. "Oh shit."

"Don't shoot the messenger." Coop shrugs, but his face remains annoyingly blank. He's my best friend, and I don't have the first clue what he's thinking. He could be pissed. Could be pleased. Fuck if I know. "Handle your business."

Maybe he's disappointed.

God knows I deserve it for putting my cock before the team. I've let them down.

I should be sorry, but I can't bring myself to regret even one moment with Kennedy. She's been a bright spot in a season wrought with challenging odds, tremendous pressure, and enough speculation to bring me to my damn knees.

"You and Carter, huh?" Parker tosses the paper on the table and crosses his arms over his chest. "Not quite the headline I was expecting."

I shove my fingers into my hair, but it does little to relieve the frustration pulsing through my skull. I owe him an explanation. Hell, I owe the whole team an explanation, but I can start here, with my friend and roommate.

I force myself to look him in the eye.

"I'm sorry I wasn't straight with you when you mentioned asking Carter out. Nothing was going on then, but…I guess I was hoping."

No need to mention we're not actually dating.

Parker stares at me for what feels like an eternity and it takes all my self-control not to fidget, but I've got years of practice being stared down by savage fuckers, so I wait him out.

Finally, he raises his fist and I knock it. "It's all good. I'm talking to a freaky little gymnast."

*Thank Christ.*

I need my roommates to have my back, because I've definitely got some explaining to do, especially if the larger news outlets pick up the story.

Which they will.

Kennedy and I are both media darlings, albeit for different reasons.

*Dammit.* The last thing I need is a bunch of reporters speculating about my personal life.

It's exactly what I didn't want, what Coach didn't want. What Kennedy didn't want.

*Kennedy.*

She's going to be pissed. I need to talk to her. She should hear about this from me, not on social media. I pull out my phone and check the time. It's late and we've got an early flight tomorrow for the Indy game. Odds are, she's home.

"Look, I need to talk to Carter. You're sure we're straight?"

"Go take care of your girl." Parker claps me on the shoulder. "Good luck. She's not gonna be happy about the article."

*Understatement of the century. I'll be lucky if she doesn't cut off my nuts.*

## 38

# KENNEDY

"WHAT ARE YOU DOING HERE?" Not my best greeting, but I'm pretty sure Austin and I don't have plans, and Becca will be home any minute.

I expect him to laugh or give me some witty retort, but his mouth remains set in a firm line.

"I take it you haven't seen the *Collegian*?" He holds up a folded newspaper.

"Who has time?" Because, let's be honest, if I've got spare time, I'm totally reading smutty romance, not snarky op-eds and sports stats. "What's up? Another puff piece on the novelty of a female kicker?"

You'd think they'd be over it by now, but not so much.

"Can I come in? It's probably better to discuss this in private." His tone is unusually serious and it's starting to freak me out.

Just what exactly is in that paper? I've been playing well and haven't missed a field goal since week five. The critics should be eating their hats and singing my praises.

I sigh and step back, swinging the door wide so he can slip past.

His biceps brushes my shoulder, and I get a whiff of his cologne. It's fresh, spicy, and speaks directly to my ovaries.

*So not the time.*

"So? What is it?" I cross my arms over my chest.

Whatever it is, it can't be good. Not if Austin's here.

His shoulders tense almost imperceptibly as he unfolds the paper and hands it to me. "Don't freak out."

I read the headline. *Waverly's Newest Couple?*

Then I read it again, forcing myself to take in the picture below.

Austin. Me. Kissing.

*Fuckity-fuck-fuck.*

My stomach bottoms out and my hands begin to shake, the paper rattling noisily.

*This can't be happening.* "Don't. Freak. Out?"

The words sound shrill and borderline hysterical to my own ears. I can only imagine how I sound to Austin.

He steps forward like he's going to wrap me in his arms. I take a step back. That's what got us into this mess in the first place.

I skim the article and the ridiculous speculation that Austin and I are Waverly's newest power couple. Like that's a real thing. This is a college campus, for fuck's sake, not Hollywood.

The last line of the article catches my eye and I read it aloud, infusing my words with all the snark the author intended. "Sorry, ladies. Looks like Waverly's sexy QB is off the market." I pause and roll my eyes for good measure. "For now."

Austin says nothing.

"This is bullshit. Who even writes this kind of trash?" I throw the paper on the couch and rub my temples. "We were so careful."

"Apparently not."

I swear to God there's a hint of amusement in his voice.

"This isn't funny."

"Never said it was." True, but I can see the corner of his mouth twitching. "Look, this isn't great press for me either, but I wanted you to hear about it from me. I didn't know anything about this, Kennedy."

I believe him. He wouldn't have wanted this any more than I do. He's got his own press headaches to deal with and they're far bigger than mine, if I'm being honest.

The media's breathing down his throat.

He doesn't talk about it, but I can see the pressure weighing on him as the hype grows each week. I can't imagine what it'll be like by the time we get to the championship game. Or the draft.

The worst part is, it'll never end.

Once he's drafted, his life will become one big spotlight, everything he says and does analyzed by the media and gossip rags. But Austin will handle it well. He's not the kind of guy who gets into trouble. He's one of the good ones.

"What's done is done." He rubs the back of his neck. "We need to figure out how we're going to handle it."

"What's there to handle?" I've totally screwed up and for what, a few good—okay, great—orgasms? Nausea churns my belly. "Coach is going to cut me and pull my scholarship. He told me as much when I joined the team."

"What?" Austin's eyes go wide. "He said that to you? Why didn't you tell me?"

"Why do you think I wanted to keep this thing between us a secret?"

He rakes a hand through his hair, as if debating his response. "Coach was bluffing. He's not going to rescind your scholarship. I won't let that happen."

I raise a brow. He might be the team captain, but I doubt he has that kind of pull.

"I've only seen him do it once, and it was drug related. Trust me, it's too far into the season for him to pull your scholarship without a damn good reason. He might bench us though." He pauses, a fleeting look of uncertainty on his face. "We need to be on the same page."

Baxter comes trotting out of Becca's room and launches himself at Austin. He scoops the dog up in his arms and begins petting him. Which is just... How the hell can I be mad at him when he looks so damn cute cuddling that ball of fur?

I can't, because this isn't his fault. We're equally responsible. We both knew the risks.

"What do you suggest?" Surely his family has more experience dealing with this sort of thing than mine.

*Mom.*

She's going to kill me.

*If she finds out.*

"We should—"

The front door opens and Becca storms in, a look of fierce determination on her face and a copy of *The Collegian* clutched in her hand.

She slams the door and wheels on us, her eyes flitting from Austin to me.

"I knew it!" she squeals, brandishing the paper. "I knew there was something going on with you two." She frowns, the wind momentarily taken out of her sails. Austin arches a questioning brow, but Becca barrels on before either of us can speak, eyes wide with disbelief. "I can't believe you were holding out on me."

"That article is bullshit," I say, searching for the words to placate her. "It's really not a big deal."

"Beg to differ."

A wide grin spreads over her face as she holds up the paper again. A hot flush creeps up the back of my neck as I realize just how many people have probably seen the picture of me locked in Austin's embrace, his tongue halfway down my throat.

How stupid could we be, thinking we were safe in the stacks?

*There's always someone watching.*

"I mean, it's not front page," Becca adds, "but it's still news. News you should have told your best friend." She pauses long enough to harrumph. "I can't believe I had to learn about it in *The Collegian*. It's all anyone's talking about on campus and on social media." She frowns. "Sorry, bae. Some of the comments are pretty harsh. But just ignore the trolls. I've got your back." She sucks in a breath, eyes going wide. "Oh, this is just like a romance novel. You remember that book where the football player—"

"Becca?" I shoot a meaningful glance at Austin, who much to my annoyance, looks like he's about to bust a gut. I suspect his grip on Baxter is the only thing preventing him from losing it. "Can we not right now?"

She glances at Austin and rolls her eyes. "Fine. But we're talking about this later. In detail."

Now it's my turn to groan. Because when Becca says detail, what she really means is excruciating, play-by-play detail.

The kind that will leave me blushing like a virgin on prom night.

"Fine. Can you give us a minute?"

Satisfied she's going to get the dirty deets later, she prances back to her room. Austin sits Baxter on the floor and he chases after her, leaving us alone in the living room.

"I can't believe this is happening." I rub my temples again, knowing it won't eliminate the pressure building between my temples.

Austin's eyes narrow and when he speaks, his tone is sharper than I've ever heard it. "Because the worst thing that could happen to you is being associated with me?"

He actually sounds hurt and I realize how careless my words came across.

"That's not what I meant." I move closer and rest my hand on his biceps, giving it what I hope is a reassuring squeeze. "It's just that I hate the idea of people speculating about us." I bite my lip as the reality of my situation hits home. "I promised my mom I wouldn't get involved with a football player. I don't know how I'm going to explain this to her."

Because she will find out, eventually.

It would be naive to assume otherwise. She'll hear about it soon enough, either from a news outlet or some well-intentioned friend on social media.

"You think this is any better for me?" Austin asks, frustration lacing his words. His eyes, which are normally clear and bright, rage like coastal storm waters. "I broke my own damn rules and lied about it to the team. How can they trust a captain that lied to them?"

Guilt strikes anew, devouring me like a lion does its prey.

He's not the only one who lied to the team.

A few months ago, I wouldn't have thought twice about it, but now?

The sharp sting of regret pierces my chest. Not regret for being with Austin—I can't bring myself to regret the hours I've spent wrapped in his arms or the pleasure he's given me—just for lying about it.

I made a promise to my mom and to the team, but it was flawed from the start. If joining the team has taught me anything, it's that maybe not all football players are asses. Austin's been nothing but patient and honest with me from the start.

He doesn't deserve to have me piling on when he already feels like shit. "This isn't your fault."

"I doubt the guys on the team would agree."

I lay my head against his chest, listening to the staccato beat of his heart. The fabric of his old Wildcats tee is soft against my cheek, and I close my eyes, soaking up his warmth and inhaling the masculine scent that's uniquely Austin. What he doesn't realize is that he's his own worst critic.

No one will ever be as hard on him as he is on himself.

"You're human," I remind him. "You're bound to make mistakes. We all are. The guys will understand. They'll forgive you if you take responsibility and apologize." I sigh. "My mom, on the other hand..."

His arms close around me, and he lowers his head so it rests on mine. The season's drawing to a close and when it's over, so is our arrangement. The realization hurts more than expected, so I force the thought from my mind and lose myself in his touch.

The quiet moment doesn't last nearly long enough.

My phone rings, and I know without looking that it's my mom. Everyone else I know texts.

"I should get that." I separate myself from Austin and smooth my shirt. Then I suck in a deep breath and square my shoulders. Better to get this over with quick, like ripping off a Band-Aid. I pick up the phone and swipe to accept the call. "Hi, Mom."

"Is it true?" Her voice is carefully controlled, no chipper greeting today.

"Is what true?" I don't know why I bother with this charade. Old habits, I suppose. We both know what she's talking about. And we both know I know.

"Kennedy."

I bite my lip, unsure how to answer.

Austin's watching me, no doubt curious to see how I'll handle the conversation with my mom. Worry lines his brow, and his lips are pressed flat. An uneasy giggle almost slips out, but I manage to stifle it. He's as nervous as I am about this call. It's kind of adorable. And it grounds me.

This is my mom. She may be disappointed in me, but she still loves me.

Always will.

"How did you find out?"

"I have Google alerts on you, dear. It was Joseph's idea." She says it almost cheerfully, like it's perfectly natural to cyberstalk your kid. "Don't change the subject. Is there something going on with you and this boy?"

"His name is Austin. And it's not what it looks like." I cringe. It's worse. "Austin and I are—" I stop, replaying her words in my head. "Wait, who's Joseph?"

"The gentleman I'm dating. Didn't I tell you? I signed up for one of those online matchmaking sites now that I have more free time on my hands."

"Uh, no. I think I'd remember that."

My mom is on a dating site? And who is Joseph?

So. Many. Questions.

Like, is this why she sounds so happy when she ought to be ripping me a new one for breaking my promise?

"Now, about this Austin," she says with less ire than I'd expect. "You know how I feel about football players, but if you're involved with him, I want to meet him."

Who is this person and what's she done with my mother?

"Um, it's not really like that."

The line is silent, and I check to make sure I haven't dropped the call.

"Then what exactly is it like, dear?"

I turn my back on Austin, who's watching me intently, hanging on every word. "We're TWB."

"TWB? Is this internet speak? You know I don't understand that crap."

"Teammates with benefits," I mutter, cheeks burning.

There's a snort of laughter behind me, but I can't bring myself to turn around. I would sooner melt into the floor at this point. My mom and I have always been open about sex, but usually my partner isn't standing right behind me, listening.

"Kennedy Lane Carter. You know I'm a proponent of women's sexual health, but even I have my limits."

Okay, so Mom's not a fan of casual sex. At least, not with football players.

Probably because that's how things started with my father.

Before I can respond, Austin snatches the phone from my hand. I try to grab it back, certain my eyes must be bugging out of my head, but he holds up a finger, asking me to give him a minute.

I shrug. "It's your funeral."

"Mrs. Carter," he says, sounding smooth, confident, and annoyingly calm. "My name is Austin Reid. I'm a senior here at Waverly, studying business administration. I also play football with Kennedy."

*Way to downplay your All-American status.*

"I think I owe you and Kennedy an apology." He turns to face me, gaze moving over me like a lover's caress. "I should've asked your daughter out on a proper date weeks ago. She deserves more than I've been able to give her, and if it weren't for her, I don't know how I'd get through this season. I know you don't have much reason to trust me, but I know how close you and Kennedy are, and I'd like your blessing to take her on a real date."

*He wants to go on a date?*

But...Austin doesn't do dates. He doesn't have the time or energy.

Not when he's so close to making his dreams come true.

Is this a ploy to placate my mother? The team? Coach?

A sour taste rises at the back of my throat.

I'm done playing games and sneaking around. I may not be ready for our time together to end, but I'm done lying. He's got another think coming if he thinks I'm going to fake date him to appease the news outlets or Coach or even my mom.

The *Collegian* article is proof of how quickly things can get out of hand.

I can't hear my mom's reply, but Austin's smile is answer enough. Clearly, he's won her over with his charm.

*Un-freaking-believable.* I get twenty-one years of lectures on douchey football players, and he's got her wrapped around his finger in less than five minutes.

Clearly I need to meet this Joseph guy because this is not the same woman who raised me.

I drop onto the arm of the couch, stewing.

They chat for a few more minutes, and I listen impatiently as Austin tells her more about himself and his upbringing. When they finally disconnect, I stare at him openmouthed.

My own mother didn't say goodbye to me.

What the hell? More importantly, what did she say to him?

"That went well." He hands me the phone, cocky grin securely in place.

His fingers brush mine, and it's a small miracle I manage to ignore the flutter of excitement that races up my arm, settling in my belly.

"What the hell are you doing?" I demand, hopping to my feet. "Asking for my mom's blessing to date me?"

"I meant every word of it." He slips an arm around my waist, pulling me close so my body is flush with his. "I want to take you on a real date. Prove to you not all football players are assholes. If you'll let me."

"You don't have anything to prove to me." I'm already convinced, but he doesn't need to know that. "And you don't have to take me on a date to, I don't know, make things right with everyone else. I'm a big girl. I chose this. Same as you. I can handle the fallout, whatever it may be."

"That didn't come out right. I'm messing this up." He releases his grip on me and scrubs a hand over his face. His large body shifts, and I can almost see the nervous energy coursing through his limbs, forcing him into motion. "I don't have much experience with relationships, and I'll probably screw up a lot, but I'm asking you out because I want to. I enjoy spending time with you and talking to you, and hell, when you're not around, all I can think about is you. You make me crazy in the best way. And I think we should go on a date. Together," he adds, as if there could be any confusion on that point.

A relationship with Austin?

I'd never let myself consider the possibility before. That wasn't the deal.

But as I look at him, at the hope in his beautiful eyes, I can't deny I want it too. A chance to see where things go. To see if maybe the chemistry we share in the bedroom could be a foundation for something more.

"What about the team? Nothing's changed with Coach or the guys."

"We'll figure it out." He grips my hip with his right hand, tugging me close. His erection is pressed to my stomach, and my body reacts in kind, desire curling low in my belly. "Is that a yes?"

"Yes." He leans down and kisses me, slow and deep, our tongues mating in a languid dance. It's nothing like the frenzied kisses that fueled our hookups, but it has the same smoldering heat. I pour myself into the kiss, enjoying the feel of his soft lips on mine. When he pulls away, disbelief rears its ugly head again. "I can't believe my mom is okay with this."

"'Okay' might be overstating things a bit." He laughs, low

and husky, the sound reverberating through my body and sending shivers down my spine. "I've met some overprotective dads, but they've got nothing on your mom. She said she'll neuter me if I break your heart."

I lean in to kiss him again, pausing when our lips are a breath apart. "So don't break my heart."

## 39

# AUSTIN

GETTING up at the ass crack of dawn to grovel wasn't exactly on my bucket list, but fuck, sometimes you have to man up. No way was I going to let Kennedy face Coach until I'd smoothed things over. Not because I don't think she can handle herself, but because that smart mouth of hers would probably get her benched and we need her for this week's game against Indiana.

Me? I'm a pro when it comes to enduring Coach's tirades.

The key is to stay quiet, show the appropriate amount of contrition, and not make the same mistake twice.

So, yeah. I came. I saw. I groveled.

Coach was pissed when he saw the article. Asked me if I was a damn moron, which I guess was fair since he'd expressly forbidden team hookups. The thing is, Coach wants to win and he's not stupid. We may have broken his rules, but we didn't violate NCAA rules and no way in hell are the boosters or the university going to want to see their top players benched for something as trivial as dating.

It's like I told Kennedy. Coach's bark is worse than his bite.

Under all that bluster, the man's really a big old teddy bear.

Coach's punishment? I've got to apologize to the team this

morning, and it'll be up to them to decide what repercussions, if any, I face. It promises to be a lively discussion. I doubt the guys will bench me—they want a national title as badly as I do—but they're sure as shit going to make me sweat it.

Fine by me. I know how to take my lumps.

Besides, I deserve whatever they throw at me.

Now I've got an hour to kill before the team hits the road. Normally, I'd enjoy having the locker room to myself, but today, not so much. I survey the pristine space, looking for anything to occupy my mind. The last thing I need is downtime to dwell on the social media shitstorm or the ass chewing my old man's gonna give me.

He's not big on distractions. Especially ones with the potential to derail my career.

His advice when I came to Waverly? No cheerleaders, no trainers, no teammates.

He labors under the delusion that as long as my hookups aren't attached to the team, the chance for fallout is nil. It's an old-school view, but I haven't bothered to correct him.

No point when I've always kept things casual.

Truth is, he'll be more concerned with bad press than anything else.

He's always trusted that the game comes first and I wouldn't let a woman—or anything else—stand between me and the dream. But bad press? It could negatively impact my draft selection, something he won't tolerate.

Not that the press has been bad. *So far.*

But I've been around sports media long enough to know it's just a matter of time.

The press thrives on scandal. All it'll take is a few trolls to stir the pot.

I scroll through my social media feeds and roll my eyes. The current narrative is sweet and sappy, a modern twist on the old QB-cheerleader cliché.

If they only knew our relationship was more like hate-fucking in the beginning.

Doesn't matter. The more time I spend with Kennedy, the more I realize how much I want her in my life. Sure, she's a spit-fire, but I wouldn't have it any other way.

She gets me. Not the cocky quarterback, but *Austin*. She calls me on my bullshit. She doesn't pander to me because I'm some hotshot football player.

Hell, I'm pretty sure she's attracted to me in spite of it.

Plus, there's the sex.

Fact is, there was no scenario where I was going to walk away at the end of the season.

The *Collegian* article created an opportunity, and I took it.

Of course, it also created a lot of headaches, but I'll handle it, just like I did with Coach. Sure he's pissed, and I would've preferred to wait out the season, but shit happens.

When the guys start pouring into the locker room, I gesture for them to huddle up.

My stomach clenches. Good thing I skipped breakfast. Facing the team is going to be more difficult than taking a verbal beating from Coach. These guys made me captain, chose me to lead the team. They expected more of me and I let them down.

I wipe my hands on my shorts.

Never let them see you sweat, my ass. It's hot as hell in here.

The coaching staff joins us, and Kennedy slips in the back door just under the wire. Can't blame her. I'd do the same in her position.

The team's uncharacteristically quiet. Even for an early morning start.

Their silence speaks volumes.

*No excuses.*

I stare out at the sea of faces, most of which are carved in stone. I don't know if it's a trick of the light or a side effect of the guilt, but whatever they're feeling, it's on me. Doesn't matter if I meant to breed hurt or mistrust, only that I did.

Because splintered teams don't win championships.

*Time to get the focus back where it belongs: on football.*

"I'm sure most of you saw the article in *The Collegian*," I say, forcing myself to meet the eyes of each and every person in the room. "I'm not here to make excuses. I knew Coach's rules and I not only broke them, I lied about it. My selfish actions have brought undue speculation and distraction to the team at a time when we can ill afford them. For that, I'm sorry. As your captain, I expect more from this team and from myself."

I pause, giving them time to process my words.

The room's so damn quiet, I can hear Langley's ragged breath. No one talks. No one moves. Not even Coach. He just watches with flattened brows, stoic expression in place.

"Coach and I had a long talk this morning and we agreed that since the entire team is impacted by my choices, the team should decide the consequences. Up to and including benching."

There are a few surprised faces in the crowd and a murmur starts at the back of the room, slowly increasing in fervor. Can't say I'm surprised. Caught me off guard too when Coach said he'd let the team decide.

I steal a glance at Kennedy. She's chewing her thumbnail, keeping a low profile at the back of the room. I know she's itching to weigh in, but I'm hoping she'll stick to her word and let me deal with the fallout.

Better me than her, captain or not.

No scout wants to recruit a player who can't follow simple directions like keep your dick in your pants, but the impact would be minimal, even if I'm benched for a game. Still, I'm hoping the guys are in a forgiving mood. The thought of riding the bench for the Indy game brings bile to the back of my throat.

I swallow it back down.

The noise in the room has reached fever pitch, and I'm laced tighter than a damn pigskin.

Finally, Daniels, one of the defensive captains, steps forward. He raises a hand and the room falls silent, all eyes pinned on me.

Man, this is fucking brutal.

I'd kind of been hoping Coop or Vaughn would speak up—they're my roommates and I know they have my back no matter what—but it's probably best to have another captain step up.

Still, it's a struggle not to fidget or wipe my hands on my pants.

Hell, it's all I can do to keep from clenching my fists.

"All right, all right," Daniels says, his deep voice carrying easily. I can't help but notice he doesn't look at me. Not a good sign. We're on opposite sides of the ball, but we've always been on good terms. Like me, he's a senior. I can't believe he'd want to see our season blown to shit over a team hookup. "We've got a plane to catch, so if you've got something to say, let's hear it."

Langley's the first one to step forward. "How can we trust you to lead us when you've been lying to us for weeks?"

There's a rumble of assent from the group, and my conviction waivers. He's right. A good leader would've been honest from the start and accepted the consequences.

"We could bench him for a week," Smith suggests, shaking his head in disappointment. "Or two."

*Two weeks?* We'd be out of contention for sure.

"I don't know. You think that's punishment enough?" Tate asks. "He should suffer."

The suggestion is met with cheers.

"There's always the captaincy," Johnson offers with a smirk. "It's not too late to name a new captain."

My palms are sweating in earnest now.

I knew they'd be upset, but I didn't expect it to be this bad. Even Coach wasn't this angry.

"Are we seriously talking about stripping Reid of captaincy?" Daniels asks, scanning the room, expression unreadable.

"You know what I think?" Vaughn says, face grim. "Love means never having to say you're sorry."

There's a snicker from the back of the room, and before I can ask what the hell he's talking about, Smith is up in my personal space, fist raised. I knock it.

"You had me at hello," he croons.

Then Jones is coming at me with puppy-dog eyes. "Losing your kicker, Reid, it was the best thing that ever happened to you. It brought you to Carter."

There's something familiar about his words, like I've heard them before. Then it hits me. They're movie quotes.

Yeah, it takes me a while to catch on. I'm quick like that.

Meanwhile, Kennedy's bent over laughing in the back of the room, a hysterical fit of giggles shaking her entire body.

*Sell out.*

I rub the back of my neck, refusing to acknowledge the heat creeping across my skin. "Any other words of wisdom?"

"Yeah," Coop shouts, a big-ass grin on his face. "Don't have sex, because you will get pregnant and die!"

Parker approaches, doing a creepy little shimmy with his fists up in the air. "You think she's gorgeous. You want to kiss her. You want to hug her. You want to—"

"What kind of movies have you guys been watching?" I ask, sidestepping him as he tries to drag me into his godawful dance.

"All right, cut the shit!" Coach bellows, arms crossed over his chest.

Someone in the back yells, "As you wish!" and the raucous laughter starts anew.

When it finally quiets down, Coach tries again. "Am I to understand we're moving on?"

"Yes, sir." Daniels claps me on the back with a hearty grin. "We chose Reid to lead us, and we stand by that decision." To me he whispers, "You're not half the sneaky bastard you think. The team's known about you and Carter for weeks." My jaw nearly hits the floor. They've known all this time? Daniels turns back to Coach. "Reid's suffered enough. And if he hasn't, we figure Carter will see to his punishment."

I could kiss the fucker.

# 40

# KENNEDY

I WATCH as Austin's taillights recede down the circular drive. Part of me wants to chase after him, beg him to stay. Or better yet, whisk me back to the safety of my apartment. I fidget with the waistband of my black skirt and smooth my white blouse.

*It's not too late to call Uber.*

What the hell made me think I could do this alone?

I sigh. Oh, right. The endorphins from our win over Indy.

*Stupid hormones*. Should've known it wouldn't last.

Now I'm on the hook for dinner with my dad.

After weeks of dodging his calls and texts, I caved. I can't remember the last time I was this freaking nervous. My stomach is tangled in knots.

And the knots? They have knots.

I won't be able to eat a thing.

I look down at my black ballet flats and then up at the sprawling, white brick hotel where he's staying. It's a landmark in College Park, the kind of place Mom and I could never afford to stay. Not even for a night.

Anger punches through me, but I force it down.

I don't have a clue how my dad's paying for it, and I don't

care. I'm not here to slash open old wounds. I'm here to see if there's anything salvageable in our relationship.

The prospect scares the crap out of me.

*Maybe I can stop at the bar for a drink.*

Or not. The biting November wind swirls around me like a twister, raising goose bumps on my legs and destroying my neatly combed hair. Several strands get stuck in my lip gloss. Of course they do. I pull them free and trudge up the steps to the massive double doors.

Once inside, I'm greeted with warmth and light and an overly helpful concierge who personally escorts me to the restaurant.

I give the hostess my name and am pleasantly surprised when she moves to seat me immediately. My father's on time. It's probably a first.

That has to be a good sign, right?

I smooth my hair, determined to make a good impression. I haven't seen my father in almost four years. When he told Mom and me he couldn't afford to help with my college tuition—despite years of not paying child support—and wished me the best of luck.

Like luck would pay the bills.

But a lot's changed since then. I've changed.

The fact that we're about to share a meal is testament to that fact.

Spending time with Austin, getting to know him, has me questioning everything I thought I knew about football players, about my father. Wondering if maybe I should give my dad a second chance. Wondering if he deserves it, if perhaps he's changed too.

What would it be like to have my father in my life?

I have no idea. And that scares the hell out of me because I'm not a little girl anymore.

I'm a grown woman. One who doesn't really even know her father, although I can't deny I want to. Some sad, desperate part of me still wants him in my life, despite everything. To have him love me unconditionally. To support my hopes and dreams. To walk me down the aisle one day.

*To be a meaningful part of my life.*

I want it so badly it's become a dull ache in my chest.

It might be too much to hope for after everything he's put Mom and me through. Which is why I didn't tell her I was seeing him. She wouldn't approve. And I don't want to hurt her —she's been my mother, my father, and my best friend for twenty-one years—but I can't deny this is something I need to do.

*For me.*

I'll know soon enough if it was the right choice.

The hostess leads me to a table in the back corner of the restaurant, our feet padding silently over the plush carpet. We weave through a sea of empty tables set with crisp white linens, blue napkins, and enough silverware to give me a panic attack. She stops, and I nearly crash into her.

*Focus.*

The hostess steps aside and gestures to an empty chair, leaving me face-to-face with my dad. I'd forgotten how much we look alike. Same wavy hair, same dark eyes, same broad smile. One that shows all his teeth, although I suspect he shares his more freely. The years have been good to him—despite his life-style—and I'm hit with another stab of resentment.

Mom would probably have a few less worry lines if he'd ever bothered to help out.

But tonight is about second chances, not dredging up the past. If he's really changed, if he truly wants to start over, maybe I could forgive him. Maybe I could make a place for him in my life.

After all, he is my father.

He stands and embraces me in an awkward hug, his long arms wrapped around my shoulders. I return the gesture, but it's a relief when we break apart.

Fuck. We can't even hug properly. This meal has disaster written all over it.

*Be. Positive.*

"Kenny." He gestures for me to sit and slides smoothly back into his own chair. "It's so good to see you."

"Kennedy," I say, correcting him as I drop into my seat and cross my ankles.

The hostess scurries off to find the server and the urge to follow her is strong.

"Kennedy." He nods in acknowledgment. "How have you been?"

Talk about a loaded question. Where do I even start?

My stomach clenches, and I reach for my water and take an uncivilized gulp. My mouth is suddenly parched. This feels all wrong, but I force myself to paste on a smile and try. Otherwise, what was the point?

"School's going well, although I'm looking forward to graduation in the spring."

His smile is encouraging, and we make small talk as we look over the menu.

When the server finally arrives to recite the daily specials, I'm relieved my father suggests we place our orders. He doesn't want this meal to drag out any more than I do. Which isn't necessarily a bad thing.

It just means we're both being cautious, wading slowly into uncertain waters.

I should be thrilled we're on the same page, right?

Once our orders are placed, the conversation turns to football. I should've expected as much. It might be the one thing we actually have in common.

The irony isn't lost on me.

"So, how do you like playing football at Waverly?" He leans forward, resting his forearms on the table. "The team treating you well?"

I bite my lip, contemplating my response.

"I only joined the team because they offered me a full scholarship, but I enjoy the game more than I thought I would." I would swear his eyes darken, but when I blink, they remain bright and interested. "I'm not, however, a fan of the pressure that comes with kicking a field goal when the game's on the line. That part kind of sucks."

"You think that's bad? Try being the QB. Every loss hangs on your shoulders." He sips his whiskey. "One day you're the prized bull, the next you're sent to slaughter."

I know he's talking about his experience, but it's Austin I picture in my mind's eye. Austin who carries the weight of the team on his shoulders, whether anyone expects him to or not.

Frankly, I'm surprised my father felt that same burden.

God knows the only side of him I've seen in the past is a selfish one.

Tonight's different, though. He's showing interest in my life, trying to connect with me.

"Don't get me wrong. I know how lucky I am to be playing D1 football, and I certainly don't think I have the toughest job on the team. I'm just not used to being in the spotlight like that. It's different in soccer."

My father levels his gaze at me. "Speaking of the spotlight, I should probably congratulate you on being the first woman to land a D1 football scholarship. That's a big deal."

I feel a blush creep over my cheeks. I'd rather he compliment me on making the Dean's List. At least that was a goal I actively worked toward.

"Thanks, but it's less of an accomplishment than the result of a perfect storm."

He raises a hand dismissively. "Sometimes it's about being in the right place at the right time. And how you leverage the opportunity."

I chew my lip, considering.

"You're probably right. The scholarship's allowed me to drop work study and spend more time on my entry for the ACME design competition." I'm practically beaming now, my lips spread thin over my teeth. I can't help it. Enzo and I have been working so hard, and I have a good feeling about this year's competition. "It's *the* design competition for mechanical engineers. The winners are pretty much guaranteed jobs at one of the top firms after graduation."

He drums his fingers on the table, unmoved by my enthusiasm.

I get it. Engineering isn't for everyone. I just figured he'd be excited for me.

"Kennedy, I think you're missing the bigger picture here."

Bigger picture? What could be bigger than my future?

He leans in close, as if he's sharing something confidential. "You've got one shot to turn your fifteen minutes of fame into a sustainable platform. You're the first woman to get a D1 scholarship and clock meaningful game time. Plus, you've got a pretty face. The media loves you."

My belly rolls like a ship in a storm.

*Goddamn pirate books.*

This is so not the time for pirate similes. Not when his every word lands like a blow, shattering everything I've worked so hard to build.

"Leave the engineering stuff to the geeks and focus on your

brand. You're underleveraged. You should be doing interviews every week to attract endorsement deals. Hell, you guys win a national championship, you might even be able to play in one of the semi-pro leagues."

He looks at me expectantly, completely unaware his dismissal of all my hard work—of my dreams—has gutted me. I don't want to be a pretty face or a football player or a brand ambassador. I want to make a name for myself in the world of STEM, where I'll be recognized for my ability to use my brain.

*Is that really so hard to understand?*

I clench my napkin in my fist as heat spreads across my face. Anger claws at the back of my throat, but the words don't come.

He's so wrapped up in his sales pitch, he's oblivious to the harm his words have caused.

"I'm telling you, Kenny. What you need is a manager to hook you up with prime time media. Someone with connections. Someone who'd have the networks eating out of their hand." He pauses and tips a glass of whiskey to his lips, draining it. His cheeks are flushed, a sure sign it's not his first drink of the evening. "Your mom dropped the ball here, but I can fix it. My fifteen percent fee is nothing compared to the money you'll rake in."

*How dare he.*

I see red at the mention of my mom, and a vein in my forehead begins to pulse. This was a mistake. I never should have agreed to dinner.

"Especially now that you've hooked a big fish," he continues, unfazed. "Number one draft prospect? Not bad, kid. Not bad at all."

I'm trembling with rage, and it's all I can do not to climb over the table and strangle him with his own napkin.

"You're disgusting," I hiss, climbing to my feet. My voice wavers, but not my resolution. I've got years of pent-up rage and he deserves every last bit of it. "I should've known you weren't here for me, just a quick buck. You haven't changed at all. You're the same selfish, self-absorbed asshole you've been my whole life."

I'm breathing hard, nostrils flared, but I can't stop.

Not even when he glares at me and hardens his jaw.

"You know what the worst part is? I wanted it to be true. I wanted so badly for you to give a damn about me, despite twenty-one years of evidence to the contrary. And you know what? The only mistake my mother ever made was not kicking your sorry ass to the curb the minute she realized what a selfish bastard you are."

I turn on my heel, not bothering to wait for a response.

I've had enough of his bullshit to last a lifetime.

The hostess stares openmouthed as I stalk past. This sort of thing probably doesn't happen often at the Four Diamond hotel, but I'll be damned before I apologize.

The night is crisp and cold when I step outside, but I gulp the cool air down like it's the remedy for my burning anger. I'm not sure if it helps, but there's no denying the shift in my emotions as fury gives way to hurt. Tears stream down my face before I can stop them, and the tiny bubble of hope I'd nurtured fractures, vanishing like any possibility of a relationship with my father.

I pull my phone from my purse and text Austin through tear-filled eyes.

At times like this, I usually call my mom, but that's out of the question.

Knowing I met with my dad would only hurt her.

She'd probably hunt him down and castrate him if she knew how he'd behaved. How he hurt me.

No, the only person I can count on right now is Austin.

Turns out, he's waiting at a coffee shop just up the street. The headlights of the Jeep round the drive in less than three minutes, and he's at my side before I can open the passenger door. He reaches for me, a grim expression on his face, and I tumble into his arms, a streaky, tearstained mess.

I doubt this is how he pictured spending his Sunday evening, but Austin holds me tight, wrapping me in his warm embrace as he kisses the top of my head. He doesn't bother with meaningless platitudes or apologies, and I'm thankful for it. I just need to be held, to inhale the scent of his spicy cologne and listen to the steady beat of his heart.

He seems to understand exactly what I need, even without words, and I marvel at how far we've come since that day on the soccer field. How could I have ever believed he was like my father?

# 41

## AUSTIN

"YOU'RE KILLING ME."

Kennedy bends over, her perfect ass on display in a pair of leggings that look like they might be painted on. I'm pretty sure she's not wearing underwear, which does nothing to help my current semihard situation.

We're hanging at her apartment, and I'm counting down the minutes until Enzo leaves so I can have my way with my woman. Enzo and Kennedy are mostly just ignoring me and trying to work out the bugs on their robot. It's a squat little fucker with googly eyes, lots of moving parts, and a remote they won't let me touch, because, and I quote, *"It's sensitive."*

Like I'm going to manhandle it or something.

I've got great hands, as evidenced by my performance against Indiana. Nailed their asses to the wall, putting us one step closer to the championship game. More importantly, I'm pretty sure the only person in the apartment who's ever gone full Hulk mode is Kennedy.

But I don't point it out because I want to get laid later.

"Hush." She gets down on her knees to inspect the robot and

I watch, transfixed, as she presses her cheek to the floor with her ass up in the air.

*For the love of God, is she trying to kill me?*

So much for semihard. My cock is now pressed uncomfortably against my zipper, and this little study group has shown no signs of fatigue.

It's going to be a long fucking night.

My only consolation?

It won't be nearly as long as the evening I spent in the coffee shop, tapping my boot on the tile floor, hoping Kennedy's father wouldn't prove to be a grade A piece of shit. I wanted so badly for it to work out for her. She deserves better than the hand she's been dealt, and I know it wasn't easy for her to give him another chance. To let herself be vulnerable.

I still can't believe that asshole came sniffing around just to make a buck off her.

Just the thought of it heats my blood.

She's his only kid, for fuck's sake.

My old man might push me, but I know he loves me. He'd never try to take advantage of me, and he'd squash anyone who did. That's what it means to be family.

Obviously, her father doesn't get the concept.

*His loss.* If he can't see what an amazing woman his daughter is, he doesn't deserve her.

Still, I hope we never cross paths.

He hurt Kennedy. No way I'll give him the chance to do it again.

A wave of protectiveness surges through me.

I abandon my Global Marketing text and join them in the tiny kitchen. The robot is rolling around, knocking down one plastic tube after another. I'm no expert, but I'm pretty sure it's not supposed to be doing that. I watch as the bot takes down another tube, the ball atop hitting the floor and rolling toward the stove where it joins six other balls of varying sizes.

"Dammit." Kennedy plants her fists on her hips, an adorable little wrinkle forming on her brow. Can't say I blame her for being frustrated. They've been tinkering with the robot for hours. "I really thought we had it that time."

"Can I try?"

There's a resounding "No!" and they start bickering about whether the issue is the robot's response time or the sensitivity of the remote.

Me? I think it's the drivers.

It's clear they haven't played Mario Kart a day in their lives.

Enzo sits the remote down and starts jotting down notes. I grab it and set the little fucker to task.

I collect two balls and drop them in the designated box without knocking over a single tube.

"How'd you do that?" Kennedy demands.

I smirk. "Years of practice."

She narrows her eyes, and I shrug. "What? I play a lot of video games. We can't all have your STEM-loving brainpower."

"Go again," Enzo says, putting his notes aside.

He resets the grid, righting the fallen tubes and balls with a practiced hand.

When he's done, I maneuver the robot around the kitchen—taking a long, indirect route to better showcase my mad driving skills—and select two more balls and deposit them in the bin as they watch in disbelief.

"Show off." Kennedy sighs, toying with the end of her braid. "So, basically we just need to practice."

"That's a good thing." Enzo grins. "It means the problem isn't the design."

"Nope," I say, cheerfully handing over the remote. "It's your total lack of skill with a joystick."

They both glare at me.

"You know, this thing would be way cooler if it could battle. Did you think about putting like a cutting tool or a hammer or something on it? When I was a kid, I used to watch this show—"

"Absolutely not." Kennedy rolls her eyes, but it's all for show. She wants to laugh. I can see it in the tilt of her lips. And after the week she's had? She deserves it. Of course, I can think of better ways to work the tension from her body, but Enzo's got to go. "No BattleBots."

"Too bad. It would be better that way." I hook a thumb at Enzo. "Ask him. He knows what I'm saying."

"Man, leave me out of this." Enzo flicks his attention to Kennedy. "Don't listen to him. The design is perfect just the way it is."

"Thank you." She hops to her feet and turns her attention on me. She gets up in my personal space, poking me in the chest with her finger. "This is important. It's my last chance to final." She's so close I can smell her flowery shampoo. "I've been close before, but never made it." She looks up at me with those big, dark eyes, excitement flaring in their depths. "I need to be on that stage."

"You will be." I snake a hand around her waist so it rests just above her ass. "But I can't help it if all this sexy nerd power gets me excited."

"We've got work to do," Enzo chides, keeping his eyes glued to the robot. "Don't go getting my partner all hot and bothered."

"Too late." His head jerks toward me. I wink at him for good measure. It's a total Coop move, but I can't deny it's effective.

"That's it. I'm calling it a night." Enzo grabs his backpack and begins shoving books and leftover parts inside. "It's getting too damn weird up in here." He turns to Kennedy. "If you're cool with it, I'll take the bot home and practice my moves tonight?"

"Sure."

I lower my mouth to her ear and whisper, "Don't worry, gorgeous. You can practice your moves on me."

# 42

## KENNEDY

True to his word, Austin gives me free rein over his body once Enzo is gone. I waste no time stripping him of his white tee, although I leave his track pants on. After that crack about my robot driving skills, which were admittedly terrible, he's due for a little punishment. Those pants aren't coming off until I say so, and I intend to inflict plenty of sweet torture between now and then.

We're making out on the couch, and I'm lavishing kisses over his rock-solid pecs, teasing him with my tongue, when my phone rings.

"Let it go to voice mail."

Austin grinds his hips against mine. The hard swell of his erection teases my clit through the thin fabric of my leggings. It's a convincing argument, and I'm tempted to ignore the phone.

Then I remember the robot.

I slide my hand between our bodies, grasping his cock in my hand. I give a gentle squeeze and drag my fingers up the length of his shaft. He makes a sound that's half growl, half moan.

I smile sweetly. "You want me to ride your cock?"

"Fuck, yeah."

"Sorry, babe. You'll have to wait." I give him another languid stroke. "That's my mom's ringtone. She'll worry if I don't answer."

"Jesus, Kennedy." He struggles to sit up with me on top of him. "You're cruel."

I pat his chest and reach for the phone. "What was that you were saying about my skill with a joystick?"

He rolls his eyes. "I take it all back. Just please don't ever mention your mom when you've got your hand on my dick. No offense, but it's a total boner killer."

"Don't make fun of my driving skills and I won't." I swipe to answer the call and slide off his lap, settling in next to him. "Hi, Mom."

"Hi, sweetie. What are you up to?"

"Not much. Just hanging out with Austin. He's helping me with my stick handling." His eyes nearly bug out of his head, and it's all I can do not to laugh. "Apparently I didn't play enough video games growing up, so he's giving me pointers on using a joystick to maneuver the robot."

"Sounds like fun," she says, a cheerful note in her voice. "Tell him I said hello."

Okay. I really need to meet this Joseph guy she's dating, because that's so not the reaction I was expecting. A horrific realization hits to me. Is she having sex with this guy? Is that why she's so happy all the time?

*Nopenopenope.*

Don't even go there. I'm thrilled Mom's found someone she enjoys spending time with, but I am in no way prepared to think about her getting down and dirty with some internet dude.

Just. No.

"Speaking of which," she says, putting an end to my speculation about her hopefully nonexistent sex life and dragging me back to the conversation at hand. *Crap.* What were we talking about anyway? "I wasn't able to get Friday off, so I'll have to miss the first day of the competition. But I'll be there Saturday and Sunday, so I'll get to see you compete and catch the Michigan game."

My heart sinks. Should've known getting three days off would be impossible.

"Coach was concerned about Enzo and me competing on game day." I pause and lick my lips. They're dry as bone. "So the contest runners agreed to move us to a Friday time slot."

The line goes quiet.

She's probably beating herself up. Which is ridiculous. Sure, she's missed games and competitions over the years, but it couldn't be helped. Priority one had to be keeping a roof over our heads and food on the table. Besides, I'm twenty-one freaking years old. Next year I'll be on my own. I shouldn't need my mother in the crowd cheering me on.

But I do.

The idea of presenting in front of so many people scares the hell out of me.

It doesn't matter how many times I do it, it never gets any easier. The anxiety was so bad last year I thought I was going to pass out. And that was after Becca's mom prescribed me anti-anxiety pills for the occasion.

Not that I can tell Mom any of that. She probably feels bad enough as it is.

"Don't worry." I force a half-hearted smile to my lips. "The awards ceremony is on Sunday, so you'll get to see Enzo and me up onstage when we win. That's the most important thing."

She sighs, and I can practically hear the relief in her words. "Thank you for understanding, sweetie. You know I'd be there if I could. You're going to do great."

I nod before remembering she can't see me. "Of course. We've been busting our butts."

"All right, well, don't let me keep you from your...what did you call it? Stick handling?"

I can't help it. I laugh out loud. Apparently I'm not as mature as I like to think. "Yeah. Stick handling."

"Is Austin treating you well?"

*There's the woman I know and love.*

"The best," I say truthfully.

Any doubts I had about Austin being boyfriend material vanished when he scraped me up off the ground after dinner with my dad. If it weren't for Austin's support, I probably would've spent the week in bed eating Dove Promises and crying into my pillow. The thing is, I know my dad is the one with a problem, not me, but that doesn't make it hurt any less.

"Good. I look forward to meeting him when I come to visit."

"Meeting him?" I steal a glance at Austin.

He doesn't look overly concerned about the prospect, but of course, he's faced worse. Or so he thinks. Maybe he's forgotten about my mom's threat to neuter him. Just as well, I guess. She's using her no-nonsense voice, which means she's not going to let this go.

"Of course. How about I take you both to dinner Sunday after the awards ceremony?"

I mouth *Dinner Sunday?* and Austin nods his head. "Sure, Mom. Sounds great."

We wrap up the call and I sink back into the cushions of the couch. Austin kisses my neck, but I'm not into it. Which makes no sense, because, hello, he's hot AF.

It doesn't take him long to notice my total lack of enthusiasm.

He pulls back, cupping my cheek in his hand. "What's wrong?"

I toy with the hem of my shirt, hands shaking.

"I'm worried about the competition. My mom just found out

she's not going to be able to make it on Friday to see me compete. It's not her fault," I say, the words flowing like word vomit. God forbid he thinks both of my parents are selfish assholes. "She has to work. But I have a really hard time with public speaking and...the prospect of presenting to such a large crowd without any support is terrifying. Last year I almost passed out."

I don't mention that while I didn't pass out, I did puke my guts out in the bathroom before the competition started.

"Hey." He tucks a loose strand of hair behind my ear. "You're going to be amazing. You play ball in front of a much larger audience every week. It's no different."

I laugh, but it's hollow and devoid of humor.

"Trust me when I say it's very different. If it was as easy as going out there and kicking a ball, something I've done countless times, I'd be money." He doesn't look convinced, so I try to explain it to him as best I can. "When I'm on the field, I'm just another pair of cleats, a player hidden by a helmet. Sure, the fans know it's me. But they can't see my face and I can't see theirs. It's all a blur. I'm practically anonymous." I snuggle under his arm, letting his body heat warm my skin. "During the competition, I have to speak. To look the judging panel in the eye and present my ideas. Answer questions about the design and mechanics while they score my responses and assess my competency. What if I choke?"

It's a real possibility. I'm the world's worst public speaker.

Sweaty palms, shaky voice, fifty-fifty shot of projectile vomiting.

The added pressure of knowing it's my last chance to final isn't helping.

For four years, I've been dreaming of winning this competition. It's my version of a national football championship and I want it so badly I can taste it. This must be how Austin feels every time he steps onto the field, knowing even one loss could keep him from his dream.

I have no clue how he shoulders this kind of pressure every day. He makes it look easy. Meanwhile, I'm over here contemplating a nervous breakdown.

"You won't choke." He says it with such conviction I almost believe him. "I'll be there with you every step of the way."

I look up at him from under my lashes. I've only really ever put my trust in my mom. This is a small gesture on his part, but it feels like a big one.

It feels like a turning point.

"Promise?"

"There's nowhere else I'd rather be."

## 43

## AUSTIN

I JOG across the parking lot and duck into the grocery store, hoping they'll have a decent floral department. I've never bought a woman flowers before, and I don't have a clue what I'm doing. Which means there's a good chance I'll screw it up.

Are there rules about colors? And flower types?

The last thing I want to do is send the wrong message.

*Should've checked Google.*

It's times like this I miss my mom the most. She was big on philanthropy and was always planning one high-society fundraiser or another. She knew all about this kind of stuff. Hell, she would've been thrilled to give me advice on how to be relationship goals, because she would've accepted nothing less from her only son.

*Relationship.*

The word still feels awkward and clumsy.

I've been labeled a lot of things: All-American, son, quarterback, friend, captain, hookup. But never boyfriend. It's not a label I expected.

Not this year, anyway.

A thrill races up my spine. Being able to say Kennedy is mine and mine alone tends to have that effect. Although they'll never have the chance to meet, I know my mom would love her. Would love her brains and wit and the way she doesn't take crap from anyone. Would love her giant heart and the fact that after so much hurt, she was still willing to give her old man a second chance, whether he deserved it or not.

I approach the floral department, taking in the rainbow of blossoms that fill the racks, and hope for the best. Because no way in hell am I going to text my roommates for advice. I'd never hear the end of it.

Plus, I'm tight on time, despite cutting my last class of the day.

I can't afford to miss classes, but it'll be worth it to see the smile on my girl's face.

Kennedy's worked so hard on this competition. She's even taught me a thing or two about puppet robots and pressure sensors. She deserves to celebrate her accomplishment, win or lose.

Not that she'll lose.

She's been practicing with the robot every spare minute. Possibly to distract herself from the thought of public speaking. Either way, it's paid off. She maneuvered it around the kitchen with expert precision last night while Becca and I cheered her on.

I scan the floral department, dismissing the potted plants and bouquets that look like Thanksgiving centerpieces. I choose a bouquet wrapped in brown paper. Orchids and roses, according to the shelf tag. They're the palest shade of pink I've ever seen—almost ivory—and they're perfect. I tuck them under my arm and head for the register.

I need to hustle. I've only got a few hours to catch the competition and get to practice.

We've been busting our asses this week, preparing for

tomorrow's game against Michigan. It's a big one and alumni are already descending on College Park, making traffic a nightmare. Waverly has a long-standing rivalry with the Wolverines and the games are always close, the stadium filled to capacity. With an 8-1 record, we're leading the conference and even though the only thing I should be thinking about is tomorrow's game, Kennedy rules my thoughts as I tap my card at the self-checkout.

I'm grinning like a fool by the time I slide behind the wheel of the Jeep. It doesn't matter. Things are going my way, and I've got the rare opportunity to spend a couple of hours with my girl on a Friday afternoon.

Plenty of time to worry about football later.

My phone rings and Dad flashes on the screen. I punch the accept button on the steering wheel, a sense of dread seeping into my bones.

"Where are you?" he demands without preamble.

"On campus." He doesn't need to know I ditched Global Marketing.

He's slow to respond. "You didn't forget about lunch with John, did you? I told you to write it on the calendar."

*Fuck.*

How could I have forgotten? Coach's been riding me about the scout visits all week, trying to get me to commit to the Sunday workout. It's all anyone's been talking about in the locker room and on the field. Even the underclassmen are hoping to make an impression.

Me? I've been trying to block out the noise and ignore the spectators.

I grit my teeth and grip the wheel tighter.

Maybe I was a little too focused because I completely forgot about lunch with Hays.

I glance down at my clothes. A Waverly polo and jeans.

My father will expect better, but there's no time to go home and change. It'll have to do. I check my rearview mirror and swing a U-turn.

The sooner I get there, the sooner I can leave.

"No, of course not," I lie, feeling like an asshole. "I'm on my way, but I can't stay long. Kennedy's competing in a mechanical engineering contest this afternoon and I promised to be there."

When I arrive at the restaurant, my father and Hays are already seated with drinks in hand, no doubt toasting the good old days. The scent of seared beef hangs in the air, but even so, I'm not a fan of the place. It's got an old-school vibe: heavy wood trim, leather-back chairs, pristine white linens. It's dark and stuffy and I'd be just as happy grabbing a burger at the Diner, but it's not up to me.

They stand to greet me and I apologize for being late. Pittsburgh may not be my first choice, but I don't want Hays to think I'm an entitled asshole. He's a scout for one of the best teams in the NFL, and I know his time is valuable.

"Don't sweat it." He claps me on the back and takes a swig of his beer. I can't help but notice he's wearing the team colors. "We just got here ourselves."

We make small talk as we wait for the server to come by, discussing Pittsburgh's chances of making the playoffs. My foot is tapping a nervous beat under the table, every minute feeling like an eternity as the clock ticks down to Kennedy's three-thirty presentation. I'll be cutting it close, but she won't care if I miss her competitors as long as I'm there for her.

Once we've ordered, talk turns to Waverly's performance.

Hays crosses his arms and studies me. "You look good, Austin."

"I feel good, sir."

"I should think so." Hays exchanges a conspiratorial look with my father. "You're eight and one. Plenty of guys in the conference who'd kill for that record."

"They've got a real shot at the national championship," my father agrees.

I shrug. "I've got a great team. It's easy to win games when you're playing with a first-rate offense."

Hays laughs and slaps his knee. "You sure this is your kid, Reid? God knows you don't have a humble bone in your body."

My dad laughs good-naturedly, but when he turns to me, there's sadness in his eyes. "He gets it from his mother. He got all the good stuff from her."

My throat closes up. I want—*need*—to say something, but I'm not sure how to respond. It's the first time I can ever remember my father comparing me to my mother. It means more than he realizes. But this isn't the time or the place to unpack all our baggage. I'm not sure it'll ever be the right time. There are too many unspoken truths between us, and I don't have the first clue where to start.

Fortunately, Hays easily steers the conversation back to football.

"Glad to hear it. I'm always on the lookout for players with a good head on their shoulders. So many kids these days have big egos and bigger attitudes. That doesn't fly in Pittsburgh." Hays sips his beer. "Coach Collins tells me that won't be an issue for you."

"No, sir. I take my role as a team leader very seriously. I just want to play ball for a good program."

I'm careful not to express interest in Pittsburgh, not that it matters since it's assumed.

"Don't sweat the draft. You'll land in a good program." Hays chuckles and shakes his head. "Doesn't matter if the worst team in the league gets first pick. There'll be plenty of trades made behind the scenes. Hell, things go right, you could end up playing for your old man's team if you finish the season strong."

"Austin won't settle for anything less than a national title, isn't that right?"

"Yes, sir." I drum my fingers on the table.

*Where the hell is our food?*

It's midafternoon, and the place isn't exactly busy. We've already burned twenty minutes.

I take a deep breath, willing the tension to leave my body. I can still make it to the competition. It's doable.

"Well, leadership wants you, the coaching staff wants you, and so do the fans," Hays says, toying with his beer. "You're a legacy."

The waitress stops at the table to let us know our food will be up shortly. My father and Hays order another round of drinks. I order another water. I need to stay hydrated for practice, even if I am desperate to get this over with.

It's another fifteen minutes until our food arrives.

Hays and my dad are still discussing my prospects in Pittsburgh, but I can't concentrate. Twice Hays has to repeat himself because I'm not paying attention. It's the longest fucking meal of my life, and yet the minutes continue to tick by, my anxiety increasing each time I check my phone.

There's a text from Kennedy.

*Kennedy: Where are you?*

I glance at Hays, confirming he and my father are too deep in their hypothetical draft to care if I'm texting, and shoot her a quick reply.

*Me: Finishing up lunch with my dad and the scout from Pittsburgh. Don't worry, gorgeous. I'll be there.*

It's a bit of an exaggeration considering Hays has only eaten half his entrée, but I don't want her to worry. I force myself to join the conversation, hoping if I do more of the talking, Hays will do more eating.

It works. To a point.

The man is the slowest eater on the planet. How have I never noticed this before?

I check the time again, a cold sweat breaking out on the back of my neck. I'm running out of time. If I don't get on the road soon, I'm going to miss Kennedy's presentation. My tapping foot has reached a breakneck pace, but I can't seem to slow it down.

*I can't be late. I promised her I'd be there. She needs me.*

After what feels like an eternity, the server finally clears our plates.

*Hallelujah.*

When Hays orders another round of drinks for the table, I go into full-on panic mode.

I pride myself on staying calm under pressure, but something's gotta give.

Hays excuses himself to hit the head and I turn to my dad, already half out of my chair. "I need to go. If I leave now, I can still make it in time for Kennedy's presentation."

His eyes widen in surprise, but his voice is carefully controlled when he speaks. It's his media voice, the one he always uses when talking to the press. Doesn't matter if it's good news or bad news or something in between, he's mastered the art of playing it cool.

"Absolutely not. If you leave now, it's an insult to the organization." He gestures for me to sit down. "The least you can do is stay until John finishes his drink."

"But—"

"No buts." He drills the table with his pointer finger. "What could be more important than achieving your dream?"

I falter. I know he means well. That he wants the best for me, but I'm not entirely sure he knows what that is.

Hell, I'm not even sure if I know.

"Kennedy needs me."

"This girl again?" My father arches a disapproving brow, the closest he'll come to showing displeasure in public. He's made it clear he thinks a relationship is an unnecessary distraction, but we've agreed to disagree. As long as my performance doesn't suffer. "Look, son, if this girl really cares about you, she'll understand. This meeting? It's about securing your future and maybe hers too, if she's that important to you."

I slide back into my chair, weighing my father's words.

My entire life he's been my biggest fan. We may not agree on everything, but he's always supported me. Without him, I wouldn't be half the athlete I am. Sure, there are days I wish we could be a normal family, but it's not in the cards.

We're a football family, and I can't throw it all away now.

Kennedy will understand, won't she?

I'm not sure, but in the end, I acquiesce to my father's wishes. Just as I've done for the last twenty-one years. Just as he knew I would. Hays returns and as they continue reminiscing about their glory days, I can't help but wonder if I've just made the biggest mistake of my life.

## 44

## KENNEDY

*Where the eff is Austin?* He promised he'd be here and we're on in five minutes. I straighten my skirt and smooth my hair. My heart is hammering in my chest and it's entirely possible I'm going to pass out. I already warned Enzo. He swears he'll catch me, though, if I go down, I might be better off cracking my head open so I have an excuse to leave.

No way I'd be able to get back up and finish the presentation after that kind of humiliation.

The arena is packed, most of the students anxious to check out the competition.

Bodies press in on all sides, the hum of conversation an incessant buzz that's impossible to block out. I follow Enzo's lead as he shoulders his way to the front of the crowd gathered around ring number three. It's one of five identical rings that's been set up for the timed trials.

It's also where we'll be presenting.

I scan the faces circling the makeshift arena, noting most wear ACME badges around their necks. While I'm verging on a panic attack, everyone else looks so cool and collected.

*How is that possible?*

The idea of facing the judges scares the crap out of me.

I draw a deep breath and blow it out through my nose, trying to channel some of Enzo's calm. He's on his own—Emma has a late class—and he's not freaking out. The difference is, he's not terrified of speaking in front of a crowd.

*Unlike me.*

It doesn't matter if it's in the classroom or in competition, I *hate* public speaking. Unfortunately, it's a key component of the ACME Student Design Competition. All team members must participate in the presentation.

*Shit. I really should've gotten my prescription for anti-anxiety meds refilled.*

Too late now.

I just need to focus. I got through the presentation last year and I can do it again. I just have to finish.

It doesn't matter if my voice shakes as long as the robot kicks ass.

I sneak a peek at the group currently competing. Their bot is doing well, and they've only knocked over one tube. Not bad, but I've seen others complete the task more quickly.

They're no threat.

I won't be either if I pass out.

"Relax." Enzo lays his free hand on my shoulder. The other holds our sizing box, which houses our robot, replacement batteries, and other supplies we might need while competing. "We're going to kill it."

"I like your confidence." God knows one of us needs to have some. I press my hands to my thighs, wiping my sweaty palms on my black dress pants. This can't be over soon enough. "I couldn't have done this without you. Thanks for saving my butt."

"Please." He waves me off. "When we win first place and I add it to my resume, I'll be thanking you."

The team ahead of us collects their robot and vacates the arena.

I swallow and force myself to put one foot in front of the other as Enzo and I move into position. The judges watch intently as we set up Sparky—Enzo's pet name for our bot—and verify its remote is synced. We only have sixty seconds to set up. Then it's on to the presentation portion.

Once Sparky is powered up, I turn to the judges.

*All eight of them.*

Which is nothing compared to the countless bodies milling around the arena, pressing closer to hear about Sparky's design.

*Oh, God.* This would be so much easier if I had a familiar face in the crowd.

But Mom's working and Becca's got an away game and Austin...Austin's abandoning me the one time I need him most. He promised to be here and he's not. I'm alone. And I'm going to pass out and ruin our chances at winning. Everything we worked so hard for, out the window because of my stupid fear. No awards ceremony. No job offers. No—

Enzo squeezes my shoulder, and I realize we're on the clock.

I lick my lips, trying to close the lid on my fear. The judges are just people. Super-smart engineering people, but people nonetheless.

Even if they hate our presentation, it'll be over soon.

I picture my mom in my mind's eye. She may not be here to see me compete, but I can't give up now. She didn't raise a quitter.

I swallow the lump in my throat and force a smile to my lips.

Enzo smiles in return.

"Good afternoon," I say, voice warbling. "I'm Kennedy Carter." My stomach rolls and I flatten my lips, praying I don't lose my lunch. "This is my partner En—Lorenzo Gonzalez. We're Team— We're Team Spark."

The judges smile and I force myself to push forward.

I've practiced this speech more than a dozen times in front of the mirror. I can do this. It's practically muscle memory at this point.

I walk them through Sparky's key design elements, while Enzo showcases the robot. My hands shake, but I don't pass out and I breathe a sigh of relief when it's over. The Q&A goes quickly and Enzo fields a particularly difficult question about the balance system, but otherwise, we survive unscathed and move on to the timed trial.

My hands are still shaking, so despite all the prep work I've done to master the art of pick and place, I give Enzo the remote.

"You sure?" he asks, surprise etched on his face. "This is your baby."

"Absolutely." He's worked just as hard as I have to prepare, and I trust him to have a steadier hand. "If we advance to the head-to-head round, I'll get my shot."

I watch, chewing my thumbnail, as he races to collect the balls one at a time and deposit them in the drop box. He does well, not dropping a single ball, but times won't be posted until tomorrow afternoon, so it's a waiting game. My gut says we'll advance, but it could be wishful thinking.

Once Sparky is packed securely in his box, we decide to head out.

No point hanging around to watch other teams compete, and we have practice soon. Besides, now that the adrenaline's faded, a familiar sense of disappointment's creeped in to take its place.

*Austin didn't show.*

He promised he'd be here to support me, and he didn't show up.

I check my phone, confirming what I already know.

No missed calls. No texts. Nothing.

The eternally naive part of my brain argues that maybe it's

not his fault. Maybe something happened, like a car accident, preventing him from being at the competition.

The more experienced part of my brain scoffs.

After all, I have enough experience with football players to know what it means to be stood up. To be left waiting with hope so powerful it cuts like a knife. I should have known better than to expect more from Austin. But no, I had to go and learn the hard way because maybe—just maybe—he'd be different.

*I will not cry.*

It's the promise I make myself as Enzo and I push through the arena doors to the parking lot.

The wind howls, but I hardly feel it as it scrapes across my skin.

My eyes are stinging and tension rolls off my body in palpable waves. Enzo must feel it too because he's gone silent.

We're halfway to his car when I spot Austin jogging across the lot, cutting between rows of cars. My heart slams against my rib cage at the sight of him, and I'm reminded of the first time we met, when he chased me down to recruit me for the team. So much has changed since then, but not everything. Austin's still as sexy as ever with his tone body, cocky grin, and crystalline blue eyes.

There's no denying he's perfection.

*Except in the way that matters most.*

He slows to a stop in front of us, a bouquet hanging limply by his side.

"Sorry I'm late."

He offers me the flowers, but I make no move to accept them.

"Late?" My tone is scathing, but I refuse to feel bad about it. I'm not the one who broke my promise; he is. If anyone here should feel like shit, it's definitely him. "You missed the entire presentation."

He rakes a hand through his hair. "I wanted to be here."

I snort. "Yes, well, you weren't, were you?" I glance at Enzo, who looks like he's about to cut and run. "What's the old saying? Actions speak louder than words?"

Enzo doesn't answer my question, but offers to give us some space.

He doesn't go far, and I know he'll wait for me. However long this takes.

Austin steps forward and reaches for my arm. I shrug off his touch.

"I'm sorry, Kennedy. I completely forgot about the meeting with the Pittsburgh scout. My dad set the whole thing up and lunch took long than expected." He pauses, gaze locked on mine. "I really did want to be here."

"You know what?" Hurt lances through my chest all over again at his meaningless platitude. If he wanted to be here, he would've been. Must've been a riveting meal if he couldn't excuse himself early. "Don't apologize. This is on me. I should've known better. It was stupid to think you'd be different."

"I am different." Hurt flashes in his eyes, but I steel my resolve. I'm hurting too and my heart's pretty full up on pain at the moment. "I'm not like him."

"Aren't you?" I wrap my arms around my waist. "You knew this was important to me, to my future. You promised to be here for me and then you bailed. And for what? Lunch with a team you don't even want to play for."

"I didn't have a choice." His voice is pleading as he reaches for my arm again.

"There's always a choice, Austin." I take a step back. "It's just as well I found out what kind of man you are now, before..."

I can't even finish the sentence.

Before I fall head over heels for him? Before I give him my heart?

*Too late for that.*

The realization makes the pressure in my chest a thousand times worse because I know what I have to do. I can't be with someone who will always put the game before me. I saw what it did to my mom growing up. What it did to me.

I can't put myself through that again. *I won't.* I deserve to come first.

And I won't settle for anything less.

I blink back the tears that threaten to escape. I will not cry. Not in front of Austin.

"Look, we gave it a shot, but this thing between you and me, it was never going to work. We're too different. We live in completely different worlds."

Austin's jaw hardens and he flexes his fingers. It's the first time I've seen his carefully crafted mask of control slip outside the bedroom. "So, what? You're going to break up with me over one little mistake?"

"Little?" I scoff, tossing my hair over my shoulder. "I'd hardly call breaking your promise little. But it doesn't matter, because this is exactly what I'm talking about. We're too different."

He growls. Actually freaking growls.

Which would probably be hot except for the fact that he's breaking my heart and I kind of want to throat punch him.

"Okay, poor choice of words. That doesn't change the fact that I screw up one time and you're using it to break things off because you're too scared to see where this thing between us might lead. Too afraid I might be like your old man to actually give me a real chance to prove I'm not." He throws up his hands. "If this is how things were always going to end, why'd you even bother? Why let me think I had a chance to build something real with you?"

"I'm too scared?" My nostrils flare and it's possible my unshed tears will evaporate into steam because I'm fired up now. I should walk away and go cool off, but I don't have it in me to walk away from a fight. Not when I have so much to say. "You should talk. You're going to spend your life living in your father's shadow because you're afraid to tell him you don't want to play ball in Pittsburgh! At least I'm doing what I want and pursuing my dreams."

Austin narrows his eyes. His shoulders are wrought with tension and the muscles of his forearms ripple as he clenches and unclenches his fists.

"Are you though? You can't even admit you care about me because what if it doesn't work out, right? It's easier to just write me off as another playboy asshole than to put your heart on the line."

"We're done here. I have to get to practice."

I turn on my heel and stalk toward Enzo.

What the hell does Austin know about my heart? He's never even been in a relationship before. He's wrong. I'm not afraid; I'm hurt.

I repeat it like a mantra as I walk away from the man who holds the shards of my broken heart in his hands.

"We're not done, Kennedy," the stubborn bastard calls after me. Like it's his choice to make. "Not by a long shot."

# 45

# AUSTIN

I STAND on the sideline with my helmet in my hand, watching as our defense tries to hold off Michigan with less than two minutes on the clock. The whole game's been a cluster, and I got picked off on the last drive. Michigan's not only got the ball, they've got momentum. They're driving down the field, and every yard they gain is a nail in my coffin.

If our defense can't keep them out of field goal range, we're fucked.

All because I turned the ball over.

I was up half the night replaying my fight with Kennedy when I should've been resting up for one of the biggest games of the season. Not that I could've slept if I wanted to. She won't answer my calls or texts.

The result? I'm playing like shit today and the team's noticed.

Everyone's feeling the tension between Kennedy and me.

How could they not when she's avoiding me like I gave her the clap? I can't get within five yards of her. Every time I try, she makes a break for it, so I've given up chasing her around the sideline.

*For now.*

I want nothing more than to pick up where we left off yesterday—I refuse to accept her declaration that we're broken up—but I owe it to the team to get my fuckin' head in the game.

Between our drama and the three-point spread on the scoreboard, everyone's feeling the pressure. Stress is high and tempers are short. Coach is giving the linesman shit over a bad spot, waving his arms like a nut.

Fortunately, one of the offensive coordinators relieved him of his clipboard.

The last thing we need is for Coach to get ejected.

I steal a glance at Kennedy. She's warming up her leg, totally oblivious to my attention.

If she'd just give me a chance to explain, I know I could fix what I broke.

But first we have to get through this game.

Michigan's third and long. I tighten my grip on my helmet and clench the collar of my jersey with my other hand. We need a stop here. If we can hold them, they'll be forced to go for it on the fourth down. They're still a few yards out of field goal range, and the fans are doing their part to keep it that way. The noise in the stadium is deafening, fans hoping to drown out the play call or draw a false start.

*We should be so lucky.*

The ball is snapped and Wyant leaps forward like his ass is on fire, breaking right through the O-line and sacking the quarterback. *Holy shit.* I can hardly believe my eyes.

I pump my fist in the air as a cheer goes up from the crowd.

If Daniels's guys can deliver one more like that, we gain possession. There's not a lot of time left on the clock, but we can run it down and eke out a win with a three-point lead.

"That's what I'm talking about!" Parker claps me on the back. "That's how you win games!"

We watch with bated breath as both teams return to the line of scrimmage.

"Come on, Daniels."

In all my years at Waverly, I don't know if I've ever been so desperate for our D to hold the line.

Michigan snaps the ball. The coverage is solid. The QB drops back and, finding no receivers, attempts to run the ball.

He's tackled at the line of scrimmage and the crowd goes berserk.

"Hell, yeah!" Parker shouts, jumping in the air.

I pat his stomach and pull on my helmet, relief flooding my veins. "Time to work."

By the time the game clock reaches zero, I'm mentally and physically exhausted, but Coop and I get tagged for interviews, so we hang back as the rest of the team hits the locker room, riding high on our 10-1 record. We give the reporters the usual fluff about playing as a team, maintaining discipline, and how we're focused on winning one game at a time.

That last part? Total bullshit.

Of course we're thinking about bowl games and the national championship. How could we not?

We're halfway down the tunnel, away from the prying eyes of fans and reporters, when Coop stops me with a hand on my chest.

"What's the deal with you and Carter?" he asks, spinning to face me.

"Nothing." I force myself to meet his stare. "Everything's fine."

"Yeah, I'm calling bullshit." He crosses his arms over his chest. "She wouldn't even look at you today. Don't think I didn't notice you watching her like a lost puppy when you should've been focused on the game. What gives?"

"What do you care?" I snap, regretting the words immediately. Just because I'm in a bad mood doesn't mean I can be a dick to my best friend. I adjust my headband and push my sweat-slicked hair back. "Sorry. I didn't mean that. I didn't get much sleep last night. It's messing with my head."

"Lack of sleep isn't the only thing messing with your head."

He's not wrong.

It's more than Kennedy being pissed at me or the fact that I'm disappointed in myself for letting her down and playing right into her low opinion of football players.

I can't stop thinking about what she said. About living in my father's shadow because I'm too afraid to speak up for myself.

I was so angry when she said it, but she's right.

Four years at Waverly and nothing's changed. I graduate in the spring. I'll be signing a multimillion-dollar contract, and I've resigned myself to a future I don't want because I'm afraid of letting my parents down.

What kind of life is that?

I tip my head back and close my eyes, taking a minute to lose myself in darkness.

*Why does everything have to be so fucking complicated?*

"Dude, what'd you do?" Coop asks, snapping me back to the conversation. "It can't be that bad."

"I broke a promise. An important one."

"And she dumped you?" I nod and Coop smirks. "Must've been a doozy. I figured you'd at least make it until the end of the season before she dumped your ass."

"Yeah, well, you figured wrong." I shift my weight, trying to figure out how I can explain the situation without breaking Kennedy's trust. Or at least, any more than I have already. It's not my place to tell her secrets, and I'd ride the bench before I ever hurt her intentionally. "Let's just say she has a history of being let down and the first time I had a chance to be there for her, I blew it."

"So apologize."

"It's not that simple. Look, I know I fucked up, okay? I tried to apologize, but she doesn't want to hear it."

"Doesn't want to or can't?" Coop shrugs. "Talk's cheap. Especially if you've already given her a reason to doubt you."

"Thanks, Dr. Phil." I hate that he's right.

Hell, Kennedy said as much when she broke things off.

"Dude, I'm just saying you need to take care of your shit. Whatever's going on with you two can't affect the team. We've worked too hard to piss it all away now. We barely pulled out the win today." He frowns. It's a look I've rarely seen on his face in the four years I've known him. Coop's the kind of guy that lets everything roll off his back. "We got lucky today."

"I know." Just like I know I need to fix things with Kennedy.

Not only for the team, but for myself.

I can't let her go. I won't. Not without a fight.

In a few short months, she's become my world. I want to wake up to her beautiful smile every day. And worship her gorgeous body every night. I want to be the one to hold her tight when things go wrong and kiss her senseless when everything goes right. She's the only one who gets me—really gets me—and appreciates me for more than my washboard abs and ability to throw a ball. I don't want to go another day without her sexy, STEM-loving nerd power in my life.

Problem is, I don't have a clue how to make things right if she's not willing to accept my apology or even talk to me.

"I just..." I trail off, scrubbing a hand over my face. "I'll figure it out."

"You don't have a clue what you're doing, do you?"

"Nope." I must sound as miserable as I feel, because he laughs, the sound echoing down the tunnel, like my imploding love life is a fucking comedy. "Thanks a lot, asshole. I'm glad you're amused by my pain."

"Dude. This isn't that complicated. You hurt her." He slaps me on the chest, but I barely feel it through my pads. "Now you've got to sacrifice if you want to win her back. Women love that shit."

"And how would you know?"

Coop's never had a girlfriend that I'm aware of, so there's a good chance he's getting his advice from talk shows or reality shows or whatever crap he watches on TV.

But I have to admit, it kind of makes sense.

*Oh, for fuck's sake.* I can't believe I'm taking relationship advice from Cooper One-night-stand Virgins-need-not-apply DeLaurentis.

He opens his mouth to respond, but I wave him off. I'm probably better off not knowing.

"Never mind. More importantly, what would you suggest? What exactly do I have to sacrifice to make this right?"

"How the hell should I know?" Coop smirks and starts for the locker room. "But I suggest starting with your dignity."

# 46

## KENNEDY

"Ready to go, sweetie?" Mom pokes her head in the bedroom door, and I nearly stab myself in the eye with the mascara wand. I don't usually put much effort into my makeup—thus the near blinding—but since I look like a puffy, spent-the-night-crying-into-my-pillow zombie, it's probably best if I give it the old college try today.

I check my reflection.

*Definitely can't get any worse.*

"I'll be ready in a few minutes."

Total lie. It'll take more than a few minutes for me to mentally prepare to leave the apartment. After Friday's fight with Austin and last night's sob fest, I'm tapped.

Completely and emotionally drained.

And I have no interest in hearing *I told you so* from my mom, which is why I can't let her see I've been crying.

I swipe on another coat of mascara like it's war paint.

True to form, Mom doesn't wait for an invitation and makes herself at home on the edge of the bed. "Is everything okay? You were awfully quiet at dinner last night."

"Everything's great. Just nervous about the ACME competition."

That's true enough. Our timed trial was good enough to advance to the head-to-head round, so we'll be in direct competition during this morning's finals.

Which means we still have a shot at winning.

What more could I ask for?

*How about a boyfriend who keeps his promises?*

Mom's silent so long I turn to look at her. Regret kicks in immediately. Her lips are pressed into a thin line and her eyes are pinched at the corners. She knows I'm holding out.

I should've known she'd see right through me. She always does.

She pats the spot next to her on the bed.

I slink over, dropping down with a sigh. Because, yes, apparently I am that dramatic. At least when it comes to Austin.

I still can't believe he was a no-show for the competition. And if I'm being honest, I'm more pissed at myself for trusting him to keep his word than anything. For letting myself fall for a guy who will always put football first.

Just like my dad.

Mom takes my hands in hers and tilts my chin so I'm forced to look her in the eye. "Spill."

It's not exactly a request, but I hesitate.

Mom's been doing so well, cutting back her hours, dating, having an honest-to-God life. I don't want to drag her down with talk of unreliable football players and shattered hearts.

Because my heart is shattered.

I let myself believe in Austin—in us—and he let me down. *Hard.*

We can come back from this. Not when forgiving him means setting myself up for more of the same in the future.

I've seen this pattern before. I've lived it for twenty-one years.

Whether he means to or not, he'll trample my heart, leaving it a bitter husk with no room for love or hope. I refuse to spend my life wondering if I'll ever come before the game. And I refuse to stand by and watch Austin walk away from his own hopes and dreams just to make his father happy.

"Kennedy Lane Carter. You tell me what's wrong this instant or I'm going to assume the worst." She pauses, eyes going wide in panic. "You aren't pregnant, are you?"

I snort and my defenses falter. A tear slips down my cheek.

*So much for war paint.*

"Me being pregnant is the worst thing you can think of?" I swipe at the tear. "You're seriously lacking in imagination."

She slips an arm around my back and pulls me close so my shoulder is pressed to hers. "What is it, sweetie?"

"You were right. About everything." I crack like a glow stick, and the truth comes pouring out. The whole luminescent mess of it. Austin and I bickering all season. Stolen kisses in the stacks. Hooking up on the DL. Dinner with Dad. Austin's broken promise. The fight that followed. "Austin's just like Dad. The game will always come first."

I'm so relieved to get it all out, it's like I can breathe for the first time in days.

"Oh, Kennedy." Mom brushes my hair back from my face with her fingertips. "Why didn't you tell me any of this before? You've been so distant, but I chalked it up to a busy schedule."

I chew my bottom lip. "I was afraid to tell you. I didn't want you to be disappointed in me."

"I could never be disappointed in you," she says, her words a balm to my aching heart. "If anything, I'm disappointed in myself. I've made you so wary of football players, passing my bias and bad experiences on to you without a thought for how that might affect your view of love and relationships. The truth is, your father's shortcomings have nothing to do with his profession and everything to do with being weak and selfish. It was just easier to make it about the game because that's what he loved most." She sighs and strokes my hair again. "I put too much of my own baggage on you, treating you like my best friend instead of my daughter. That wasn't fair. I'm sorry, sweetie."

"You have nothing to apologize for. You were a single mom. You did the best you could." I sniff and give her a squeeze. "And for the record, you are my best friend."

"That doesn't mean I didn't make mistakes. I leaned on you too much." She turns her body so she's facing me, a smile curving her lips. "But you're so much brighter and smarter than I ever was. Much more levelheaded too. If you fell in love with this boy, he must have some redeeming qualities."

I pull back, shock rippling through my body.

"What makes you think I'm in love with him?"

She smiles, and it's one of these annoying, knowing smiles. "The way your face lights up when you say his name. The wistful tone of your voice when you talk about him. The way you're trying to hide your pain, even though it's written plain as day on your face."

Well, hell. Am I always this transparent? I only just figured it out myself.

"Are you saying I should give Austin another chance?" I ask, uncertain which answer I want to hear.

"I'm saying you know him best. Only you can decide if he deserves a second chance." She shakes her head. "I can't believe I'm saying this, but from where I'm sitting, it sounds like he cares about you very much. He risked a lot to be with you. I don't condone the two of you sneaking around against your coach's wishes—or mine—but I admit it was an unfair ask on my part. I never should have put you in a position where you didn't feel you could come to me, whether it was about your father or anything else. I'm so sorry for the pain your father's caused you, and I'm glad Austin was by your side, but I will always be here for you, Kennedy. Always." She says the last part with force, gripping my hands in hers as if she can will me to understand and keep this sentiment close to my heart.

There's a sob building at the back of my throat, and I'm afraid if I speak, it'll break free. So I hug her, squeezing her tight and burying my face in her hair like I did when I was young. She smells like lavender and lemongrass, a scent I'll always associate with home, no matter how old I get.

Several minutes pass before I can bring myself to let her go.

I want to stay here all day, wrapped in the comfort of her arms, but I'm an adult and, broken heart or not, I have responsibilities.

"We should probably get going. I don't want to be late for the finals."

We stand and she cups my cheek.

"You're so young and you're faced with pressures my generation never had to endure. The world's not the same as it was twenty years ago. I don't know if that's a good thing or a bad thing, but I do know you have to give yourself the space to make mistakes and learn from them. Austin too. I tried so hard to protect you from making the same mistakes I did, I nearly took that experience away from you. None of us is perfect, Kennedy. Not me. Not you. Not Austin. But no matter what happens today, I am so proud of you, and I will always love you."

I watch her retreat and flop back down on the bed, her words replaying in my head.

*I love Austin. With all my heart.*

He's taught me it's not a weakness to ask for help. He makes me feel special in a way no one else ever has, with his boundless faith in my abilities and his appreciation of my so-called nerd power.

And the way he worships my body? That doesn't exactly hurt either.

But...can I forgive him?

God knows we've both made plenty of mistakes, but have we learned from them?

# 47

## AUSTIN

I MAY HAVE FUCKED up my relationship with Kennedy, but if football has taught me anything, it's endurance. No way am I going to let her eject me for a personal foul. I'm going to fix this, no matter what it takes, because I'm in it for the long game.

After my talk with Coop, I spent the night organizing my playbook.

First up is breakfast with my father.

I'm nervous as hell and it won't be easy, but it's time to man up. I can't call myself a leader if I don't even have the balls to advocate for myself. My old man may not like what I have to say, but this conversation is long past due and whatever the outcome, I'll deal with it.

He's waiting in the hotel dining room when I arrive, the sports section spread out on the table in front of him. The place is busy, nearly every table full. No surprise there. Probably booked solid due to the Michigan game.

He looks up as I approach and folds the paper, setting it off to the side. "Did you see Georgia got knocked off yesterday?"

"Yes, sir." I pull out a chair and join him at the table, my stomach raging like a category five hurricane. “I was starting to think they might go undefeated.”

He considers. “They’re overrated, but it doesn’t change the fact that they’re leading the SEC.”

We talk shop until the server comes over. She recognizes my dad and starts gushing about how she grew up watching him play. When she finally gets hold of herself, she asks him for his autograph and then takes our orders. My father orders half the breakfast menu, but I stick with eggs and toast, barely able to stomach the idea of food.

I want to get this over with as quickly as possible.

“We need to talk,” I blurt out as soon as the server leaves the table.

My father arches a brow and tilts his head. “Something wrong, son?”

“No—” I stop myself. I need to be honest. My need for approval is what got me into this mess in the first place. “Yes. I don’t want to play ball in Pittsburgh.”

He goes rigid, face hard as stone. His blue eyes, so like my own, search my face as if he thinks this might be a joke.

“I don’t understand,” he finally says, lifting a hand from the table.

It’s not a dismissive wave, more like a gesture to signal confusion.

I can hardly fault him. I’ve never said the words to anyone but Kennedy before.

“I don’t want to play ball in Pittsburgh,” I repeat. “Pittsburgh is your legacy, Dad. I’ll always love the city and the fans and the franchise, but I want to make my own mark in the NFL.”

“It’s always been your dream to play ball in Pittsburgh. What’s changed?” He frowns, the expression cutting deep lines into his forehead. “Is this about that girl?”

My temper flares, but I swallow it down.

"This has nothing to do with Kennedy." It's a struggle to keep my voice even, but the last thing we need is a scene. The papers would be all over it. "This is about me and what I want. It's never been my dream to play ball in Pittsburgh. That was your dream. And Mom's."

He leans back, deflating faster than a New England football. "But we thought you wanted it too."

"I know. I should've spoken up sooner." I wipe my palms on my thighs. "I didn't want to let you guys down. Especially Mom."

My voice cracks on the last word. My father's eyes lock on mine, and I know we're both remembering her as she was before the cancer ravaged her body, vibrant and full of energy. Our biggest fan.

"Your mother and I just wanted what was best for you."

"Pittsburgh isn't what's best for me." I reach across the table and rest my hand on top of his. It's clumsy and awkward and it just reinforces the gap Mom left in our family. "I don't want to spend my life living in your shadow. Do you know what it's like being compared to you week in and week out? You're a legend. You hold so many records and you've done so much philanthropy. The fans love you. It's a lot of pressure to live up to."

He blinks and understanding dawns in his eyes. "It will only intensify if you're playing for my old franchise."

I pull my hand back and shrug. My silence speaks volumes.

"Son, you're one hell of a football player. You'll probably break every record I set one day, and nothing would make me prouder." He gives me a faint smile. "I guess I never stopped to think about the pressure you're under."

"It's not your fault—"

He raises a hand to cut me off.

"Yes, it is. Your mother and I wanted what's best for you, but we should've asked what you wanted—I should have asked what you wanted—because you're our son first and foremost." His voice hitches when he speaks again. "Losing your mom was the hardest thing I've ever gone through and I...I threw myself into making that dream come true because it felt like keeping a piece of her alive. But I know that more than anything, she'd want you to be happy."

Tears prick the back of my eyes.

It's probably the most honest conversation we've had in the six years since my mom died.

"What a mess we've made," he says, shaking his head. It's rare my father admits making a mistake. This feels like a big admission, but it's not just his mistake. It's mine too. I should've been honest from the start, but I've learned my lesson. From now on, no holding back. I'm going to speak from the heart, even if it makes me the sappiest SOB to play the game. "All this time. Well, I'll support you no matter where you play ball, but there's always a chance Pittsburgh will draft you."

"I know." I drum my fingers on the table. "If it happens, I'll sign with a smile. Just...don't interfere. Let things play out naturally, okay?"

"Of course." He narrows his eyes. "Is there a team you've got your eye on?"

I laugh, the sound exploding from my chest as the weight of the conversation is lifted.

"Let's just say I'd look pretty damn good in orange and navy."

After breakfast, I swing by the football building.

Coach's optional workout doesn't start for another hour, so I should be able to catch him before he hits the field. I pass by the guys suiting up in the locker room and head straight for his office. I knock on the open door and he looks up, a wide grin spreading across his face.

"You decided to come out after all."

"I'm not here to practice." His face falls and he gestures for me to take a seat, but I remain standing. I won't be here long and

I'm pressed for time. "I'm here to thank you for your advice, sir. I appreciate your thoughts on the potential in Chicago and your unwavering confidence in me." I pause, gathering my courage. "I know I said my future was in Pittsburgh, but I've come to realize there's no one path to success. I'd like to meet with Chicago's coaching staff at the combine, and I'd be honored if they call my name in April, but there's something more important than football I need to do today."

Coach's brows knit in an angry V. "What the hell could be more important than football?"

"My future." He looks perplexed, but I doubt he'd be impressed by the truth. The man eats, sleeps, and breathes football. I doubt he's ever loved anyone or anything as much as he loves the game. It's a mistake I don't plan on making. "I hope you'll give my regards to the Chicago scout."

He throws up his hands in defeat, and I take it as a good sign.

"Thanks, Coach."

I start dialing my teammates as soon as I leave Coach's office, my mood lighter than it's been in ages. I've got some recruiting to do if I'm going to win back my girl.

## 48

## KENNEDY

THE AUDITORIUM IS PACKED as we take our seats in the third row. I'm wedged in between Enzo and Mom, but that doesn't stop Becca from reaching over to pat me on the leg.

"Third row for the win. You won't have to walk as far when they call your name," she says with her usual optimism. I kind of want to hug her face for giving up her day off to come support me. Fall semester's been rough. Between soccer and football, we've hardly spent any time together, but our friendship is as strong as ever and I know I can always count on Becca to be there for me when I need her. "You've got this."

"Here's hoping."

Enzo and I won our heat, but with five heats, it's impossible to know the overall winners since times weren't posted. I swear the ACME judges are masochists. This has been the longest weekend of my life, although if I'm being honest, the competition is only half to blame.

I'm doing my best not to think about the other reason, all six foot four of him.

*The struggle is real.*

We wait with bated breath as the rest of the crowd files into the auditorium.

I'm too nervous to make small talk, although my mom and Becca don't share my affliction.

Enzo nudges my shoulder. "Don't forget to breathe."

I flash him a shaky smile. "Only sixty of the original seven hundred and eighty-six teams competing advanced to the finals. I'll take those odds."

The minute the words are out of my mouth, I want to stuff them back in, because in truth, the odds aren't great.

Which is why I need to focus on the positive.

I already lost my boyfriend this weekend. Losing the competition is not an option.

*Good vibes only.*

Right. A win today will give us a chance to compete at the international level. It will also open a lot of professional doors, doors that might otherwise be closed to us.

I can't speak for Enzo, but I don't have connections, and in a field that's heavily dominated by men, I need every advantage I can get.

Besides, how freaking cool would it be to work for one of the top engineering companies, like Gamut, where I could help drive change and inspire other girls to pursue STEM careers? That's the kind of influence I want to have in my field. Sort of like the amazing opportunity football has given me to show girls they truly can do anything.

My chest tightens at the thought of football. And Austin.

He believed I could play D1 football even when I didn't.

He was also the one who helped me see what a great platform I was building to change the narrative about girls in male-dominated sports and STEM fields.

For that, I'll always be grateful.

The lights go down and the emcee takes the stage.

I try not to fidget as he runs through the usual minutia, talking about all the work ACME's doing in the industry and the hard work of all the competitors.

"Yeah, yeah. No one's a loser. We get it," I whisper to Enzo. "Can't they get to the awards already? I'm dying over here."

"Same."

After twenty minutes of lip service, the emcee finally invites the judges to the stage.

I sit up straight, my pulse pounding. Mom grabs my hand and gives it a quick squeeze.

"The third-place runner-up from Cornell University is... Team KISS!"

The crowd applauds, and we watch as the students make their way to the stage to collect their crystal trophy and have their picture taken. I'm clutching the arm of the chair so hard my fingernails are digging into the soft wood.

The applause dies down and Team KISS moves to the back of the stage.

Then the emcee announces the second-place runner-up from MIT: Team Awesome.

We applaud again and watch as they go through the same routine.

The tension in the room is so thick it's a wonder we don't choke on it.

This is it. Our last chance to final.

My heart slams against my rib cage, and I can hardly draw a breath.

I grab my mom's hand, this time not letting go.

"And finally, the first-place winners of the ACME Student Design Competition, from right here at Waverly..." I'm on the edge of my seat now, squeezing my mom's hand so tight it's a wonder she doesn't cry out. "Team Spark!"

I clasp my hands over my mouth, but it does little to contain my celebratory scream.

*We did it! We actually won!*

There's a thunderous round of applause complete with whooping and cheering, but I can't focus on any of it. I'm on sensory overload. Or celebratory overload. Or maybe I'm in complete shock. Enzo and I exchange a quick embrace before I turn to my mom and Becca, who lean in and hug me at the same time, shouting their congratulations over the noise of the crowd.

My mom's crying and Enzo's tugging at my hand and it's all happening so fast.

I suck in a breath to center myself, square my shoulders, and follow Enzo to the stage on shaky legs, emotions running high. We climb the steps on the left side of the stage and—thankfully—I manage not to face-plant.

It's so bright on the stage I have to squint to see.

We shake hands with the judges, and my eyes finally begin to adjust as we pose for pictures.

The photographer snaps pics from several angles, but at least he doesn't have to tell us to smile. I'm grinning like a fool. So is Enzo.

Doesn't matter. We've earned the right, busting our butts day in and day out to build the fastest robot in the competition. Of course, we probably wouldn't be standing here without the meddling of a certain cocky QB. His driving tips were invaluable, if not infuriating.

My chest squeezes at the thought of Austin and my smile falters, but I force it back into place.

I will not let my broken heart dampen this moment.

The emcee congratulates us once again, and another round of applause breaks out in the audience. It's loud and raucous and wholly inappropriate.

I squint, focusing on the back corner of the auditorium.

"Holy shit." Enzo nudges me with his elbow. "Is that the football team?"

*Holy shit.* It *is* the football team. They've taken over the last couple of rows, loud and proud in their Waverly jerseys.

And they have signs. The homemade kind. With glitter.

It's an amazing show of support from our teammates.

Actually, no, it's sweet as hell.

And I know without a doubt this is Austin's handiwork.

Is he here? Now?

I try to locate him in the crowd, but it's hard to see their faces from this distance, so I scan the signs, my chest warming as I read the sappy messages.

My heart skips a beat when I spot one that says: *Kennedy Carter: #93 on the field, #1 in my <3!*

He came, and he brought the whole damn team.

My throat begins to close up, and tears build at the corners of my eyes.

Austin lifts the sign over his head, reminding me of that old movie where the guy rocks a boom box to woo the girl he loves. But unlike the guy in the movie, he's not down and out. He wears a brilliant smile. Which I guess makes sense, since he refused to acknowledge the fact that I broke up with him.

*Cocky bastard.*

I laugh in spite of myself, a spark igniting low in my belly.

*He came. For me.*

Despite everything. Despite the fact that I broke up with him. Despite the fact that I called him a coward when it was my own fear talking.

It's impossible to focus on the closing ceremonies, so I don't bother to try. I keep my eyes locked on Austin. I can feel his beautiful blue eyes boring into me, so I'm not surprised in the least when he stands for the remainder of the ceremony, declaration held stubbornly over his head.

When the emcee finally wraps up, I'm down the steps like a shot, fighting through the sea of bodies to get to the back of the auditorium.

Because Austin was right about one thing. We have unfinished business.

## 49

## AUSTIN

THE SEA of people exiting the auditorium makes it damn near impossible to get to the stage. Which is ridiculous. At six-four, I should be able to shoulder my way right on through, but fighting against the tide of bodies is no easy feat. Especially with the giant poster board I'm toting. The thing's massive, but no way was I leaving it behind.

It's part of my grand gesture.

I'm halfway to the stage when I spot her.

*Kennedy.*

She floats toward me, caught up in the mass exodus, determination burning in her eyes. She's beautiful and fierce and she's meeting me halfway.

*That has to be a good sign, right?*

My heart beats double time as the distance between us closes.

This is right. I can feel it in my gut.

We meet midway up the aisle and there are so many things I want to say to her, but I'm not sure where to start. I've given hundreds of speeches—to the team, in class, at fundraisers—but it's hardly the same as pouring my heart out. The fact is, I suck at expressing my emotions.

I probably should've practiced at home, but it's too late for that now.

"Kennedy."

"Nice sign. Love the glitter."

She gives me a tentative smile, but her arms are crossed over her chest. It doesn't take a genius to figure out her guard's up.

Doesn't matter. She's here. I can work with it.

"Thanks. I made it myself."

"I can tell." Her lips begin to quiver and she presses them flat like it'd be the worst thing in the world to share a laugh right now.

The distance between us is like a kick in the gut.

I sit the sign on an empty chair and take a step closer to her. She inches back like she thinks I'm going to go all caveman and sling her over my shoulder.

Which is ridiculous, because that would totally be a last resort.

"I know you said we're over, but the thing is, I can't accept that. I've never given up on anything in my life, and I'm sure as hell not going to give up on us. Not without a fight."

She arches a brow, but I plow ahead before she can argue.

"The last couple of months have been some of the hardest of my life, but they've been made easier by having you at my side. Whether we're fighting or playing ball or kissing, it doesn't matter. You bring out the best in me and you make all the insanity—the press, the pressure, the speculation—easier to bear. Because it's just static. None of it matters. Not when I'm with you."

"Austin—"

Whatever she's going to say, the words die on her tongue and she bites her lip as if she can trap the rest inside. Fine by me, because I'm not finished yet. Hell, I'm just getting warmed up.

My blood's pumping fast and my skin's hot and the desire to take her in my arms is so fucking strong it requires all my self-control not to act on it. As desperate as I am to touch her right now, she's made it clear she needs space. I can respect that.

*For now.*

The last of the crowd trickles out of the auditorium, and I'm vaguely aware of the team gathering around us with their sparkly signs. It doesn't matter. They should hear what I have to say. Because with all the fanfare around the game, it's easy to lose sight of what's important, what really matters.

"I get it. I screwed up. I put the game before you, before my promise, and I broke your trust. I hurt you. Even though it's the last thing I ever wanted to do, it doesn't change the fact that I did it. I'm sorry. For all of it."

She blinks up at me, her big dark eyes covered in a glassy sheen.

*Fuck.* She's going to cry. It's probably not the first time. And it's my fault.

The knowledge is like a knife jammed between my ribs.

"You broke your promise and missed the competition for a meeting you didn't even care about." Her voice wavers. "How exactly do you think I should feel about that?"

"You should be angry. So be angry. Throw up your hands. Rage at me. Tell me I'm a selfish bastard. Just don't walk away from me. Please." I pause, my breath coming fast and hard. "We both know you're not breaking up with me because you don't care about me. You're breaking up with me because you care too much. You're afraid I'll hurt you again, like your father did. But I'm not him, Kennedy. If you give me the chance, I'll prove it. Over and over. Every day. I'll do whatever it takes to earn back your trust."

"I—" She falters, a tiny crease appearing between her brows. "I don't know what to say. I want to believe you, but nothing's changed. If you can't even put your own dreams before the pressures of football, how can I expect to compete?"

Is that what she thinks? That this is some kind of game to me?

"There's no competition. I'll always choose you."

She throws up her hands and plants them on her hips. "Football is your life. It's what you were born to do and you're going to be freaking unstoppable when you get to the NFL. I would never ask you to choose between me and your future. But I won't play second string. I can't stand by and watch you give up on your dreams to make someone else's come true."

My breath whistles through my teeth. "I told my father the truth."

She freezes, eyes wide. "You did?"

I nod. "This morning. A pretty smart woman made me realize that living someone else's dream is no way to live."

Her face softens and she takes a step closer. "How'd it go?"

"Better than expected." I rake a hand through my hair. "My dad's going to back off, let things play out how they will. It was a good talk, actually."

"And Chicago? What about the optional practice?"

"I asked Coach to pass my regards to the scout and let him know I look forward to speaking with the coaching staff in the spring, when my eligibility expires. Being here for you today was more important than running drills. You were right about my priorities being screwed up, but I think I've got it all figured out now."

I take a step closer, letting my hand skate over her cheek.

She leans into my touch, eyes drifting shut. Her skin is flushed, her chest rising and falling in rapid succession, but it's the softness of her skin that does me in. She pretends to be so tough, so untouchable, but the truth is, underneath it all she's vulnerable, in need of love and support, just like the rest of us.

"You did all that for me?"

I tilt her chin up to mine. I want her to see the truth of my words in my eyes.

"For us. So we can start fresh. No more secrets. No more lies. No more half-truths."

"For us," she says slowly, as if trying out the words. "I like the sound of that."

The smile that lights up her face is glorious. I can't imagine going another day without it in my life. This moment is so damn perfect I don't care who's watching or listening. The guys might bust my balls for the rest of the season, but it'll be worth it just to see that smile on her face. "I love you, Kennedy."

# 50

# KENNEDY

*He loves me?* Warmth spreads through my body, and the words plant themselves deep in my chest, taking root immediately. It almost feels too good to be true. I told myself it was too much to hope for, that he might feel the same way. I thought— Well, I guess it doesn't matter what I thought.

Not now. Not when he's just laid his heart bare in front of the entire team.

*Austin loves me.*

It's clear in the way he looks at me, with such tenderness and adoration. I don't know how I missed it before when it's so obvious now. I'm full to bursting with happiness, and when he smiles, I want to pepper his dimple with kisses.

But we have an audience, and I doubt they're here for the PDA.

I look around at the smiling faces of our friends—our teammates—and my heart swells with pride. And not just because they have mad skills when it comes to glittery posters. I never expected to be a real part of this team, but the fact that they're here is proof I'm one of them.

Proof that everything I thought I knew about football players was wrong.

Sure, our comradery is different from what I shared with the women on the soccer team, but it's no less precious to me. I'm so grateful I have the opportunity to be part of such a close-knit team. I've learned a lot this season, about football, about life, even about myself.

I wouldn't trade the experience for the world.

"Put the man out of his misery," Coop says, giving me a playful wink. "Hasn't he suffered enough?"

He's right. Austin's made himself vulnerable. With his father, the team, and with me.

I love him all the more for it, and I owe him the same in return.

My heart thunders in my chest as I turn back to Austin, taking his hands in mine.

I can see the tension in his shoulders, but if we're going to wipe the slate clean, I need to get this off my chest.

"I owe you an apology too. I shouldn't have walked away the other day." I take a steadying breath. "It was easier to lash out than admit that all this time, from the first day we met on the soccer field, I've been projecting all the hurt and disappointment of my childhood onto you. It was easier to believe that given the chance, you'd hurt me just like my father did."

Austin flinches, and I squeeze his hand.

"It was unfair of me to lay his mistakes at your feet in an attempt to protect myself. Especially when you've been nothing but supportive. You believed in me when I didn't even believe in myself. If it weren't for you, I wouldn't have a full scholarship or a place on the team. I wouldn't have won first place today, because I wouldn't have had Enzo to help me get Sparky ready in time. And if it weren't for you, I wouldn't have tried to reconnect with my dad."

He starts to protest, but I raise a hand to silence him.

I steal a quick glance at my mom. She's smiling, so I can't be doing too terrible a job with my apology. It's not sparkly poster-board, but it's the best I've got.

"Just because it didn't work out the way I'd hoped, doesn't make the lesson any less valuable. You've shown me it's okay to be vulnerable and to take chances. And I love you for it."

Austin's breath hitches, and when I look into his eyes, I see myself reflected across a summer sky. I lay a hand over his heart. It beats a steady rhythm under my palm and it centers me.

"I love you for your sense of compassion and your need to protect the people you care about. I love you for your sense of humor and your desire to always do the right thing. I love the way you challenge me when I'm being stubborn, the way you hold me when we're watching tv, and the way you always kiss me good night. I love you for being you."

We stare at each other for a beat.

I'm not sure which of us moves first, maybe we move at the same time, but then our lips are crashing together, his mouth moving hungrily over mine as I press my body to his, trying to get closer to the man I love.

Behind us, I hear the opening chords of "In Your Eyes" and I have a brief moment of validation before I dismiss it and pour myself into the kiss.

The guys cheer and whistle, but Becca's voice is loudest of them all as I claim my man, and when we finally break apart, I'm breathless.

Austin pulls me to his side, tucking me under his arm as he turns to the rest of the team.

"Who knew you all were such romantics?" I tease.

"You ever need help with a completely over-the-top romantic gesture," Parker says, ruffling Vaughn's hair. "This is your man."

Coop shakes his head, awestruck. "Dude, I feel like your

extensive knowledge of chick flicks is totally wasted. This shit is gold. It should get you laid every weekend." He winks. "Even with the beard."

"What's wrong with his beard?" Becca asks, which sets off a whole new round of razzing.

Vaughn's cheeks flush a deep shade of scarlet, and I'm pretty sure it's only the presence of my mom that keeps him from responding.

"Hey, now. Vaughn doesn't get all the credit." Austin puffs out his chest. "The signs were my idea."

"Of course they were." I grab his hand and pull him toward my mom.

Might as well get the introductions out of the way now that she's been subjected to our big, sloppy makeup kiss.

Speaking of making up...I am so having dirty, loud makeup sex with the man I love tonight.

Just the thought has me squeezing my thighs together in anticipation.

I must be making horny eyes, because Austin lowers his lips to my ear and whispers, "Don't worry, gorgeous. I promise to make it worth the wait."

The words remind me of our first night together, and desire coils low in my belly.

Which is so not appropriate when I'm about to introduce the man to my mom.

Fortunately, Austin takes the lead, giving me a moment to get my ovaries under control.

"Mrs. Carter." He extends his hand, flashing a thousand-watt smile. "It's nice to finally meet you in person."

"Austin." She looks him over from head to toe as if assessing him for flaws. Good luck. The man has none that I've been able to find. And I've explored every inch of his rock-hard body. "I was starting to think you weren't going to make it."

"You and me both. The glitter took a little longer to dry than I expected."

They laugh like old friends, and I look from Austin to my mom. "You knew about this?"

"Of course. Austin called me this morning while you were getting ready." She reaches over and pats my arm. "Don't worry, sweetie. I gave him the business for breaking your heart, but he sounded so contrite. I thought he might deserve one more chance." She cuts her eyes at him. "But only one. Next time, I won't be so forgiving."

Damn, my mom is scary intimidating.

Austin must think so too because he says, "Yes, ma'am."

"I'll give you two a minute alone." She smiles and backs away. "Just meet me at the car when you're done."

Mom retreats up the aisle, and I can't help but wonder if Austin called her before or after I spilled my guts this morning. It doesn't matter. I'm done holding on to the past.

I want to move forward and focus on the future, a future I hope includes a national title, my dream job, and the cocky QB who's stolen my heart.

It's a tall order, but I'm a modern woman and you know what?

I'm starting to think I really can have it all.

I lace my arms around Austin's neck and pull him in close, inhaling the spicy scent of his cologne as he slips his arms around my waist. His hands rest just above my ass, and I'm pretty sure he's teasing me on purpose, but I don't mind because I know he'll make good on his promise later. When he lowers his mouth to mine, the kiss is slow, sultry, and anything but chaste.

It's the kind of slow burn that could incinerate my panties—if I were wearing any—and I know without a doubt I've met my match. After all, if we can get through senior year, we can get through anything.

# EPILOGUE

## AUSTIN

It's draft day and I'm nervous as hell.

All my life I've dreamed of hearing my name called and walking up on that stage to shake hands with the commissioner. I've imagined a lot of different teams over the years and a lot of different picks, but it doesn't matter if I go number one or number ten. It's a huge honor just to be here.

Oh, who am I kidding? My ego totally wants to be drafted first overall.

My heart wants to go number three.

Under the table, my leg's going a mile a minute and it's all I can do to keep a smile on my face. I've seen enough draft days to know there are cameras everywhere. Appearances and all that. My suit is custom-made, but my tie is so tight I can't fucking breathe.

That'd be my luck. I'll pass out before they even call my name.

Kennedy reaches over and takes my hand in hers, giving it a gentle squeeze.

She always looks stunning, but today she's wearing a sexy ivory dress that showcases her gorgeous legs. Paired with her sun-kissed skin, she looks like a goddess.

What I wouldn't give to sling her over my shoulder and go find an empty closet.

God knows I'd rather pass the time worshipping my woman than sitting here like a caged animal.

"Almost showtime," my father says, pride shining in his eyes. "I remember my draft day. Man, every minute felt like an hour."

"Thanks, Dad." I loosen my tie. "This is brutal."

My old man snorts. "I don't want to hear it. In my day, we didn't get to enjoy spring break in Cabo before the draft. You should be plenty relaxed."

If he only knew. Kennedy and I spent most of the trip naked.

She must be thinking the same thing because there's a flush in her cheeks. From embarrassment or arousal, I can't tell. Then her foot finds mine under the table, and I'm certain it's the latter.

God, I love this woman.

The last five months have been incredible and if I have my way, it's just the beginning.

We haven't talked much about what we're going to do after graduation in May. There's too much uncertainty for both of us. I have a decent idea of my top draft prospects, but there wasn't much point making plans until we know for certain. Kennedy's had a number of interviews, including a second interview with Gamut last week, but she's still waiting for an offer.

"Here we go," Dad whispers.

We all sit up straighter and turn our attention to the screen where the NFL commissioner has taken the stage. I barely hear a word he says before the clock starts running on Cleveland. They've got a decent QB, but you never know what might happen in the draft.

After weeks of mock drafts and pre-draft visits, I'm as uncertain as ever. This moment is the culmination of my life's work. All the practices, the bowl games, the championship run.

It's all brought me here, to this moment.

Now it's up to the football gods to decide where I go next.

My father's been true to his word, remaining hands-off in the pre-draft maneuvering. In the months since my eligibility expired, I've visited Cleveland, New York, and Chicago, all teams with early draft picks. Any one of them could call my name.

And I haven't counted Pittsburgh out.

They could be trading picks even now. But no matter which team calls my number, I know it'll be okay because I've got all the love and support I need right here at this table.

It doesn't take Cleveland long to decide and relief surges through me when they select a running back from USC.

Then New York is on the clock.

I grip Kennedy's hand so tight her eyes go wide and she lets out a tiny squeak. "Sorry."

I try to pull my hand away, but she holds on. I appreciate that she doesn't tell me to relax or have faith or trust the process. It's impossible at this point.

My old man wasn't kidding. The process is brutal.

Every second feels like a minute. Every minute like an hour.

My father eyes the phone on the table. "Quiet phone's a good sign. They usually call before officially announcing the pick," he explains to Kennedy. "But not always."

*Not always.*

The commissioner leans toward the mic. My heart's thundering so loud I barely hear the words coming out of his mouth. "With the second pick of this year's NFL Draft, New York selects D'Andre Wilson, University of Georgia."

My dad pats me on the back, and Kennedy's smile is so wide I can see all her teeth. To the casual observer, it probably looks like they're trying to keep my spirits up. After all, most people expected me to be the number one pick.

But this scenario might work out even better.

Sweat trickles down the back of my neck.

Chicago's on the clock. Like my dad, my eyes are glued to the phone on the table.

I silently will it to ring. Each passing second feels like an eternity, and when the commissioner returns to the mic, my confidence falters.

"With the third pick of this year's NFL Draft, Chicago selects Austin Reid, Quarterback, Waverly University."

I fly out of my chair, forgetting to maintain decorum, and sling my arms around my father.

"Congratulations, son. I'm proud of you and I know your mother would be too."

Pride surges in my chest because I know he means every word.

"Thanks, Dad."

When I turn to Kennedy, I figure the hell with decorum and kiss her on the lips. The little vixen slips me the tongue.

Oh yeah, she's definitely turned on.

I hold her tight and whisper, "I love you."

"I love you too, babe. I'm so proud of you for staying true to yourself. Now get up there and claim your jersey."

When I turn to go, she slaps me on the ass for good measure.

I can't believe I'm going to Chicago. It's a dream come true.

One of the attendants hands me a Chicago hat. I pull it on as I climb the steps to the stage. The lights are bright and the bill does little to cut down the blinding glare, but nothing can bring me down right now.

I stride toward the commissioner as he extends his hand to me.

I give it a few good pumps, and we pose for pictures with my new Chicago jersey.

*Lucky number seven.*

But is it lucky enough to convince Kennedy to come to Chicago with me?

~

## KENNEDY

My feet are screaming for relief, so I kick off my heels the moment we're alone in the hotel room.

I knew there would be lots of celebrating after the draft, but I didn't realize quite how intense it would be. I guess I'll have to get used to schmoozing, *erm*, socializing, but if it's the price I have to pay for loving Austin, so be it.

It doesn't hurt that he looks like a wet dream in his crisp black suit.

He flips on the bedside lamp and strips off his jacket, tossing it over the back of a chair. The suite is a little extravagant for my taste, but I'm slowly getting used to Austin's world. Plus, even I have to admit the soaking tub is divine.

Someday I'm going to have one just like it.

Austin sinks down on the edge of the bed, and I wedge myself between his thighs.

It's been a long night. He looks exhausted, but in the best possible way. "How're you feeling?"

"Like everything I ever wanted might finally be within reach."

He slips a hand under my skirt, the rough pads of his fingers skating up my outer thigh. His touch is featherlight, sending a shiver down my spine. I close my eyes and tip my head back, savoring the feel of his hands on my bare flesh. He has the best hands. I could never tire of them, not when every touch feels like the first.

When I open my eyes, he's staring up at me, a self-satisfied smile on his face.

"You deserve it." I stroke his cheek, my fingers scraping over the fine stubble that's begun to show. "Which is why I've got one more signing bonus for you."

"A signing bonus?" Desire flares in his eyes, and my ovaries stand at attention. "Hell, yeah. I've been dying to rip this dress off you all night. It's driving me fucking crazy."

"I'm flattered, but that's not exactly what I had in mind."

I laugh and push him back on the bed, but he doesn't stay down long and props himself up on his elbows.

"So, we're not talking about sex then?" He grins, flashing his dimple.

"Keep your pants on—for now. I've got something even better lined up."

He doesn't bother to hide his skepticism. "What could be better than sex?"

"You'll see."

I grab my bag off the desk and pull out the offer letter from Gamut. It came in a few days ago, but I didn't want to say anything until all the details were ironed out. I climb into bed with him and hand him the first page of the offer.

He scans the letter twice and then turns to me, confusion in his eyes.

"Why didn't you tell me you got a job offer? This is great news. We should celebrate."

The man was just selected number three in the NFL draft. He'll probably make more money on his first contract than I'll make in a lifetime, and he thinks we should celebrate my job offer?

I lean down and kiss him, slow and soft. When he slips his hand under my skirt, I sit up.

"Wait, there's more. I didn't even tell you the best part. I'll be working in Chicago, so we can be together after graduation."

It's a full ten seconds before he reacts—I totally counted—but when he does, his smile is the brightest I've ever seen. And it's all for me.

"You're right," he says, a mischievous gleam in his eyes. "This is way better because it means I can have sex with you every day."

"Wow. If I didn't know better, I'd think you're just using me for my body."

I climb atop him, straddling his hips as he considers.

He pushes up the hem of my skirt, but his gaze stays fixed on mine.

"Then I'll have to do a better job of showing you how much I love you. I was going to ask you to come with me, but I wasn't sure if you'd say yes." He pauses. "You're sure this is what you want?"

Is he kidding? Of course it's what I want. These last months together have been the best of my life. I can't imagine my life after college not including Austin.

He's become as essential to me as air.

"Yes. I'll get to work on clean energy systems. It's a win-win for me. I get my dream job and my dream man."

"But how did you know I'd end up in Chicago?"

"I didn't. I negotiated a clause in my contract that would allow me to choose my location after the draft. They've got offices in New York and Chicago." I shrug. "It was a calculated risk. It paid off."

He laughs and I can feel the low rumble reverberate through his chest.

"Smart, gorgeous woman. I love it when you talk nerdy to me."

"So shut up and kiss me."

~

**Thank you for reading Claiming Carter! Need more Wildcat shenanigans in your life? Grab Coop's story, Catching Quinn!**

**www.jenniferbonds.com**

## ALSO BY JENNIFER BONDS

**Waverly Wildcats**

Holding Harper

Claiming Carter

Catching Quinn

Scoring Sutton

Protecting Piper

**The Harts**

Miles and Miles of You

Not Today, Cupid

**Royally Engaged**

A Royal Disaster

Royal Trouble

A Royal Mistake

**The Risky Business Series**

Once Upon a Dare

Once Upon a Power Play

Seducing the Fireman

# ABOUT THE AUTHOR

Jennifer Bonds writes sizzling contemporary romance with sassy heroines, sexy heroes, and a whole lot of mischief. She's a sucker for enemies-to-lovers stories, laugh-out-loud banter, over-the-top grand gestures and counts herself lucky to spend her days writing swoonworthy romance thanks to the support of amazing readers like you!

Jen lives in Pennsylvania, where her overactive imagination and weakness for reality TV keep life interesting. She's lucky enough to live with her own real-life hero, two adorable (and sometimes crazy) children, and one rambunctious K9. Loves Buffy, Mexican food, a solid Netflix binge, the Winchester brothers, cupcakes, and all things zombie. Sings off-key.

To connect with Jen online, visit www.jenniferbonds.com to sign up for her newsletter and be the first to know about new releases, giveaways, and exclusive content! You can also find her on Facebook, TikTok, and Instagram @jbondswrites.

Made in the USA
Monee, IL
03 November 2024